A self-confessed reading addict, Ella Allbright writes commercial women's fiction set in her beautiful home county of Dorset. Her first novel in this genre, *The Last Charm*, will be published in August 2020 by One More Chapter, an imprint of HarperCollins, and she's currently hard at work on her next book. Ella is represented by agent Hattie Grünewald at The Blair Partnership, who represent J.K. Rowling.

Ella also writes as Nikki Moore, the author of the popular #LoveLondon romance series. A number of the novellas featured in the Top 100 short story charts on Kobo and the Top 20 in the Amazon UK bestsellers Holiday chart, and in 2018 the collection was released in Italy. Her first published work was the short story *A Night to Remember* in the bestselling Mills & Boon / RNA anthology *Truly, Madly, Deeply*. Her debut romance *Crazy, Undercover, Love* was shortlisted for the RNA Joan Hessayon Award 2015.

When not writing or reading, she can usually be found working in her HR day job, walking the family's cute beagle puppy or watching a Netflix series!

You can connect with Ella/Nikki on:

🐦 @NikkiMoore_Auth

D0552924

The Last Charm

Ella Allbright

OneMoreChapter

One More Chapter
a division of HarperCollins*Publishers*
The News Building
1 London Bridge Street
London SE1 9GF

www.harpercollins.co.uk

This paperback edition 2020

First published in Great Britain in ebook format by
HarperCollins*Publishers* 2020

A catalogue record for this book
is available from the British Library

Ebook ISBN: 978-0-00-838656-6
Paperback ISBN: 978-0-00-838657-3

Set in Birka by Palimpsest Book Production Ltd, Falkirk
Stirlingshire

Printed and bound in Great Britain by
CPI Group (UK) Ltd, Croydon CR0 4YY

This book is dedicated to my gorgeous Fiancé, who has always championed me, supported me, challenged me and loved me, in the best possible ways. Mark, this story is my love letter to you.

This book is also dedicated to anyone who has ever felt lost. We're all in it together, and you're not alone. No matter how dark it is, there will always be stars in the sky, guiding us on.

LOST:
One precious charm bracelet with
great sentimental value.
Last seen near Lulworth Cove,
Dorset on 31 August.
If found, **please** get in touch –
REWARD ON OFFER.
Contact LeilaJones@LJ-Art.co.uk

Leila

December 2017

From: *LeilaJones@LJ-Art.co.uk*
To: *Winterjewel@outlook.net*

Subject: *Re. My Charm Bracelet*
Today at 12:32 p.m.

Dear Caitlin,

Thank you so much for getting in touch about finding my bracelet. You've no idea how much it means to me. I've been checking my phone about a hundred times a day ever since I put up the posters and plastered the ad all over social media. The feeling of relief is almost indescribable.

It was gifted to me on the eve of my eleventh birthday, and without the bracelet, I haven't felt like myself. Each and every charm on the silver link chain with its little heart-shaped locket clasp is significant, marking a special memory which has the power to make me laugh, smile, or cry.

Caitlin, have you ever loved someone so much that every time you look at them, a piece of your heart swells with joy simply because they're in the world? Well, that's who Jake is to me. Each charm on the bracelet is a part of our story. My life, his life, our lives … and how they've intertwined over the past fifteen years. I need the bracelet back, and to convince you it's mine I'm going to tell you all about the precious memories that come with those special charms.

I'll start before our beginning, because you need to know how I got the bracelet and how that day affected my whole life. By the end of this re-telling, I hope you'll find it in your heart to return my bracelet to me, so I can finish the birthday treasure hunt Jake created, find the last charm, and put it where it belongs.

Mine and Jake's story isn't over yet, no matter what other people might think.

Leila

30 August 2001

The Charm Bracelet & The Heart Charm

There's glistening jewellery lying on my bedspread when I get in from seeing Eloise – a silver charm bracelet with a heart-shaped locket holding the clasp together and a tiny chain dangling from it. Turning it over between my fingers, I see a plain silver heart charm hanging down halfway around it. I frown. It's my eleventh birthday tomorrow so maybe the bracelet's an early present? But why isn't it wrapped? And who is it from? There's no label. I can't picture Dad buying it, going around shops after spending all day at work plumbing. It can't be from Mum, because she always wraps presents she says are 'fit for royalty' with carefully folded paper, tape sticking the edges down neatly, and a ribbon tied in a bow with the ends curled into spirals.

Sitting down on the bed as I undo the bracelet to see if it fits me, a scrunching sound echoes around the room. Frowning, I look down and pull a piece of paper from under my leg. Unfolding it on my bare knees, I smooth it out and see a single word and a kiss. It's both the simplest and the hardest note I've ever read.

Sorry. X

A heavy thudding sounds up the stairs and Dad bursts into my room, eyes wide, blond hair sticking to his sweaty forehead. He's clutching a crumpled note in his hand, and the paper matches the note I'm holding. 'It's your mum,' he whispers brokenly, 'she's gone.'

I actually feel my eyes widen with shock, and my breath catches in my throat, choking me.

How *could* she? How can she leave us? Leave me? I trusted her.

I hate her. I hate her. I *hate* her.

Jake

February 2002

The motorway that's whizzed by for most of the journey melts away into grey pavements and red-roofed houses, and Jake can see his reflection in the car window. He turns away. His mum always says he's striking looking, but Jake's not sure that's a good thing, even though she tries to make it sound that way. The last time his dad, Terry, caught her saying it, he'd said Jake was a freak. That it was her fault their son had been born with a cleft palate and different coloured eyes. Having a normal healthy baby, he'd yelled, was more than she was capable of.

The car journey's taken *forever*. They'd left Birmingham as dawn was breaking and Jake can't wait to get to their destination. He's fed up of moving houses. He's twelve or thirteen – he doesn't know his actual age because his dad won't let them celebrate his birthday, even though his mum has tried to – and they've moved at least six times that he can remember.

Finally, they roar up outside a white house with pebbles on the bottom half and a red front door. It has double-glazed windows, and the small front garden has trimmed grass. It's nice. Hopefully it'll last more than a few months. His dad called their last house a shithole, but it hadn't been when they first moved in. Even Jake knows that if you don't mow the lawn, if you leave rubbish in the grass, and kick in the walls and doors when you're angry, a house will soon fall apart. Just like a family will if you don't care for it.

A few minutes later, he's following his dad up the beige-carpeted stairs with a heavy box in his arms. 'You're probably not going to be happy about this, because you're a moaner like your mum,' Terry smirks, 'but your bedroom is at the back of the house, and well ... Follow me.'

There's a sinking feeling in Jake's stomach as he trudges along behind his dad's bulky body. Opening the white door at the end of the corridor, Terry makes a sweeping gesture with his arm. As Jake walks in, the first wall he sees is candy-floss pink. The carpet is thin, also pink, with coloured dashes and dots of what looks like dried paint ground into it in patches. Purple, green, brown, black, yellow, grey and blue. The room is babyish and girly, and he looks at his dad questioningly. He tries not to flush with discomfort but knows he hasn't succeeded when his dad lets out a nasty laugh.

'It was the daughter's bedroom. I know it's going to embarrass you when you have mates around – if you manage to make any this time, that is – but you'll just have to wait until I have time to paint it another colour.' The gleam in his eye says he's enjoying this.

Jake can feel his jaw quivering with rage. One day he'll be strong enough to punch his dad right in his big, stupid mouth.

Then he steps around the corner and his mouth drops open. There are doors painted on the two walls nearest the window. He thinks the first set of doors is supposed to be the wardrobe leading to Narnia, but he doesn't recognise the others. What he does know is that they're really cool. He longs to step through one of them into another world, but he rearranges his face so his dad can't tell, shrugging his shoulders the way he's learnt to. Like he's not bothered. 'I'll have to wait until you're ready then, I guess.' He tries to inject a note of disappointment into his voice and turns away to traipse over to the window.

'Come on, boy.' His dad yanks him backward so he nearly trips over and bumps his head on a set of empty bookshelves screwed into the wall. 'Lots to do. Get a move on.'

Setting the box down on the single bed in the opposite corner of the room, Jake lopes down the stairs after Terry, thinking about the painted doors and wondering what other magical places they lead to.

***

Later, Jake's straightening up from the car with the last box in his arms when he glances up and sees her. She's sitting in the front of a van a few cars down, staring at him. He sucks in a breath. Everything seems to go into slow motion.

She looks a couple of years younger than him, although because he's small for his age they're probably the same height. A white-blonde ponytail is sticking out from under a baseball cap and she has milky skin with dark eyes. He'd have to get closer to see what colour they are. She looks like an angel. He bets her dad doesn't breathe booze all over her or use his belt on her legs 'til they bleed. As Jake's wondering about going over and saying hello, hoping his clothes aren't too scruffy, she pulls the cap down low and turns away. She obviously saw his scar and eyes. He doesn't know what he was thinking. He's not good enough to be friends with someone like her.

'What are you doing just standing there? You're bloody useless.' His dad cuffs him hard around the side of the head, catching him by surprise. He stumbles over his own feet and shoots into the house before he can get hit again, face red as he realises the girl must've seen. Racing up the stairs, he kicks open the door to his pink bedroom, throws the box on the floor and rubs his ear. It throbs. Swinging around, he frowns at the door. No lock. That means he'll be out on the roof tonight, depending on his dad's mood later. Hopefully, he'll be too drunk to climb up after him. Or if he does, maybe he'll fall off. That would be something.

As Jake drops to the floor with a thud, he notices scuff marks on the base of the bed and a few loose pieces of stitching hanging down. Frowning, he lies down on his back and shuffles to push himself along until he's lying directly below where he'll sleep. There's enough daylight coming in through the bare windows to illuminate the underside of the bed. As Jake looks up, his eyes widen at the picture stuck there. It's childish, but altogether beautiful.

Something about the magic and imagination of it makes him feel fearless.

***

A few minutes later, ignoring his throbbing ear and the chance his dad will cuff him again, Jake runs back downstairs and onto the street.

Racing down the road, he takes a deep breath and goes up to the window of the scuffed white van, knocking on the door with a dull metallic clang. The girl stares at him through the glass, fair eyebrows drawn together, dark eyes unreadable. She bites her bottom lip but after a moment, opens the door. Jake steps back as she climbs down onto the pavement. She's in baggy blue jeans and a plain white T-shirt.

'Hello,' he says, keeping his voice steady even though inside he is quivering. What if she doesn't like him? What if she turns away?

But 'Hi,' she replies quietly.

'I moved into the neighbourhood today.' He can smell strawberries and is sure it's coming from her. It reminds him of the time he and his mum went strawberry picking, just the two of them. It's a good memory, a rare one.

'Yeah,' the girl scowls, 'into my house.'

'It's yours?' He thinks of what he just discovered under the bed, and the painted walls. 'I mean, sorry. Didn't you want to move then?'

'No, I didn't. It's Mum's fault.' Her scowl deepens. 'We're leaving at the end of the week.'

'Oh.' His stomach drops with disappointment. 'Where is she?'

'Not here. I don't know.' A sigh this time.

'Sorry.' This isn't going well. He's upsetting her. Jake takes a step back and rubs his scar. It used to pull his lip up when he was little, but his mum managed to get him into a hospital for surgery, so it's now just a straight vertical line cutting down into his top lip on the right-hand side. 'What's wrong with your mouth?' she asks.

'Um ... I was born with a defect. But it's fixed now.'

'Huh.' She stares at his face. 'I can still see the scar though.'

'Yeah.' He blushes then stares at the ground. When he looks up, she's studying him, her eyes warmer.

'Don't worry, it's not that bad. Besides, I think it's good to be different.'

'Thanks,' he mutters. Though he is touched by her kind words, he wants to change the subject, so he nods to her wrist. 'That's a nice bracelet. Who gave it to you?'

'Mum, before she ran off.' Her face twists. 'I guess it's something to remember her by. It sucks that she left but the bracelet's my favourite thing, even though I'm cross with her.'

He feels privileged she's sharing her feelings with him. Or maybe she's just so angry at her mum she'll talk to anyone about this. 'Well, maybe—'

'Oi, what do you think you're doing? Get inside, now.' A large hand hauls Jake backwards.

'Dad. I just—'

'Back in the van, little girl.' Jake's dad smirks at Leila, his voice rough. 'Didn't your dad ever teach you not to talk to strangers?'

With a start, she scrambles into the van and slams the door shut, her eyes round.

The last thing Jake sees before he's frogmarched inside is her face, full of fear and disgust. He realises he doesn't even know her name.

Leila

February 2002

We only have five days left in Bournemouth and then we're leaving for good. I hate going to bed every night because I know when I wake in the morning, we'll be one day closer to moving out of Grandad Ray's, to a town I've never been to and where I don't know anyone. Starting mid-term at a secondary school where all the other kids will know each other makes me feel sick, and the thought of saying goodbye to Eloise makes me even sicker. She's my best friend. I didn't even get to spend this half-term with her because she's on holiday with her family. It's totally rubbish. Dad says we'll come back and visit sometimes but it won't be the same.

I roll over and curl into the rumpled quilt as morning winter sunshine creeps through the curtains, but my mind is on the house a few doors away. Our old house, the one I had to part with yesterday. I hope that whenever I close my eyes and imagine it, it'll always be there in my head, waiting for me. I'll open the front door and pass the doors to the kitchen and lounge, thundering up the stairs to my bedroom, which is exactly how it's supposed to be. My bed will be tucked against the wall covered in stuffed toys and sketch books, the

11

bookshelves crammed full of different-sized paperbacks, and all my posters will be hanging on the walls. A white wardrobe is in the corner and my white dressing table is covered with pencils, charcoals, and paint pots, as well as a hairbrush Mum used to brush my hair with every night. Before she left.

The doors to Narnia and Hogwarts are still painted on the walls, along with other entryways like the Gates of Argonath from *The Lord of the Rings*. I'll slide under my bed and my charm bracelet will swing against my wrist as I lift my hand to smooth the wooden bed slats. My wonderland will still be there, a picture I worked on for two weeks solid when I was seven years old. I went back to it six months ago, after Mum left, to add more detail. Wanting to be swept away and distracted from the reality of my world.

I used every colour felt-tip pen I owned on that piece. In some places I used two or three colours on top of each other to make a new one. In other places I applied craft glue to stick feathers, gems, and ribbons to the scene. There are stickers too, of animals, hearts, and smiley faces. I drew a unicorn and gave it a rainbow tail. I added a peacock with green, purple, and blue glitter on its tail feathers. The sky is the biggest part and there's no sun. It's a deep, intense indigo with sticky glow-in-the-dark stars. Right in the middle, if you look for her carefully, there's a little girl with silvery blonde hair peering out from behind a tree. She has fairy wings on her back and stars in her eyes. There's a paintbrush in her left hand and a charm bracelet around that wrist, which I added recently. In her right hand she holds a magic wand, gold sparkles trailing from it.

But that was then, and this is now, and I'll probably never see my creation again. I couldn't remove it from under the bed without ruining it, and couldn't bear to do that. It's *so* unfair. I really hate Mum sometimes.

Sighing, I climb out of bed and have a quick wash in the faded green bathroom, then dress in a violet T-shirt and my favourite blue jeans with a sparkly heart on the pocket. Brushing my hair, I put it in a ponytail and feed it through the hole at the back of the baseball cap I wore yesterday, tilting the peak down over my face. I feel like hiding this morning. Maybe if I can pretend I'm invisible, none of this will be real.

A few minutes later, I step into the kitchen holding *Harry Potter and the Goblet of Fire* to my chest. I've read it three times and can't wait until the next one in the series comes out.

Dad turns to look at me from his seat at the table, his big hands curled around a cup of tea. 'Morning, princess,' he says, 'sleep okay?'

'Yes, thanks.' He used to call me princess when I was seven or eight and has started again since Mum left, usually on the days I get really upset. I know he understands how sad and angry I am at leaving everything behind, but I also know it's not his fault and he's just looking out for us. No, I blame *her*.

This morning he looks rumpled. His clothes aren't ironed, and his face is creased with lines. I feel guilty. He's been sleeping on the sofa because there are only two bedrooms.

'Morning, Leila.' Grandad Ray steps out of the pantry holding a jar of homemade strawberry jam and puts it on the table. 'I'll get some toast on. Tea?'

'Yes, please,' I say, watching as he moves around the kitchen. Everything's dark in here, even with the overhead light on. The units are dark brown wood, the floor's covered in a thin greyish carpet with navy swirls, the walls are painted damson, and the table matches the units. I wonder how he sees in here. He's so *old*. I heard him telling Dad yesterday that he's only sixty but feels much older with everything going on.

I put my book down, careful to keep it away from the crumbs on the tablecloth. I'm quiet as I eat breakfast, lost in my own thoughts until Dad clears his throat and stands up, making me jump.

'I'm off to work now,' he says gruffly, 'I have a few last jobs to finish before wrapping up the business.'

As if it's not bad enough we had to sell our home, Dad also has to lose the business he set up fifteen years ago. He explained to me that because Mum's not around to do the books or admin, and he can't afford to employ someone to do those things or to pay the mortgage alone, we're moving to Basingstoke so he can work for his friend (who I call Uncle Martin) doing the plumbing for some new housing projects.

'You'll be all right for the day, won't you, love?' Dad's looking at me with a worried expression on his face.

I paste on a bright smile and nod. The truth is, I feel adrift. Like Harry Potter when he stays at Hogwarts for the first Christmas holidays because he doesn't want to go back to the horrible Dursleys. Dad and Grandad are adults and have each other, but I have no one. No one to talk to, no one to tell how scared I am about starting a new school. No one to share my feelings with about whether I'll make new friends.

'Of course. I'll probably read or draw, watch TV or something.' My eyes drift over to the window, aching for fresh air.

'We can always go for a walk later, Leila, if you want?' Grandad offers.

'Maybe.' I drop my gaze to the table. 'Have a good day, Dad.'

'Thanks, love.' He leans over to kiss me on top of the head, which I try to dart away from because I'm way too old for that now, and then walks to the door, grabbing his tool bag on the way out.

Grandad Ray and I stare at each other. Even though we've lived along the road from him since I was little, we hardly ever came over here before Mum left. I don't know why. I'd never seen them argue; they just didn't really seem to talk.

There's a knock on the front door and he frowns. 'I wonder who that is.' He wanders off as I finish my milky tea and take my cup over to the sink. In the distance I hear him speak. 'Oh, hello.'

He's back a minute later, an amused expression on his face. 'It's for you.'

Turning around, I look at him. 'Who is it?'

'A young lad. He said he met you yesterday? He wants to know if you'll come out.'

'Oh.' I blush, feeling like I've done something wrong, or like the boy is calling on me because he's got a crush. I doubt that's what it is though. He's probably lonely because he's just moved to the neighbourhood. Into *my* house.

'Do you want to see him?' he asks. 'If you do, you could probably spend some time with him here or maybe a short visit to the park? If we agree a time you need to be back by, that is. I'm sure your dad would be okay with it.'

The thought's tempting. Eloise is away and I'm lonely without her. I don't have much else to do and would rather be out and about doing something than stuck inside. Besides, the boy seemed okay – nice – although he did ask a lot of questions.

'Leila? I can send him on his way if—'

'I'll see him,' I reply in a rush. 'Maybe we'll hang out in the garden first?'

'That's a good idea,' Grandad says. Picking up his cup of tea, he tries to hide a smile behind it but fails.

Blushing again – my pale skin is *so* stupid – I walk through the dark dining room and into the hallway, pulling open the door Grandad's left a few inches ajar. The boy is leaning against the doorframe and I surprise him so much he stumbles over the threshold and lands at my feet.

He looks up at me from the carpet, odd-coloured eyes wide, and shrugs his shoulders, laughing at himself. 'Hello, again.'

I giggle. 'Hi.'

As he picks himself up, he dusts off his faded clothes and smiles. The action pulls the scar above his lip tighter. 'I w-wondered if y-you wanted to come out? We didn't finish chatting yesterday.'

I shrug casually, 'Sure. Do you wanna go in the garden? There are some cool trees to hang in?' My cheeks scald bright red. I must sound like such a baby. I think he's older than me, so he's probably used to going down the park with gangs of kids.

'Sure,' he nods. 'I'm Jake.'
'I'm Leila,' I answer shyly.

***

Jake and I end up spending the week together. He's intriguing, different to other boys I know from school, who are all loud and loutish. He's quiet, more thoughtful. He also has a confidence I wish I had. He just seems comfortable with who he is and what he thinks about things.

After that first morning in Grandad's back garden when we sit in the lower branches of the apple tree, idly chatting and getting to know each other, we spend most days down the local park. We wrap up in parka coats (mine brand new and boxy, his worn out and too small for him) and ride our BMX bikes (mine shiny and bright, his with a broken handle and covered in rust). I don't say anything or ask any questions though, because I don't want to embarrass him.

We talk about films, music, and books when we get to the park. Jake hates school because he says he's no good at it, but he likes to read at night when his parents think he's sleeping, borrowing books from the school library. Of course, he's between schools now. Feeling sorry for him, I lend him one of my Harry Potter collection on the promise he'll return it on Friday when we leave.

White mist from the cold hangs in clouds in front of our faces while we sit on the swings chatting, hands wrapped around the icy chains. Shivering is something we become used to. On a couple of the days, Jake is quieter than usual and doesn't want to talk, wincing occasionally but not saying why, so I bring my sketchpad with me. I draw for hours on end in the wooden Wendy house that's usually for the smaller kids. It's empty save for us, because of the wintry chill.

Wearing fingerless gloves so I can draw, I share my sandwich and thermos of hot chocolate with him as he watches my left hand fly over the pages. He doesn't seem to mind the silence when I draw, just appearing relieved to be out of his house. Every afternoon when it gets closer to home time, a strange tension comes over him. His shoulders creep up, his face gets hard and he becomes even quieter. By Thursday, I feel like I know him enough to be concerned.

'Is everything all right at home?' I ask hesitantly, leaning towards him.

'Everything's fine,' he snaps, looking away.

He doesn't talk to me for the next hour, so I don't ask him about it again.

Even though we've worked out he's nearly two years older than me, he never makes me feel stupid or childish. He asks questions about my drawings and where I get my ideas from and why I enjoy it so much, and says my art is really good. I tell him stuff about Mum leaving as I twirl my bracelet around my wrist, and sometimes when we talk, Jake puts his finger out and flicks the heart charm so it swings like a pendulum. On the morning I'm leaving, I go into a panic when we're at the park, thinking I've lost it, frantically checking my wrist and pockets and looking around on the ground but not able to find it. Jake calms me down and puts his hands up inside my coat sleeve, slowly easing the bracelet into sight from where it got caught on the inside of the sleeve elastic. Beaming at him, I go to hug him a thank you, but he backs away. Awkwardly, I let my hands drop to my sides.

When it's time for me and Dad to leave, I'm sad to say goodbye to Jake, and realise I'll miss him. He's been so easy to talk to, and the thought of leaving him behind fills me with sadness.

'This week's been nice,' I say, as we stand facing each other next to Dad's loaded van. There's a lump in my throat. I'm leaving everything I know behind and going into the unknown. 'Thanks.'

Jake nods his head, putting his hands in his coat pockets. His odd-coloured eyes – one green, one brown – are solemn and the scar cutting into his lip looks paler today, especially against the starkness of his messy, thick black hair.

I'm about to gather my courage to ask if we should maybe stay in touch when Jake steps back, and Dad opens the van door behind me. We've already said our goodbyes to Grandad Ray inside the house, and he said it's better he doesn't come out. I know he finds it hard to show his feelings.

'Come on, love,' Dad chides, 'we need to get on the road. We've got a couple of hours ahead of us and unpacking to do at the other end.'

'Okay, sorry,' I murmur, my gaze still on Jake's face. I wait for him to say something but he's in one of his quieter moods again. 'Okay, bye then,' I mumble.

'Bye,' he replies, as he steps back.

Turning away, I climb up into the van. Buckling my seatbelt, I wind the window down and glance at him, checking one more time that he's not going to say anything, but his mouth is in a straight line. His eyes are blank. It's like I've already left.

As Dad starts the engine and releases the handbrake, I raise my hand to wave at Jake, and he suddenly darts forward and slams his hand on the door. In turn, Dad slams the brakes on.

'What?' I hold my breath.

'I've still got your book!' he says anxiously.

I smile, 'You're enjoying it. Finish it and then give it to Grandad Ray. I'll get it from him next time I'm back.' I nod. 'Maybe I'll see you then?' I say in a rush, holding my breath.

'You really want to?'

'Yes.'

'I'd like that.' The blankness from his eyes fades a bit. 'You sure about the book?'

Dad revs the engine.

I roll my eyes. 'Yes. Keep the book. Bye, Jake, and take care.'

I don't know it in that moment, but they'll be my last words to him for two and a half years.

Jake

31 August 2003

The Pencil Charm

Jake's sitting on the pitched red roof outside his bedroom window for the fourth day in a row. It's steep and his mum doesn't like him being out here, particularly when it's hot. The beating sun does sometimes make him feel dizzy, but it's the best place to stay out of his dad's way. Terry's less fit than he used to be, so can't get out here anymore.

Anyway, he's been out here hundreds of times over the last year and has perfected the art of climbing in and out of the window without even a wobble, just like Joey in *Dawson's Creek*. Besides, his dad is out of work after punching someone down at the yard and being fired, so he's at home a lot more. His jobs never last long, and their spare room is full of DVDs, CDs, electrical goods, and gym equipment he sells down the market or on eBay. He's always wheeling and dealing, and Jake's mum joked last month he's like that TV character Del Boy from *Only Fools and Horses*. The comment earned her a black eye, because Jake's dad prides himself on his good looks and took offence at being compared to the actor who plays Del Boy.

Jake's own ribs are still healing from a few weeks ago when Terry came home drunk from the pub and accused Jake of not being his son. He was yelling and screaming that Jake was an impostor, and his mum must have cheated.

He doesn't remember the actual punches, or what it felt like to be curled up on the kitchen floor with his dad standing over him. He only knows that once it was over, his whole body ached, a mass of sore parts and bruises. In the bathroom afterwards – the only room in the house with a lock on the door, because his dad likes privacy to shower – he spat blood into the sink and held his side. It was hard to breathe, a sharp pain stabbing at him every time he inhaled. But he's used to it now, and broken ribs heal with time.

His mum stayed in bed for two days, but he had to get up for school to see out the end of term. He didn't mind, because it was a relief to be away from home. Even though he doesn't get on with many of the kids in his classes, he stays on for as many extracurricular activities as possible, to extend the school day. He knows parents are supposed to love and protect their kids, but that's not his experience. Maybe his mum used to try and stand in his dad's way when he was little to stop him being hit, but he's not sure if that's a real memory or just wishful thinking. Nowadays, she seems to have simply accepted their life as it is. She has never done anything to change it, never taken action that he knows of to rescue them. There've been no hastily packed bags, hidden tins of cash, or bus journeys to refuge shelters. Jake and his mum are like two strangers locked in a prison together, passing the time and trying to avoid eye contact. He doesn't expect anything from her. He's simply waiting until he's big and strong enough to stop his dad. Surely if Terry sees he can stand up for himself, and for his mum, he won't bother them. He'll find someone else to take his anger out on. Jake just needs to survive until then. A couple of years ago, he'd hoped that becoming a teenager would mean the arrival of muscles. It hadn't, but he still has hope that he might shoot up at some point. It's hard to get strong and grow when some days he doesn't eat though.

He sighs, wishing he were anywhere but here. There are birds singing in the leafy trees nearby, and in the distance he can hear the buzz of a lawnmower, so he pictures a patch of bright green grass in his head. It helps pass the time. Grey smoke floats up from the garden a few houses over, and he imagines a party of people crowded around a BBQ. He can almost taste the meaty sausage, and his mouth fills with saliva. He hasn't eaten anything since last night, and his stomach is growling and clenching in spasms. If he's lucky, Terry will go out for a bit and he can sneak to the kitchen. There's no predicting the pattern of his comings and goings, so it can be difficult. And the last time his mum tried to give him some food, Terry broke her finger. 'I hope you've learnt your lesson,' he said, glaring as she cowered against the kitchen counter cupping her hand. 'If your son wants food, he can come down and get it himself.' After that Jake decided he'd rather go hungry than see his mum get hurt or get an extra bruise himself.

Now, he picks at the knee of his black shorts as a distraction. They're tattered, fraying at the edges and at least two sizes too small for him, tight around his thighs and hips. His T-shirt is a brand that went out of fashion when he was twelve. Unlike his school mates, he doesn't wear the latest trainers or sports gear. It's why he doesn't go out with anyone at weekends, or in the evenings. He's too embarrassed about his clothes, and what people might say about them. What they might think of him and his family.

The only person he trusts, who never judges him, is Ray. Leila's grandad. When he's with the older man, he knows he won't get sympathetic glances or be asked awkward questions. Ray knows Jake's situation is difficult, although not the full extent of what happens behind closed doors. He doesn't try to stick his nose in, although he mentioned once there are services that can help Jake and his mum. Jake shut down when Ray said that, and left quickly, so Ray hasn't brought it up again. Recently though, Ray has offered Jake the opportunity to do occasional chores, giving him little brown envelopes of coins, feeding him hot meals after every task he completes. Jake keeps the money at Ray's house so his dad can't take it and spend it on alcohol.

Ray's house is only three properties along, and Jake can easily see into his back garden because of the bend in the road. Jake often hears what's going on in Ray's house, particularly as he tends to leave his windows open. Most of the time, it's not much – the muted sound of a presenter talking on TV, a jazz tune on the radio, Ray telling a cold caller that no thank you, he doesn't need what they're selling – but today is different. There are two voices approaching the back of the house from inside, getting louder as they reach the garden. Ray and a large pink man with scruffy blond hair step onto the shorn grass, walking over to the green plastic circular table and matching chairs. Jake recognises Leila's dad, Henry, although they only met once in passing.

Ray's carrying a round cake with a white base, hot pink icing and matching candles, while Henry balances a tray with porcelain cups, silver spoons, a teapot, jugs and sugar, which he places on the table. It's the same set Ray uses when Jake sneaks around for tea.

His heart lifts. He's been waiting weeks for this, ever since Ray mentioned their visit. He hopes he got it right. He would have given it to her himself, but his dad gave him a black eye yesterday. He's too ashamed to show the purpling bruise and bloodshot retina to anyone. There would be too many questions. Usually his dad is more careful to hit him in places where bruises can be hidden. In the end he decided to just post the gift through the door late last night in an envelope with a simple *L* on the front.

Jake sits forward to get a better look as Leila comes into view. She's grown a little since last year. Her long silvery blonde hair is as lovely as ever. She's wearing it in a high ponytail, with her fringe pinned back in a mini-quiff. There are red and purple streaks of hair mascara in it right through to the ends. Her jeans have lines down the side of the legs and she's wearing a black T-shirt that ends a few inches above her waistband, exposing her stomach.

'Happy Birthday, Leila!' Ray smiles, holding a big knife aloft before pointing it at the cake. 'How does it feel to be thirteen? Officially a teenager?'

'Yeah, y'know. It's okay.' She shrugs, dropping down into the seat next to her dad.

'Leila, manners!' Henry says.

She flushes, 'Sorry.'

'Do you want me to light the candles?' Ray asks his granddaughter.

Jake shuffles further forward to watch, careful to dig his toes into the roof tiles.

'Yes, please.'

When Ray holds a match to them and they're all lit, her dark eyes sparkle and her pale skin flushes with excitement as she leans forward to blow them out. Managing them all in one go, she grins.

'What did you wish for?' Henry asks as she sits down, and Ray starts cutting the cake into neat slices.

Leila looks at her dad steadily for a moment, her grin fading. 'A dog,' she mutters at last.

'Really?'

'Really.' But her eyes skitter away from his, like she's lying.

'This arrived last night.' Ray produces an envelope from his back pocket.

'Thanks.' Grabbing it from his hands, she rips it open eagerly.

Jake leans further forward, watching, holding his breath, wanting to hear. A car roars along the road, at risk of drowning out her reaction. *Bugger off!*

'This is really cool,' she says, holding up a small silver charm. 'A tiny pencil! Mum must remember I like drawing. She remembered it's my birthday!' She beams, looking delighted. 'There's no note but that's okay. Oh my God, I love it!'

Oh. Jake wraps his arms around his raised knees, biting his lip.

Ray opens his mouth to say something but subsides. Henry glances at him, and they exchange a look.

Leila fastens the charm on the bracelet and grins at it, before jumping up and crossing to the apple tree on the other side of the garden. She traces a shape on the knotted bark with her finger. Jake knows there are intricate patterns carved into the tree, a series of waves, circles, and hearts. He once asked Ray what they were and who put them there, but the older man's face set into concrete lines and he changed the subject. Jake suspects it was Leila's mum who engraved the bark.

Henry and Ray settle in the chairs with cups of tea in front of them, leaving the cake on its plate in the middle of the table as they chat. Jake's stomach rumbles at the sight of it. Because he can hear and see everything, he feels somehow part of the scene. Almost there, but not quite touching. He knows that, even without a mother present, this is how a family should be. People who take care of each other and enjoy each other's company.

'We need to talk about that charm.' Ray squints at Henry in the summer sunlight. 'I'm not sure if—'

'I know,' Henry interrupts, glancing around, 'but not right now.'

'Soon,' Ray says, and Henry nods. 'So, what present did you get her this year?'

Henry lets out a short laugh. 'I didn't. She just wanted money to spend on stuff herself. CDs, clothes, and lip gloss, I think,' he sighs.

'She's growing up.' Ray's smile is wry. 'I remember those days. Except with Amelia it was the early 80s, so it was stomach-baring white T-shirts with rolled up sleeves and low-slung jeans with big hair. She used to get through so many cans of hairspray. Anna and I called it the Madonna effect.' He chuckles, before trailing off. Henry's staring at him. 'Sorry,' Ray says, 'I forgot who I was talking to.'

'No, it's okay.' Henry clears his throat. 'She was my wife. I would've liked to have known her back then. Perhaps if I'd understood her more, then what happened—'

'You can't blame yourself. My daughter is who she is, and I doubt anything you'd have said could have changed things. At the end of the day, she lived three doors down from me. You were out at work trying to earn a decent living and pay for the house, and your family. If she was struggling, she only had to come and knock on my door. I would have listened. Would have tried to help.' He pauses, 'It is a shame about the house though. I know how much you loved it.'

'It's just a building.' Henry shifts in his seat, craning his head to watch his daughter. 'My home is wherever Leila is.'

Up on the roof, Jake's hands curl into fists, and he blinks away the tears suddenly glazing his eyes. Leila's so lucky.

'It'd be nice if the house was being looked after though,' Henry adds gruffly. 'I spent lots of time on it.'

Ray exhales, fiddling with a button on the sleeve of his brushed cotton shirt before looking at his son-in-law. 'They're not the type of family to take pride in their home.'

'Really? Why's that?'

'They don't really speak to anyone, and never come to the neighbourhood BBQs. The few times someone's gone round to invite them, they've had the door slammed in their face.' He grimaces, 'You know I don't like to speak ill of people, Henry, but their only saving grace is their son.'

'The boy Leila spent that week with before we moved?'

'Yes. Jake. He's a lonely boy, but so bright and engaging. He struggles academically but whatever you tell him, he absorbs. He's a thinker. If he can get out of that situation, he'll do well.' Pausing, he adds, 'I don't think everything is quite right in that house.' Henry raises both eyebrows in question, but Ray shakes his head. 'It's not my place to say.'

'Sounds like you've spent quite some time with Jake.'

'He comes here sometimes to visit and helps me out with chores. We talk. He's a good lad.'

Jake's face heats with embarrassment at hearing the truth of his family summed up so neatly, but at the same time, Ray's words send a thrill through him. He thinks he's bright and will do something with his life.

'It's been two years since Amelia left,' Henry mutters, checking to see where Leila is before switching the topic. 'Do you think she'll ever come back? Leila still asks.'

Ray looks uncomfortable, and it's a strange expression on his face. Jake's never seen him look anything but self-assured.

'I don't know,' Ray answers Henry's question after a long pause. 'But I know she's okay.'

'How do you know that?' Henry sits forward in the chair, the plastic groaning under his weight. 'Have you spoken to her?'

29

'She sent me a letter. I don't where she is. There's no post-mark or forwarding address.'

'You've had a letter from Mum?'

They both jump in their seats.

'Leila, I didn't see you there,' Ray exclaims.

'Where is it? I want to see.' She puts her hands on her hips, stepping closer to her grandfather. 'What does it say?'

'That's probably not a good idea. I wouldn't want you to get upset.'

'I'll be upset if I don't see it. It's my *birthday*. Please. I'm old enough. I just want to see it. I swear I won't get upset.'

Henry winces. 'Is there anything ... worrying in there?'

Ray rolls his eyes up to the left, thinking. 'No. It's just general things. How she's doing, what she's doing. As I said, no location.'

Henry touches Leila's shoulder gently, and for a fleeting moment, Jake's stomach flips over in pure jealousy. 'Sure about this?' he asks.

'Yes.' She holds her dad's gaze, her lips pursed.

'Okay, then.' His fingers twitch, as if he too is aching to read the letter.

'All right.' Ray pushes himself from his chair and heads towards the back door. 'Why don't you start eating while I go and look?' he suggests, before walking into the house.

Father and daughter glance down at the birthday cake, and Leila shakes her head. Jake wonders if she's too nervous to eat. She starts twirling the ends of her purple and red pony-tail around her fingers, over and over, and Jake knows he's right.

A minute later, Ray reappears clutching a white rectangular envelope. There's handwriting on the front, but Jake's too far away to see what it looks like. Taking the letter out, he holds it toward Leila before moving to hover over her left shoulder. Henry rises to stand next to his father-in-law.

Leila unfolds the paper. Her eyes moving from left to right, she reads its slowly, mouthing the words. Her face screws up and a single tear rolls down her cheek. 'Not ready to come home yet?' she shouts, throwing the letter onto the mown lawn and stamping on it with her high-top trainer. 'She's had long enough. She's the most selfish person *ever*. That's it. I don't want anything to do with her!'

Twirling around, she flees into the house before Henry or Ray can react. But Jake's already scrambling down off the roof, sliding in through his bedroom window with little regard for the skin scraped off his back, flying down the stairs into the lounge. He wants to make sure she's okay, having forgotten about his black eye and other injuries.

Even though he's sometimes jealous of her, she's helped him and he'd like to think they're friends. Yanking the net curtain back from the window, he sees Leila throw herself against the door of her dad's van, scrabbling for the handle, sobbing. Henry follows her out, reaching for her.

Just as he does, a heavy hand clamps down on Jake's shoulder. 'There you are, son,' Terry says.

Leila

November 2004

The Shell Charm & The Book Charm

Frowning as the teacher scrawls famous Lady Macbeth quotes across the whiteboard in blue marker pen, I absent-mindedly fiddle with the new charm that arrived this morning. With a solemn nod, Dad slid the envelope across the breakfast table towards me. For a moment I thought it was from him. However, when I sliced open the envelope with a butter knife, it contained a curled-up silver conch shell with a swirly pink interior, tiny and so very cute, with a typed note. *Happy Homecoming.* It was on the tip of my tongue to ask how Mum knows we've moved back to Bournemouth and if that's the case why doesn't she just visit, but Dad stood up abruptly and left the room.

As he was closing the front door, he called over his shoulder he'd see me in time for dinner, and to try to be good at school, leaving me and my grandad staring at each other over my cornflakes and his marmalade on toast. The silence between us before I got up and tossed the dregs of my cereal and milk into the bin was uneasy. I've only seen him a handful of times since we moved away, and I never knew him that well when Mum lived with us.

I was probably a bit snappy with him as I pulled on my forest-green school blazer over my striped blouse and said I had to go, but what do people expect? I didn't ask for this. It wasn't my choice. I didn't want to be transplanted, taken away from everything I know. *Again*. I still can't believe Dad made me move back here. Although it isn't his fault Ray's ill, and coming back to look after him is the right thing to do, did we really have to move in with him? Every time I catch sight of the peeling red front door of our old house, the gaping tiled roof, or the weed-choked garden, it makes me wince. Even so, I can't stop looking. It's like a scab you shouldn't pick but do anyway, even though you know it'll leave a scar.

I wonder if Jake still lives there. I've not seen him since that half-term we spent together, which seems like a lifetime ago now.

I also wonder if Eloise – or anyone else I might recognise – will be at this school. Despite our promises to be best friends for ever, Eloise and I didn't keep in touch after I left. Still, there've been moments over the years when I've thought about her, wondering how she is.

Now, flexing my toes inside my new black flats, heels stinging and rubbed raw by the walk to school, I tune out the teacher droning on about the core themes of Shakespeare's play. Instead, I focus on the music playing in my left ear through an earphone hidden by my long hair. I've been listening to 'This Love' by Maroon 5 on loop since it came out at the beginning of the summer and haven't tired of it yet. We covered *Macbeth* at my old school last term, so I know it back to front and sideways and don't need to hear it again. Besides, I found sketching pictures of the witches more interesting than the tragedy, greed, and madness of the story.

'Miss Jones, am I boring you?' Mr Strickland's sarcasm booms and bounces off the walls.

His tone annoys me. Lifting my chin, I raise one eyebrow, careful to tuck the earphone wire out of sight. 'I'm not sure. Are you boring yourself yet?' There are titters around the room, along with the sound of pupils shifting in their seats to watch the drama unfold.

The teacher's nostrils flare as he straightens his back, his salt-and-pepper hair sitting on his forehead in an old-fashioned 50s-style wave. 'Don't be so rude. Pay attention and contribute, or else you can stay back for detention today and explain to the head teacher why you feel you're above getting a good education, and why,' his eyebrows draw together, 'you feel you're entitled to disrupt the lesson for all your classmates.'

'I'm happy to explain to the head that you can't keep me in for a DT today because you need to properly notify a parent in advance to keep a child back after school,' I respond flatly, intimately familiar with school rules and regs after the last fourteen months, feeling the burn on my lower back itch at the thought. 'Plus, I hardly think the head would be interested in my first offence on my first day, do you?'

He sucks in a breath, a puce flush washing up his neck into his face. 'It's because it's your first day here you should be trying your best to—'

The smallish, dark-haired boy behind me, whom I only

gave a cursory glance to when I rushed in late at the start of lesson, clears his throat.

The teacher's face tightens. 'Is there something you want to add, Mr Harding?'

'Nah, I just wondered whether we could get on with it now? Lady M is kind of hot for a homicidal chick and I wondered whether there are any sex scenes.'

'For God's sake—' Mr Strickland shakes his head as the class explodes with laughter. 'You know, for someone who's been held back for failure to academically achieve, despite being one of the oldest in your year group, you always have a lot to say for yourself, don't you?' The teacher marches down the aisle between the rows of laminated tables.

'Yeah, thickie,' a chunky yellow-haired boy sat leaning against the opposite wall yells, 'why don't you spend time with people your own age?'

'Good one, Davey,' his friend sniggers beside him.

I feel bad for the flack he's getting on my behalf, given that he interjected to save me, so I turn around to peer over my shoulder.

I gulp with shock. It's Jake! He looks older but it's definitely him. I take in the details of his face with my artist's eye. The scar running down into his lip. His different coloured eyes – left one brown, right one green – and the thick dark eyebrows framing them. His cheekbones and jaw seem too angular, telling me he's not eating any better than he used to. His black hair is shaggy and a touch too long.

He flicks me a quick acknowledging glance before craning his head to look up at Mr Strickland, who's now hovering above him. 'Sir, the truth is,' he says with a straight face, 'I find your lessons so inspiring that I fuck up just so I can repeat year ten and spend more quality time with you.'

I hide a snigger behind my hand. Jake's former quiet confidence has become a more daring manner, and I marvel at the chances of us being in the same class.

Switching my attention to the teacher, I watch a mixture of emotions flutter over his face. Anger, resentment, and then resignation. It's a war he either can't win or just can't be bothered fighting. 'Right, that's enough messing about,' he barks, 'let's just get back to it, shall we? You, behave.' He glares, nodding at Jake. 'You're on your last warning from me. Any more trouble and you'll be suspended again, or worse.' He nods down at me, 'And you, behave yourself too.'

He's so patronising it makes me seethe.

Mr Strickland claps his hands and strides back to the front of the room, pointing at the board. 'Now, who wants to comment on Lady Macbeth's behaviour? About the way she goads her husband into killing the Scottish King, Duncan?'

'Goads?' I mutter under my breath, yanking the earphone out and jamming it into my blazer pocket. 'Whatever happened to free will?'

'Someone tell me how she manipulates him. How she forces him into becoming a murderer. He wouldn't have done it otherwise. He was innocent in all this, wasn't he? Come on! Someone must have an opinion. Act 1, Scene 7, what does she say?'

My fingers flex and curl into fists. I need to control myself.

'You've all gone quiet. Look –' he turns his back to the

room, stabbing his finger at the quotes he's copied out '– what do these tell us about Lady Macbeth? About the female of the species and their ability to lie and deceive?'

Manipulate? Lie and deceive? The female of the species? Like only women are capable of that kind of behaviour. My teeth grind. He's a total misogynist. Although, his description does bear some resemblance to my feckless mum. After all, didn't she lie and deceive us into thinking she loved us before running out? I swallow down the rage unfurling in my chest. I swear, if Mr Strickland says one more sexist thing—

'She's greedy and forceful,' he continues, using a red marker to underline a quote, his back to the class, 'and she's willing to seduce and coax until she gets exactly what she wants. Come on, women like her have been doing this since the world began, haven't they? What about Eve in the Garden of Eden? She completely led Adam down the garden path, and some would argue that mankind has been paying for that sin ever since—'

At that, I grab the heavy hardback off my desk and hurl it across the room at his head. It misses, hits the board beside his left shoulder and drops to the floor with a thud.

'What the—' Spinning around, he sees the book on the floor and glares at the class. He picks it up and holds it aloft. There's a deathly silence. Everyone looks at each other with unease. 'Who threw this? *Who?* It could have seriously injured me.'

I swallow, immediately regretting my loss of temper. You'd have thought I'd have learnt by now, after what happened at my last school. Dad is going to be horrified. I couldn't even make it through three lessons. *Shit.* Taking a deep breath, I open my mouth and start rising to my feet, planting my hands on the table in front of me. But before I can stand, a voice behind me speaks out.

'I did it.'

'What?' Mr Strickland's eyes narrow, his gaze landing over my right shoulder.

I click my teeth shut. What the hell's Jake *doing*?

The teacher gestures to the book he's holding. '*Pandora*, by Jilly Cooper? A bit girly for you, isn't it?' His mouth curls into a smirk. 'Not the type of reading material I'd imagine you with.'

'Unfortunately, I can't reach the top shelf in the newsagent's yet. Unlike you, Sir,' Jake replies cheekily.

'I do not—' Mr Strickland splutters, eyebrows shooting up. Everyone loses it, and I can't help sniggering, even while knowing I can't let this continue.

I turn around to look at Jake again and my lips form the words to end this whole thing and take the blame, but he shakes his head slightly and talks over me, staring our teacher in the eye. 'It pissed me off, all that guff you were spouting. I thought you should shut up. If I had to ruin a book to do it, I can live with that.'

'Jake Harding, that is the final straw!' Mr Strickland bellows. 'Get out of my classroom, now. Go and find the head and explain what you've just done. You think you're so clever? Well, let's see where it gets you.'

'That's cool,' Jake shrugs, grabbing his tatty bag from the carpeted floor and sauntering to the front of the room. His

black trousers are an inch too short at the ankle, and there's
a noticeable gap between the cuffs of his blazer and his thin
wrists. 'I'll just take this with me. I might need something to
read while I wait.' Plucking my book from the gaping teacher's hands, he flings open the door and slams it shut behind
him.

***

As soon as fourth period is over – a boring physics lesson I
had no hope of following – I rush to the head's office, bag
banging against my hip as I ask people for directions. I get
lost twice before I stumble into a reception area with four
closed blue doors and matching blue carpet. There's a row of
three blue chairs and Jake's sitting in one of them, his head
resting against the wall as he gazes at the ceiling.

'Tell me you haven't seen the head yet,' I blurt.

He tips his head forward and his odd-coloured eyes flicker
as they move over me. I touch my pale hair self-consciously
when his gaze lands on the length of it hanging down a few
inches past my shoulders.

'It's still so light, almost silvery,' he muses.

'You remember me then?'

'Of course I do.' An odd smile plays on his mouth. When
he sees me looking, he lifts a hand and rubs the scar like it's
aching.

'Sorry,' I mutter, 'I didn't mean to stare.' Sighing, I step
closer. 'So, have you seen the head? I need to speak to him,
her, whoever. I need to explain it was me who threw the book.'

'It doesn't matter. Don't worry about it. It wasn't just the book – it was the stuff I said. They're used to it from me.' From the expression on his face, he doesn't much care.

'But if I hadn't thrown it,' I insist, 'you wouldn't have made the comments to cover for me.'

'I would. He was pissing me off. He deserved it.'

'It's still not up to you to take the blame, Jake.' Studying his apparent indifference, relaxed body language, and thinking back to the way he spoke to Mr Strickland, I tilt my head. 'You're pretty cocky now, aren't you?'

'If you say so. Why –' he grins '– do you like cocky?'

'Hardly,' I scoff.

'Shame.' He sucks his cheeks in, studying me.

'What happened to you?' I ask.

'Nothing. Why, what happened to you?'

It's a deflection and we both know it, and his slight rudeness makes me blush. I settle into the chair at the other end of the row, so there's an empty one between us. 'You don't need to cover for me, Jake. I appreciate what you did, but I can take care of myself. I know it'll probably only be a couple of days of detention or maybe a suspension.'

'I've already seen the head, and she's expelling me. It was my last strike. It's too late.'

I shoot out of my seat. 'What?' My eyes well up with tears. 'Why didn't you say something? I've got to go in and see her. That's not right.'

Getting up, he blocks my path, holding me back from a door with an etched sign on it. *Head teacher, Mrs Grace Irving.* 'Don't.'

Despite the fact he's a few inches shorter than me and skinny, he's pretty strong. 'You have to let me,' I insist. 'It's not fair on you.'

'No.' He shifts to the left when I try to side-step him. 'Listen! It's too late for me here. It was going to happen sooner or later. I'm no good at keeping out of trouble. And if you hadn't thrown that book then I would have done something else. Maybe something worse.' He shakes his head, tufty black hair sticking out at all angles. 'Mr Strickland's a sexist twat. But you can have a fresh start. Forget what happened today. Begin again. It's all right here, this school. Most of the teachers are cool.'

'But—'

'What's the point of you owning up and getting in trouble, when I'll probably end up getting expelled for something else tomorrow?'

I go to protest again, when he pushes me gently away and stares at me beseechingly. 'Please, Jones.'

'Why are you doing this?' I realise there's something else going on here and am taken aback at the way he uses my surname. We were only ever on first-name terms.

'It doesn't matter.' He shakes his head, looking anxious. 'Just go along with it?'

Pausing, I bite my lip. This is more like the boy I knew, and the expression on his face reminds me of the way he used to look when it was time to go home from the park. It still doesn't feel right to let him take the blame, but I'm at a complete loss and have tried my best, so after taking a deep breath and tucking away the guilt, I nod. 'Okay. Thank you.'

I shuffle from one foot to another. 'But are you going to be okay? Isn't your dad going to kill you?'

The bored expression is back on his face. He loosens the knot in his school tie and yanks the loop over his head, making his hair even messier. 'I'll be fine. Go.'

'I will, but ... why take the blame for me?'

He pauses, and then says quietly, 'I met you before I met you, and what I saw, I liked. I knew you were a good person.'

'Well, that's cryptic. What are you talking about? We met outside our houses on the day you moved in, and then spent the next five days together.'

Delving in his pocket, he unwraps a Polo, biting down on it with a distinct crunch. The smell of mint drifts over me. 'I'll tell you one day, when it's right,' he says with a shrug, before clearing his throat. He touches a finger to the heart-shaped clasp on my bracelet. 'You still have it.'

'Of course. It's important to me. Mum never came back, but at least I know she thinks of me occasionally.'

His thick eyebrows give him an air of intensity that makes me jittery. It's weird being with him again.

'Jones, I need to—'

As he's speaking, his dad flings his way into reception, curse words filling the air along with the stink of alcohol, and whatever Jake was about to say gets lost in the moment.

***

When the final bell rings, I dive out of last period before grabbing everything I need from my locker and taking a shortcut from the school grounds. I've had enough for my first day and am still unsettled by the scene I witnessed outside the head's office when Jake's dad turned up. He really is a horrible man. The only highlight of the day was running into Eloise, and after a warm hug, her introducing me to some nice girls she's friends with.

On the walk home, I stop to study a view which catches my eye. I take out my sketchpad and a piece of charcoal. There's an alleyway running between two houses, trees and bushes lining it to form an archway of foliage. The shape of the leaves and branches melding in the middle – with rays of sunshine streaming through them to make a dappled shadowy effect on the dirt path – is exquisite. I lose half an hour sketching, while leaning up against a concrete post. It's only when the light changes I realise I've drifted again, and lost time. Crap. Shoving my stuff in my bag, I run the rest of the way home.

'Sorry,' I gasp, stumbling through the front door. Moving along the dim flock-papered hallway, I flip off my shoes. The carpet is thick and frayed under my feet and has an ugly red and yellow swirly pattern.

Dad steps out of the lounge, his face strained. 'You're late. Where've you been? I left work early to be here.'

Stiffening, I try to keep my voice even. 'Sorry. Something caught my eye on the way home and I stopped to sketch it.'

'You're okay?'

'I'm fine.'

His face softens and he steps forward, putting his large hand on my shoulder and squeezing gently. 'Leila, we agreed. You can't keep wandering off. People worry.'

Sliding out from beneath his touch, I walk into the lounge. 'I told you, I was just sketching.' Propping my bag on a chair, I unzip it and reach in for my school books. I'm so sick of having this conversation with him, and don't want another argument.

Sighing as he follows me in, he sits down in the chair opposite, his navy T-shirt dirty from where he's been lying on some stranger's floor to fix their plumbing. 'You should wear the watch I bought you.'

'It makes me feel trapped,' I reply flatly. 'I don't want to spend my time counting down the minutes, always clock-watching.'

'You need to be responsible—'

'I am responsible.' Wrenching my arms out of my blazer, I lob it into the corner. 'Dad, stop! God, why can't you just give me some space? What do you think is going to happen? I'm fourteen, not four.'

He stands up, shaking his head sadly. 'With what happened at your last school ...'

His disappointment is more than I can stand, and I don't need the reminder. 'Look,' I huff, 'that's behind me. I stayed all day, okay? Can't you give me some credit? I was only half an hour late.'

My grandad – whom I refer to as Ray nowadays – strides in from the kitchen holding a cup of tea. He must be having a good day with his illness, because he normally needs a mid-afternoon nap. 'Leila, don't you speak to your father like that! Not under my roof. In my day you showed your elders some respect. And in the Navy, you were taught to obey authority – your superiors – whether you agreed with them or not. You trusted that the orders you got were for the greater good. You should give your dad the same respect.'

I cross my arms across my chest, face boiling. 'Sorry,' I mutter. He's never reprimanded me before, and although I'm tempted to flounce up to my room, his expression says it won't get me anywhere.

Stepping closer, he extends the hot drink toward me. 'Come on, take a seat.'

Relaxing at his easy acceptance of my apology, I take the cup and sit down at the old mahogany table, giving Dad a conciliatory smile and rubbing his arm as he joins me. Thankfully he returns the gesture by squeezing my hand, warming my heart. No matter how shitty I can be, he always loves me.

'Now that's done –'. Ray clears his throat, uncomfortable with the show of emotion '– is this yours?' Going over to the towering oak bookcase in the corner, he comes back with a copy of *Pandora* and passes it to me. 'Someone left it on the doorstep earlier,' he explains, 'but they were gone by the time I got there. I'm not as quick these days with my bloody lungs. Yours?'

'Yes.' Flipping to the Orlando Bloom bookmark inside, I find a tiny charm stuck to the back with tape; a book with open pages and lines scored into them to look like writing. There's an odd quiver in the pit of my stomach. It's weird getting a charm from Jake. It's mine and Mum's thing so it feels like he's intruding, and we don't really know each other well enough to exchange gifts. I suppose it is kind of sweet though. 'It's from Jake.' I look at Dad. 'He picked up the book when ... Uh, something happened today. I kind of lost my temper in class and he took the flack for me. I did try and sort it out,' I blurt, 'really, I did, but it was too late. He got expelled, and he wouldn't let me do anything to stop it.' I pause, thinking. 'It was almost like he wanted to get thrown out. Then his dad arrived, and he was horrid, yanking Jake around all over the place. I didn't get to say goodbye before they left.'

Dad frowns. 'Doesn't sound good. Now this boy knows where you live?'

'It's Jake Harding, Dad. From down the road? The one who lives in our old house?'

Ray clutches his side and goes white, before taking a deep rasping breath. 'My Jake?'

'Ray, take it easy.' Dad gets out of his chair, sliding an arm around his waist to prop him up. 'What's wrong?'

'We need to check on him,' Ray mutters urgently. 'I won't rest easy until I do. I can go knock on the door and see if Jake can come over and help with something. I pay him to mow the lawn and help me wash the car, so it shouldn't look suspicious.'

I follow uneasily as they shuffle into the hallway. Dad helps Ray put his shoes on, before pulling on his own toe-capped work boots. Since when does Ray need help with household maintenance? He's only been ill for a few weeks. As I shove my feet into my flats, Ray steps away from Dad and steadies himself. 'I can manage, thank you.' Throwing open the door, he straightens his shoulders and marches down the front path as if his pain was never there.

Dad and I rush onto the pavement behind him. We come to an abrupt halt as the peeling red front door of my old house opens and Jake's dad emerges, dragging his son along by one arm and carrying a bag over his other shoulder. 'Cut it out, boy,' he roars, 'I told you what would happen if you kept getting in trouble at school. You can go up north to my family and give them grief instead!'

Unlocking a run-down blue Ford Mondeo with rust around the arches, he thrusts Jake into the back and throws the bag in after him, hitting him square in the face. I can see it all because their car is facing us, the driver's side closest to the pavement. Jake's head disappears beneath the line of the seats, and I turn into my dad's shoulder, wincing.

Dad tenses, putting his arm across Ray's chest as he tries to step forward. 'You're not well enough, and it's not our business.'

'I have to do something.' He's agitated, his hands clenching.

Jake's mum steps out into the messy garden, greasy black hair dishevelled and a vivid scarlet mark on her cheekbone. Spotting us, she scrubs at her tearstained face and tucks shaking hands into her skirt pockets, trying hard to conceal her emotions. But I can see from the way her shoulders bow forward that her heart is breaking, and a little of my own breaks with it. No mother should be separated from their child. It's just not right. But she stands by while her husband gets in the car and starts the engine. She does nothing but watch. Says nothing. Doesn't take one step forward. My sympathy for her withers and dies. Every parent should fight for their child, doggedly, until there's not an ounce of energy left in their body, until there is no breath left. It makes me hate Mum all over again, and tears sting my eyes.

Jake's head reappears and he meets his mum's gaze, nodding once and then giving her a solemn wave goodbye. His eyes flicker our way, but he pretends not to see us. I don't blame him.

Winding the window down, Jake's dad shouts at his wife to get in the house, or else. She hastily retreats inside, the door slamming behind her. Paint flecks shower down onto the garden path with the violent force, like dried blood. Revving the engine, Jake's dad sticks his middle finger up at us, 'Enjoying the show? Fuck off, the lot of you.' With a screech, he peels away from the kerb, narrowly missing the cars parked on the other side of the road.

Ray's shaking with anger, and Dad's concerned, holding his elbow to guide him home, checking over his shoulder to make sure I'm following. As we go back inside, I picture Jake's thin face, feeling scared for him and hoping he'll be okay. I can't help feeling it's my fault.

Crossing the threshold into the dim interior of Ray's hallway, realising how thoughtful it was of Jake to return my book and give me a charm when his own situation is so bad, I wonder when I'll see him again.

I have no idea that the next time I do, I'll be saving his life.

Leila

June 2006

The Puppy Charm

'How cool is this?' Eloise spins around on the steep stone-edged steps, sapphire eyes sparkling. 'An end-of-school party at Durdle Door. Isn't it brilliant?' Flinging her arms out with enthusiasm, she starts to overbalance, alarm filling her face.

'Careful!' Grabbing her wrist to steady her, I nod my chin towards the beach below us. 'Come on, we'll chat down there.' Behind me Michelle – Shell – giggles and Chloe sighs. I know they'll both be rolling their eyes, even though we should be used to Eloise's exuberance by now. Dad calls it her *joie de vivre*.

'Do you know what's even more brilliant?' Eloise smiles, ignoring my suggestion. 'That your dad finally got you a puppy. You're so lucky – I'm majorly jealous!'

I can't help grinning, excitement fizzing through me. 'I know,' I squeak, 'she's so adorable. I've waited *so* long.' I think back to the other morning when Dad called me out to his work van and a tiny tri-coloured beagle exploded out of it. I almost cried with joy as I ran my hands over her wriggling little body and tan, white, and brown silky fur. 'Well, I did what he asked.' I nod. 'I stayed in school and took all my GCSEs. I can't believe I've only had her for three days – it already feels like for ever! It's a bit of a drag that she's not allowed out yet though. I can't wait 'til I can walk her. Are you guys still coming to see her tomorrow?' I crane my neck round to look over my shoulder at Shell and Chloe.

'I wouldn't miss meeting Fleur for the world,' Shell says, face glowing with colour from our days spent basking in Bournemouth Gardens and on the pier approach.

'I'll be there, as long as she doesn't wee on me.' Chloe replies, before raising an eyebrow. 'Fleur. You're such a Potter geek. Couldn't you think of anything more imaginative?'

I stick my tongue out at her, used to her gentle sarcasm. 'Fleur Delacour is cool, and totally owned the Triwizard Tournament. And that French accent! You wish you were that cool.'

Chloe mutters something about Harry Potter being for kids, and I stick my tongue out at her again as if to prove my childishness.

'Come on, you two,' Eloise says with a grin, 'pack it in. We're here to party.'

Someone obviously agrees with her. 'Yeah, move it along. I wanna get trashed!' A voice shouts out above us, and I notice a gaggle of people behind Chloe. We're holding things up.

'All right, we're going,' Chloe yells over her shoulder, irritated.

We pick our way carefully down the steps cut into the side of the cliff, following each other in single file. Looking up, I take in the amazing view. The rich blue sea, reminding me of Winsor and Newton's oil colour French Ultramarine, laps against the stony shore. A pale sky hovers above us, stretching into the distance. It would be so pretty to paint. My fingers itch for a graphite pencil and paper to draw an initial sketch.

As soon as we reach the beach, we take our sandals off, Chloe complaining about the millions of tiny stones beneath our feet. 'These are going to get absolutely everywhere. Why couldn't we go to Bournemouth beach?' she grumbles, pushing her newly feathered fringe from her face self-consciously and straightening the empire line of her flowing red dress. 'It's sandy there, and right next to town.'

'Not to mention there's a pier you can go hide under to snog Simon's face off,' Eloise jokes. 'You're going to tell him you like him tonight, right? If you don't, you won't see him 'til September and he's bound to have got off with someone else over the summer.'

'Shut up,' Chloe hisses, glancing around. 'One of his friends might be listening.'

'Well, I hope so. If they're not here, he's not likely to turn up either. Now, relax –' Eloise reaches into her bag, pulling out some cans of beer '– and have one of these. It'll put a smile on your face.'

I reach for a beer as Chloe shakes her head. I don't really like the taste, but I do like the floaty feeling I get after drinking a few.

Shell touches Chloe on the arm, her hazel eyes kind. 'Don't worry, he'll be here. And we'll find a way for you to talk to him. I'm sure he likes you.'

'Thanks,' Chloe mutters, pushing a lock of straight black hair behind one ear.

When I moved back home at fourteen, Chloe was trying to be a carbon copy of Eloise, with a shoulder-length wavy bob and heavily filled-in eyebrows. But for the last year or so her confidence has improved, and she's let her hair grow out, no longer plaiting it to make it kink, and wearing less make-up. She's much prettier this way, and nice with it too – despite the fact she tends to moan a lot. Maybe it's because neither of us has mums that we're so dysfunctional.

Michelle is lovely, but in a kinder, more thoughtful way than Chloe. The spots that caused her such misery when we met are long gone, and she's even taller than Eloise, with endless legs and envy-inspiring boobs. She towers above me, and I sometimes feel like a little girl compared to them all, being the shortest by at least three inches. Eloise regularly says they'd all love to be five foot, slim, and tiny-waisted, but I'm not convinced. It's no fun not being able to reach the top shelf or being constantly told I look younger than I am. I'm going to have to sort some fake ID out soon. We start Sixth Form in three months' time and Eloise is already talking about going clubbing. It would be so humiliating if I couldn't get past the doormen.

'So, why Durdle Door?' Chloe persists as I crack open my beer and take a long deep gulp, shuddering at the taste. 'I mean, it's miles away. Look how long it took us to get here, and how many types of transport we had to use.'

'Because of that,' Eloise answers, pointing at the craggy, beige limestone arch that bends over gracefully into the sea, solid and immovable. 'Later on –' she leans in, arching her eyebrows '– some kids are jumping off the top. I also heard from Megan Whateley that others are planning to go skinny-dipping. You can't do either of those things at Bournemouth beach; there's too much of a risk of the police getting called.'

'Isn't jumping a bit dangerous?' Staring up at the stone archway created by hundreds or potentially thousands of years of erosion, there's a funny dip in my stomach. I've got a bad feeling at the thought of people jumping off it, and as I slide my chunky mobile phone out of my pocket and see the low signal, the feeling gets worse. It's just past 7pm, so we've got hours to go. Eloise's older brother Max won't be here to pick us up until midnight.

'Don't worry –' Eloise catches my eye '– people do it all the time. Just enjoy,' she encourages me, smiling. 'Feel the vibe in the air.'

I must admit it's a beautiful setting for a party. The endless sea views in the evening sunshine are incredible. I can't believe I never knew this existed, right on my doorstep. There's no hint of a breeze and the sea is calm and flat. Lines of brown seaweed form lacy patches along the beach. I can hear birdsong and the waves make only a rhythmic whisper of sound against the shore. Far noisier than the elements are the couple of hundred or so pupils from our school and others from the surrounding areas. I look around, following my friend's advice and soaking up the atmosphere. Various groups of kids are unfurling blankets, setting up ice boxes and stripping down to swim shorts and bikinis before racing down to the water.

'Come on, let's go –' Eloise jiggles on the spot '– I want to find Jonny, and you never know, Chloe, Simon might be with him.' Turning to glance over her shoulder, she grins as she looks back at us. 'It's chaos. I love it!'

She sets off, sure we'll be following in her footsteps. I've always envied her vivacity and confidence. And why wouldn't she be those things, with her cloud of curly black hair, heart-shaped face, big blue eyes, and curvy figure? Looking down at my skinny knees in denim shorts and my virtually flat chest, I sigh, knowing I'll have to go in the sea later. I'll be keeping my T-shirt on when everyone else is using the excuse to strip off. *Hollyoaks* has a lot to answer for, and just under-lines how boring and sensible I am for not sleeping around or crushing on the wrong person.

If I had a mum, maybe I'd talk to her about how inadequate those TV programmes make me feel, and how my figure means I'm practically invisible to boys. Perhaps she'd pour me a cup of tea, pass me a slice of homemade cake, and say it won't last for ever. Reassure me that one day I'll blossom, and they'll notice me, and having a boyfriend isn't the most important thing in the world anyway – it just feels like it sometimes. She'd hug me tight and stroke my hair and finish off by saying that if I'm happy being single, that's all right. But I don't have a mum, and there's no way I could confide any of this to Dad. We'd both be mortified by that type of conversation.

I twist the silver bracelet around my left wrist, playing with the handful of charms hanging off it. It holds six now: a plain silver heart; a tiny pencil; a silver conch shell with a pink interior; an open book with squiggly lines etched into its pages; a round disc with the sea, a setting sun, some seagulls, and a boat engraved on it with a tiny blue gem stone on its hull; and finally, a minuscule silver dog, which arrived this morning. Despite what Dad and Grandad Ray say about Mum never being in touch with them, she must be. How else would she know to send me the dog charm today?

The only time I've ever taken the bracelet off was when I was rushed to A&E a few years ago and one of the nurses insisted I remove it when they were treating my burns. She didn't want me to lose it in the hustle and bustle of the hospital, she said, while helping me into the open-backed gown. I shudder, not liking to think about that night. There are too many bad memories.

I turn the dog charm between my fingers, a smile touching my lips. The bracelet sometimes looks bare because it has so many empty links, but I have faith Mum will send more charms to fill it up. Most of the time I resent her for leaving and never coming back, for not staying in touch on a regular basis. But at other times I'm just glad she makes the effort with the charms, even if it's only every few years. It means that every so often, she thinks about me. That she cares, even if her stubbornly continued absence says the complete opposite.

I try and shrug off the thoughts which could lead me into a black cycle of pain and despair. The blare of music is rising, and as we trudge along the beach to find Jonny and his friends, I realise there isn't one central source of sound. My ears pick out different tunes blaring from a variety of speakers and the contrasting beats and tempos thrum through my body. With them, my spirits rise. We're free at last. School's over, my uniform's in the big black refuse bin. We're done.

And when we go back in September, it'll be different; we'll be treated like adults.

As we move from one group of kids to the next I raise my hand and wave at people, smiling and nodding. Tipping my head back to swallow more beer, I gaze up at the peaks and dips of the chalk cliffs towering above us, the tops and sides of them covered with vibrant green grass. The pockmarked cliff face sweeps down to the beach, and in some places, I can make out small caves running along the base. Some kids are already climbing up to explore them. Three points for guessing what the caves will be used for later.

A giggle escapes me. After months of feeling somehow apart from others, with the pressure of revision, exams, and my future on my shoulders – things only *I* could do something about – I suddenly feel part of something bigger, unified in something amazing with the people around me. There's a crackle of energy in the air, like electricity. I grin. This is going to be fun. What could possibly go wrong?

***

It's getting late. The sun's rays have dimmed, and a couple of campfires have been built with driftwood to provide flickering light. It's past 10pm, and everyone has gathered into one big mass, a knot of teenagers in a jagged circle. Music's still playing, voices rising and falling in unpredictable patterns above the melodies. The day's still muggy but the air isn't quite as warm on our skin. My bum is going numb from sitting on the shingle, but I've had a great time. It *has* been fun. We've eaten, danced, drunk, laughed, and played. We swam, we splashed each other, and Jonny shocked us all by stripping off and jumping into the waves naked in front of everyone – a challenge to Eloise in his eyes. I honestly didn't know where to look, so instead dove into the salty green-blue of the waves, closing my eyes against the image.

The fabric of my T-shirt drifted against my skin over my swimsuit, and for a moment I pretended I was a mermaid and that if I kept swimming, I'd find a magical world out there under the sea. It was a fanciful thought, and I was embarrassed by it – I'm nearly sixteen, for God's sake – but as soon as it flowed through my head, a vivid picture formed, and I knew I'd be painting that mermaid someday. For a moment I wondered if I was drunk, but I'd only had one can of beer. I'm glad of it now as I don't have that floaty, out-of-touch feeling I get after three or four.

Huddling in my beach towel next to Shell, our eyes meet. We share a smile before looking over at Eloise and Jonny kissing, and then at Chloe, who's curled up shyly within the semi-circle of Simon's arm. She's gazing up at him in adoration. I'm both happy for her and sad at the same time, with a hint of jealousy thrown in which I immediately feel bad about.

'Hey, isn't that Jake Harding?' Shell asks suddenly, gazing across the fire at a small group that's broken off from the rest of us.

Tension runs through my body. 'What? Where?' I squint across at them.

'Yeah, he came with Owen Plaitford.' Eloise finally detaches her mouth from Jonny's and looks at me as I twist back to face her. 'They stayed friends after he left. I spoke to Owen earlier.'

'What?' I squeak. She could have said. Then, I scowl. If he's stayed in touch with Owen, why hasn't he stayed in touch with me? I thought he liked me, but maybe I was fooling myself and it was just a passing friendship, like the intense ones when you meet people on holiday, sharing secrets with them, and then never seeing them again.

I've always wondered what happened to Jake after his dad tore him away that day, feeling guilty for my part in it. Now, every time I see *Pandora* sitting on my packed bookshelf or catch sight of my book charm, I remember that short skinny boy and I'm caught between a mixture of gratitude and annoyance. If it all meant nothing, why did he give me the charm, especially when he knew how important the bracelet was to me?

'So, Leila, are you going to make my night, or what?' A pair of wet shorts appear in front of my face, their owner thrusting his groin towards me.

I rear back. 'Urgh! Leave it out, Shaun,' I groan, shaking my head.

He's Jonny's friend, and thinks it's hysterical to pretend he fancies me and try it on. At school, he'll sneak up behind me and grab me around the waist to pick me up or pluck my bag off my shoulder and make me chase him for it. Once he stuck his face in my neck and pretended to snog me loudly in front of everyone. I laughed and half-heartedly pushed him off, knowing we're just friends, noticing how he watched for Shell's reaction from the corner of his eye.

Leaning over, Shaun lifts me off the sand, bringing me in tight for a big hug, soaking my T-shirt and swimsuit all over again.

'Shaun, you git!' I yelp. 'I only just dried off!'

'Git?' He mock roars. 'I'll teach you, you uppity little cow!' Bending his knees, he tries to scoop me up over his shoulder, but I leap out of the way squealing.

Just as I open my mouth to laugh, a hand yanks Shaun backwards by the shoulder, sending him flying with the unexpected strength of it. 'Leave her alone!' A deep voice yells. I see Shaun's feet leave the ground and he actually sails through the air like something out of a cartoon, his back arched. There's a muffled '*oof*' as he lands on the shingle not far from the fire. The breath whooshes from him and he curls over onto his side.

'Shaun!' Shell and I run over as Chloe and Eloise spring to their feet. He's lying on the ground, red-faced and groaning.

Shell drops to her knees and rolls him over, moving his head onto her lap, her hair streaming down around their faces. 'Are you okay?'

'Shit.' Wheezing, he takes a deep breath. 'Yeah, think ... so ...' he mutters. 'Just winded. What the fuck happened?'

'I don't know. Some guy just went postal.' Frowning, she glances up at me. I look around, shrugging my shoulders in bewilderment.

Shaun's breathing is coming a little easier as Shell helps him sit up, dusting him off with a gentle hand. She winces. 'You've got some cuts and grazes on your back from the stones. We should put some antiseptic cream on them. I've got some in my bag.' She gets to her feet, holding out her hand. 'Come on. Can you walk?'

'Yeah, I think so.' As he stands up unsteadily, he puts an arm around her shoulder, leaning in. 'If I knew all I had to do for your attention was get shoved around at a party, I would've done it months ago.'

Shell rolls her eyes. 'That's tragic.' But there's a little smile on her lips.

It looks like all my friends are coupled off, and the thought stings. But I ignore it, and seeing Shaun's okay, I spin around. 'Did anyone see anything?' Everyone's standing there watching, hands over their mouths whispering and gossiping. 'Who did that?' People shake their heads, watching as Shaun limps off with Shell. 'Anyone?'

'It was me.' A voice with a faint northern twang says from amongst a crowd of heads, before the bodies part and a tall form walks through. 'Are you okay?'

I can't see much of his face as the only light is from two nearby fires, but it's enough to recognise him, even though he's about a foot taller than the last time we saw each other. I take in the familiar scar, the sharp cheekbones, heavy eyebrows, and thick black hair. 'Jake.' I gulp. He looks like a stranger but also familiar at the same time. 'Why the hell did you do that?' He's not a short skinny teenager any more. He's much taller than I remember and with him in swimming shorts, I can also see a lot of muscles. I force myself to focus on his face and pray my fair skin won't betray me. 'What were you thinking?'

'I thought he was hurting you, Jones. I heard him call you a cow, and he was trying to grab you.'

Something about the way he uses my surname grates on me, just like it did when I was fourteen. 'He's my friend. We were messing around. We always do.' He flinches and opens his mouth, but I get there first. 'You can't just shove people around!' I point my finger at him, uncaring of the crowd watching our little drama. 'You could have seriously hurt him. What's *wrong* with you?'

'Quite a lot, it seems.' His lips curl back over his teeth. 'Including sticking up for spoilt little girls.' He holds his arms out to his sides, 'So the next time I see someone who needs help, I won't bother—'

'*Spoilt?*' I screech, staring at him. 'Well, I didn't need help, and I definitely don't need yours. You have no right to just come charging in.' My volume climbs, my face getting hotter. 'Jeez, when did you turn into such a feminist?'

I gape at him, expecting better from him than that, before realising the look in his eyes isn't anger. It's pain.

'After all,' he continues, 'you were happy enough to accept my help last time.'

He's got me, and it puts me on the defensive. 'W-well, I didn't ask for it then,' I shoot back, 'and I'm not asking for it now.' I put my hands on my hips. 'Anyway, since when did you adopt a "violence solves everything" ethos? Don't be like your dad and go—'

'What?' His mouth drops open, wounded, before rallying. 'I was just trying to protect you. We're friends.'

That stings. 'No, Jake. We were friends once. And barely that. *Then you left.*'

His jaw tenses, a pulse beating. 'If that's how you feel, fine.'

Spinning around, he marches off through a gap in the crowd, churning up shingle along the ground as he goes.

Eloise and Chloe appear next to me. 'Bloody hell, Leila,' Eloise says, eyes wide. 'I know you're loyal to your friends and he hurt Shaun, but you sort of lost it with him.'

Chloe nods in agreement, 'It's not like you at all. You okay?'

'Yeah, of course,' I say with a nod. As I turn to them, the anger drains away, leaving me shaking. Embarrassment fills me for losing control, especially so publicly. They've never seen this side of me. Dad would be so disappointed. We thought I'd left my temper behind when we moved back to the south coast.

I simmer with resentment at Jake for bringing back memories of emotions past. Yet he didn't deserve what I said, and I *really* shouldn't have made that comment about his dad. I cringe. Then I burst into tears.

***

Nearly two hours later I'm propped against Chloe, my head resting on her shoulder as we listen to 'Don't Look Back in Anger' by Oasis. She's smiling as she watches Simon and Jonny pretend to strum guitars in front of the fire, miming the way Liam Gallagher sings with his mouth practically kissing the microphone.

I've calmed down and the atmosphere is muted now, not many of us left at the beauty spot. I hate ugly scenes, and it's soured the evening. I wanted to go home straight afterwards, but Eloise couldn't get any signal to call Max, and I could see my friends enjoying themselves, so I wiped the tears away and pretended I was fine. And I am – or at least I will be. I can't understand why Jake behaved like that, or why my reaction was so strong. I overheard Eloise muttering to Chloe that in a way it was sweet he was trying to protect me, but I disagree. I'm not his to protect. Still, I wonder if he's okay after our disagreement, and regret causes my stomach to churn.

My attention turns towards the water, and the stone arch of the Door. There's a dark figure on top of the high rocky outcrop. It disappears and then I hear a splash. Scouring the sea for a swimmer in the fading light, I see nothing. For a moment I turn away as Eloise waves at me, holding out a can of beer, but I shake my head. Michelle glances at me from beside Shaun and mouths *okay?* so I nod and give her a double thumbs up.

I turn back to the sea, scanning it again for a swimmer, and then the shoreline for someone getting out. Nothing. Maybe I imagined it. But I feel uneasy. I uncurl my legs, pushing myself off the ground and moving away from the fire. It goes unnoticed as someone turns the volume to maximum and everyone stands up to sing together, voices raised as they throw their arms around each other's waists and shoulders, shouting out about how Sally can wait, and that she knows it's too late.

Striding with effort over the multi-coloured pebbles to the water's edge, I can't get rid of the feeling that someone was— There! Squinting in the half-light, I spot a small dot in the sea at the bottom of the arch, and moments later, a pair of flailing arms. They look like they're clawing at the sky. Whoever it is, they're in trouble. Casting a look over my shoulder, I see everyone's occupied, noisily singing, their heads thrown back. They don't realise that a drama is unfolding only a dozen feet away, silent and unseen.

'Hey!' I shout, turning to the crowd and trying to get someone's attention. 'Hey, there's someone in trouble!' But they can't hear. As I hesitate, I notice the arms sink beneath the glassy surface of the sea and realise I haven't got time. I've wasted too much already.

If nothing else, I'm a good swimmer – one of the few skills Mum instilled in me before she disappeared. My instincts take over. Taking deep breaths, I wade into the water, ignoring the slight chill. The sea hasn't had the whole summer to warm up yet. As soon as it's deep enough, I dive in, my arms arching over and alternating in firm, precise strokes. *Hang on*, I think hazily, *just wait for me.*

It takes for ever but at the same time feels like only an instant, and then my left hand's connecting with a struggling body, and I'm grabbing an arm and heaving them to the surface, both of us gasping for breath. Their fight for survival is making it hard for me to get a grip.

'Stop it!' I order, briny water filling my mouth. Turning my head, I spit it out. Salty water is splashing in my face and stinging my eyes. I can hardly see. I try hooking my right arm around their chest so I can get them to lie on their back and tow them in, but they – *he*, I realise from the width of his shoulders and shape of his skull – is dipping down below the water again. He can't kick properly for some reason. There's a current beneath us trying to pull us out to dangerous depths, but I resist it. *Not today*, I think fiercely, *and not like this.*

Yanking him back up to the surface, I calm myself down, inhaling deeply to make sure I have enough air in my lungs to keep us both afloat. 'Stop moving. Relax!' I bellow in his ear through a mop of dark hair, trying to get through to him. 'It's okay. I've got you.'

Thankfully he quietens, and I hook my arm around under his armpit across to his opposite shoulder so he's floating in front of me, both of us on our backs. I draw him closer, noticing his right leg is dead straight, toes curled over tight. His chest is solid and broad beneath my hand, and I try to ignore the feeling of my boobs squashed against his back, working on keeping our lower bodies apart so our legs don't tangle. Apart from the play-fighting with Shaun, this is the closest I've ever been to a guy. *Nearly sweet sixteen and never been kissed*, I think regretfully.

Shaking off the thought, I set out for the beach in a slow but steady back-crawl, using my left arm, tilting my head back in the sea, and gazing up at the darkened sky as I swim. My long, pale hair floats to the top of the water, fanning out around our heads. The only sounds audible with my ears beneath the surface are the stones shifting against each other, as if in a sigh. Night's fallen during the last few minutes, and sparkling stars have appeared in the velvet sky. It looks like there are a thousand at least, twinkling and saying hello. Telling us they're here and that they see us too.

There's something magical about the moment despite the circumstances, and I can't help but take in the view. The starry sky stretches above us, no end in sight. It's like this boy and I are the only two people in the world. There's just us, in the water. Everyone else has faded away and been forgotten. But strangely that's okay. It's comfortable. Right.

The moment lingers. 'Beautiful,' I whisper, tilting my head to see more stars.

'Yeah' echoes back, and I know I've spoken in his ear again.

'Jake!' I recognise his voice, and for a brief pause I stop swimming. Even though I'm in chilly water, the warmth of embarrassment creeps over my skin. I wince. This isn't how I'd imagined seeing him again, especially after earlier. Talk about awkward.

He doesn't reply, but I hear him mutter *shit* under his breath as I resume swimming.

Before I'm ready for it, I feel smooth hard points beneath my legs and realise I've swum us all the way to shore with barely any effort. Planting my feet on the bottom, I stand up, helping him wade in. The water comes up to my hips and his thighs. It's so dark, the night air is like a blanket, and the fire is too far away to let me see his expression.

Bending over at the waist, he coughs a few times and inhales sharply before stumbling to the water's edge. I follow him, hovering uncertainly and watching as he collapses in a heap, straightening his leg out before grabbing his foot and pulling his toes up toward his body. Muttering some swear words under his breath that would make even Grandad with his Navy background flinch, he massages the arch of his foot with a groan. The longer he works on it, the more it returns to its normal shape. His thick black hair is plastered to his head, and he rakes both hands through it, leaving it stuck up in damp tufts. At last, he looks up at me. One of the clouds covering the moon passes, and it shines down on us, painting his face a ghostly white.

'Jake,' I whisper hesitantly. 'Are you okay?' Given how I just helped him, he doesn't look pleased to see me. 'Are you hurt? What happened? That was scary.' For both of us, I add silently. Not to mention unsettling. I close my eyes, blushing. I was right up against him, our bodies touching. There's a weird feeling in my stomach, but I don't like him in that way.

'I'm fine,' he says through gritted teeth, as I open my eyes, 'stop fussing.'

'S-sorry,' I stutter in a high voice, too shocked to say anything else.

Stepping away, I shiver in the night air. My white T-shirt's soaked and sticking to my body. Pulling it away from my swimsuit helps a little, but not much. I need a towel and some dry clothes. Glancing along the beach, I notice everyone's still singing, their choral voices soaring. For all intents and purposes, Jake and I might as well be alone together on the beach in the shadow of Durdle Door. It's weird – only ten minutes have passed since I realised someone was in trouble and dove in after them, but I feel like I've aged ten years. Like the girl who came out of the sea is a different one to the girl who went in. Maybe that's what happens when you save a life – you change your own.

The thought makes me cross. I did a good thing, so why's Jake being like this? Why's he acting like I tried to drown him, rather than help him? He could have easily been swept out by the current that tried to steal us away. 'You know, you could at least say thank you,' I hurl at him, teeth chattering. 'Without me, you'd have been in real trouble.'

He pushes himself off the ground, avoiding my eyes. 'No, I wouldn't. I didn't need any help. I'd have been fine as soon as I got rid of the cramp.' Shrugging his broad shoulders, he bunches up fistfuls of his black swimming shorts, squeezing out the water.

'That's rubbish! You were sinking fast, and the current was strong. You would've been gone before anyone knew it. And what were you doing jumping off the top of the Door anyway? It's practically suicide. Have you got a death wish?'

'No.' His voice turns cold, the new depth in it making him sound like a man. Then I realise he must be almost eighteen so he *is* practically a man. 'I just thought it would be a cool thing to do. Owen dared me. You sound like my mum,' he drawls, in a bored tone, 'and I don't need another one of those. Thanks, though.'

I glare at him. 'I thought I was too hard on you earlier – I felt bad about it actually – but you are *so* rude, and an idiot too if you think a dare is worth risking your life for!'

'If you say so.'

The final cloud drifts away and the moon shines its cool light more brightly on his face. The planes are smooth and hard, but there's still some softness around his chin. The scar leading down into his top lip seems fainter than it used to. His eyes glint as they look me up and down.

Hugging my arms around my middle, the breeze drifting across the beach makes me shiver again. Suddenly I'm cold and tired, longing for a hot shower and my bed. There's salt drying in crusty zig-zags along my skin and my hair is dripping cool water down my spine. Shaking my head, I stare at him. I want to go home. I'm done with this. 'Whatever,' I reply, swinging around to leave. 'If you're not even going to say thank you … or apologise for earlier … See you around.'

'Me, apologise?' His voice makes me jolt. 'You were the one who said we're not friends.'

'We're not,' I flash. He didn't stay in touch, so how can we be friends? Well, I'm not spelling it out for him.

'So why did you help then? And why bawl me out for saving you earlier, but think that it's okay to do the same for me? It's a bit hypocritical, isn't it?'

Turning, I gaze at him, pulling the hem of my T-shirt down. 'I didn't know who I was saving at the time, did I?' As soon as it leaves my mouth, I realise how awful it sounds. That if I'd known it was him, I'd have left him there to drown. I rush on. 'And maybe it does make me a hypocrite, but all I knew was someone was in trouble, and no one else had realised. I didn't have a choice; I had to help.'

'There's always a choice.'

'Not for me. What was I supposed to do, let someone drown?' He opens his mouth, but I keep talking. 'Anyway, now I know it's you, I'm glad. Now you can consider us even.' They feel right, those last few sentences on my lips, the shape and sound of them. I've just very probably saved his life, and when he took the blame for me that day at school, he unknowingly saved mine. Our school, my friends, the stability I've had with Dad and Grandad over the last few years, saved me. No more running away, no more losing control of my rage and frustration, no more silly decisions with disastrous consequences. I feel the skin on my lower back itch despite my drenched T-shirt, and wish for the hundredth time I'd been left unmarked by that night. Not just physically, but mentally too.

'We're not even. We don't need to be. You don't owe me anything,' Jake snaps. 'I used you.'

'Used me how?' The moon is swallowed up by another cloud and his face flickers back into darkness. 'Jake?' I demand, stepping forward.

'I wanted out of there,' he says. 'Getting expelled from school was how I was going to do it. Mum was in on it. Luckily for me, it worked.'

'So, you took the blame as part of some grand plan? I could have been anyone?'

'Yes.'

He sounds so cocky, and I don't like it. 'I don't believe you.' I yank my T-shirt off over my head, hoping the breeze will take the dampness from my bare skin and help dry out my swimsuit. 'I just don't. That day at school, you made that weird comment about how you met me before you met me. It meant something; it was personal. And later, you brought *Pandora* back with the book charm.'

'You remember what I said?'

'Of course. So, what did you mean?'

He sighs. 'Is there any chance you're going to let this drop?'

'No. Plus, if you don't explain it to me, I'm going to tell everyone I had to fish you out of the sea. That wouldn't do your bad-boy image much good, would it?'

'That's blackmail.' The northern edge in his voice sharpens. I shrug, waiting.

At my silence, he huffs. 'Fine. Yes. The day we first met—'

'The day you moved into my old house,' I murmur, still able to recall how furious I was at Mum for leaving, holding her responsible for us selling up and leaving town, and all my friends, behind. 'What about it?' I prompt, embarrassed to remember how resentful I was of the new family moving into *my* house. 'Come on.'

'I was out front, and you were in your dad's van. We spoke—'

'Yes. I was worried about you.'

'You were?' An odd note creeps into his voice.

'Yeah,' I admit. 'I watched you and your dad. I didn't like what I saw. I thought he was scary.' It makes me feel bad all over again about the comment I made earlier when we argued. Sure, Jake grabbed Shaun, but he didn't beat him to a pulp or enjoy the scene the way I suspect his dad would have.

'I know.' He sighs, clearing his throat. 'Well, before that conversation, I'd been in the house for the first time. Dad had put me in your old bedroom; he thought that was funny because it was pink. But when I went upstairs and saw the paintings of all the doors on the walls, and how many worlds you'd imagined stepping into ... it made me feel hope. Not something I was used to. I also discovered what was under the bed. I saw what you'd created there. It was like a magical place I could e-escape to ...' He stumbles over his words. 'I felt like I was walking in your footsteps. It made me feel like I already knew you.'

There's so much pain in his voice when he talks about

escaping that I daren't ask any more questions. But, God ... Squirming, I recall the picture he's talking about, the one under the bed. I think of the fairy who was based on me, with silvery hair and starry eyes, holding a magic wand and a paint brush. That piece is so deeply personal and childish. The thought of another person seeing it makes me feel a bit sick. It feels intrusive, like he's seen parts of me he shouldn't have. On the other hand, there's something about his confession that touches me. He used my creation to escape a world he didn't want to live in, just like I did after Mum left. Perhaps we're not so different, and maybe he's not as hard-faced and cocky as he sometimes appears.

'So, when I had the opportunity to help you in return,' he continues, 'at the same time as helping myself, I took it. Happy now?' Before I can answer, the moon reappears, lighting the beach around us. I glance around. While we've been talking, the party has broken up, the music's been turned off and a few kids are drifting towards us, heading for the steps carved into the grassy cliff. As he notices them, Jake shifts away, shoving his hands in his pockets. 'Anyway, enough of all that,' he says, breaking the mood. 'You've had your explanation.'

I stare at him, confused at his abrupt turnaround, my mouth open as I search for the right thing to say. 'Well, thanks for telling me,' I reply, uncomfortable. The moonlight catches my bracelet with a glimmer as I move my arm, and I spin it around my left wrist, rubbing the dog charm between two fingers. To fill the silence, I start babbling. 'My dad finally bought me a puppy as a reward for taking all my exams,' I blurt. 'I've been on at him to get me a dog for years. As an only child I always wanted company growing up. Anyway, I got her the other day and her name's Fleur. She's really cute. She keeps following me around and wanting to play.'

'That's nice.' Tilting his head to the side, he asks, 'After the character in Harry Potter?'

'Yes,' I say, surprised by his observation. 'The charm arrived this morning. Grandad found it in an envelope that came through the door.' I press on, wanting another answer from him. 'You know him, right? The day you left he wanted to go after you, to stop your dad taking you.'

'He didn't need to; he knows that.'

'What?' I glance at him sharply. 'How does he know? Have you been in touch with him?' Hot jealousy shoots though me. I'm not sure whether that's about Grandad, or Jake.

'You don't need to worry about that. Jones, look, there's something I need to—'

'Jake!' A voice shouts above us on the stairs, and I recognise Owen's lanky frame and shaggy hair. 'We need to go,' he hollers. 'We've got a problem. Your dad—'

'Coming,' Jake calls back, interrupting his friend. He starts backing away and I go to follow, but he holds his hands up, palms out, to stop me. 'Don't. If it's about my dad, I've gotta go now.'

'Jake, wait—'

'I can't.'

'But what did you mean about my grandad?'

'It doesn't matter.' He darts off to the side, grabbing a black rucksack from a pile of bags. Slinging it on his shoulder, he lopes up the steps. 'Just for the record,' he says in a rush, 'I would have been okay without you. There was no need to help me. I'm a strong swimmer and I know my way around the sea. Really.' As he starts climbing, he gives me a half-salute, touching a hand to his forehead. 'But thank you. Not bad for a feminist,' he smirks. 'And by the way, Jones, I'm glad you grew your hair.' He points at the sodden ropes hanging almost to my waist. Before I can reply, he nods to the screwed-up T-shirt I'm clutching in front of me. 'And nice top, but I preferred it on. It definitely looked better on.' Spinning, he leaps up the steps, taking two at a time without once glancing back.

'What?' I stare after him, embarrassment colouring my face. Why did I ever think we were friends?

Jake

November 2007

The Car Charm & The Sea Charm

'Holy Fuck, what the hell?' Jake stomps his trainer on the brake pedal, the BMW juddering to a stop.

Whipping his head round, he glares between the head rests, a green car filling his rear-view window. He yanks the handbrake on and leaps out of the door. Racing to the rear end of what he sees now is an old VW Beetle, he slaps an open palm against the back window. 'Stop. Stop moving, for God's sake.'

The car halts and the driver's window is rolled down, a blonde head emerging. The hair is so pale it's almost silver. 'Huh?' Turning her head, she flinches, 'Oh, Jake. It's you.'

Jake's heart jolts in his chest. *Leila*. He figured she'd have gone to college in town to study art by now. The last time they'd seen each other was eighteen months before, when she'd dragged him from the sea. After he'd made an idiot of himself laying into her friend, and she'd accused him of being like his dad. Not his finest hour, but he'd been embarrassed and, to his shame, his pride had got in the way of manners.

The shock of seeing her now unexpectedly, unprepared for

the emotions it causes, adds to his anger. 'Yep, it's me.' His voice rises, a slight northern lilt coating it. 'And don't play the innocent. You backed into my car and were trying to drive off. We need to exchange insurance details. Also, it looks like the bumpers are caught on each other, so you're only doing more damage trying to pull them apart.'

'Okay, calm down.' Her head disappears, and she rolls the window up. She clambers from the car as he comes around the front bonnet of the VW to meet her. 'Actually, you backed into me. The spaces are opposite each other and there's no right of way, but I started reversing first—'

'I don't think so, Jones,' he drawls.

Her eyes narrow. 'Don't patronise me, Jake, and don't be an arse.' Her tone is mild, but the comment stings. 'Oh no, I'd better be careful in case you think I'm being a feminist again.' She raises both eyebrows, more confident than before. 'And how was I supposed to know the bumpers were caught on each other? I don't have Supergirl's x-ray vision.'

'That's a shame, because if you did, it might improve your driving skills. I clearly had the right of way because contrary to what you think, I was reversing first. I checked my mirror twice.' But even as he says it, he knows he was distracted by the visit to his friend Owen, by all the things that've changed but not changed while he's been away.

Inhaling deeply through her nose, which is sporting a tiny diamond stud these days, she draws herself up to her full height – which is still a good few inches below his chin – before steadily releasing the air from her mouth. If he had to guess, he'd say she was praying for patience. 'Well, the insurance companies can argue it out.' She nods. 'The main thing is no one got hurt.'

'Until I get home,' Jake mutters.

'Huh?'

'Nothing. Don't worry about it.' It's not her fault his dad's how he is. Still, at least now he's the same size as his father.

He studies Leila. She's short and slender, although the grey fake fur jacket with black jeans and ankle boots bulks her out. There are three earrings in her left lobe. A star, a moon, and a garnet. 'Nice outfit,' he says.

'Right.' She blinks. 'Are you trying to be funny?'

'Excuse me?'

'About my outfit,' she replies coolly. 'Last summer you were pretty clear that my body should be covered up.'

He barks out a laugh. 'You misunderstood me. I thought the wet T-shirt suited you.' She'd been gorgeous that night, all big dark eyes and pale, moonlit skin.

'Oh.' She steps back, a frown pulling her eyebrows together. '*Oh*,' she says in an odd tone, blushing.

Now her pale hair rests on her shoulders, the tips dyed lilac. It's just like her to do something different, something outside the mainstream, but with her blonde eyebrows, light complexion, and petal-patterned grey irises, the overall effect is curiously bland. She needs a brighter colour. He always thinks of her as so vivid. Plus, he can't believe she cut her hair. It was so amazing.

'Jake?' She's watching him, cheeks reddening further as he stares at her. When she brushes her hair back from her face with a small graceful hand, tucking it behind one ear, the scent of strawberries fills the air. He also notices charcoal smudges on her index finger and thumb, and is glad she still draws.

Feeling self-conscious, he rubs a finger over his scar and forces a twisted smile. 'Sorry. I was just thinking. You've cut all your hair off.'

'Not all of it. But yeah, I needed a change.' She gazes at his face, 'Your scar's a bit more pronounced than it used to be, because you're so tanned.'

'And?' he queries, self-conscious and wishing she hadn't brought attention to it.

She frowns. 'Nothing. It's very *Pirates of the Caribbean*. It's quirky, and you know I don't have a problem with quirky.' Holding her arms out to point at her outfit.

In the distance, a high-pitched bell lets out three sharp shrills. 'Oh, shit. I need to get to class.' She throws a panicky look at the redbrick buildings behind them. 'We should sort the cars out. Do you want me to try and drive forward again or—?'

'No. Let's take a proper look first.' Striding to the back of her car, he leans over to inspect where it's attached to the rear end of his.

As Jake is running his hands along the hooked bumpers, a member of school staff appears, shooing away all the gossiping students scattered across the car park. 'Haven't you all got lessons to get to? Come on, clear off, the bell's gone,' he barks. 'Are you both all right?' he asks, marching over to them. 'Do I need to call an ambulance or inform the police?'

Jake shakes his head. 'It's under control. Give me five

minutes and it'll be sorted.' Glancing up, he straightens to full height. 'Bloody hell. Mr Strickland.' He pauses, then adds, 'I thought you'd be retired by now.'

Leila snorts, before turning it into a cough.

'How do you—' The teacher's eyes squint as he concentrates. 'Jake Harding. I remember you.'

'Yes, Sir.' Jake grins. He can't help it. The man looks horrified.

'What are you doing here?'

'Oh, I was thinking of coming back to do my A-levels. I know it's a bit delayed, but still, it's always worth a shot. I thought I'd try English. You'd enjoy that, right?'

'I ... ah ...' Mr Strickland's face whitens.

'Stop torturing him, Jake,' Leila admonishes, 'we both know that's rubbish. You couldn't wait to get out of here.' She gives him a sideways look.

Jake shoves his hands into the pockets of his jeans. 'She's right. I was just here to see a friend for lunch. Owen Plaitford? We'd just said goodbye and I was leaving when Leila and I bumped cars. I'm not applying to come back, don't worry.'

Mr Strickland relaxes, his chest puffing out as the anxiety slips away. 'So, what are you doing these days? I can't imagine you've made anything of yourself, after the way you behaved at school.'

Jake's grin falls away at the derisive tone, and he stares at the older man. 'You haven't changed much, have you?' He stands straighter. 'But actually, I have. I got the basic qualifications I needed, left school, and joined the Marines. I was in officer training last year, all five phases, and went on my first mission a couple of months ago. So, whatever you might think of me or who I was back then, these days I'm proud to serve my Queen and country, and help keep others safe.'

Leila's eyebrows rise, but she says nothing.

'Oh.' Mr Strickland's mouth opens and closes like a vacant goldfish before he pulls himself together. 'In that case, if I'm right to believe you, then well done.'

Jake's face goes blank, but he manages a nod and then his chin tilts up, just by an extra millimetre. 'Thank you,' he replies in a low voice. He steps away. 'Anyway, we'd better separate these cars and exchange details. We won't be long; I'll be gone soon.'

'All right,' the teacher agrees, 'as you were then. Try not to be too late for English,' he shoots at Leila, before hurrying from the car park.

'Well, that was weird,' she remarks, watching the man's departing back. 'It's not like him to be nice.' Jake's already crouched down by the bumpers as she turns around. 'Don't you think, Jake? It was nice of him to say that to you, right?'

'Whatever,' he mutters. Bending back a piece of metal with a grunt, he stands and moves around to the driver's side of his car, wiping his dirty hands on his jeans.

'Whatever?' She looks perplexed. 'He said well done; he acted like he was proud of you. What's not to like about that?'

'It's not him who should be proud of me. Look, just forget it.'

'Oh. Right, I see. It's about your dad.' A beat of silence.

'Look, Jake, what I said about you being like your dad at the beach party. I shouldn't have. I never got the chance to say sorry properly. And I am sorry.'

'Don't worry about it,' he says, looking over her shoulder, but his voice is terse, betraying him.

'But, I really didn't—'

'I said, let it go.'

She sucks in a breath. 'Okay, if that's what you want.'

'It is.' Getting into the BMW, he slams the car door and starts the engine. Reversing it carefully by a couple of centimetres, he slams it into first gear and shoots forward a metre or so. With a shearing sound, the cars break apart. He climbs back out and comes around to inspect the damage, wincing. After a moment, he shrugs. 'It could be worse, I guess.'

Leila studies the buckled chrome bumper, her lips twisting. 'Grandad's not going to be happy with me. I've only had it a few weeks.'

'I'm sure he'll forgive you.'

'Hopefully. Anyway –' she changes the subject abruptly, spinning round to face him '– it doesn't matter, does it? About what Mr Strickland said. Because you were making it up, right? You're not in the Marines. It was a load of rubbish.'

He frowns. 'Why would you say that?'

'You're the most rebellious person I know, Jake. Answering back and getting into fights. Jumping off Durdle Door. Getting thrown out of school. Plus, you're here, not halfway across the world. So come on, stop being stupid, what have you actually been up to?'

For a second, his frown deepens but then he laughs and

crosses his arms across his broad chest. 'Yeah, you're right. You got me. I've actually been in a youth offending detention centre for the last eighteen months.'

'What ... what for?' Her eyes widen.

'You're unbelievable.' He chuckles. 'You'd rather believe I broke the law and was sent away than believe I might've found something worth doing with my life. Because of course people can never change, and there's no way the rebellious stuff could've been a phase I was going through, or a reaction to an unhappy home life, could it?' Her mouth drops open, but he carries on. 'There's no way that talking to someone I looked up to and respected as I was growing up, someone who'd served in the Navy and said it was the making of him, inspired me to want to do something better, to be someone better than my dad. And of course, leaving home, finding a purpose and something I'm good at and a family I belong in, isn't a possibility you'd consider for me.'

'Woah. Quite the soliloquy. Okay, I apologise if I got it wrong.' She cocks her head, studying his face. 'You do look different. More grown up.' Then her gaze drifts down to his muscular forearms. Even though it's a crisp November day, he's wearing a black T-shirt. She shivers in the breeze whipping brown and auburn leaves around them, the wind sending them whistling along the concrete to form in damp piles in corners of the car park.

'I believe you –' her expression smooths out '– about the Navy, I mean. I shouldn't have jumped to conclusions. I was just surprised. How come the visit?'

'We're allowed shore leave. I wanted to see my mum, and

my old stomping ground.' He clears his throat. 'You seem irritated with me sometimes. Why is that?'

'Well, you can be pretty annoying. Cocky, and overprotective.'

'Please,' he says wryly, 'you'll give me a big head if you're not careful.'

'Sorry, but it's just the way you can come across.'

'I don't mean to. I guess cheekiness can edge into cockiness, and as for overprotective, I'm just looking out for you.'

'I appreciate that, Jake,' she says, nodding, 'but I find it a bit much, especially when it's done without asking.'

'Okay, noted. I'll try not to do that,' he says stiffly.

'Don't be like that. But you also called me spoilt at the party, and I didn't really get it.'

Flushing, he shoves his hands in his pockets. 'Sorry. Heat of the moment. I didn't mean it. It's just that I don't always think you realise how lucky you are, and maybe sometimes you take things for granted.'

'In what way?' She frowns.

'You've got a family—'

'With a mum who buggered off, pretty much on my birthday,' she replies flatly.

'Maybe, but the family you do have protect, love, and care for you. Whereas I have both my parents but—'

'You don't have what I have,' she finishes slowly. 'Oh. I see. I never thought of it like that. I'm sorry. It must be hard.' She looks sympathetic, reaching a hand out towards him.

Jake waves her words, and comfort, away. 'Let's not get into that.' He can't bear her pity. Besides, he's not that beaten little boy anymore. 'You were talking about all my worst traits?'

She laughs, casting him a wry smile. 'Honestly? It's not even that. This isn't easy for me to say, but I've been annoyed at you for years for another reason.'

'Really?' He moves closer. 'Why?'

'I guess I was just surprised and disappointed that after you left town you never got in touch again. I never got to say thank you for returning *Pandora* and leaving me the book charm –' she looks discomfited, and softens her voice kindly '– which, by the way, was really nice, but it's mine and Mum's thing so I'd rather you didn't, thank you.' Her voice hardens, 'You stayed in touch with Owen after you left and hinted that you did with Grandad too. Then we just ran into each other by chance at the beach party. It's not like you were looking for me.'

'But I—' he blurts, before grinding to a halt.

'What?' she leaps in.

How can he tell her that all the charms bar one have been from him, when he knows it will break her heart? For the last six years he's bought her charms based on what Ray's dropped into conversation about her life, whereas she's believed her mum sends them. She draws comfort and hope from that belief.

Now it's gone on so long he feels trapped by his own lies. If he stops sending them, she'll be devastated, because it'll mean no contact from her mum at all and she'll feel like she's losing her all over again.

At last, he mutters, 'I'm sorry I didn't stay in touch. I should have done. I'm not back for long but I promise next time I'm home on leave I'll look you up. Okay? To be honest, I didn't think it would matter that much to you.'

A wave of heat surges up her neck and into her face, mottling her skin. She steps back. 'It didn't, don't worry about it.' Averting her gaze, she gabbles, 'Look, I've got to run. Mr Strickland will be wondering where I am. Let me grab my insurance details.'

He watches her dive into the front of her car as he pulls his wallet out. A minute later she's pressed her details into his hand on a scrappy bit of paper. It's written in blue pencil and is barely legible. He squints at it, trying to read. The details he's given her are in neat block writing on the back of a business card someone once gave him, noted down in case of an accident.

She mouths the insurance company name and number as she reads it. 'You came well prepared.'

'Maybe Navy life has given me self-discipline and now I prepare in advance.'

'There's that chip again.' She moves closer and pretends to brush it off his shoulder, before awkwardly stepping back.

He laughs, defusing the tension between them.

'Preparing in advance sounds a bit boring to me,' she says. 'I'd rather not waste time doing things now that I might not have to worry about doing at all.' She folds the card in half and shoves it carelessly in her pocket. 'To be honest, you always struck me as independent, so it doesn't surprise me you're organised. I guess you were used to looking after yourself.' She straightens. 'Anyway, make sure you tell the insurance company the accident was your fault before heading off again overseas. I could do without having to wait months for this to be sorted.'

'Oh, don't worry, I'll call them –' he raises one eyebrow '– to confirm it was your fault, and that you need to pay for the damage.'

'I reversed first,' she retorts, 'so it was your fault. You should take responsibility.'

'I don't think so. Got any witnesses who are going to agree with you?'

They both look around at the empty car park.

She groans. 'Jake, you might be earning an annual salary, but I'm not. I'm just a poor student who spends all her money on art supplies and petrol. Come on. You owe me.' She pulls a hopeful expression. 'Don't forget I saved your life once.'

'Don't forget I saved you from being expelled once. I'd call it even, as you said that night on the beach. No deal.'

'You said it didn't make us even, that you used me to get what you wanted, to leave home.'

'I said a lot of things back then.' He sighs. 'I shouldn't have said I used you. I've grown up since.'

'Sounds boring,' she mutters, looking down and fiddling with her charm bracelet.

He flicks the tiny car charm, knowing he's tempting fate. He's not ready to say goodbye yet though. 'You got another one.'

She looks up. 'Yeah. Grandad started teaching me to drive on his friend's farm just after my sixteenth. It was in the New Forest, so great scenery and lots of private land to practise on. I studied hard to pass the theory test as soon as I hit seventeen, and then took a few lessons to help pass the driving test. The charm arrived a few weeks later.'

'You like it then?' He holds his breath.

'Yeah, it's cute.' She grins.

He nods. 'You passed your test quite quickly.'

'Not something you usually associate with me, huh?' Her mouth quirks up on one side. 'I really wanted a car to get around on my own. There are loads of amazing places I want to paint and taking an easel on the bus is no fun. My friends didn't exactly relish driving me to deserted places and waiting around for hours on end either.' She rolls her eyes. 'But after I passed my test, Dad and Grandad clubbed together and matched some savings I had, and we bought this rust bucket.' She kicks the vintage Beetle's back tyre fondly.

'You're lucky they did that for you.'

'Yeah. But I'm also the youngest in my year and having to wait nearly twelve months while all my friends got cars has been crap. The thirty-first of August is the worst day *ever* to be born on; I'm just lagging behind constantly. The least Mum could've done was cross her legs for an extra couple of days. Then I'd be the oldest in my year instead of the youngest.'

'You're right, she was completely selfish,' he says, with a straight face. 'But I don't think the thirty-first of August is all bad.'

'Why's that?'

Jake starts walking backwards, taking one last look at her, waving her insurance details in the air. 'Because someone born on that day is paying for my dad's car to be repaired.'

'That's not funny,' she hollers as he gets in the BMW and reverses around in an arc to face the exit.

He rolls down his window and gives Leila a cheerful wave.

'Take care, Jones. My insurance company will be in touch soon.'

'Jake, you sod!' she howls as he drives off, revving the engine. 'God. You're always so cocky!'

The sight of her fills his rear-view mirror as he leaves the school grounds. She wraps her arms around her waist, the fur on her collar bunching up around her glowering face. The clouds part and a ray of sunlight shines through, glinting off the diamond stud in her nose. 'The other thing about the thirty-first of August,' Jake says to himself as he presses on the accelerator, 'is that I think someone born on that day is pretty spectacular.'

Leila

30 August 2008

The 18th Birthday Charm

'Urgh, I can't believe my eighteenth is on a Sunday,' I moan to Eloise, tugging the short prom-style dress down over my thighs. Desperately trying to create some cleavage, I reposition the pads inside my strapless push-up bra.

'Yeah, it sucks,' she agrees, mouth dropping open as she applies mascara to her long, dark lashes. 'It's pretty much the most boring day of the week. Only Mondays are worse.' Her big blue eyes find mine in the mirror. 'But on the other hand, you get to party Saturday night and be hung over tomorrow. You've also convinced your dad to let it just be us on the boat, no parents, only crew. That's cool because they're pretty much just there to make sure we have a good time, given how much you're paying for the cruise. So, it should be one hell of a party.' She wiggles her eyebrows.

I gulp, 'I hope so.' In all honesty, El is the one who's talked me into this party. I'm an introvert at heart. I love spending time with my close friends but I'm never happier than when I'm alone drawing, painting, or reading. After six months of being worn down by her, and how excited she was at the thought of a boat party, I gave in. I didn't think many people would come, and I suspect most of them are only doing so because El is so popular and there's free booze, but I'm sure it'll be fine.

'Plus, you'll get loads of cool swag,' she continues. 'You're bound to with, like, eighty people coming.'

'Maybe.' Then, coming up behind her, I frown at my reflection. 'I'm eighteen tomorrow. We're off to uni soon. When the hell are my boobs going to come in?'

'You've got a gorgeous figure. Don't try and change it.'

'Easy for you to say,' I grumble, 'you're, as Jonny says, bootylicious.' I stare at her curvy body and the cleavage spilling from her tight white top worn with a silver sequin miniskirt. Totally impractical platform heels are on her feet and she's wearing a boho headband she's seen Mischa Barton off *The O.C.* wear to some awards event. The combination of pop, hippy, and disco styles should look ridiculous, but as usual my friend pulls it off, effortlessly cool.

'I mean it.' She spins to face me. 'You've got the same figure as Taylor Swift. Slim, graceful. You're lucky.'

'Really?'

'Yeah, exactly like T-Swift,' she says with a straight face, before ruining it by snorting, 'just three-quarters of a foot shorter.'

'Thanks!' I'm rolling my eyes as Chloe and Shell spill into Eloise's room, both laughing. We always get ready here because she has the biggest bedroom of all our houses. Plus, neither Eloise nor her parents mind us slinging bags in the corner or leaving a trail of girly devastation behind us. My dad would have a heart attack if we left my room in this state. Leaving from here also means I don't need to face a long list of questions from him just before my party. We did our father-daughter chat earlier. He's still pretty protective, even though I've reminded him every day for the last few weeks about my impending adulthood.

'What are you talking about?' Chloe asks, sitting down on the striped duvet. She looks stunning with her light blue eyes rimmed with black eyeliner and her shoulder-length brown bob styled in flicks around her face.

'Leila's worrying her petite little body will put Cameron off tonight,' Eloise drawls, tipping her head at me. 'You guys *are* planning to finally have sex, aren't you? I mean, you've made the poor guy wait long enough.'

I flush. 'Shut up, El.'

'Leave her alone,' Shell immediately defends, looking like a blonde-highlighted goddess in denim shorts, a floaty babydoll top and gladiator sandals. 'She doesn't need you on her back.'

'All right, calm down,' Eloise jokes. Unaffected, she turns back to the mirror and her make-up.

Shell glances at me, mouthing, '*You okay?*' I nod in reply, but my stomach sinks.

***

A while later we've boarded *The Dorset Princess* for my party, a three-hour cruise around Poole Harbour, past stunning

Sandbanks and beautiful Brownsea Island. I've chosen prosecco for drinks (it feels so grown up) and we're having a fish and chip supper people can eat straight out of the wrapping. There's also a fully staffed bar below decks. It turns out there's one good thing about being the youngest person in my year after all. Everyone else is already eighteen, and they've got ID to prove it, so there's no need to worry about smuggling alcohol on board tonight. The crew have agreed to turn a blind eye if I have a few alcoholic drinks before midnight, especially as we'll be out at sea.

Cameron comes up, slinging his arm around me as I lean against the rail watching the crew members undoing ropes and getting ready to cast off. 'Hey, gorgeous,' he murmurs in my ear, 'happy birthday for tomorrow. Are you ready for your birthday surprise later?' His breath is hot on my earlobe and I squirm slightly.

'Sure,' I reply, staring fixedly at the concrete quayside.

He huffs, 'You could sound a bit more excited. I've booked us a hotel room for tonight. It's not cheap, you know.'

'You have?' I can't quite keep the dismay out of my voice as I turn in his arms to gaze into his eyes. They're usually a warm brown, but now they look cold and hard.

'Problem?' His eyes narrow.

'No, of c-course not. It's just Dad's expecting me back tonight and I was going to have a birthday breakfast with him in the morning. Plus, I'm not seeing Grandad until tomorrow afternoon when he gets back from his fishing trip. I wanted to be home when he got in.' In my head, I add, *and you haven't even asked if staying in a hotel is what I want, if taking our relationship to the next level is what's right for me.*

'Well, sorry if our sex life is getting in the way of your plans,' he replies snarkily. 'It's not like I've been patient or anything.'

I start shaking. 'Cameron, please don't be like this.' I twist my multi-coloured cocktail ring around my finger and then readjust my chunky statement necklace. It suddenly feels like it's choking me. He can be so sweet, and I do like spending time with him, even if we're very different. His family are rich, posh, and live in a massive house. It's in marked contrast to my family's modest lifestyle. 'You don't need lots of money,' Grandad once told me when I complained about not having the newest model of mobile phone, 'if the job you do has value and the people around you add wealth to your life.' It sounded cheesy at the time, and I flounced out of the room, but I get it now. It's your purpose in life and your family and friends that count, not material things.

Cameron, on the other hand, just doesn't understand living on a budget or working hard to get decent A-levels, because he's lined up to run the family business. It can make him a bit spoilt sometimes, and more and more recently I've felt the sharp edge of his short temper.

'You know –' he removes his arm from around my shoulders and steps away, gazing past my left ear '– your friends are looking good tonight. Michelle in particular is really hot. Look at that top on her. I mean, wow,' he says in a low voice.

Winded, I spin around to face them, knowing he's trying to punish me. 'They do look nice,' I reply in a neutral tone, not wanting to start an argument or get upset at my own party. Chloe and Shell are chatting with their heads together, and Eloise is standing a few feet away, laughing up at something Jonny's saying. His surfer-style hair is getting shaggy and she reaches up to tuck it behind his ear. He catches hold of her hand, kissing her open palm. Neither of them cares that they're in a crowded room surrounded by kids their own age; they just love each other. It must be nice, and I feel a pang of something unnameable, knowing I don't feel that way about Cameron.

Plus, he's wrong. My friends aren't hot. They're beautiful, inside and out. And none of them, not one, would betray me. Do I really want to stay with someone who hurts me on purpose, because he's not getting his own way? *But you do like him*, a voice whispers in my head, *and you can't throw away seven months of happiness over one comment*. I ignore the other voice saying this is far from the first time he's upset me recently. Still, I'm not going to act all needy or give him the apology he obviously wants.

'Whatever,' he snaps, 'I'm getting a beer.'

I shrug and raise the glass of prosecco to my lips, turning my back on my boyfriend while I wait for my eyes to stop stinging.

Switching my attention from the pubs, cafés, and the small amusement arcade lining Poole Quay and back to the dock, I notice the last member of the crew running along the metal plank from the corner of my eye. Once he's reached the deck, the plank is pulled in. All ropes have been cast off. The boat's engines growl to life and there's motion beneath our feet. A diesel smell wafts through the air. As I gulp down fizzing alcohol, the boat moves away from shore and my friends join me at the rail so we're standing in a row. Shell puts a hand over my clenched fingers, telling me without words she's noticed Cameron's strop. Eloise leans over the top rail, adventurous as ever, and bends to look at the name of the boat painted on its side. 'Jonny says I'm his princess,' she announces.

Chloe makes a clicking sound with her tongue. 'I'd rather be someone's boss than their princess.'

'Each to their own.' Eloise smiles. 'You'll be a high flier in the City in no time.'

Slipping into silence, we watch the distance between boat and quay grow as we chug away. As we do, two figures come racing into view.

'Wait!' A man's voice shouts, cutting through the evening air.

'Hang on!' Another guy yells, and I recognise Owen Plaitford with his long legs and lanky frame. I invited him because he's older than us – at uni now – and cool, but he never RSVP'd. A mutual friend said they thought he'd gone skiing to Val d'Isère or something. It crossed my mind that if Owen came, Jake might do too, if he's due shore leave.

Without slowing, they pump their arms and legs harder, speeding up as one falls in behind the other on approach to the boat. Taking a running leap across the churning water, Owen makes it safely on deck as a quick-thinking crew member opens the gate for him. As he does so, I catch sight of the other guy. My stomach dips as I realise it *is* Jake. My heart's in my mouth as I watch him stretch his legs and jump even further. There's no way he can possibly make it. Shell gasps. Eloise mutters, 'Wow!' And Chloe mutters, 'Impressive,' as with barely any effort he lands next to Owen. Casually straightening his top, he shakes hands with the crew member and clasps him on the shoulder in thanks. We all stare.

'It's like watching Daniel Craig,' Chloe muses, referring to the newest James Bond. 'Except he's dark, not blond. I wonder what he looks like with slicked-back hair, coming out of the water in tiny shorts?'

Eloise snickers, covering her mouth with her hand.

My cheeks burn. Last year when we bumped cars, I thought Jake looked gorgeous in his jeans and tight black T-shirt with his height and toned arms. He looks even better now. But I have a boyfriend and it's not like that between me and Jake. I still can't believe I said that stuff to him about being annoyed because he didn't stay in touch. As soon as I'd shared it, I wanted the ground to open up and swallow me whole. What was I thinking? It sounded like I was practically begging for his friendship, or attention. He's never shown any sign of liking me as anything other than a friend. I mean, he doesn't even call me by my first name. Plus, it's been ages since I last saw him and if someone likes you, they stay in your life. Whereas he keeps leaving. Though I guess, there *are* the postcards. He sends them to keep in touch. Just once every four months or so, with a picture of whatever country he's in, and a few scribbled lines on the back. I keep them in a bundle in my top drawer, tied together with a purple ribbon. There's never a return address, so I can't reply.

'He's all right,' I say casually, 'if you like the broad-shouldered, muscular, cocky type.'

Chloe raises her eyebrows but says nothing.

Eloise smirks. 'If you say so.' Circling around Shell and Chloe to stand next to me, she casts a look over at Cameron who's propping up the bar in white shorts and an open-necked shirt, talking to one of his mates with a pint in his hand. Switching her attention back to the new arrivals, she arches one eyebrow. 'This ought to be fun. I'm sure Cameron's going to love this.'

'I don't know what you mean.' I down the rest of my prosecco, immediately reaching for another. 'Jake doesn't think of me that way. And he made me take liability for the accident, the sod.'

***

'Happy Birthday, Jones. How many drinks have *you* had?' A deep voice says at my elbow an hour later, making me jump.

'What do you want?' I say flatly, not in the mood for judgement, especially after Cameron's behaviour tonight. I'm half-cut on prosecco and perfectly willing to go the whole way. The alcohol's making me feel addled and short-tempered, harking back to my thirteen-year-old self. The one who was angry at the world. The one who made a horrific mistake. The silvery burn on my lower back is itching like mad.

'I just came to say happy birthday, and catch up,' he says, surprised. His odd-coloured eyes give me an appraising look and I bristle, feeling as if he can see right through me. I don't like it at all.

'Oh. Sorry.' Grabbing another prosecco from a passing friend, I notice Jake's faint northern accent is less pronounced than it used to be. He's standing close, talking straight in my ear above the music and jostling bodies. I ignore the heat coming off his solid frame, putting the glass to my mouth and gulping the rest of it down. It's my fourth. Or maybe fifth. I've lost track somewhere. All I know is that someone's turned Razorlight up on the speakers, and my boyfriend is acting like a shit. Hmm, the room is blurring at the edges. Maybe I should get some air.

Twisting around, I head up the wooden stairs, tripping over the top one onto the deck before righting myself by grabbing the railing. Jake follows me out. Taking a moment to admire the view, I breathe deeply, feeling more drunk in the fresh air rather than less. It's barely 10pm. Twilight's fallen while I was below deck talking, dancing, and drinking, and night is swiftly approaching. The pink sun – reminding me of Winsor and Newton's Permanent Rose – has almost settled below the horizon and the lights along the Sandbanks peninsula from the row of hotels, bars, and houses are becoming more noticeable. They look, I think hazily, like a constellation of twinkling stars.

Where's my prosecco gone? I notice Jake holding an empty glass and wonder if he took it. I also notice he's wearing dark blue jeans and a plain grey T-shirt that fits him perfectly without being too tight. It suits him, with his black hair and chiselled face. And the scar too; I really like his scar. Each time I see him, he seems to get better looking. *Wait, what?* I shake my head. *Stop it.*

'Have you got any idea,' I blurt drunkenly, 'how much my insurance premiums shot up after the accident? It cost me a fortune.'

'It wasn't personal, Jones, it was the principle. You caused the accident, so it was right you pay for it. I'm sorry if it's hit your petrol and art-supply budget. But I'm sure you found a way of dealing with it.'

'I thought you were joking when you said you'd be claiming against me. From what I remember, it was both our faults.'

'You know it wasn't.' He stares at me, unblinking. 'Besides, what good would it do for me to let you off? You're not going to learn about consequences or about taking more care that way, are you?'

'Just because you're in the Marines it doesn't mean you can order me around. You're not my dad!' We stop and stare at each other. My cheeks tingle with warmth. 'Sorry, I've had a few drinks.'

'Yeah,' Jake nods, 'I can see that.' His face softens. 'Look, I'm just trying to keep you safe.'

'But you're not my brother, or my boyfriend,' I reply, 'so it's not your job to do that. I've told you before.' Immediately I go crimson. Why the hell did I mention him being my boyfriend? Sighing, I flex my shoulders to release the tension. The truth is, Jake turned twenty earlier this year, and just the thought he's so ahead of me in life makes me feel hopelessly inadequate. Despite his upbringing, I always feel like he's got it together, while I float around in a bit of a haze. It probably doesn't help that Dad always seems so worried about me. But I don't need people hovering; it makes me feel suffocated.

Makes me want to run. I try not to do that – try not to be like Mum.

'Okay.' He holds his hands up, palms out in surrender. 'I get it. Look, the accident happened, and hopefully it'll never happen again, so let's drop it, okay? Did you get good A-level results?'

'Yes, so I'm off to uni soon.'

'What about your drawings? I always thought you should try and sell them.'

'You did?' The only stuff he's seen are the doors on my old bedroom wall, the hidden piece under my bed and the stuff I sketched down the park when were young. 'Thanks. Well, I did some pieces for my art coursework, and they were displayed in the hall, but I'd never try to sell them.'

'Why not?'

'Because they're not good enough.'

'Really? We'll have to agree to disagree. You look lovely, by the way.' He gestures to my dress. 'Strapless suits you.'

'It does?'

'Yes. You have great collarbones, even if they're buried under that necklace.'

My mouth drops open. 'What?' I squeak. 'Did you just compliment my *collarbones*?'

He screws up his odd-coloured eyes, before opening them again. 'I did. And I sounded like an idiot.' He laughs self-consciously.

It wrong-foots me, and I let out a giggle. Then I go to lean on the railing with my elbow and almost miss. I grab a tight hold of it instead. 'Yeah, smooth.' I'm not just referring to him. I pause to look into his eyes. At least he seemed sincere about my collarbones, and from the glimpses I caught of him downstairs, he doesn't leer into cleavages the way Cameron has been.

He clears his throat. 'So, that guy you were with? Is he your boyfriend?'

'Yeah.' I tighten my hand around the rail, and sway with the motion of the waves. I'm beginning to feel sick. A surge of fury at Cameron's behaviour boils in my chest. How could he humiliate me at my own party? Losing his temper, treating me as worthless because I won't sleep with him, and making me crave his attention by withdrawing it. So immature.

'Only he doesn't seem very into you – or at least, he's trying to give that impression.'

'Oh, bugger off, Jake. I don't need you picking holes in my relationship. What's it got to do with you, anyway?'

'I was just going to say you deserve better.'

'Well, don't.' His comment and concern catch me on the raw. Maybe I don't deserve better. Because if what people deserve directly correlates to what they get, then Mum wouldn't have left. Or at least, she would have come back well before now. So, I can't be that much of a good person. I can't deserve to be happy, can I? My brain is muddled by the alcohol; I can't make sense of anything. I'm just angry, angry, angry. At her, at Cameron, at the world, at Jake. People are always letting me down or leaving.

'Jones—' He steps towards me, raising his hand toward my cheek, compassion in his eyes.

He feels sorry for me, and it makes it all worse. 'Don't!' I bat his fingers away. 'I told you, don't say anything. *Please.*' Reaching for the railing beside me, I miss, just as the wake from a passing ship sends the boat rocking. Stumbling backwards with the force, nearly falling over, another layer of embarrassment is heaped onto my existing humiliation.

Jake's hand steadies my elbow and tugs me towards the railing so I can grab it. 'Thank you,' I mutter, while the skin of my elbow tingles at his touch. His hand slips away, and he buries both hands in his pockets.

Standing shoulder to shoulder for several long minutes, we fall into silence. He seems to know I need it, and my stomach is pitching and rolling all over the place, so I use the time to steady myself, afraid I might throw up on his trainers.

I stare out into the darkness of the waves until I'm calmer. Jake, I realise, helps me feel better. There's a reassuring confidence and solidity about him.

To lighten the mood, I tease, 'So, taken up any more dares recently?'

'Like what?'

'Oh, I don't know.' I think for a moment before saying playfully, 'Like swimming to land to prove what a good swimmer you are, as you once boasted.'

'You don't believe I could? Come on, I'm a Marine.'

Tilting my head to the side, I squint at the distant land, pursing my lips. 'You couldn't,' I say. 'It's way too far.'

'Wanna bet?' He crosses his arms over his chest.

Laughing, I shake my head. 'No, don't be so s-silly,' I slur.

'What's it worth?'

'Nothing.'

'A kiss?' He raises one eyebrow, a dimple flashing in one cheek.

For a moment I'm both breathless and speechless at his question, and don't know what to say. Did he just say a kiss? No, I'm drunk, I must've imagined it. Like when you're ill with flu and don't know what's real or not. Still, the thought of kissing him makes me feel ... odd, and my stomach somersaults. I don't like the feeling; it's like being out of control. Like when you spin around and around and when you stop you can't walk straight and the world just tilts crazily.

At my silence, he throws back his head and laughs, 'Don't look so horrified! I'm only joking!' He gives me a little mock punch on the arm, before backing away.

'Oh.' Embarrassed, I let out a giggle. Relieved. *Disappointed?* Confused.

'I will take the bet though.' He whips his top off over his head.

'What?' I gape at his toned body and broad shoulders, open-mouthed.

Digging his mobile phone out of his pocket and thrusting it into my hand, he strips down to his boxers.

'Jake! What the hell are you d-doing?' I hiccup.

'Proving a point.' He grins. 'I rarely back down from a dare. Tell Owen I'll meet him on shore later. Happy Birthday, Jones.' With that, he leaps over the rail and plunges into the choppy blue sea which appears almost black in the darkness.

I watch in astonishment as he swims away from the boat with long, steady strokes. Not once does he look back. His head is turned toward shore and he simply keeps going. I have a moment of utter terror during which I wonder whether to throw in a life jacket or summon one of the crew. But then I realise that he *is* a Marine and we're probably only anchored a mile or so off the peninsula. His dark hair blends into the inky darkness of the sea and I can no longer see him. Shaking my head, my stomach lurches. What do I do?

Owen wanders onto deck and picks up Jake's top and jeans, squinting after his friend. 'Is that Jake swimming back toward land?'

'Erm, yeah.' I push Jake's phone into his hand. 'Here. He ... he said he'd see you on shore.'

'Right,' he muses, shoving the phone in his pocket and pulling on his earlobe.

'Should I be worried? Should we tell someone?' I bite my lip.

'Nah, he's more than capable of taking care of himself. He'll be fine.' He tugs on his ear again, lanky frame towering above me. 'Um, why exactly did he jump overboard?'

Hesitating, I grab my hair from where it's flying into my eyes and tie it into a knot. 'It's possible I dared him.' I pause. 'Didn't think he'd actually do it though.'

He laughs and then looks at me searchingly. 'Well, he never could resist a challenge. Plus, he is a bit of a show-off sometimes, when he's trying to impress.'

'Don't know why he'd be trying to impress me.' Holding a hand to my mouth, a burning feeling rises up my throat. Turning around, I bend over the railing and am violently sick. As I do so, I realise I never thanked Jake for the postcards.

***

Ugh, I behaved like a complete idiot last night. I feel awful. Physically, emotionally, mentally. I look awful too. My skin is normally milky pale, but this morning it's practically transparent. My hair is lank despite me drunkenly washing it at 1am to get the sick out of it. Holding the vanity mirror from my handbag up to my face, the grey circles under my eyes almost match the shade of my irises. I'm eighteen today, at last, and should be bouncing around with a grin on my face. Instead, I'm lying in bed wishing for a quick death. 'Why did I keep on drinking?' I ask my bedroom ceiling with a groan, thinking of last night's drunken text-message argument with Cameron. He'd disappeared once we docked, and had stopped answering his phone to me too. What a dick. But I know I came across as desperate and paranoid; not attractive.

I trudge into the kitchen half an hour later in a cotton skirt and vest top, my hair in a loose plait. I feel more human, but it's still touch and go. Guess you're not really supposed to drink your own body weight in prosecco, especially when you only have about a metre and a half in height and eight stone to absorb it all.

'Happy eighteenth, love!' Dad exclaims as I enter the kitchen, holding a cup of tea towards me. Fleur leaps from her bed, wagging her tail and spinning around, her triangular shaped ears flapping out behind her. Yapping away as if she too is wishing me happy birthday.

'Ugh,' I grunt, grimacing. 'Shhh.' I wave my hand at Fleur and push her gently away, ignoring her sad eyes. Bless Dad. There are purple balloons and *Happy 18th Birthday* bunting hanging from the walls and ceiling.

He blanches, putting the tea down. 'You okay, love? You look ...'

'Like crap?'

'I was going to say green.'

Letting out a snort, I walk over and give him a big hug, even though it doesn't help with the nausea. 'I know. Thanks, Dad. I appreciate the effort.' Stepping back, I sit down gingerly at the table, accepting the glass of orange juice he pours. Fleur pads over and sits beside me, resting her silky little head on my knee. Taking pity on her, I stroke her velvety tan ears from top to bottom, just the way she likes it. I feel soothed straightaway, as I always do. She's got such an adorable little face.

'Was your party good?'

'The party –' I take a sip of juice and nod as the sugar hits my system '– was eventful.' His face drops at my tone. 'But great, yeah,' I add hastily, 'amazing, thank you.' He and Grandad shelled out a lot of money for me to have the birthday I wanted. Or rather, that El wanted for me. It's not his fault I got hideously drunk and argued with my boyfriend, dared Jake to jump off the boat, was sick everywhere, and generally made a pain of myself. That's all on me. Once I'm feeling better, I need to text my friends and say sorry, as well as find a number for Owen or Jake. I'll deal with Cameron later. 'The staff were really nice, and we had fun. We danced, the music and food were good, and everyone loved the prosecco.' Especially me. 'I got in just before one,' I explain, continuing to stroke Fleur's ears rhythmically, 'and the others went back to El's.'

'Well, glad you had fun, and got home safe. That's good. Breakfast?'

'I can't face it at the moment. Sorry.'

'Not a problem. Maybe later?' Sinking into the sturdy wooden chair next to me, he hands me a thick envelope. 'Happy Birthday, Leila. I know it's not very personal, but it's what you wanted, right?'

'Yes. Thank you.' I hug him gratefully, knowing there's a wad of notes in the envelope. I've been desperate for some new oil paints and supplies to take with me to uni. 'Absolutely perfect.'

'This arrived for you yesterday too,' he says quietly, producing another white envelope from his pocket with an *L* on the front.

Gulping, I take it from him, noticing there's no stamp on the envelope. She's close then, must have delivered it by hand or got someone else to. Sometimes my full name and address are typed on the envelope along with stamps and postmarks. Those times, I realise she must be travelling. I don't know which one is worse. When she's so far away, or that when she's in the neighbourhood she never knocks on the door. Taking a deep breath, I tear open the flap with my left index finger, wondering if this time, finally there'll be a note. Peering into the envelope I see there isn't, but—

I gasp. Nestled inside is a little key charm in solid platinum, with '18' set into the circular part of it, the part you'd hold if it was a real key. The one and eight are made up of sparkling jewels. 'They're real diamonds, aren't they?' I whisper.

He leans over to examine the charm as I hold it up so the

jewels twinkle and refract the sunlight coming in through the window. 'Looks like it,' he murmurs, smiling sadly.

'I'm sorry, Dad. It must be hard for you too.' He looks like he's going to say something as I lean over and hug him again, but then Fleur lets out a protesting whine because I've stopped pandering to her. 'Oh, stop it, you,' I say softly as I sit back in my chair. I'm going to miss her when I'm gone.

'I can't believe you're off to uni soon,' Dad says with a catch in his voice.

Something catches in my throat too. 'I know, it'll be weird.'

'I don't know what I'm going to do without you here to cook and clean up after us.'

'I know,' I say miserably, the familiar guilt rising. 'I'm sorry.'

'I was joking, love! We'll be fine. Ray and I can cook for ourselves and divvy the chores up. I'm getting someone in once a week to clean from top to bottom too. You've done a great job looking after us the past couple of years but now it's your time to fly. You need to live your life. Neither of us wants to get in the way of that. Don't think about it for another minute. We're just going to miss you, that's all.'

'Me too.' Blinking back tears, I extend my left arm. 'Can you put the charm on, please?' My hate and resentment of my mother have slowly diminished over the last couple of years, replaced by something like gratitude that she left if she couldn't care for me the way Dad has done so brilliantly for the past seven years. There are still times when I miss having a mum, and other moments when the old familiar anger creeps back in, but it's faded – like a patch of sunlight when the sun goes behind the clouds.

It only takes a moment for Dad to attach the new charm to my bracelet, and when I shake my wrist to admire it, it's like it's always been there. Like it's always belonged and was simply waiting for me to catch up. The thought is bittersweet, but I choose to focus on the feeling of joy.

'Now –' Dad breaks our sombre mood '– your grandad isn't back until later, and you don't want to eat. It's your birthday. What shall we do?'

Standing up, I drain my glass and force myself to swallow. I feel like I'm still at sea, swaying. How long does the feeling take to go away? 'I have an idea,' I say. 'If you promise to drive very slowly and we can have the windows down the entire journey.'

'Of course.' Grabbing his van keys off the side, he stands expectantly.

***

Forty-five minutes later, we roll up in the car park at Durdle Door.

'Oof, thank God that's over.' I tumble out of the van and turn to Dad. 'You coming for a walk on the beach? The views are amazing.'

'If you don't mind, I'll sit here and read the paper with my tea.' He holds up his thermos.

'Okay.'

'That's unless you want company?'

'No, it's fine. Honestly.' The sun is blinding, and I've had to put sunglasses on to deal with it. Neither of us has ever been great in the heat with our fair hair. 'Besides, if I was desperate for company, I could have brought Fleur.' With my hangover, I couldn't face the thought of trying to rein in her exuberance. For a moment I wonder if this is the best idea, but the thought of sitting on the stones with the Door to my left and the sea gently lapping the shore with a fresh breeze in my face pulls at me. I grab a bottle of water and a flapjack from the cool-box in the footwell. 'See you in a bit.'

A short while later, I descend the steps set into the hill to the side of the famous archway, panting lightly. I can't wait to collapse on the beach. My legs are trembling and it's possible the water I drank on the way down will make a reappearance. But the sea is relatively calm, the breeze I was longing for stirring my hair and kissing my cheeks. The cool air is refreshing and for a split second before the nausea returns, I don't feel so rotten.

Taking a deep breath as I step down onto the shingled beach, I gaze across the multi-coloured stones and pause. 'Great.' Someone else I need to apologise to, for acting like an idiot last night. On the upside, at least I know he's not dead.

Jake

31 August 2008

Jake's listening to music when he sees her. Sitting upright, he groans. He came here to think. What she's doing here? He needs more time to come up with a proper excuse for jumping overboard before seeing her again. He still can't understand why he did something so showy and embarrassing. He stripped in front of her for God's sake. It's not as if he'd had too much to drink. He'd only had a pint, to pace himself. He's lost the taste for alcohol while at sea. Not like some of his fellow officers.

Being in the Marines has taught him to think strategically and see the bigger picture, not to act on impulse. He makes quick decisions under fire if he needs to. But she wasn't holding a gun to his head, was she? He can't use that excuse.

He pulls the buds from his ears as she traipses towards him.

'Hi. Mind if I sit?' She points to the stones beside him.

To Jake, she looks weary and pale, but the floaty white skirt and red vest top suit her. Wearing sunglasses, with her silvery hair in a loose plait hanging over one shoulder, she also looks younger. Like when they first met. 'Sure,' he replies.

She sits down facing the horizon, chucking a bottle of water and a plastic-wrapped flapjack between them. 'Thanks.'

They're silent a moment, both staring out to sea and watching the sunlight glimmer on the caps of the water. A few people are walking along the shore, but it's too early for the arrival of families, so it's not that busy. The white breakers are crashing onto the shore along the gently curved bay.

'It's so beautiful,' she whispers.

'Yeah,' he agrees, tilting his head to sneak a peek at her. 'It is. What are you doing here?'

Looking down, she gathers up a handful of tiny stones, transferring them idly from one hand to the other, watching as the browns, beiges, and whites blend together and then fall apart. After a moment, she drops them and glances at him. 'I come here quite a lot. It's a bit of a drive, and the climb back to the car park is a bitch, but the views and sense of calm are amazing. Sometimes I come to draw or paint if I need a change of scenery from our back garden.'

'Cool.' He nods slowly, not wanting to tell her it's one of his favourite places in the world, in case it feels like he's stealing it from her.

Her gaze flits up over his trainers, jeans, and grey T-shirt. She frowns. 'Is that last night's outfit?'

'No!' But he rubs a hand over his stubble, checking to make sure he's not too shaggy. He's not going to tell her he spent half the night on the beach, unable to settle at the B&B just along the coastal path.

'Yes, it is.' Leila insists. 'You didn't, like, swim all the way from the boat to Durdle Door, did you?'

'Don't be silly, Jones. I'm a strong swimmer, but that would be bloody ridiculous.'

'Don't call me silly!' She snaps, before wincing and putting a hand to her forehead. 'Sorry. I feel terrible, I'm not in the best mood. Still ... *that would be bloody ridiculous,*' she imitates him, 'you sound like a head teacher sometimes. How's that even possible when you came from up north originally?'

'We moved around a lot,' he replies. 'Okay?'

'O-kay.' She drawls it in an American accent, like she's off some teen soap. 'So, what are you listening to?' Nodding to the leads looped around his neck.

'Oasis. I'm going back to my Britpop roots. I've been listening to it a lot on the ship.'

'You can't go wrong with Britpop.' She smiles, before flinching and putting a hand up to massage her temple. 'But aren't you a bit young? I mean, we were hardly teenagers when Oasis, Blur, and Pulp were having their day. I wasn't even school age for most of it.'

'I'm nearly two years older than you,' he reminds her, 'and it was what Dad listened to.'

'How *are* things with him?'

He can feel his face drop. 'Not good,' he says curtly.

'And your mum? Does she ever ... think of leaving?' She asks in a hesitant voice, watching his expression.

He's never told Leila everything, but from her question he knows that she knows, and he feels a burning sensation spread across his face.

'I saw the way he was with you,' she adds gently, 'and a mark on your mum's face once. Sometimes I hear raised voices, and she hardly ever leaves the house. It doesn't take a genius to work out what goes on.'

The flush on his face burns brighter. He shouldn't be embarrassed, but he is.

He studies Leila's face. There's nothing but compassion in it and her dark grey eyes are soft. Taking a breath, he decides to trust her. 'She won't go – she's too scared he might track her down – and she won't let me call the police. That's not the way we do things in our family.' He sighs, 'We did try once, last year. I sent her my signing-up bonus. It was a lot. Would have been enough for her to start a new life, rent somewhere while she looked for a new job or signed up for a qualification. But he took it all –' he shakes his head '– every last penny. I'm saving up again, but it'll take a while. I pay the mortgage so there's not always a lot left.'

'You pay their mortgage?'

Jake laughs bitterly. 'As soon as I joined the Navy and he worked out I was earning a decent living, he told me I had to unless I wanted something to happen to her.'

She gasps. 'Oh, Jake. I'm so sorry. That's awful. What an absolute ... Actually, there aren't even words to describe him, are there?'

'No,' he says grimly, 'there really aren't. So, the best I can do is visit when I can and keep working towards a way to set her free. It's difficult.'

'I hardly ever see you home on shore leave.'

'That's because most of the time I stay in the house. He doesn't go out much, just drinks.'

'Oh, Jake,' she repeats. Pulling a face, 'Have you ever confronted him?'

'No.'

'How come?' She turns to face him more fully, frowning. 'I mean, you must be trained and everything—'

'Because, Jones,' he shoots back, her questions making him defensive, 'I'm worried that if it began it wouldn't end, and I might kill him.'

A silence falls, and she gulps, her eyes wide. He closes his, unable to believe he admitted the thought out loud. Unable to believe he has let her see him for who he really is. Damaged, angry.

'Sorry.' They speak at the same time, and he opens his eyes.

'I'm sorry – I wasn't judging you.' She shuffles closer, tilting her face up to his, surprising him. 'I understand, and I don't blame you for feeling that way. Most people would.'

'You're not disgusted? I thought you'd be morally outraged, Jones. Especially after that time at the beach, when you accused me of being like him.'

'That's different,' she answers in a low voice. 'Defending someone else isn't the same as beating someone to a pulp because you want to show off, have lost control, or get a kick out of being a bully. Besides, I told you I should never have said that. I was just angry that night. Anyway, the point is you're not the bad guy here.'

He shifts on the stones, creating distance between them. The last thing he wants is her pity. He hates the idea of her thinking of him as powerless against his father. Plus, he doesn't want her getting dragged into the mess that is his family. 'Look, I appreciate you listening, but can we talk about something else? Something a bit happier?'

She crosses her arms and looks away from him to the rocks poking out of the slate sea. 'Sure,' she whispers, 'and don't worry, I won't say anything.'

'Thanks.' He didn't think for a moment she would. Trustworthiness is one of the things he likes about her. He also likes how kind she is. He clears his throat. 'So, happy actual birthday, Jones. Did you have fun last night?'

'Thanks. I think so.' She grimaces, reaching for the bottle of water between them. 'I'm not sure I remember all of it. I know I had a lot to drink, because I feel pretty crap this morning. But I'm sure it'll pass eventually.' Her skin pales further as she unscrews the bottle lid and takes a swig.

Smiling, he grabs a stone and pulls his arm right back to hurl it into the curling waves. 'Most things do.'

'Yeah.' Sighing, she adjusts her sunglasses. 'Listen—'

At the same time, he says, 'About last night—'

Laughing uneasily, they fall silent. 'Go on,' he prompts.

She removes her glasses and squints at him, looking shamefaced. 'I was going to say I'm sorry. For daring you to swim to shore. I was drunk and shouldn't have said it. It was stupid, and I should have known you'd want to prove your point. I can't believe you actually did it though.' She pauses, staring at him. 'I was worried.'

'You've nothing to say sorry for. I'm in charge of my own destiny. If I didn't want to jump, I wouldn't have. I must admit though, it was a bit of a dick move. I mean, stripping and everything ...' He laughs uncomfortably. 'I don't know what I was thinking. But it made you laugh, right?'

'I did find it pretty amusing, if not a little scary.' Shaking her head. 'I may not owe you a sorry, but I had to send a lot of apology texts out this morning.'

He says nothing, just cocks his head and waits.

'You're not going to ask who to?'

'Well, I won't pretend I'm not curious. But if you want to tell me, you will.'

'Wait. Is there a sensitive soul hiding under that rough exterior?' she teases.

He self-consciously rubs a finger over his scar. 'Absolutely not. Don't be stupid.'

Her eyes track the movement of his finger, and he drops his hand. 'You can deny it, Jake, but you do everything you can to help your mum. You've got a good heart.'

He doesn't reply, having no intention of following the rabbit down that particular conversational hole again. He leans back to look up at the sky. The sun's getting brighter and hotter, and he thinks Leila feels it too, a line of sweat beading on her top lip. She wipes it away with the back of her hand when she catches him looking. Closing her eyes, she sways.

'Are you going to be sick?' he asks. 'If you are, try not to do it in my direction.'

'Thanks for the reminder. I'll try my best,' she says wryly. 'It's just hot and I'm hung over. This wasn't the way I planned to spend my birthday, you know. Still, at least I can look forward to seeing Grandad later.'

'Ray.' He smiles. 'He's on a fishing trip today, right?'

'Yep. How do you know?' She gazes at him.

'I saw him packing up his fishing gear yesterday morning.'

'Oh. Right.'

'So, this year's charm?' Putting a finger out, he traces a line down the little key where it hangs from the bracelet. 'The most expensive one so far.'

'Looks like it.' Moving her arm away, she touches a hand to her wrist, tugging on the clasp to make sure it's secure.

It annoys him how she pulls away from him. He knows he has his off days, and his scar, but he's not that hideous, is he?

'Well, you're quite the golden girl, aren't you?' He mocks in retaliation. 'After doing so well with your A-levels, uni place, posh boyfriend, and everything. Let me guess, you're going to the same uni and will stay in halls together until you can afford your own flat. Then you'll get married,' he clasps his hands, puts them under his chin and flutters his eyelashes, 'and have the perfect two-point-four children and live happily ever—'

'Jake, that's enough. It's my birthday and I feel like shit.' She blinks rapidly and sticks her sunglasses back on. 'FYI, Cameron and I are going to different universities, and right now I'm really not sure if a long-distance relationship is going to work.' She sucks in her cheeks. 'Maybe I'll just go and sit by myself. I don't need these kinds of comments today.' Planting her hands either side of her, she pushes off the stones.

At the same time, he grabs a handful of her red top, and yanks her straight back down.

'Hey!'

'I'm sorry, I'll be nice,' he says quickly. 'I've only got a few days' shore leave, and everything feels a bit weird. Like I don't quite fit. I hope my jumping off the boat didn't cause any trouble?'

'Yeah, I get that feeling most of the time,' she admits, to his surprise. 'And don't worry, your night-time excursion just gave people something to talk about. Owen couldn't wait to go down and tell everyone what you'd done. And Chloe was gutted she missed you taking your clothes off.'

'She was?' He arches an eyebrow.

'Yep, something about James Bond,' she murmurs, switching her attention back to the horizon, and clearly not wanting to go into it.

'You really feel like you don't fit in?' He holds up the bottle of water, nudging her to drink again.

She slides it from his hand and takes some small sips. 'Oh, all the time.'

'But, why?'

She squints. 'It's hard to explain.' Holding a hand to her mouth, she gulps. 'Ugh, this hangover can't be over soon enough.'

'Have some of this; you'll feel better for it.' Unwrapping the flapjack, he offers it to her.

She takes a bite, chewing carefully. Once she's swallowed, she stares at him, about to say something. But at that moment, Henry comes tripping down the stairs, panting and red-faced. His fringe is stuck sweatily to his forehead and he's waving a mobile phone in the air. 'Love. I've been trying to get hold of you. What were you doing? You, you weren't ... answering ... your ... phone ...'

'Dad? What is it?' Racing up to him with Jake in pursuit, she grabs her dad's arm.

'It's Ray.' Henry's face says it all.

'What?' Leila demands, fingers tightening on his wrist.

'He had a heart attack, on the boat. They've brought him back to shore.'

Jake and Leila stare at Henry in horror.

'A-and?' Leila is trembling.

Her dad puts his arm around her shoulders, face crumpling. 'He's on the way to Dorchester Hospital. We've got to go. Now.'

Leila

September 2008

The Bereavement Charm

The melodic piano intro of Avril Lavigne's 'When You're Gone' begins and I feel my heart spasm and thud-thud-thud in my chest. Swaying, I clutch the dark wooden pew in front of me. I can't see it because of the tears blinding my vision, but know it's there because I can touch it. There are some things in this world you can't touch though; you just need to rely on faith that they're there. Like Grandad, gone too soon. I hope he's watching over us.

Six ushers, mostly ex-military men, are carrying Grandad's coffin towards the altar on their shoulders in slow measured steps. I wonder idly if their deliberate gait is the same as the one brides use to make their way up the aisle, and realise that if I'm ever a bride my grandad won't be around to see it. He'll never see me paint new scenes, or have children if I decide I want them, or live my life. A sob rises from my stomach, up through my chest, and falls out of my mouth. The coffin hasn't reached us yet, but it will soon.

'I can't believe he's gone,' I choke, shifting my gaze to Dad, standing beside me still and silent. 'How can he be gone?'

'I know, love.' When he puts his arm around me, stretching the already snug formal black suit across his wide body, I lean into him, drawing strength from his solid presence.

Chloe, Eloise, and Shell are standing in the row behind us in silent support, and one of them reaches forwards to stroke my hair. Then other hands land on my shoulders, squeezing. They don't have to say anything. They're here. I turn to them and smile gratefully. Like me, they're wearing blue dresses. It was Grandad's favourite colour and seemed a good way to honour him.

The church is full, and people shuffle along pews to make room for each other. It's packed out with neighbours and friends, as well as men Grandad served with in the Navy. Everyone's brought their families along, so there are as many children as there are OAPs. Near the back, a baby wails over the music. The piano continues playing, the chords striking shards of grief into my body. A small child pipes up somewhere, 'Why is Ray in a box, though?' He's immediately shushed but there's an uncomfortable titter of laughter in the seats surrounding him. I stifle a weird sound in my throat, not sure whether to laugh or cry. At least the little boy's curiosity helps defuse some of the tension.

Unlike a normal church, it's not cool and dark in here; it's stifling and bright. It's an unusually warm September day, and it is wrong, wrong, wrong that the sun's out and the air's balmy when Grandad's dead.

I still can't believe he's dead.

A red carpet runs up the central aisle. Two huge vases of white lilies stand just in front of the altar, along with a giant picture. Instead of Grandad's face, it's adorned with a photo of his favourite ship – the one he was on for his longest tour – and around the edges are photographs of all the countries he visited in the late sixties and early seventies. Iran, Bahrain, Fiji, Singapore ... Dad said Jake helped make it, and I'm touched. He should have left five days ago, but he applied for extended shore leave for compassionate reasons, and they let him stay. I've hardly seen him though. I've barely left my room since it happened. I just couldn't face it, him, anyone. This morning is the first time I've spoken to Cameron for a week and a half. I was on a slow burn of anger, too proud to call him first, and too buried in my grief to make the effort. He didn't turn up that Sunday to comfort me after I called from the hospital and left a voicemail. He didn't call or come round to say how sorry he was. To see if there was anything he could do, even if it was just holding me while I cried. It wasn't until he finally called me earlier today that I understood why. Now I'm glad he stayed away.

'Are you sure you're up to this?' Dad asks.

'I have to be,' I murmur. 'Someone has to do it.' We decided a few days ago that I would read the eulogy. Grandad has no blood relatives other than a few distant cousins, Mum, and me. It didn't seem right to ask any of his three cousins – people he hadn't seen for over forty years – to talk about him. What would they say, other than telling fuzzy misremembered stories about their childhood? They only knew him up to his early twenties. He lived a whole life after that. He had a wife he adored, if only for a few short years, and he built a home and raised a family.

Of course, we can't find Mum. We have no way of tracking her down so she doesn't even know her own father is dead. Every time I think about it, I grit my teeth. This is what she's left us with. The legacy of the missing. The sad knowledge that she doesn't know the man who gave her life no longer walks the earth, and she may not find out for years. The fact she didn't get to say goodbye will probably haunt her. But it's not my problem. No, my problem is that I must get up in front of all these people and talk about Grandad without crying.

As I think this, the coffin finally moves past us and I notice one of the ushers is taller than the rest, with a straighter bearing. As they place the coffin down gently on the trestles, and I realise who it is, my nose stings. 'Jake,' I murmur.

He's in full formal navy-blue uniform with gold buttons on his jacket and gold circles round the sleeves. He looks like he's aged about five years. Nodding, as the other ushers go and sit with friends and family, he walks over to me. 'Jones.' His face is grave, his odd-coloured eyes dull but sympathetic. Unspeaking, Dad moves down the pew so Jake can slide in next to me.

I can't speak. My mouth is dry and empty.

'I know.' He mutters under his breath, handing me a tissue from his inside pocket.

As the song comes to an end, a hysterical bubble of laughter erupts from my mouth. This is ridiculous. It can't be Grandad's funeral, it's about twenty years too early. Unthinkingly and uncharacteristically, I bury my face in Jake's shoulder to muffle the sound. What will everyone think of me if they see me laughing? They'll think I'm a monster. Or at the least, completely inappropriate.

His arm lands around my shoulders, squeezing in comfort. The threat of tears tingles in my nose. Taking control of myself, I stand upright, fiddling with my charm bracelet. In a daze, I hold my arm out so it captures a ray of sunshine coming in through the stained-glass windows. Absently, I twist my left wrist back and forth, studying the charms as they catch the light and create rainbow prisms. The bracelet is something I'll always hold close to my heart, so much more than a simple possession.

Dad coughs next to me. On the other side, Jake takes my hand and tucks it into the crook of his arm. I let it rest there, drawing comfort from him. The priest, a man who hardly knew Grandad because he wasn't religious, is talking. I hadn't even noticed. How long has he been speaking? Staring vacantly at the wall behind the altar, where Jesus is hanging on the cross, time loses meaning. I drift through hymns and pages of orders of service being turned over. Then Dad and Jake are calling me.

'Leila. Leila?' Dad is whispering in my ear.

I snap out of my daze, realising it's time for the eulogy. Heat swarms up my spine, a patch of sweat collecting in the small of my back. I'm not ready.

'We'll be right here,' Jake tells me. 'You can do this.' Standing aside, he points to the altar, where a pine lectern stands. The church is hushed, and everyone's waiting.

I'm having an out-of-body experience. My legs are moving, despite my knees shaking, and then I'm standing facing everyone. I don't remember getting here. The sea of faces is blurred. There are so many people.

'Ray's beloved granddaughter Leila is now going to give the eulogy.' The priest, his silver hair curling around his ears and brown eyes kind over the top of his wire-rimmed glasses, nods at me.

Where's my speech? Glancing down, I run my hands down my dress. There are no pockets. What did I do with it? As panic hits, I see my three best friends shuffle sideways out of their pew and walk toward me. Climbing up the white marble steps, they gather around.

'What's wrong?' Eloise asks from the corner of her mouth.

'I can't find it!' The microphone picks this up and a concerned ripple runs through the congregation.

'Speak from the heart,' Shell murmurs. 'Just say how you feel. We're here.' They form a semi-circle behind me. Chloe reaches over and squeezes my hand. They've got my back, literally.

I switch my attention to Dad, who's chewing on his lip. Then Jake gives me an imperceptible nod, and mouths, 'Go, Jones.' He believes in me, I can do this.

'Sorry, everyone,' I croak, 'Sorry. I was all prepared, and now I can't even find the eulogy.' Clearing my throat, I begin. The strength of my friends and family gives *me* strength. 'Okay, so, I'll do my best.' Taking a deep breath, I follow Shell's advice, and let my heart do the talking. 'The day my Grandad – Ray to you – had a massive, catastrophic heart attack was my eighteenth birthday.' I see sympathetic glances cast my way, and people looking at each other and shaking their heads. 'I know, you're thinking *poor girl*, right? Well, I won't lie, it was devastating. We are still devastated. And every year on my birthday, I'll remember what happened, and I'll be devastated again. But – and there is a but – it'll also be an excuse to celebrate. Not how many years I'll have been around for, but how many years we got to have him.' I gulp, but force myself on. 'Dad and I had to leave Bournemouth when I was eleven due to personal circumstances.' A few people who know our story share understanding looks. 'We only saw Grandad a few times during the years that followed. We weren't particularly close, and I was cross with him for reasons I won't bore you with. I used to annoy the hell out of him by calling him Ray or Grandad Ray sometimes.' The priest clears his throat, and I realise that referring to the fiery place in a place of worship isn't the done thing. 'Oops, sorry,' I mutter. 'Anyway, he hated me using his name, and on one occasion told me off for being disrespectful.' A sob escapes, followed by a mangled laugh. 'Anyone who served under him in the Royal Navy will know what it was like to be on the wrong side of him. He could be really stern and had a certain way of looking at you that said he was really disappointed, and you should be disappointed in yourself too ... It was pretty scary.' There are a few stifled smiles, and some nods of agreement from a group of men sitting in the pews over on the right.

'When I was fourteen, we moved back to Bournemouth because Grandad got ill, and we needed to care for him. Some of you won't know this, because he hid it so well, but for a year or so he had lung cancer. He came through it, but it was unexpected to say the least. I'll be honest –' I gaze out at them, trying to focus on one face at a time to calm my nerves '– I was a brat about coming back halfway through secondary school, and I blamed Dad, and Grandad, for making me. The thing is though,' I carry on, 'that we moved back to the street I grew up on thinking he probably didn't have long to live, and instead we got the greatest gift. Because we got the last four years with him. No one could have predicted that. During that time, he went from being Ray to properly being my grandad, and I started calling him that. I got to spend precious time with the most stubborn, but also principled, and wisest man I've ever known.' A tear rolls down my cheek, and I puff out a shaky breath. 'No one could have predicted he'd ruin it all by having a fatal heart attack while out at sea. But, I mean, talk about picking your moments.' I point at the collage with the ship. 'He loved the sea. He spent most of his working life at sea, and he died at sea. It's where he would have wanted to go, even if it was too soon.' Gulping, I wipe my damp face with both hands. 'I know it's where I'll always find him.'

My eyes search and hold Jake's. There are tears streaming down his face too. Why is he crying so hard? 'And so, our family has decided his ashes are going to be scattered off the coast. It's what's right.' Pausing, I drop my hands to grip the edges of the lectern. 'He led a good life. We have to hold onto that. Hold onto the fact that, if you were lucky enough to know him, you were lucky enough to have been taught something by him. He was a man of strong values, integrity, and sheer determination. Along with my dad, my grandad taught me about the kind of person I want to be.' I taste the salt on my lips, feel the heaviness in my heart from his absence. 'A good person. Someone who can look at themselves in the mirror and be proud. Someone,' I finish, my voice echoing through the church, 'who makes the people around them better just for knowing them. That's what he gave me,' I say in a fierce voice. 'That's who he was. I'll miss him, but he'll still be with us all, because every time one of us does something good that we can be proud of, and every time we look in the mirror and feel it, he'll be there. He'll be there,' I repeat. 'He always will be.' I release my breath and look at the priest.

'Thank you, Leila,' he says, reclaiming his place. Leaning forward into the microphone, he repeats, 'Thank you. That was a moving eulogy. He would be proud. He *is* here.'

'Thank you,' I whisper. The breath leaves my body and I go down the stairs to rejoin Jake and Dad. My friends resume their places behind me and as they do, I see Chloe has a tissue bunched in her hand, and Eloise is gulping back tiny sobs. Shell smiles, murmuring, 'Well done, you did him proud.'

I turn to face the altar as 'Eternal Father', better known as the Naval Hymn, starts playing. Jake threads his fingers through mine, holding tight. 'I miss him too.'

For a brief minute I let him comfort me, before pulling my hand from his and looking at him in confusion. 'Why? You hardly knew him.'

He shakes his head, eyes shining, one green, one brown. 'Leila,' he starts, then stops. 'Never mind. Think what you like.' Undoing the top button of his jacket, he places the hymn book down on the bench and leaves the church. Even above the hymn and people singing, the slam of the doors echoes through the building.

Catching Dad looking at me, I turn to him. 'What?' There's an expression on his face I can't read. It's not one I'm used to seeing nowadays. Disappointment.

***

Leaning against the metal balcony railing with a glass of white wine in my left hand, I gaze out to where the line of the dark blue sea meets the pale blue horizon.

It was expensive, but we decided to have the wake at a hotel on the Sandbanks peninsula overlooking the sea. We feel closer to Grandad if we can see the waves and caps, and watch the swirls and eddies of the currents and tides. The sun's still shining, and the air is balmy. You'd think it was the summer holidays rather than mid-September. It's hard to believe in a few weeks I'll be packing up and travelling to Brighton to start uni. It's even harder to believe life is simply meant to go on, when for me it feels like it stopped eleven days ago. But I need to take my own advice from Grandad's eulogy. I need to go out into the world, be a good person, and make him proud. Which means there's something I need to do.

Spotting his dark head in the crowd, I catch Jake's eye and beckon him over with my free hand. He says something to the man he's talking to, pats him on the shoulder, and makes his way over to me. He's still wearing his military uniform and I gulp as he approaches. I can't deny he looks handsome, especially with his black hair against the formal dark jacket, even though having such thoughts at Grandad's wake feels completely inappropriate. Plus, this is Jake, a boy I've known since I was eleven, and who doesn't see *me* that way. Even if he did, he wouldn't be right for me. He's far too overprotective; it would drive me mad. Plus, he's always leaving town and is out of touch for months on end. I couldn't live like that, or love like that. I need someone who's here for me. Who sticks around. Basically, the opposite of my mother.

No, it's better if we're just friends.

'Hi,' I say hesitantly as he reaches my side.

'Hi,' he replies. 'How are you doing?'

Taking a deep breath, 'Not great. You?' I ask, trying to be conciliatory.

He doesn't reply, shrugging one shoulder and turning to face the coast.

'That good, huh?' Taking a deep gulp of my wine before balancing the glass on the railing, I turn my attention to the sea. His behaviour upset me at the funeral, especially the way he left. But he was obviously upset too. I'm so confused. I do appreciate him doing the picture for Grandad and sticking around to help, but the way he acted in church it was like he thought Grandad was his too. I just don't get it. I ache to ask Jake about it, but on the other hand I'm not sure I'm ready to take on someone else's pain. My own is already too much to bear. Immediately, I feel selfish. Why does life have to be so complicated?

'So, Brighton?' He breaks the silence, and I know my attempt to make peace has been accepted.

'Yes.'

'Studying art?'

'Yeah.' Keeping my eyes on the shimmering waves, I gulp down more wine, the floral, tangy taste strong on my tongue. Other people's chatter drifts up from the balcony below us. I'm glad he's decided not to bring up the subject of him leaving the funeral. Perhaps he feels it's best left for another day.

'You must be excited? Brighton's a great place to live.'

'I guess.'

He sighs. 'You're not the best conversationalist today, Jones.'

'I'm trying my best to hold it together, Jake,' I admit softly. 'It's difficult to even breathe. If you want to go and talk to someone else, I'll understand.'

'Sorry. That was insensitive.' He shoves his hands into his uniform pockets, frowning. His sunglasses are pushed back into his thick black hair, which has grown out a bit over the past couple of weeks. He undoes a few of the buttons on his military jacket and leans against the railing. How does he always look so calm and composed, when everyone around him is falling apart? 'People are worried about you,' he adds. 'You've been out here for the last two hours. Are you going to come in soon?'

'I don't feel like talking,' I murmur. 'It's not a social event. They're acting like it's a wedding, drinking and standing around gossiping. It's disrespectful.'

'They're not gossiping, Jones,' he answers mildly, 'they're catching up. Some of them haven't seen each other for years. It's not meant to be disrespectful. But it is a chance to remember Ray and share memories. To celebrate his life. He would have been fine with it.' Raising one eyebrow, 'Would you rather they stood around eyeballing each other in silence, drinking water?'

'Oh, for fuck's sake!' It bursts out of me; I can't contain it. His words make me feel ridiculous. The last thing I need is him launching grenades at me. I need his understanding, not his judgement. 'I'm always in the wrong, aren't I?' I just can't handle this, I want the world to disappear. 'It's always me that's the problem. You guys are all the same.'

'What the hell do you mean by that?' He straightens away from the railing and turns to me, looking astounded.

'Always wanting to blame someone else. Cameron dumped me this morning. *On the morning of my grandad's funeral*. A week and a half of silence and then he calls. Do you know what he said? He told me he slept with a big-breasted blonde after my birthday party and that he was sorry, but it wasn't going to work out. He wants to enjoy uni and doesn't need a girlfriend who's going to be sitting around moping all the time and calling him in tears. He said he didn't need someone who's such a mess. He just wants to have fun.' I down the rest of my wine before snatching a glass from the tray of a passing waiter. The guy looks startled, but smoothly walks on.

'Well then, he's a heartless twat and a waste of space, and I'm sorry he hurt you so badly.' Jake's face darkens. 'If it wouldn't get me thrown out of the Marines, I'd punch him in the mouth for saying all that to you. But if that's the way he thinks, you don't want him, trust me.'

'You don't have to defend my honour, Jake. And please don't

tell me what I should and shouldn't want.' My fingers clench around the stem of the wine glass. It feels brittle between my fingers, as if it might snap. Like me. 'Why are you always so overprotective? It makes me feel *suffocated.*' Furious tears cloud my eyes, a ball of heat scrunching up in my chest. He flinches, but I carry on. 'And how could you say earlier that you miss Grandad? *My* grandad? You only met him a handful of times.' I'm a runaway train on fast tracks, inevitable and deadly. 'What would you know about missing him?'

I'm *so* furious at both Cameron and Grandad for leaving me. Without thinking, I hurl my wine glass to the floor. There's a loud tinkling crash and wine sprays up onto Jake's trousers, shards of glass flying everywhere.

There are gasps, and with a sinking heart I notice the patio doors leading out to the balcony crowded with guests from the wake. My friends and Dad are at the front, watching in dismay.

'Leila!' Dad thunders, looking horrified. He never shouts or raises his voice at me.

My bottom lip starts wobbling as anger and adrenaline drain away to be replaced by a sick, shaky feeling. 'Sorry, Dad,' I choke. This must remind him of the year I was thirteen, and I know how much it will hurt him to think I've regressed to that rage-filled girl again.

'Not me you should be apologising to.' He crosses his arms.

My eyes widen as I turn back to Jake, seeing the shocked and embarrassed expression on his face. What have I done? Oh, shit. 'S-sorry, Jake. I shouldn't have done that.'

'Don't worry about it,' he bites.

'Jake—' I hold my hand out toward him but he steps back. I feel awful for taking my grief, and anger at my ex-boyfriend, out on him. He doesn't deserve it.

'I'll leave,' he says quietly. 'I'm obviously not wanted here.' Lifting his chin, he pushes his way through the gawking crowd and into the room beyond. His broad shoulders are the last thing I see before regretful sobs overcome me, and I crumple into a ball on the floor, the glass cutting into my skin. I don't feel it. I just want Grandad.

He was also my link to a mum whose memory becomes more distant every day. The charm bracelet is now the only thing I have left of her. I cradle my left wrist to my chest, protecting it.

***

'How are you feeling today?' Dad asks in a stilted tone.

'You're still cross with me then?' I rest back against the kitchen unit as he wanders over to the sink to rinse his cup. Even Fleur doesn't seem to like me much this morning, giving me a baleful look when I came down earlier before pointedly turning her back on me.

'Cross isn't the right word, love.'

I wait, but nothing else is forthcoming. 'Well, what *is* the right word then?'

Placing the cup on the counter with a little clink, he sits down at the kitchen table. Staring at the dark wood, he frowns. 'Disappointed. Shocked you'd act like that at your grandad's wake. Ashamed you'd think it okay to treat Jake that way.' He shakes his head. 'Those things. But not cross.'

'I know.' Joining him at the table, I squeeze his hand. 'I acted like a spoilt brat, and I'm genuinely sorry.' I sigh. 'People will remember the day, but for the wrong reasons. The wake kind of went downhill after that little scene, huh?'

Lifting his head, his frown deepens. Lines bracket his mouth and a deep groove forms between his eyebrows.

'Okay, it's not funny.' I suck my cheeks in. 'But, please Dad, you have to understand. I was grief-stricken over Grandad, and Cameron had just dumped me. I was gutted. Then Jake comes along and starts acting like Ray was his grandad too … I haven't been sleeping well recently either, so that didn't help,' I admit. 'But I feel better now. Clearer.'

'Love,' he says gently, 'I'm glad you feel better. And I *do* understand. But you're eighteen now, an adult.'

Puffing out a massive breath, I lace my hands together on the table. 'You're right. It's no excuse.' I nod. 'I have to take responsibility for causing such embarrassment. *I* was an embarrassment.' I still have plasters covering the tiny cuts on my shins and ankles to prove it.

'So how will you make it right? Texts to the guests are fine, and people will understand you were distraught. But what about Jake?'

I squeeze my fingers tighter together. 'I'll go and say sorry.'

Dad's hand lands on mine, giving me reassurance. 'Good. But let's have a cuppa in the garden first. Get the tray ready, I've got to pop upstairs. There are some things I want to show you, and some things you should know. Maybe then you'll start to understand Jake, and his relationship with your grandad, better.'

What relationship? I wonder. What's Dad talking about?

***

Ten minutes later we're sitting with cups of tea at the table in the back garden. There's no breeze, and like yesterday the sun is beating down on our heads. It's got to be mid-twenties, and I've dressed all wrong for the climate in baggy jeans and a yellow off-the-shoulder T-shirt. I'm baking, and can feel the skin on my exposed shoulder, arms, and face prickling in the heat, tender to the touch. The apple tree Mum carved patterns into the trunk of is laden with fruit. Idly, I wonder if the branches are still strong enough to bear my weight. It's been a few years. On the other hand, at a little over five foot and a size eight, there are some days I feel like I could blow away in a puff of wind.

'This is for you,' Dad says gruffly, pushing a jewellery box across the table. 'It's from Ray. It was your eighteenth birthday present. Jake helped him pick it out. They went to the shops together.'

'They did?' I frown. 'When? Why?' It doesn't make sense.

Dad doesn't answer, instead saying, 'Your grandad was planning to give this to you when he got home that day. The hospital found it in his pocket and gave it to me for safekeeping. I've been holding onto it, until you were ready.'

I gaze at the box, then at him, my eyes shining and a lump lodged in my throat. Fleur takes pity on me and bounds off the porch and through the green grass to lay her soft chin on my knee. I smile at her, silently thanking her for the comfort. 'I should have seen him before my party,' I gulp, 'or been waiting for him down on the quay rather than hungover down at Durdle Door—'

'Don't be silly, love,' Dad says firmly. 'You had every right to have fun for your birthday, and Ray wanted that for you too. Don't forget he was happy fishing with his friends. No one could have known what would happen.'

'I know. I just ...' Closing my eyes, I picture Granddad's face, which could be stern one moment and kind the next. Opening my eyelids, I scrutinise the box. 'Okay. Yes,' I say, answering the unspoken question. 'I can handle it. I'm ready.' Picking up the velvet box, I flip the lid open. Nestled on the cushion are three tiny charms for my bracelet, connected together on one tiny loop. A cross inlaid with diamonds, but with curled ends rather than straight lines, an anchor, and a solid unadorned heart, not unlike the one Mum left me all those years ago with the bracelet.

'It's beautiful,' I breathe.

'I think it's a military thing. They represent faith, hope, and love,' Dad explains. 'I suppose that's what he wanted for you.'

'Oh.' A tear slides down my cheek. 'That's lovely. Yes. They're the three most important things, I think he would have said that. But I still don't understand, why did Jake help him pick it out?'

'You'd need to ask Jake about that.' He takes a gulp of his tea, his expression troubled. 'There's something else. When I went out the other day, it was to the solicitor's. It was the reading of the will. I didn't think you'd be able to cope.'

Inhaling sharply, I dip my chin in acknowledgement. 'That's okay. It probably would have been too soon.' Picking up my cup of tea, I take a mouthful and screw up my face. 'There's a load of sugar in this. Are you trying to prepare me for a shock or something?' I joke. His face says it all. Clinking the cup down on the saucer, I lean forward. 'Dad, what is it?'

'He's left you some money. Not a lot, but enough to pay for the first year of uni at least.'

'That's –' I sniff '– I ... that's so kind.' I can't process all the emotions flowing through me at the thought of using Grandad's money, so I focus on my father instead, on how uncomfortable he looks. 'Why do you look so worried?'

'He left us the house, Leila.'

'Oh. I ... but I don't ...' I founder. 'But shouldn't it go to Mum? Isn't she his next of kin? I mean, unless ...' Covering my mouth with my hand, 'Oh my God, do you think he thought she's dead? Or did he *know* she was?' I start to cry. Now I'll never know her. No matter how angry I've been with her over the years, there's always been a part of me hoping she'd come back. Hoping we could rebuild our relationship, make up for all the lost time. Imagining I'd finally get answers for why she left us the way she did.

'Love, no! Stop.' Coming around the table, he puts an arm around my shoulder. 'Don't cry. It isn't that. He left a letter explaining he's never known exactly where she was, and he's never been sure if she'll return, but this house is our home and he wants us to have it. I think he felt that because she walked away, she ...'

Wiping my face, I ease away to look up into his face. 'Forfeited the right?'

Re-taking his seat, he shrugs. 'Something like that.'

'So, what are we going to do? Why did you look so worried?'

'I don't find it easy to talk about my feelings—'

'I know. You're like him that way.'

'But,' he continues, 'it is more rightly her house than mine. With him gone, I feel like a bit of an impostor. I always thought when he did eventually go, I'd move on.'

'Have a fresh start, you mean? Is that what you want?' I demand. He looks uncertain, so I play on it. 'Well, I think you're wrong. It's your house as much as hers. Because of her, we lost our home, remember?' Flinging my arms out, I gesture in the direction of the house down the street, the one I grew up in. Jake's house now. 'And you're not an impostor; you're my family and we're still tied together. Plus, what will happen to the house if we say no? We can't just leave it to get run down and neglected.'

'Maybe so.' Dad looks uneasy. 'Anyway, we don't have to make any decisions yet. We have some time to think.' Pulling a long velvet navy box from the chair beside him, he places it on the table. 'This is something else I wanted to show you. His medals.'

'I've seen them before. He used to show them to me a lot, the first year we came back to live here. It was his way of showing me what true courage and honour meant, remember? When I was behaving like a ratty teenager and being up

142

myself. *You'll impress me, young lady, when you've earned yourself a medal.'*

Dad smiles at my imitation of Grandad, and I laugh softly in response, before it catches in my throat. I'll never hear his voice again. 'Why did you want to show them to me?'

'He left them to Jake.'

'Wh-what?' I gasp. 'But they were so precious to him.'

'I think Jake was too, love. I'm not sure you've ever really understood it before, but they were friends. He mentioned Jake a few times when we came back, remember? And that day Jake left, when he was nearly sixteen and his dad manhandled him into the car, Ray was so upset.'

'But I ... I never really took it seriously. I mean, I did wonder why he was so concerned that day, but Jake was never around here visiting or anything.'

'Before we moved back, he was, more often than not. He spent hours here. Then we returned, didn't we?'

I feel guilty. If it's true, then we pushed Jake out. Yet he's never said anything or made me feel bad. Unless that's why he called me spoilt that time on the beach? Maybe all along he felt I didn't appreciate what I had in Dad and Grandad, when it was something he didn't have himself. He said as much once. Did he used to come here to seek solace from his volatile dad? Hide away somewhere he felt safe? And then he lost it because of us. The thought makes me want to cry. Poor Jake.

'But for the last four years, Jake's been away from home,' I exclaim. 'They've hardly seen each other. If they were friends once then they're not any more, surely?'

'Love, think about how upset Jake was at the funeral. He created the picture for your grandad. He came in full dress and carried your grandad's coffin. That's not someone who's a stranger. He's as devastated about losing Ray as we are.' He pauses, 'I think Jake saw Ray as a surrogate dad or grandad.'

'Really?' Surely there's no way Jake and Grandad could have been so close without me knowing. Is there?

'I know you feel Jake was too involved at the funeral, Leila, but there's something you should know.'

'What?' Leaning forward in my seat.

'Jake didn't come into the hospital with us that Sunday, when I came to get you on the beach. But he did follow us there, and he waited in the car until we left. He didn't want to intrude on our private family time, but he wanted to say his own goodbye. When we left to come home, he went in and saw Ray.'

'He did? How? He's not family.'

'I gave my permission.'

'You did?' I choke, the thought of Jake alone with his grief making me sad.

'Yes. They had a special bond. It was the right thing to do. Why do you think I invited him to sit in the front pew with us?'

'You did?' My mouth drops open. I thought Jake was there for me and realise how much I've started to take his friendship for granted.

He shakes his head at me. 'Maybe this will help you understand.' Reaching down next to him, he brings up a plastic storage box, plopping it in the middle of the table next to the teapot. Opening the lid, he points at the contents, rows and rows of white envelopes. Their tops are sliced open, odd triangular bits of paper sticking up here and there where the flaps have torn unevenly. 'Jake and Ray wrote letters to each other when Jake was away. These are the letters he sent your grandad. They're private, but I think Ray would've been okay with you reading one, if it helps convince you of their friendship.'

Standing up, I peer in, running my fingers along the rows of paper, making a rippling sound. I see the censure on Dad's face and feel ashamed. 'Have I been really dim?' I ask in a small voice.

'You could never be that. I'll leave you in peace to do some reading. Also, I didn't want to upset you or leave you alone until you were ready, but a customer has pipes that need fixing. I need to go. See you later, love.' As he heaves himself up from the table, he presses a kiss to my forehead. Idly, I stroke the nubby bit on the centre of Fleur's glossy head and watch Dad walk away, realising he's wearing one of his cotton work tops. He obviously feels it's time to get on with things, and of course he's been losing money by not working over the past two weeks. Such is the life of a self-employed plumber, with no holiday or sick pay. I curse myself for being so insensitive. Why don't I notice what's going on around me?

Sighing, I dig my fingers into the envelopes. 'Okay, let's see what we have here, Fleur.' She gazes up at me before lifting her chin off my knee and loping over to the border to have a dig around for something interesting. As a beagle, her nose always rules her head. I smile ruefully and shake mine.

Whatever happens, whatever crisis befalls us, life always carries on. Some things remain constant. There's a comfort in that.

My phone beeps with a text message, but I ignore it. It's probably Eloise, Shell, or Chloe checking up on me. Right now, Dad's words, and finding out the truth, are far more important. Sliding the folded paper out of the envelope, I settle back in my chair and start reading, the sun warming my skin.

May 2007

Dear Ray,

Hope you're keeping well? Thanks for your last letter – it was a great read, and even greater to hear all about that twenty-pound Common Carp you caught. I'm jealous! Maybe next time I'm back on shore leave, we can go fishing together.

I know it's been a while. We've been on a training exercise, which of course I can't talk about, and things went to shit for a while when we had some unexpected company. But it's done now, and afterwards we stopped off in a part of the Indian Ocean in need of extra security which had some pretty spectacular views, so it wasn't all bad.

Being on a ship day after day feels more monotonous than being on land. At least on land, you get the change of scenery between work and home, or places you go to hang out or stretch your legs. The equivalent here is above deck versus below. It's either the wind on your face or the rumble of engines vibrating through your stomach. You know what I'm talking about. I'm not complaining though. I enjoy the challenge of what we do, of never knowing what's going to happen and what we'll be faced with from one day to the next. The lads are great (when they're not stealing my stuff and hiding it for a laugh) and hot bunking works okay unless some joker decides to spread jam on the sheets … Still, there's a lot of mutual respect and I'm slowly getting to know the other guys. I was on officer training with some of them so it's been good. At the end of the day, we've got each other's backs. We must, because it's part of the job, but also because it's the right thing to do. If we don't look out for each other, it could be the difference between life and death. It's that simple, and that important. I know I don't have to tell you of all people how proud I am to serve my country, because you've done it yourself. But I am. It's also given me something I've never had before. A purpose. A passion. A family. Plus, something I'm finally good at. I'll never be able to properly thank you for all the stories you told me as I was growing up. They changed me, giving me a perspective of the world I wouldn't have had otherwise, showing me there were opportunities out there I never would have dreamt of.

Just like you felt, it's a privilege and an honour to keep international waters safe, whether our own or our allies', and to stop bad people doing worse things. Most importantly, to help people in need when there's been a crisis or disaster. Those are the hardest jobs, but also the most fulfilling.

As much as I talk about monotony, I don't feel trapped like I did back home. Ironic, given that on a ship, I'm more trapped (physically anyway) than I ever was before. Let's be honest, if I wanted a change of scenery from the ship, other than when we make port, my only option is shark-infested waters …

It's funny though, when you have a rigid routine, it makes you think about time. It makes you feel like you have more. I've been reading loads, and one of the engineers is into philosophy and recommended Seneca's Letters From a Stoic. Yeah, I'd never heard of him either. Turns out he was this Roman scholar who had a challenging life by all accounts, but he had some interesting thoughts about the important stuff. There was one thing that struck me in his letter on saving time. 'Make yourself believe the truth of my words – that certain moments are torn from us, that some are gently removed, and that others glide beyond our reach.' I know I've let time, and parts of my life, slip through my fingers and it's like I never realised before that time is finite. There will never be enough of it, and our lives are limited. Seneca said that nothing is ours except time. Not possessions, not money, not love. Just time. It's the one thing we have control over, that we can choose to use wisely and well, or fritter away on unimportant things.

It made me think about my dad, and what you said last time we spoke. I know I need to sort things out with him. I'm just not ready. It isn't time yet. But one day, it will be. It'll be the right moment to look him in the eye and confront what he is and ask him why. To try again to make him stop. For now, please continue keeping an eye on my mum, if you can. I trust you, and I have another plan to try and

get her away from him. I feel guilty for leaving them both,
but she told me once that I had to get out. On the day I
left, she told me to run away. Far, far away. And I did, but
maybe I went too far.

But enough of that maudlin stuff. Write back and tell
me what you've been up to. How are Henry and Leila? Is
Leila painting? She's so talented. I bet she's studying hard
on her A-level courses.

Your letters might take a while to get to me, but I look
forward to them. Don't wait too long – remember what I
said about time.

Jake

As I finish reading the letter, tears are streaming down my
face. I don't need any more convincing. I remember Grandad's
joy at catching that fish, the thrilling story he told us about
how he landed it. It'd taken him two and a half hours and
the moral support of his fishing buddies. Earlier this year,
after I helped him set up an account, he posted a picture on
Facebook of him cradling the carp against his stomach like
a baby. Until then he'd been a massive technophobe, but once
he was on there, he got all excited about tracking his old
Navy friends down and started sharing stories with them.
Now I wonder if he and Jake used social media to keep in
touch. Does that mean they stopped writing letters? It would
be a shame if they did, looking at the number of envelopes
Jake sent over the years. There's something so much more
meaningful and personal about letters, compared to texts or
messages.

The way Jake asked Grandad to keep an eye on his mum and talked about his relationship with his dad so freely ... it's obvious they meant a lot to each other. Even if I feel horribly ashamed about how oblivious I've been, it's the truth. Jake and Grandad were close, and he deserved to mourn him as much as the rest of us. He deserved to be there in the church with us, and at the wake.

And there's something else. Something surprising. Along with his confession about his family on the day Grandad died, the letter offers me more insight into how Jake thinks, and what he does every day. And it strikes me he might be many things – exasperating, sometimes cocky, a bit of a know-it-all – but above everything, he's a good man. A brave one. Grandad admired him, I know it.

Jake's got hidden depths, I've just never seen them all, I acknowledge.

'Shit.' I feel sick when I think about my behaviour in telling Jake he barely knew Grandad and being so angry with him at the wake. No wonder Dad thinks poorly of me.

Throwing the letter on the table, I race from the garden and through the house, stopping only to shove my bare feet into flip-flops in the dark hallway. Flinging the front door open, I jog clumsily along the pavement, before pounding on the peeling red door. 'Come on, come on.' I keep knocking until there's an answer.

'Yes?' Jake's mum looks tired and worn, black hair dull and pulled back in a ponytail. Her skin is patchy and there's a fading bruise under one eye. I've never met her properly, have only ever seen her from a distance. I know more about her than she thinks, and I long to say something about how she could escape this life, but I don't know how to broach the subject – and now isn't the time.

'Hi. I'm Leila, from down the road?'

'I know who you are.'

I flush, and I'm not sure why. 'Is Jake here?'

She looks defeated. 'He left. Yesterday. He came back from the wake –' she pauses '– packed his kit, and went. I haven't heard from him since. I assume he got back okay. Don't think he'll be back for a while, by the look of him,' she finishes in a whisper.

My stomach rolls at her sadness and I want to give her a hug and offer help. But it's not my place. Besides, I'm only eighteen, what can I do? What kind of difference can I make, if she's never been able to help herself? And if capable Jake hasn't been able to? Then I feel awful for the thought. If she hasn't left, it's because she's petrified or hasn't been offered the right help yet. Surely there's something Dad and I can do, living just along the road?

'Who's at the door?' an irritated voice yells from inside. 'Is the boy back again? I'd like to teach him some manners after the way he spoke to me yesterday.' His speech is slurred in a halfway-through-a-bottle-of-whisky kind of way.

'No one,' she calls quickly, 'Jehovah's Witnesses.' Leaning toward me, she blinks, a nervous twitch. 'You need to go,' she says, before raising her voice. 'No, thank you.' Shooing me away with a thin hand with chipped nails, she slams the door in my face.

I watch as flecks of red paint drift to the floor, looking for all the world like dried blood. It reminds me of the day Jake first left, an echo of a similar thought. I frown as I realise he's left once again, and I have no idea when I'll next see him. The thought makes me feel bereft. I'm not sure why it affects me so strongly.

Jake

June 2009

There's a knock on the bedroom door. Before Jake can answer, it flies open and his mum comes stumbling in.

'What is it? Is everything okay?' He springs off the bed where he's been reading a book and digging up the courage to go and see Leila. He hasn't seen her since Ray's funeral the previous September. 'Is it Dad?'

'No.' She twists her hands together. 'He's passed out on the sofa.'

'Then why do you look so worried?' There are frown lines on her forehead and her mouth is pursed.

'Leila's dad is here, asking if we've seen her.'

'What? Why would she be here?' His brain fills in the gaps. 'Wait, she's missing? Move, please.' Rushing past her, he charges down the stairs and sees Henry waiting at the door, face screwed up with concern. 'Henry. What's going on?'

'Have you seen Leila?' His broad shoulders are hunched over, his big hands twisting anxiously together.

'No. I only got back from shore leave yesterday and wasn't sure what kind of reception I'd get, after the way we left things.' He rubs a hand around the back of his neck, recalling every single detail of the scene at the wake, of how shit the whole day had been. Although it's been nearly ten months, and he considers himself a tolerant person, there's still a little part of him that hasn't forgiven her for that scene. He still misses Ray too. Misses hearing his voice and reading his letters. He misses writing them back as well. Writing allows him to think, to crystallise his thoughts in a way talking never has. He hasn't sent Leila any postcards either, given their falling out.

Henry makes to leave, but then looking awkward, he stops. 'For what it's worth, she did come by to apologise the next day but you'd already left.'

'She did?'

'I told her about Ray leaving you his medals and then she understood about your friendship. Did you receive them safely? I had to send them to the base, and they called me to ask a lot of questions.'

'Oh.' Jake shifts uneasily from one foot to another. 'Yes, thank you. It meant a lot. I should have contacted you, sorry.'

'Don't worry, I knew it would.' Henry turns once again, but then blurts. 'Can you help, Jake? I'll understand if you don't want to, if you're still cross with her, but—'

'That doesn't matter now.' Jake waves the comment away. Besides, he already feels lighter at the idea of Leila trying to build bridges. He'll also never forget the kindness this man showed by inviting him to be part of the celebration of Ray's life. 'Although I'm not sure why it's me you want help from?'

'I thought that with your job, being a Marine, you'd be good at finding people.'

'Ah, I see.' Jake hides how much that stings. It's not because Henry sees his daughter and Jake as friends, but because Jake has skills other people don't. 'Of course I'll help. Tell me what's going on.'

Henry steps back. 'Leila left the house just after lunch and I can't get hold of her. She's been gone for seven hours. None of her friends have heard from her either.'

'Well, maybe she's out of battery, or is somewhere painting? She likes peace and quiet for that, right?'

'I've texted asking her to let me know she's safe. No reply. That's not like her.'

'You really think she's in danger?'

'I don't know. It's just that ...'

Jake leans forward, 'Just what?'

'Her mother had a habit of running away, and Leila did too in her early teens, before we moved back here. She was very upset when she left earlier. We'd argued.'

'About?'

Henry clears his throat, and peers around. His eyes flicker to the kitchen doorway behind Jake. 'It's delicate.'

'Okay, let's talk at yours.' Grabbing his keys off the side and shoving his feet into trainers, Jake hollers through to the kitchen, 'Mum, I'll be back later.' As Henry strides down the path, Jake locks the front door and follows the older man.

A minute later they're standing in Henry's kitchen. 'We have privacy now. Tell me, Henry. What is it? If I'm going to find her, I need to know.'

The older man sinks down into a chair at the table and starts talking in short sentences. As he does, a tear spills down his cheek. After some muffled explanations, he finishes with, 'And then I said I was disappointed in her, and Ray would be too.' Henry looks up, shamefaced. 'I was too hard on her, Jake. I was just so shocked. She ran out crying. What if she's done something silly? Doesn't come back?'

Jake pushes away from the cabinet he's been leaning against. He puts his best poker face on, the one his squadron say makes him a great leader, because they never worry they're in trouble, even if they should be bricking it. 'She won't do anything silly, and of course she'll come back. We just need to find her. No clues as to her whereabouts? Do you think her friends might lie for her, say she isn't there when she is?'

Henry shakes his head, expression anguished. 'I know she's nearly nineteen and has been living her own life in Brighton, but they could all tell how worried I was, so I don't think they would. They were genuinely worried and have all been texting for news for the last two hours. No one can get hold of her.'

'Okay,' Jake nods. 'Stay there.' Taking the stairs two at a time, he searches her room, thinking, looking for clues. Henry said she'd been back for the summer break for a few weeks. There aren't many belongings in her room. Apparently, she left the bulk of her stuff at the shared digs. She never went into halls during her first year, Henry had told him; she used some of Ray's inheritance to house-share with other students. It's part of the reason father and daughter have fallen out, not only because he considers it a waste of money, but because living with other students away from campus, she's got mixed up with a guy on another course who sounds like a liability.

Jake doesn't want to think too much about who Leila may or may not be sleeping with, so concentrates on her room instead. There's a shelf of assorted paperbacks and some clothes piled up on a chair in the corner, a pair of discarded sandals on the floor, an unmade four-poster bed, a glass of half-finished water on the bedside cabinet, a few stray hair bands, a lip-gloss in shimmering raspberry, and a sketch pad.

'Where are you, Jones?' Something tickles his memory, a comment she made once, but he can't focus on it. The more he tries to remember, the more it slips out of reach. He thumbs rapidly through the pages of the sketchpad. Inside are charcoal pictures of Brighton. The first, is one of the lanes with a homeless woman in the doorway, clutching a small dog, her sadness apparent; then there's the main pier with the amusements on it, stretching out to sea above a stony beach; the final one is a row of narrow houses lined up on a street leading down to the sea. They're beautiful, and perfectly capture the vibrancy of the city, but they're not helpful. 'Damn it!'

Then he has a thought. Dropping to the carpeted floor, he wriggles around until he can get under the bed. 'Aren't we both starting to get a bit old for this, Jones?' He mutters. 'Or too big, at least.' Using his phone screen as a torch, he shines it onto the wooden boards above his head. There's a tiny pencil sketch taped there. The sea is still, with only a few waves, and the archway is surrounded by water, stoic and strong. 'Of course,' he smiles. 'Got it.'

Racing down the stairs, he almost knocks into Henry, who's standing in the hallway holding his phone and looking anxious.

'It's okay.' Jake clasps his shoulder and squeezes. 'I know where she is. I'll get her.'

'I should come—'

'If she's upset with you, that might not be the best thing. Let me go. I'll bring her back, I promise.'

'Are you sure?' Henry's eyes are watery.

'Absolutely.' Jake grabs his keys and opens the door. 'See you soon. Oh, by the way –' he pauses with his foot on the doorstep, his back to Henry '– I know where she is because I know your daughter. Not because of my job.'

He doesn't expect an answer, but as he swings round to pull the door closed, the other man is looking straight at him, a small smile curving his mouth.

'I know that, Jake. Why do you really think I asked for your help?'

Leila

June 2009

The Rainbow Charm

Lowering myself onto the beach, I shiver. The day has been warm and the sun's still up despite it being gone nine at night, but the multi-coloured stones feel cold beneath my thighs. Perhaps they simply match the ice surrounding my heart. I'm afraid to feel, because if I let the numbness slide away, I'll be left heartbroken. Or maybe just broken, full stop. A fragility is simmering just beneath the surface and I can't let it take over.

But it's all just been such a huge shock. I'll never forget the dread and disbelief on the day I took the pregnancy test. The way I gulped and slumped to the floor, curling up on the grotty bathmat in my student digs as I stared at the two lines declaring the result positive. I couldn't be pregnant. It couldn't be true. I was on the pill, and while I might be flighty about some things and get caught staring off into the distance more often than not – particularly when I was working on a painting – contraception formed part of my daily routine. How was it possible? And why? Why me, and why now? I was about to finish the first year of uni. It was all going well. Despite losing Grandad last year, and how awful I felt during the autumn and winter, by the time spring came around I felt settled and happy, interested in my studies, and getting great marks. I was also in a relationship with someone I could see myself perhaps falling in love with one day.

Every swear word I knew had filled my head, blasting from my mouth. It was the wrong time; it was absolutely impossible. I wasn't ready to have a baby, and neither was Ricky. We'd only been together a few months, and there was no way we could become parents.

It was typical. I'd only taken the test because I kept being sick but was gaining weight, and wanted to rule pregnancy out as an option before darkening the GP's doorway with fears about something sinister. But it was a baby. Ridiculous.

No, no, no. Sweaty panic had gripped me tightly as I wrapped the test in loo roll, put it back in its box, and secured it in the chemist's paper bag. Running out of the house, I shoved it deep into the refuse bin under black bags packed with stinky food rubbish. If I couldn't see it, it wasn't happening. Casting a nervous look up and down the street, I wheeled the bin out a day early just to make sure Brighton and Hove Council took it away.

Although a quick calculation told me I might already be a couple of months along, I chose to bury myself in my course and concentrate on painting in my spare time. I made excuses not to see Ricky. How the hell could I decide what to tell him and cope with how he'd deal with it, when I couldn't even face it myself? I managed to pull it off for a whole two weeks, ignoring every wave of nausea, every tingling ache in my boobs, every moment my nose twitched at an odd smell. It's funny what desperation can make you do.

And now, here I am, where I belong. Getting what I deserve, my eyes staring blankly out to the horizon, past the graceful arch of Durdle Door.

Reaching into my pocket, I take out the ancient iPod I've somehow never been able to let go of and select the playlist El started for me years ago. She occasionally adds to it, mostly when I get dumped. She's really good at finding great break-up songs. I laugh bitterly as I realise there are quite a few on the list. Unwinding the earphones, I tuck the buds into my ears, hoping if the music is loud enough it'll drown out the guilty voice threatening to occupy my head. As soon as 'You Could Be Happy' by Snow Patrol starts, I know I've made a mistake. Tears fill my eyes as every jagged bit of hurt and loss I've been shying away from fills my head, clenching around my heart. My eyes screw up, my throat closes, and silent sobs choke me. Tears roll down my face, unwanted, unbidden. It physically aches – God, it feels like I can't breathe – and I want to curl in on myself and disappear. The pain in my chest is what I imagine a heart attack feels like. I bring my knees up to my chin and wrap my arms around them, holding onto myself because no one else can, or is here to. Pressing the button to loop the song on repeat, I play it again, letting the music and words release my grief.

During the fourth repeat, a hand lands on the shoulder of my thin denim jacket. I jump. Whipping the earphones out, I look up, at the same time realising the light is dimming.

'Jake. What are you doing here?' I ask, scrubbing my swollen face self-consciously with my hands.

Sitting down beside me, he drapes a tartan blanket around my shoulders. '*I know,*' he says simply, gazing out to sea where dusk is starting to fall. 'And your dad was worried because he couldn't get hold of you. He was worried you'd done a runner like your mum. Sorry if that sounds insensitive. His words, not mine.' Then he adds quietly. 'I also thought you might need someone.'

'I'm nothing like her,' I reply in a taut voice, pulling the blanket closer. 'Maybe I used to go missing for a few hours occasionally when I was in my early teens, but it was mostly when I needed space, or was painting or drawing.' Even as I say it, shame fills me. I'm not telling the whole truth, not by a long way. I think of that night at my first secondary school, the heat and smoky darkness which filled the room. 'Dad has nothing to worry about. And what do you *know?*'

'That you're pregnant,' he answers. 'Also, that you're not sure what you're going to do about it, but you may not keep it. Your dad was rough on you, and he's sorry.' He pauses, and looks at me thoughtfully. 'He is *truly* sorry, Jones.'

Open-mouthed, I can't speak for a moment. Dad told him? But it was *private*. Then I grasp that given Dad's one of the most intensely private people I know, he must've been frantic to tell Jake. I deliberately left my mobile phone in the car so I could avoid the calls and messages. I couldn't face anyone. I just needed the quiet. Now I feel guilty, but it's soon swamped by the tsunami of emotions I'm battling. The fact that Jake just sits there patiently waiting unravels me.

'I was pregnant,' I murmur brokenly. 'But I'm not any more.'

His eyes widen – one green, one brown – and I see in them a compassion I don't deserve. 'What happened?'

'I started bleeding this morning, after my argument with Dad.' I speak in a factual tone, trying to get through it. It's the type of stuff I wouldn't usually share with a guy, but for some reason I'm completely comfortable telling Jake. 'It carried on, got heavier, got worse. I started getting cramps, so I went to hospital. I was in A&E for half the day. It's part of the reason I didn't answer my phone. And then afterwards, at the hospital, when they'd told me I'd suffered a miscarriage ...' I trail off. 'I didn't much feel like talking to anyone.'

'God, Jones. You went through that alone?'

'Don't. Don't feel sorry for me, don't sympathise. I c-can't,' I cry. 'I didn't want it. Or at least, I didn't think I did. I don't want to talk about it, okay?'

He nods easily, switching his attention to the archway in front of us. The sun is setting, and is positioned so it's shining right through the arch, like a key in a hole.

Before I know it, and maybe because he's not looking at me, it all spills out. 'You must think I'm an awful person, because I didn't want the baby –' my breath catches, but I press on '– or at least, I wasn't sure if I did. And now it's gone, before it even had a chance, because I failed. I couldn't do the one thing women are made for. I didn't keep it safe,' I sob, 'maybe because I didn't want to.' His hand finds mine, but he says nothing and so I hold on, talking. Talking because I can't stop. 'It's not fair. I ... I didn't know, I didn't want to hurt it, I didn't know what I wanted.' I choke, salty tears filling my mouth. 'Now it's gone, and I feel empty. My stomach hurts but I still feel sick, and I just want the whole thing to go away. I want it behind me, but I can't think of anything else! Everything is a big fat mess, and the last time I saw you, I was horrible and now here you are being so sweet. And I don't deserve it. I can't take it!'

Grabbing a handful of stones, I throw them across the beach, narrowly missing a seagull perched on a piece of drift-wood watching us. The sight sends me into hysterics, and I burst into tears. Jake places a steadying hand on my back, letting me weep. After several long minutes, my crying quietens and the beat of the waves on the shore soothes me. The worst of it is over for now, and relief is the strongest emotion, closely followed by exhaustion. I hide my face in the blanket and whisper a subdued thanks. When I lift my head, Jake's watching me with concern.

His shoulder nudges mine. 'Your dad said you were involved with another student, that you have a boyfriend,' he says gently. 'What did *he* want?'

'Well, when I finally told him, it turned out he didn't want either of us,' I say in a bleak tone. 'Guess now he's off the hook.'

'Well, it's not easy. It's a difficult situation.' Ignoring my tear-streaked face, he looks me in the eye. 'I'm sure he didn't mean—'

His words churn my stomach. Is he on Ricky's side? 'So, now you're defending him? There was no misunderstanding what he said. He meant it. He was clear.' Fury whips through me, lashing me, making me strike out. It's just too much. It piles on top of the anger I already feel. The A&E doctor said the pregnancy hormones will take a few weeks to leave my system, so my moods will be up and down for a while. A horrible irony. You still get the symptoms, even after the reason for them has gone. 'Why do men always stick together? Ricky told me to stop crying and get it sorted, and Dad can barely look at me.' Scrambling to my feet, I toss the blanket at his feet and start backing away. All I want to do is leave.

Jake stands, coming towards me, his shoulders broad against the sunset. 'Jones. Wait. Where are you going?'

Holding my hands out in front of me, I shake my head. 'I need my friends, not you. Not someone who's going to make excuses for a guy he doesn't even know.' I'm hurt, and desperate to push him away. He shouldn't be around me right now; I'm no good. 'And after all, we're not friends, are we? Because you left me *again*, without saying goodbye, and again haven't been in touch. You can't just keep slipping in and out of my life, Jake, and then expect to carry on where we left off. I never know where I stand with you.'

He flinches. 'That's not fair. It's my job!'

'I understand that,' I say, wrapping my arms around my middle, 'but it shouldn't stop you getting in touch. You found a way to do that with Grandad, by writing those letters to him. What about the postcards you used to send me? They just stopped!'

'I'm sorry.' He stares at me. 'But there's no way I could've known you'd want me to carry on. The last time we were together you were pretty clear I'd pissed you off and was overstepping the mark. If I'd known you felt differently, well ... You say you don't know where you stand,' he speaks into my silence, 'but you must know I'm your friend. We've had a few clashes over the years, but we have history. Plus, I like you Jones. You must know that.'

'Why? Why would you like me?' I laugh harshly, feeling like the worst person in the world right now. Shamed. Sad. If I could climb out of my own skin, I would. The emotions running through me are almost unbearable. And something about his use of the word 'friend' stings.

Coming closer, he grabs my hands and holds tight.

'Because you have a wonderful eye and a brilliant imagination – if you didn't, you couldn't draw and paint the way you do.' His eyes gleam in the rays of the setting sun. 'I love the way you see the world. Your art is always full of hope and magic. You're kind too. It's in the way you shared your food with me in the park that first week and didn't push me to talk about stuff I wasn't ready to. The way you've always looked after your dad and Ray. And the compassion you showed when I told you about my parents on the morning of Ray's death. Your words at the funeral, about Ray, they were heartfelt and lovely – he would have been so proud. Everyone in that church was proud, Jones. Yes, you can be spiky and stubborn, and you have a bit of a temper and can be ditzy – and you have the worst taste in men – but you have a beautiful soul.'

Wrenching my hands away, I scowl, only able to focus on the bad bits. It's like he can see the worst parts of me, and is using them against me. My temper's something I've worked so hard to contain, and it hurts he'd mention it. I know I'm ditzy. I don't always listen – there are moments when my common sense disappears because I'm often daydreaming about things I'm going to paint, and I have a hard time concentrating, but still ... 'You don't know me at all, do you?' He can't, if he doesn't understand how much his words would burn me.

'If don't know you, how did I know you'd be here, of all places?'

'Lucky guess,' I spit, throwing my arms out to the side, 'so why don't you just bugger off? You're good at that!'

But he doesn't. He just walks a few feet away and stares out at the blue-green sea, which is calm now with no white-caps. I notice the resigned sigh which runs through his body, the way his shoulders tense then relax, and how his broad chest puffs out.

What am I doing? Just because I'm hurting, it doesn't give me the right to hurt someone else. Despite the pain in my heart, I'd like to think I've learnt something over the past year. Deflating like a balloon emptied of air, I go after Jake, traipsing doggedly towards the sea's edge. The physical effort it takes is immense. The memory of his letter to Grandad and my realisation that Jake's a good guy give me the strength I need. 'I shouldn't have said that,' I murmur, standing next to him. 'My boyfriend betrayed me, my body's betrayed me, and I didn't even have the chance to decide what to do about the baby; the choice was taken from me. I'm sorry. Maybe we're not close friends, but you always seem to be there for me, even though I don't always appreciate it.' His chin dips in a nod of acknowledgement. 'The truth is,' I rush on, touching the plain heart charm on the bracelet round my wrist, 'I'm angry with her too. My mum. She should be here for this, to help me through it. To listen, to give comfort, to say whatever it is that mums say at times like these. But she's not.' Sighing, my eyes search his face in the falling darkness. 'Dad loves me, but he doesn't understand, and I can't bear to see the look of disappointment on his face. He's worked so hard to raise me, to provide, to give me a good education, and as far as he was concerned, I was considering throwing it away on an unplanned baby.'

Jake finally turns to me. 'Just because something isn't planned, it doesn't mean it's a mistake.'

'Well, I'll never know now, will I?' Tears fill my eyes again and trickle down my face. I'm so sick of crying. Over the past year I've shed so many tears, and I'm ready for it to end. So ready.

'Come here.' Opening his arms, Jake wraps them around me before I can reply.

Stiffening, I try to pull away, but he raises one hand and starts to stroke my hair soothingly.

'It's okay,' he murmurs against the top of my head. 'You'll be okay.'

I don't mean to, but the warmth of his body is a comfort and I relax into him. He's so tall, so much bigger than me. I feel safe and secure. It's okay to lean on him. To let him absorb my pain. It's reassuring, and I bury my face in his chest. He keeps stroking my hair and the tears keep flowing but I feel better. After a while the teardrops slow, and the worst of it has passed.

Edging back in his arms, I gaze up at him. His eyes are dark, his features hidden by the twilight. He looks dangerous and like a stranger, even though I've known him since I was eleven.

'What are you thinking?' he asks.

One of his palms is warm against my lower back, and the other hand is still stroking my hair. It feels nice, but something's changed.

He looks at my mouth and brings me closer. 'Jones?'

I feel sick, and there's a twinge in my stomach. 'Jake—'

Then he drops his head and kisses me, his lips firm on mine. Breaking away, I push both hands against his chest, forcing him back. I must have caught him unawares because he stumbles backwards and lands on the stones.

'What the hell are you doing?' I cry. 'I thought you said we were friends.'

It's hard to see his face as he leaps to his feet, but his anguished voice says it all. 'I'm sorry. I didn't mean to ... I was just trying to comfort you.'

'Well, don't!' Spinning around, I stride towards the steps, shingle churning beneath me. I'm not capable of running. 'And don't even think about following me. Just leave me alone!' I hiss.

My heartbeat thrums in my chest, my cheeks burning with heat. How *could* he? After being so sweet about the baby and comforting me, how could he do that when I'm at my most vulnerable? When I'm so confused?

I trudge up the hill, exhausted, the evening moonlight shining down on Durdle Door behind me, leaving Jake on the beach alone.

***

It's close to eleven by the time I get home. I called Dad to say I was safe, and coming back. I apologised for worrying him and asked him to text my friends and let them know I'm okay. He insisted on staying up to wait for me, so I had to get tough and insist he go to sleep, saying I was too upset to see him. He made me promise we'd talk properly tomorrow though.

Unfortunately, it's not a promise I can keep. My head's too full of the argument with Dad this morning, losing the baby, what I'm going to do about Ricky, how shit I feel physically, and then Jake kissing me.

It's too much to deal with, and so although I came home, I'm not staying. I can't. I need some time and space. I can't be here, but I also can't go back to Brighton. I'm not ready to be around my uni friends, or face Ricky yet. I'll find somewhere else, just for a little while. I'm going to drive through the night until I end up somewhere that feels right, then hide away for a week or two. Despite what Dad believes, I still have a significant amount of money left from Grandad, and it's not as if I'm intending to grab my bag and flee to the French Riviera for the high life or anything. I just want somewhere pretty, quiet, and still. Grabbing my duffel bag, I stuff some clothes into it, shove in a book, take my spare art set from the bottom of the wardrobe, and sneak out of the house. I'll call Dad in the morning so he doesn't worry. I'll explain what happened with the baby. I take a deep breath and let it shudder out. I will tell him I'm fine but need time to myself.

Climbing into my VW Beetle, I wonder if I should be driving but I'm wide awake and amped up with all the upset of today, so I'll make a start. If I get tired, I'll pull over. Switching the CD player on, a Coldplay song comes on, and I massage my lower stomach. Taking two ibuprofen with an old bottle of water from the footwell, I start the engine, watching as a set of lights sweep onto our road. Instinctively, I know it's Jake. He was only ten minutes behind me. I don't want to see him.

Backing up slowly, I reverse down the drive and wait until I'm at the end of the road before putting my headlights on.

***

I arrive back in Brighton three weeks later. I ended up staying in a village in North Devon called Sheepwash. It was tiny. Ten or so houses around a pretty little flowered square serving as residents' parking, a small grey church, a local pub with strong pale beer, and a small shop with a post-office counter. It was also exactly what I needed: self-contained, quiet, with little else to focus my energy on.

I stayed in a beautiful thatched cottage painted pale blue, with a large wildflower garden and a double bedroom overlooking the village square. My room filled with sunlight each morning despite the old wooden shutters inside the window, but I woke up feeling rested despite the early starts. I slept well, ate cake, went for walks on Bude beach, and watched films at the cinema in Okehampton. I spent time in the leafy green garden too, painting all my hurt away: a watercolour of my favourite view from Hengistbury Head, right from the top and overlooking the spit, filled with rows of colourful beach huts and with Mudeford Quay in the background; Bournemouth Pier stretching out from its sandy beach in oils, their colours vibrant on the paper. I turned a few of my charcoal sketches of Brighton into bigger pieces rich with detail. I painted until my back ached and my fingers were stiff, but it was a release and felt like falling in love again.

I thought a lot and got my head straight. Checking in with Dad daily by sending a quick text meant he didn't worry, and I spoke with Eloise, Shell, and Chloe to tell them each what'd happened. We cried together and they all offered to come and see me, but I wanted to be alone. El texted me rude pictures every day to cheer me up, Chloe sent me inspirational quotes, and Shell somehow tracked down where I was and posted me extra art supplies. Having good friends, I realised, is so important. As Jake would say, I'm lucky.

During my second week in Sheepwash, I felt strong enough to call Ricky and have The Talk. We ended it. The pregnancy and losing a baby were too much for our relationship to endure, and I no longer felt any excitement at the idea of seeing him. He sounded relieved, which caused a small twist of hurt, but at least he said sorry for the way he'd reacted.

Jake is another matter. I'm not sure what to do about him. I still can't believe he kissed me. What was he *thinking*? I keep going back over it in my mind, even when I try my hardest not to let thoughts stray to him. Maybe when I cried in his arms, I held him too tightly, or gave off a signal or something? That must be it. He's never given me any reason to believe he has feelings for me.

At least things are normal with Dad again. I dropped in at home this morning before driving onward to Brighton. We had a big heart-to-heart and apologised to each other, and things are back on track. My plan now is to find a job to fill the rest of the summer until term starts again in the autumn.

Letting myself in through the front door of the narrow, terraced house, painted a cheery lemon yellow as if to compensate for its squashed tininess, I heave my case and portfolio of new work into the hallway and lean them against the wall. I stop and listen. Thank God Ricky has moved out. I hold a hand to the middle of my chest. Physically I've pretty much recovered, but I know it will take a while for my heart to do the same.

Dropping the wad of envelopes Dad gave me onto the kitchen table, I scoop up a note from my housemates inviting me to join them at the beach. Sighing, I drop into one of the kitchen chairs. I may as well open my post – no doubt a heap of depressing bills – before sorting out the kitchen and unpacking. I'll decide whether to join my uni friends later. Sifting through the envelopes, I spot a handwritten one. The handwriting is small and neat, almost printed.

I tear it open and unfold the lined paper. As I do, a small charm drops onto the faded lino of the kitchen floor. Leaning over, I retrieve the piece of metal and stare at it, biting my lip. It's a tiny multi-hued rainbow with a cloud at either end. Is it from her? Does she know how much, more than ever, I need her?

Frowning, I straighten the paper and start reading. By the time I finish, tears are rolling down my face.

Jake
June 2009

The Rainbow Charm

Jones,

You told me off for not writing to you, so now you're getting your wish.

I've just got back from Durdle Door, and I'm glad you got home safely too. Although you wanted me to hang back, I needed to make sure you made it okay, so I followed at a distance.

I hope as you're reading this, whenever it might be, you're better than the last time I saw you. That you're not feeling as raw, sad, and angry. That you've figured a few things out.

I tried to help on the beach, and wanted to be there for you, but instead I added to your pain. I'm sorrier than you'll ever know. I shouldn't have kissed you; my timing sucked. It's the one thing that's always been off about us, and our friendship – timing. And we are friends. I believe it, even if you don't. The first time I saw you sitting in your dad's van with a pink baseball cap on and an odd look on your face, I knew you were going to be important to me, and I was right.

Look, I'll be gone for a while. I'm shipping out, and won't be back for at least six months, and who knows what will happen after that. So, I wanted to send you something to cheer you up because I know you'll be gutted that I won't be on British soil :) Is that the sound of you telling me to shut up and stop being cocky I can hear in my head? ;)

Anyway, the charm with this letter is for a rainbow baby – the ones that come along after those that are lost. I believe one day you'll have the chance to be a mum, and next time the tale will have a happier ending. He or she will be your rainbow baby. For now, I know you won't forget what you've lost, and I won't either. I'm sorry the choice was taken from you, but whatever you'd have decided, it would have been the right thing for you.

The other thing about rainbows is they only appear while there's both sunshine and rain. So, the charm is also to remind you that while life is full of darkness, when there are disappointments and people make mistakes and let you down, there is always light too, and something beautiful that remains. You still have a lot to be grateful for: family, friends, your health, a bright future, and endless possibilities. Just know that I'll always be here for you, no matter what.

Always look for the rainbow, Jones. You have to treasure life – no one else is going to do it for you.

I'll try to be better at staying in touch and hope you still want me to.

J x

Leila

November 2011

The Graduation Charm

'Well done, Leila, I'm proud of you.'

Dad's hearty slap on the shoulder, intended as a sign of affection and pride, almost knocks me over. He always forgets how strong he is. I might not get my physical size from him – he's broad where I'm narrow, and tall where I'm short – but I'm grateful for inheriting, or more accurately *learning*, his emotional strength. If I didn't have that, I wouldn't have made it through the last two years. After losing the baby, I shut myself off from the world for a while and for the best part of a year buried myself in hours of exhausting uni work and painting, juggling them alongside a series of part-time jobs because of the perpetual financial worries dogging me after I'd decided to donate the rest of Grandad's money to a good cause. If I was more like my mum, I would've run away from the situation, but instead I stayed. On my good days, that makes me proud.

'Thanks, Dad.' I lean into him and smile, before spinning round to take in the sight greeting us from the balcony. He's never been one for extravagance, so when he called and said he was staying in a seafront hotel while in town for my graduation ceremony, I was surprised. But if there was ever a reason to justify the expense, he explained, it was staying somewhere decent while coming to see his daughter graduate.

'Not a bad view.' He nods to the scene below us. 'Even with what's coming.'

The throbbing wind, beating with the rhythm of a heart as it builds towards a storm, whips the ends of my long hair across my face. Typical of the south coast of England to pull some freak weather out of the bag. I pull my hair away from my red-lipsticked mouth with a roll of my eyes. I know I should have taken the time to get it cut, but I've just been too busy. So instead I plaited part of it around the crown of my head, leaving the rest down. 'No, Dad,' I reply with a grin, 'not a bad view at all.' He's putting me up here too, as a treat for my final night in Brighton. After deciding to stay on for a few months until I'd graduated formally, I'm reluctant to leave. I've loved it here: the people, the city, the buildings, the beach. Still, it's time to go home. I know that much, even if I don't know what I'm doing next.

Gripping the balcony railing, my eyes take in the busy road stretching along the promenade. The wide shingle beach is dotted with a straggle of brave visitors bracing themselves against the weather as they trudge along the stones. Brighton Palace Pier extends into the sea, with the distinctive dome housing the amusements leading along its length to fairground rides.

It's a special place, and I'll miss it. While I've lived here, I've learnt it takes a team three months to repaint the pier every year. I've watched them working on the mammoth task in between lectures and working in a local bar. I know too that it's 1,722 feet long and was officially opened in May 1899 after eighteen years of building works, hindered in part by a catastrophic storm. More, what I know is when I'm sad, homesick, tired, or just need my spirits lifting, if I go and stand on the pier and look out to the horizon, I feel better. And even though it might seem counterintuitive to most people because who knows what lurks in the darkness, sitting under the pier on the sliding pebbles makes me feel safe and calm.

'I've lost you again.' Dad's voice jolts me from my thoughts.

'Sorry.' Shaking my head, I raise my eyes. Beyond the pier, the sun's slowly setting into the peaty sea. It's cold, stark, and beautiful and I know back home the view is even better. 'I was just thinking.'

Dad clears his throat. 'You're like your mum in that way. She used to stare off into space sometimes. It would have been useful to know what was going on in her head.'

'I'm nothing like Mum,' I snap. 'For a start I'd be here for my daughter's graduation.'

We both fall silent.

'Sorry, love. I didn't mean anything by it.'

He's lovely. I'm lucky. There's a pang in my chest when I think about the raw deal Jake got with his dad. What a sorry excuse for a parent. I really should appreciate mine more. 'That's okay. Sorry for snapping.' Shivering, I wrap my cheap olive parka coat more tightly around me, feeling dwarfed by its puffy material.

'Here.' Digging into his jacket pocket, he holds out an envelope towards me. 'This arrived a couple of days ago.' Frowning, he adds, 'Be careful of the wind, it's strong.'

'I will. I hope you haven't got me anything. I told you not to.'

He chuckles. 'Well, I can't promise there won't be something waiting for you at home – along with Fleur, a doggy who's really missed you – but it won't be a charm. I know that's you and your mum's thing.'

'Hmmm.' I study the envelope, an unfamiliar postmark in the top left-hand side joining the typed address. 'Looks like she's travelling the world again,' I say bitterly. But one side of my mouth's already hitching up in a reluctant smile, wiping away the negative thoughts about my wayward mother as I open it. 'Aw, it's sweet.' I pluck the tiny graduation cap charm from the otherwise empty envelope. There's a small tassel hanging off the mortarboard and seeing it on my bracelet will remind me of my achievement more than having a row of letters after my name or a certificate in a folder. There'll be a daily reminder on my wrist that I passed my Arts degree with a First, and that all the agony and hours of slog were worth it. My lecturer says I have a promising career and tremendous talent if I can channel it in the right way. Great to hear, but easy for him to say. I still have to pay the bills. Even moving back in with Dad, I need to pay my own way. I want to. I'm aware – not because he would ever tell me but because last time I was home I saw a bank statement – that he's struggling financially.

I give him a brief hug and step back, noticing with a frown

that his hair is thinning and there are more lines fanning out from his eyes. I'll look after him when we get home. I can cook and clean again, make sure he's taken care of.

He dips into the jacket's inside pocket, bringing out another envelope. 'Here. This also arrived the other day.'

'Thanks.' Examining the small neat script on the front, I know immediately who it's from, and my stomach twirls. I shove it in my coat to open later. I haven't seen Jake since that evening at Durdle Door when he kissed me, although he did at least start sending postcards again. Just a few a year: one of Alexandria Port in Egypt, one from Dubai, one from an island in the Indian Ocean. Each time they held just a couple of bland sentences about the weather and wishing me well. A bit cold, really. But I bundle them all carefully together and tie them with a purple ribbon, keeping them in the top drawer of my dresser, where I can reach for them if I need to.

***

The following day, a few hours after an underwhelming graduation ceremony and an overwhelming amount of tears and hugging as I said goodbye to my housemates and other uni friends, Dad and I walk through our front door in Bournemouth. After dinner last night we both agreed on an early night, given the anticipated excitement of today and the heaving around of boxes as we packed me up to come home. Still, despite a solid ten hours of sleep and an easy drive back, it's been a bit of a whirlwind and we're both weary.

After greeting an ecstatic Fleur, who was looked after by

a neighbour while Dad was away, I trudge upstairs with a box under one arm and a bin liner hanging from the other hand. I told Dad to leave everything else for later and put the kettle on. I need a moment on my own. As I kick my bedroom door open and drop my belongings, a feeling of unease creeps over me. While I've been home for weekends or even weeks at a time between terms, the idea I'm back here for good fills me with dread. I don't know why. I should be pleased to be here, with Dad, in the house I grew up in from the age of fourteen, in the town I love so much. But instead I feel stifled, powerless.

Going over to the window, I pull back the curtain and peek into next door's garden, and then at our other neighbour's patio. My shoulders drop as I see they both look exactly the same as when I left for uni. I don't usually check; it's never important. But today, it is. Resting my forehead against the window, I sigh. I guess when I visited before, I knew I was escaping sooner or later. Now I don't have that. But why should I need to escape? What am I escaping from exactly? I can't put my finger on why I feel this way.

Rising on tiptoes, I crane my neck to see the sloped red roof of Jake's house – my childhood home. I can't manage it; the angle isn't right. Backing up, I pull my arms out of my parka and slide the envelope from the inside pocket, letting my coat slither to the carpet. The card's been burning a hole against my ribs ever since last night, but Brighton didn't feel like the right place to read it. Inserting a nail into the flap at the back, I rip it open.

It's a graduation card. 'Happy Graduation Smart Arse' is

emblazoned in black across a glossy white front with a picture of a donkey underneath it. Despite myself, and the fact I want to be cross with him for his soulless postcards, I chuckle. Opening it up, I'm intrigued to see what he's written this time. I can't imagine anything will ever touch me the way his last beautiful letter did, but even if it's only half as good, it'll be enough. The right-hand side of the inside of the card holds a simple message.

Well done, I knew you could do it.
(You're lucky you didn't get a 'You're a Fucking Genius' card
– it was a close call),
   Jake x

But the left-hand side is crammed with tiny printed writing. Taking a deep breath, I lie back against my pillows and begin to read. Before long, I'm thinking Jake has an uncanny ability to read my mind.

Jones,
   I know it's been a long time, but I figured you needed your space, and I've been all over the world on a series of overseas tours. I can't tell you much about what I've been doing, but I've seen some incredible sights and done important things. Things that needed doing to keep people safe.
   It's been more than two years and I think it'll be a while longer yet until I see you, but at least now I know you're home I can picture you walking along our street, or painting

183

in your back garden, or hanging out with your friends somewhere.

I know it's going to be weird being back. You might feel out of place, out of sorts, being home permanently. Perhaps you feel like you've gone backwards, circling back to where you began. But you need to remember you're a different person from the volatile grief-stricken girl who set off for uni. I could see changes that night on the beach even though you were so upset, and I bet you're stronger because of all you've been through.

Last time I was on shore leave your dad and I caught up. I still miss Ray and writing to him, so it was nice talking to Henry and hearing what he's been up to, including how you've been doing. It's obvious he's proud of how hard you've worked, what you've achieved, and how independent you've become. He knows you've got a bright future ahead of you. So, don't be deflated – don't feel like coming home is a bad thing. Think of it as the next chapter in your story. It won't be for ever. It's a stepping stone while you find out what you're supposed to do, until you find your own way. One day you'll have your own house with your own family, and your dad will be a part of that too. For now, you need to make a plan and get stuck in. Good luck with whatever you decide to do and I look forward to catching up. At the moment, it's likely to be next year at some point; I've just asked for a career intermission so I can take six months out to work on a voluntary project in Africa.

I don't know whether you're still pissed off at me for trying to kiss you, but if you want to get in touch, even by text, my number's below. I shouldn't have done it – as I said, the timing was off – but I don't completely regret it, and maybe one day you'll want to give it another try.

Jake x

As I finish reading his message, the breath shudders in my throat. The timing was off? Maybe one day I'll want to try kissing him again? The thought of it makes me squirm. That night on the beach it was wrong for him to kiss me, for so many reasons. Ricky, the baby, my grief. And since then I've just been angry at him for it, and for breaking my trust, and have never stopped to consider whether, if those things weren't in the way, I'd have wanted him to kiss me.

I just don't know. The thought is odd, like trying to jam a piece of a puzzle into a hole it can't quite fit. Jake's the kid down the road who I hung around the park with, and who stopped me from being expelled from school, who now just happens to be a man. I can concede he's good-looking, and he's also caring, compassionate, a great leader, someone who can be relied on, sensitive, and intelligent. But he also has a tendency towards cockiness, is overprotective and overbearing, tells me what he thinks even when I don't invite his opinion, is uncomfortably honest about my faults, and can be a bit of a show-off.

I also don't like the way he can see through me, as if every part of me is exposed. It's unnerving. Vulnerability isn't something that sits easily with me.

Plus, I can't risk the on-off friendship we do have. I've come to realise I treasure that, no matter how much I've tried to deny it in the past. Because I've missed seeing him over the past two years. I've missed our moments together. Before he kissed me on the beach, he was being incredibly sweet and supportive.

It already hurts when he leaves with us being sort of friends; I can't imagine how it would feel being with him, with him touring the world all the time, out of touch for months on end. Never knowing if he was coming back or not. Exactly like Mum. No, there's no way I could handle that. It's too much.

It's all a bit irrelevant though, isn't it? Because '*I don't completely regret it*' is hardly a declaration of love. Perhaps I'm just the one girl who's pushed him away. A challenge. I'm sure he's not wearing his chastity belt while he's serving overseas. The thought makes me feel a bit sick. I bet he's literally got a girl in every port. Picturing his tall, broad-shouldered body in his uniform, I frown. A splinter of annoyance works its way under my skin, piercing me.

How dare he do this? How dare he put these thoughts in my head? I don't need this right now, with everything else going on.

Kiss him? 'Arghh! Not likely,' I mutter, stabbing his number into my phone. I press send on the text before I can think too much about it. Before I can admit I'm being irrational, hurtful, and unfair.

Harding, thanks for the card but get on with your own life instead of trying to run mine. Jones.
P.S. It's a no thanks to giving the kiss another try

The irritation spurs me on to race down the stairs and bring all my stuff up, unpacking in a white-hot rush of frustration and adrenaline. When I'm done, I sit down, make a list, and pin it to the cork-board above my dressing table so I can see it every day.

1) Get a job
2) Help Dad pay the bills
3) Clean, cook and look after Dad
4) Paint
5) See El & Co

For the next few hours, I put an ache in my wrist and give myself burning eyes squinting at the drawing of fire and flames I sketch across my pad in charcoal. When I sit back, satisfied, my fingers are black and my head's pounding but my annoyance with Jake is spent, the emotions channelled onto the paper.

Three weeks later, after pounding the pavements and unable to find any job connected with my degree, I accept a role in an office-supply company, co-ordinating stock. I've also caught up with El, Shell, and Chloe – surprisingly, she's dating Jake's friend Owen – and have folded neatly back into our friendship group. In some ways I feel more grown up, but in other ways it feels like I never left.

I comfort myself that at least there is one thing that remains uncomplicated, as I spin the bracelet around my wrist and run my finger over each of my precious charms.

Jake

August 2012

The Music Charm

'Man, it's been so long since I last saw you. Welcome home.' Owen slaps Jake's shoulder, before opening the van's side door. 'After you.'

'Thanks. Great to be back, even if only for a few weeks.' He grins at his shaggy-haired friend as he takes a seat, and for the first time in ages his smile feels genuine. That saying about a weight being lifted is true. He can't believe his dad's gone. The fucker has left, taken away in the middle of the night by the police for his involvement in some dodgy deal, and then warned off by his mum's cousin Doug with threats of violence hanging over him if he ever returns to Bournemouth. Jake seriously doubts he'll come back now his mum's got Doug involved, given his reputation up north. So the guilt, worry, and creeping sense of doom have all vanished. His mum's back in the house where she belongs, after a protracted absence, and has finally explained Leila's original part in it all, breaking the promise she'd made not to tell. About a generous gesture almost three years ago that gave her the opportunity to be somewhere safe for a while, to break free of her husband's hold. He'll always be grateful, and can't wait to see Leila today to thank her in person. The annoyance he felt at the lack of reply to his postcards, and the harsh text she sent after his graduation card, are forgotten.

Glancing at his watch, he sees they're set to leave in five minutes. Is she going to make it?

Owen climbs in behind the wheel, and Chloe snuggles in next to him, squealing with excitement. 'Road trip to Cardiff! Coldplay here we come!' Jake remembers her as a bit of a grumbler, but being in a relationship with laid-back Owen has mellowed her. Maybe it's true that being with the right person makes you a better one.

Jake cranes his head to look out of the open van door as Owen starts the engine, and sees her come running up.

'Sorry, sorry,' she pants, climbing into the van and sliding in next to him. Her long, tanned legs are bare in a short black skirt, and she's wearing totally impractical high wedges. 'I got caught up. But I'm here now, and I'm worth the wait, right?' Leaning forward, she plants a mushy kiss on him.

Owen chortles in the background and Chloe lets out a snort, but Jake's eyes are open and as Simone presses her lips harder against his, he sees movement from the corner of his eye and detaches himself.

'Oh.' Leila halts in the act of hoisting herself into the back of the van. 'Jake, I didn't see you there.' Her expression is wary.

'Hi.' Jake smiles to put Leila at ease, 'Long time, no see.'

Leila looks confused, nodding once as she clambers in.

Simone turns to look down her nose at the new arrival. 'Who's she?' Curling her nails around Jake's wrist and digging in.

With a frown, he eases her hand away. They've only dated a few times, and he doesn't like how territorial she is. The only reason she's here is because Owen unthinkingly mentioned in front of her that they had a spare ticket because someone dropped out. 'This is Leila; she lives down the road. Jones, meet Simone.'

'Hello,' Leila mutters, sitting on the bench on the other side of the minibus.

She's in cut-off denim shorts and a plain white V-neck T-shirt. The outfit is simple but it suits her, showcasing her lithe body and dark eyes. She's wearing her charm bracelet, and a platinum pendant hangs down between her breasts. As she crosses her legs, Jake sees a thin chain around her ankle too. His eyes sweep over her, and he notices a new tattoo on the back of her right hand, a scattering of stars and swirls. She looks sexy and carefree. He's missed her. It's been years with all his tours and time in Africa, and trying to stay away from his dad, who was living in the house alone while his mum was in hiding.

Leila knocks on the window to someone outside. 'Come on!'

'Sorry, almost birthday girl!' A tall guy with stark red hair and bright blue eyes swings into the back of the van. Jake's irritated just looking at him. He's like a male model off some cheesy aftershave ad.

'Hi, Craig,' Owen and Chloe chorus from the front seat.

Simone puffs her chest out and simpers, 'Hello.' Jake simply nods in greeting.

Craig bends his head to fit into the minibus before claiming his place beside Leila.

Owen puts the vehicle in gear. 'Right, let's get going. We've got nearly three hours ahead of us.'

Chloe lets out a whoop and Leila joins in laughingly, but her expression is strained. She's had a blunt fringe cut in, and Jake thinks it makes her look older than she is. Craig wraps his arm around her shoulder and tucks her long silvery-blonde hair behind her ear. She smiles, her expression easing, and turns to gaze out of the window.

Jake's stomach lurches and he grabs hold of Simone's hand, squeezing hard.

***

The Millennium Stadium is teeming with lines and crowds of people, pulsing with energy and anticipation, and the noise level makes Jake wonder if his hearing will ever be okay again. The atmosphere is dense, the heat stifling, and Jake's weather antennae – something you develop when you spend so much time at sea – are twitching. Owen, Craig, and Jake are standing in line for beer while the support act plays.

The girls have gone to the toilets together, although the way Leila and Chloe linked arms and walked ahead of Simone made Jake feel a bit sorry for her. He promises himself he'll make more of an effort with his date when she returns. It doesn't help that he slept the whole way here, partly to avoid seeing Craig and Leila snuggled up together and partly because he's knackered. He's learnt to sleep anywhere during his years with the Navy.

The way Simone's eyes were rolling in her head and the amount of empty cans of wine she'd discarded in the bin on arrival don't bode well for the rest of the evening.

'So, how long have you and Jones been dating?' Jake turns to Craig, keeping his tone casual.

'A few months.' Craig raises one perfectly arched eyebrow. 'Jones?'

'I've been calling her that since we were teenagers.'

'You've known her that long?'

'Yeah. I lived on her road, in her old house.'

'She never mentioned you. Sorry, mate,' he says condescendingly, slapping a hand on Jake's shoulder, enough strength behind it to be a warning.

It doesn't sting as much as Leila's omission does. 'It's fine, *mate*.' Jake's voice is light, but he uses the full force of his arm muscles to return the gesture. 'I'm away a lot for work.'

Craig stumbles forward then looks at Jake warily before righting himself. Owen stifles a snigger beside them.

'Our turn.' Jake motions to the serving window. 'I'll be back in a minute, get me a beer?'

'Sure,' Owen nods. Craig simply scowls.

Coming out of the toilets a few minutes later, Jake sees Leila a few steps ahead of him, making her way back to the others. Reaching out, he touches her left shoulder blade, his fingers accidentally tangling in her long pale hair.

Frowning, she stops and spins around. 'Oh. Hi.'

'Sorry, didn't mean to try and lasso you.'

'Are you comparing me to a wild horse?' she asks, while being jostled by passers-by.

'Nah, they're too headstrong and untameable. You're not *that* bad.'

'Hah! Thanks. What would you compare me to then?' she asks watchfully, grey eyes dark as she moves closer to hear him speak.

'A unicorn. They're pretty magical.' Jesus, he sounds like a ten-year-old, which is pretty much the way he always feels around her. The twenty-three-year-old guy who travels around the world on ships, carries a gun most days, and commands troops ceases to exist. It's like the man haunted by his father and scarred by his upbringing disappears, leaving behind someone fresh, whole, and full of hope.

She throws back her head and laughs. 'A unicorn? Oh, brilliant. Thanks, Jake. You've made my day.'

'Glad to be of service.' He bends over in a mock bow, covering up his embarrassment.

'So, how are you? You seem ... different. Lighter somehow.'

'I'm good. I am lighter. And it's thanks to you.'

'Oh?' she responds warily, pushing her hair back behind one ear to reveal a dangling silver multi-earring of stars and moons.

He moves nearer, edging her over to lean against the wall and out of the path of the crowd. He lowers his voice. 'Mum told me what you did for her, with the money, helping her get out back then. She also thinks you had something to do with the police appearing last week. You know she's back home now?'

'It wasn't hard to call in an anonymous tip, seeing vans coming and going at all hours. And I'm glad she's back, but she wasn't supposed to say anything.' Crossing her arms, she drops her voice to a whisper. 'I didn't want you to know.'

Jake has to lean forward to hear her. 'Why?'

'I wanted to help her because it was the right thing to do, and because I could. Plus, I didn't want you feeling you owed me anything. And as much as you annoy me at times, it was partly in thanks for your letter, and the rainbow charm. They really helped me through a tough time.' She hesitates, then says, 'I hate to admit it because you can be a bit big-headed, but when I'm having a shitty day, your letter reconnects me to what's important. It reminds me not to let the day-to-day stresses become everything, to remember there's a bigger picture and that I have a lot to be grateful for.'

'I'm glad.' He feels emotion swell in his throat but chooses not to make her uncomfortable with any further comment. 'And as for Mum, she kept your secret for years, but was feeling emotional being back in Bournemouth in our house, with me turning up for a visit. She accidentally spilled, but wouldn't share the details. So tell me, how did you manage it? All I knew at the time was that she was somewhere safe.'

Leila bites her lip. 'I was home from uni for a weekend and waited until your dad went out one day. I took a chance he wouldn't be back for a bit. I went to her with a rucksack full of banknotes and said she had five minutes to pack up anything she couldn't live without, and then we were going. She was shocked, but I held the front door open and told her she had this one chance to walk through it. I'd spoken with a refuge beforehand, near Woking, and arranged it all. She was really scared, but I somehow convinced her to be brave. And she was.'

'That's pretty impressive, and courageous. A bit Daenerys really.' He refers to the Mother of Dragons from *Game of Thrones*, who most of his troop have a massive crush on.

'Cavorting around half naked with Drogo?' she jokes. 'It's funny because Eloise calls me that sometimes.'

'Well, you have got the silvery hair, and you're both small ...'

She slaps him lightly on the arm. 'Oi!'

He grins, then becomes sombre. 'Look, in all seriousness, thank you for everything you did for Mum. I mean it. Are we friends now? Even if I annoy you sometimes? You did more or less tell me to bugger off in that text ...'

She winces, 'Sorry about that. I wasn't in a good place after graduating. I shouldn't have been so harsh. It just annoyed me that you seemed to get exactly how I was feeling.' She smiles, raising her eyebrows. 'No one likes a know-it-all.'

'Touché.' Jake smiles back.

'I was also annoyed that your postcards were so ... cold.' She raises her voice above the increasing volume, excitement thrumming down the hallway as the crowd surges towards the doors leading to the stage, the supporting act nearing the end of their set.

He stares at her. 'They weren't meant to be, but I often wrote them in a rush and –' he pushes a hand through his black hair '– you have to be careful what you put in written correspondence. Both for security reasons and because the lads will rip you to shreds if they see anything too soppy. Sorry.'

'Oh,' she mutters, looking away and playing with her charm bracelet, spinning it around her wrist. 'I didn't think of that. Not that you'd write anything soppy to me anyway. We're just friends.'

'Yes,' he states firmly, wanting the acknowledgement, 'we are.'

'Cool.' She smiles faintly but a frown lingers on her forehead.

He thinks about her earlier comment. 'You really think I'm big-headed?'

'Cocky is the word I've always used.'

'Hmmm. Well, just remember there's a difference between bolshiness as a teenager to cover up your inadequacies, and cockiness because you think you're God's gift.'

'Pfft! What have you possibly got to be inadequate about? You're one of the most confident people I know. I mean, you spent six months in Africa helping dig wells and build villages, right? And your day job is as responsible and worthy as it gets.'

'Maybe I'm confident now because I've found my place in the world, but not back then.' He realises the food and drink stands are nearly empty and the crowd is dissipating. 'We'd better get going.'

'Wait. I've been wondering ... You looked pleased to see me earlier but Owen said you'd been back a week. Is there a reason you haven't dropped round to say hello?'

'The last time we actually spoke was after the mis— After

the baby,' he murmurs. 'You were angry because I kissed you, and made out we weren't friends. You also never replied to my postcards. So, I wasn't sure whether to come around or not.' Straightening up, he shakes his head. 'Look, I fucked up on the beach. I'm really sorry.'

She acknowledges his words with a nod. 'So, you weren't sure about what kind of welcome you'd get?'

'Something like that.'

'Look, it was a horrible time, but I understand you were trying to do a good thing coming to find me at Durdle Door. I took my frustrations out on you. I won't deny your timing sucked, but I'm willing to let it go if you are. Life's too short, right? All we have is time.' Her face softens.

The phrasing chimes a bell in Jake's mind. A letter he wrote years ago. 'Is that ... Are you ...? Is that a quote from something you read?' He asks, his back stiffening.

'I, uh ...' She closes her eyes, then opens them again, and takes a deep breath. 'Yes. It's from a letter you sent Ray. After he died –' she flinches, eyes pained '– Dad gave me a box of letters you wrote him.'

'They may have become your property, but you didn't have any right to read them. They were private.' It feels like an invasion; the letters are so deeply personal, so full of his thoughts and fears.

'I know, I'm sorry.' She holds her hands up, palms out. 'I only read one after the funeral, I promise. Dad was so disappointed with how I treated you and wanted me to understand how close the two of you were, how important you were to each other, and how –' she nods '– you had every right to grieve for him. I came to see you, but you'd already left. You can have the letters back if you want?'

'Yes, please. Mum can store them at the house.'

'Okay. Sorry, I didn't mean to upset you.'

'You haven't. Don't worry.' He rubs his top lip, where his scar is aching. The weather is quickly closing in. 'Come on,' he yells above a sudden wave of noise from the stage, 'they're on, let's go.' The powerful, beautiful, and distinctive opening notes of 'The Scientist' echo through a nearby archway and he grabs her hand, pulling her through into the main arena. Scanning the crowds, the standing room in front of the stage which he and his friends have bought tickets for, he knows they've got no hope of finding them, at least until they have a break in the set later. Pulling Leila in front of him so he can keep an eye on her, he nudges her forward until they find a tiny space in the crowd to stand.

'I can't see!' She jumps around trying to catch a glimpse above people's heads. But she's still happy, singing along with Chris Martin as he tells a story about going back to the start.

'We can put that right,' he mutters, and without waiting for a reply, he puts his hands around her narrow waist and hoists her over his head, settling her onto his shoulders.

'Jake!' she squawks, looking down at him from her perch. 'You can't do that,' she yells, yanking his head around by his hair so he's looking up at her.

'Why not?'

'I'm too heavy, we're too ... close.' She looks flustered, indicating where his hands are gripping her bare knees to keep her secure.

'I carry kit and gear far heavier than you every day,' he scoffs, tightening his grip. 'And we're friends, remember?' He tries not to let any edge show in his voice.

'But—'

'Can you see when you're standing on the ground?' He gazes up at her impatiently.

'No.'

'Do you want to see them perform?'

'Yes!'

'Then shut up, Jones, and enjoy the song.' He hears her say something under her breath, but it's lost as the heaving, throbbing crowd join in with Coldplay's frontman singing so eloquently.

After a moment, he feels her relax as she sways to the music. He watches the big screens at either side of the stage as the cameras pan around, filming the massive crowd and this iconic performance as everyone sings about nobody saying it was going to be easy.

Suddenly, the clouds above them, heavy with moisture, open up and send a downpour onto everyone's heads. The audience are drenched within seconds, and people gasp and judder at the chill, but keep bopping around and singing as Chris Martin thanks them for coming to the concert and apologises for the weather. Jake can feel droplets hitting his cheeks and dripping down from his hair through his short stubble, and his scar aches with the charged atmosphere. His finger strokes Leila's knee idly and he can feel the heat of her body around the back of his neck, down over his shoulders and over his chest.

She laughs giddily as the rain intensifies but she keeps singing and swaying. As Jake flicks a glance back to the huge screen to the right of the stage, he sees the camera is on them, showing Jake's soaked dark hair, odd eyes, and scarred lip, with Leila on his broad shoulders. Her white T-shirt is clinging and nearly see-through, her streaming hair darkened by the rain but flaxen, and the milky pale skin, fair eyebrows, and grey eyes making her look like a fairy. They don't look like they belong together. He is dark and she is light, like beauty and the beast. But her face is lit up with joy, and Jake doesn't blame them for wanting to film her. She's stunning, the beauty shining out of her.

Laughing, she points at the screen. 'Jake! It's us! Oh, God.' She covers her face for a moment and then touches a hand to her sopping hair, but with a shrug lifts her hands in the air and begins singing again. The crowd around her smile and join in. The camera pans away.

A moment later, when 'Fix You' starts playing and the line about lights guiding you home rings out, Leila squeezes Jake's shoulder. He wonders if she's having the same thought as him. About the baby she lost and the comfort he tried to offer her, before he cocked it all up by kissing her.

***

Her back is damp with sweat and rainwater as he follows her inside during intermission, his hand gripping her T-shirt so as not to lose her. Her face is glowing, and he can't keep the grin off his face. He knows they'll have to look for the others now, but he can't regret the time they shared, accompanied by a crowd of thousands but somehow alone together.

Spinning around, she shocks him with a quick hug, before stepping back self-consciously. 'Thanks for having me on your shoulders. I know I was shitty about it at first, but it made all the difference. It was amazing; God, the view I had! I wouldn't have seen anything otherwise. I hope you're not sore?'

He makes a show of rolling his shoulders and groaning. 'I'll be injured for days, and will probably need surgery and heaps of back massages.'

'Ha, ha.' She smiles impishly. 'No, you're definitely enough of a lug to carry me. I could feel how strong you are. The way you picked me up!' She eyes up his muscular shoulders and arms. 'You must beat everyone else out in the field and on the assault courses.'

'Well, I'm not sure about that.'

'Jake Harding being modest, what's the world coming to?'

'I couldn't say,' he replies, nudging her out of the way of a group of lads carrying one of their own in the middle of the huddle.

'What was your favourite song?' she quizzes him as they make their way towards the bar.

'"Fix You",' he says as they arrive, gazing around for Owen's shaggy head.

'Me too,' she agrees, nodding as she pulls her damp top away from her body.

'It reminds me of you,' admits Jake, looking down at her, 'or at least it used to. I used to feel like I needed to try and fix you, but I can see that's not the case now. You seem like you've got everything sorted. You're happy, settled with a boyfriend and a job, living with your dad. You've fixed herself.'

She frowns and then touches a finger to the rainbow charm on her bracelet – his charm. 'I'm sorry you felt responsible for me. I wasn't aware I needed fixing. Was I broken then?' But before he can reply, Leila carries on, 'I guess there have been times when I lost my way ... and you always seemed to be around to help. But if you're asking if I'm okay, then fundamentally, yes. But it's not all perfect, not by a long way. I don't want to live with Dad for ever, as much as I love him. And while it's great he's letting me redecorate and has agreed I can paint a mural somewhere in the house, it's not quite what I had in mind when I dreamt of a career in art. The call-centre job is slowly killing me too ...'

'No one's life is perfect,' Jake responds, 'despite whatever outward appearances people try to create. And if it was perfect it would be boring, and where's the fun in that?'

He waves a hand above his head as he catches sight of Owen in the sea of heads. Their spell is about to be broken.

'I don't know how you can always be so self-assured,' she says. 'It's like you know everything is always going to be all right.'

'It's the exact opposite,' Jakes says, surprised. 'It comes from knowing shit is bound to happen, but if you can get through it then there's always something better on the other side. Because there has to be.'

'So, you're basically saying that shit is inevitable?'

'Yes,' Jake says with a grin, 'pretty much. And that's fun too.'

Shaking her head, she grins back, her face turned up towards his. 'Jake Harding, you are an odd one sometimes.'

'In a good way?'

'Well, remembering the times you jumped off Durdle Door, and a boat, I—' Her answer is cut off as a hand snakes over her shoulder and Craig says in her ear, 'Leila, a word, please.'

At the same time, Simone storms up with Chloe and Owen in tow, her eyes blazing. 'What the fuck was that?' she sneers, alcohol fumes slapping Jake straight in the face.

Yes, the spell is well and truly broken.

***

Simone's still simmering with anger when they stop off for a late dinner at a motorway diner on the way home.

Jake sits at the table, exasperated and yearning for the night to be over. He should be on a high from the concert after how utterly brilliant it was, but instead the trip has been soured by Simone blasting him for having Leila up on his shoulders.

'That's the kind of thing you do with your girlfriend, not some girl from down the road,' she'd raged. 'You brought me along, but you've hardly spoken to me, and then you go off with *her*. And you get filmed together, looking all starry-eyed and coupled up.'

Despite being royally pissed off, and knowing she was completely over-reacting, he'd apologised and reassured her it wasn't how it looked, and that she was seeing more than was there. Right now, it was about damage control and getting her home without any further upset to anyone. They all had to share a van.

From the wary expression on Leila's face and Craig's exaggerated jokes and chat, things aren't rosy between them either.

'So –' Chloe pushes her half-eaten burger aside and leans forward, smiling at her friend '– I know it's a few days early, but we wanted to give you this while we're all together.' Rooting around in her handbag, she produces a card and a small neatly wrapped present with a red ribbon on top. She pushes them both across the table and her smile widens. 'Happy Birthday.'

'Oh, thanks.' Leila looks frozen, her eyes pinned to the gift. She picks it up and carefully undoes the ribbon, teasing one end of it so it undoes smoothly, before peeling the paper away to reveal a little red box.

'We know it's not the norm, and you usually get your charms from your mum,' Chloe says quickly as Leila flips open the lid, casting a worried look at Owen, who squeezes her hand. 'We just thought it would be nice to have something to remind you of the concert.'

Leila plucks the charm from the box, the musical note dangling between her fingers and shining under the harsh strip-lights of the diner. 'Thank you,' she says warmly, although her smile is forced, 'it's lovely.'

'We all chipped in,' Chloe rattles on.

'Obviously it was all my idea,' Craig brags, putting a proprietary hand on Leila's back. 'I know how much you love that bracelet. Even more than me,' he guffaws, as if the idea is absurd.

Leila's eyes flash and Jake can almost read the thought

going through her mind. *Who says I love you at all?* Or maybe that's just wishful thinking on his part.

Chloe rolls her eyes. 'Yeah, right. Actually, it was—'

Jake jumps up, catching the edge of the table with his thighs, rattling the bottles and plates. 'We need to set off, don't we?' He motions through the window to the car park.

The rest of the group mutter their agreement and stand, grabbing bags and coats, having paid when they ordered. Owen nudges Jake's arm with his elbow as they walk to the door. 'You okay?'

'Yeah, fine. Thanks for bringing us.'

'No problem. Got to make the most of seeing my best mate before he flies – or, should I say, sails – off again.'

But Jake isn't really listening to Owen's banter. He's tuned into a conversation going on behind them.

'Why don't you buy yourself charms for your bracelet?' Simone is slurring at Leila. 'Too expensive?' she asks cattily, obviously questioning Leila's financial situation. 'You still live at home, don't you?'

Jake can hear Leila's indrawn breath and goes to turn around to tell Simone to shut up, but Chloe gets there first.

'Leila has enough money to spend on charms if she wants to,' she says sharply, 'she just chooses not to.'

'Why?'

'Because my mum normally sends them to me,' Leila replies, 'so I don't need to.'

'Sends them? Why not gives them?' Simone demands.

'None of your bloody business!' It's clear Leila has run out of patience. 'Okay?'

'You—'

'Come on.' Jake turns and puts an arm around Simone's shoulders, drawing her away. 'Let's get you home.' He mouths a *sorry* to Leila above his date's head.

A grateful smile curves Leila's mouth, and he nods in acknowledgement before leading Simone to the van, talking about the concert to keep her distracted as he buckles her in. Sitting down, he notices Craig pull away from Leila's touch when she settles next to him, and grimaces.

He and Leila don't talk on the way home, but hours later when they park up and say their goodbyes, the way she looks at him tells Jake that something has changed between them.

Leila

December 2012

The Christmas Tree Charm

The Christmas tree is up in the corner, bedecked with turquoise and purple baubles and dripping with tinsel. It twinkles with flashing LED lights, and sits in a large red ceramic pot to hold it steady. A red velvet ribbon is fastened to its top branch rather than the more traditional gold star. I'd have preferred a real tree, but the first year we had Fleur and got one she kept spinning around beneath it rapturously, snuffling and trying to hoover the pine needles up. She obviously didn't realise they're toxic for dogs, and within a day Dad had to donate our gorgeous tree to a family down the road. I really can't see the attraction of putting something sharp in your mouth, even if you think it tastes good. Mad beagle.

I look around the lounge from where I'm digging our stockings out of an ancient box. Winterberry-scented candles are dotted around the room, brightening the dark walls and ancient furniture, and covering up the smell of emulsion from upstairs. I started redecorating months ago, but have only managed to do mine and Dad's bedrooms so far, what with work and Craig ... I shudder, steering my thoughts away. The point is, it's taken far longer than planned to create the new vision I had for our house. Even Dad's getting impatient with me now, and he's usually the most laid-back person going. He's at a Saturday job, so I'm all alone. El and Chloe are both busy with their lovely boyfriends, and Edwin has given me a rare weekend off as a reward for increasing sales at the gallery. Although I've got Fleur's waggy company, I can feel the sharp edge of loneliness digging into my skin, so an MTV Christmas channel is playing seasonal songs to create background noise, and the smell of cinnamon and aromatic alcohol wafts from the kitchen where mulled wine's slowly simmering on the hob.

I've done everything I can to create a Christmassy spirit in the house, to make it nice and festive for us. The weather's even joining in, the winter wind rattling the draughty windows, shimmering frost coating the leaves on the trees like they've been breathed on by Jack Frost. A thick carpet of snow coats the ground from where icy flakes fell and settled overnight. I've also been to two Christmas parties, eaten turkey with cranberry sauce and all the trimmings, and gone to a fete with Eloise, surrounded by adorable children dressed as elves, reindeer, and shepherds, running around high on excitement and sugar in the form of minty striped candy canes. In a surprising turn of events, El has swerved away from her previous career choice as a tabloid journalist to complete her PGCE on top of her English degree and become a primary school teacher. She says that life as an NQT is tough but she's getting a lot out of it, even though the school is sort of incestuous and everyone is either sleeping with someone they work with or getting involved in other people's business. Jonny is there calmly in the background to cheer her on, and I know she'll be fine if the happy glow in her big blue eyes is anything to go by.

I've had plenty of opportunity to gear myself up for the season, but I'm not feeling it. At. All. If anything, it's making me feel worse, as if I'm trying too hard. It's forced and faked. I'm starting to hate Christmas and everything that comes with it. Maybe it's because I was expecting to share Christmas Day with a boyfriend this year, looking forward to finally having someone else by my side. Don't get me wrong, I love Dad, but it's not the same, is it? He should have someone, and I should too. My bloody mother ... Her running off is the reason Dad's never found anyone else, and why I'm too scared to commit – apparently. At least, Craig thinks so.

Craig, it turns out, thinks a lot of things. I wince as I hear his voice spinning through my head, shying away from the accusations he threw at me before thundering out. It wasn't a pretty scene. Two weeks have passed, and I expected him to contact me and apologise, but I've heard nothing and from the look of his Facebook page he's already moved on with someone else. My nose stings and tears fill my eyes, but I blink them away as I find the padded penguin stockings and hang them together above the fireplace. Stepping back, I take in the overall scene. Yep, completely overdone. Frowning, I move toward the kitchen. Time for a drink.

There's a loud knock at the front door and I seize upon

the distraction from my brooding. 'Fleur! Wait!' I call as she bolts down the hallway, rolling my eyes when she ignores me as usual. She's sitting on the mat, eagerly waiting, pink tongue lolling out of her mouth. She always looks like she's grinning when she does that. Bending over to grab her collar, I open the door.

'Oh, hey, Jake,' I say shyly.

'Hi.' He lifts a hand in greeting, stamping the snow from his boots. 'Can I come in? I'm only back for a few days; can't stay for Christmas unfortunately.'

'Sure.' I step back, still hanging on to Fleur, as Jake takes his boots off. I feel awkward and self-conscious, and it's hard to talk to him, hard to know what to say. We agreed we were friends at the concert, and I felt so at ease with him that day, but I haven't seen him for almost four months. Plus, we have so much history between us. Not to mention *that* kiss, when I rejected him. I wonder if I'd feel more at ease if he was home more often, if we saw each other every weekend. If I got to spend quality time with him, then maybe the strangeness I feel around him would disappear. The strangeness which only intensified when I sat on his broad shoulders listening to our favourite songs at the concert. He was so strong, and warm, and I felt so safe. But I also felt strangely jumpy too.

He clears his throat and looks pointedly down the hallway. I realise I'm just standing here staring at him.

'Sorry.' I let go of Fleur's collar without thinking and she launches herself at him in delight, jumping up with her paws on his thighs, trying to get to his face. 'Don't—' I start saying as he picks her up to hold her against his chest, but it's too late. As he makes baby talk at her, she leans forward and swipes her long saliva-covered tongue right from the tip of his chin, up over his mouth and nose, halfway to his forehead. I wait for him to put her down or explode the way Craig used to, but instead he grins and screws up his face.

'You've got doggy breath,' he tells her, 'but thanks for the kisses, Fleur.' Adjusting his hold, he pops her under one arm so he can tickle her chin with the other hand as he walks through to the lounge. I stare at him in amazement, wondering what just happened. She obviously knows him. Maybe he visited more often than I realised when I was away at uni.

'Smells great,' Jake calls from the other room. 'Any chance of a drink?'

Shaking myself out of my daze, I carry on through to the kitchen to rustle up some mugs. Finding some Christmas ones with mistletoe painted on them in the back of the cupboard, I pour some mulled wine into both, garnishing them with a cinnamon stick. If I keep making the effort, perhaps I'll start feeling Christmassy at some point.

'Thanks.' He takes the warm mugs from my hands as I enter the lounge, and sets them both on the mantelpiece to cool down. Seeing the design, he lifts one eyebrow. 'Is that a hint? Mistletoe – are you after a Christmas kiss?' He raises both eyebrows.

'From you?' I snort, going red despite myself. 'Hardly. Honestly Jake, do you ever stop?' I shake my head. 'I'm sworn off men for now anyway.'

'Thinking of swapping to the other team?' As he sits on

the sofa, Fleur immediately climbs into his lap and makes herself at home. He stretches out long, muscular legs encased in jeans, and starts stroking her soothingly. Her eyelids start to droop, and she settles her snout on his upper thigh. The twinkling Christmas tree lights glint off his thick black hair and the navy cable-knit jumper shows off his mismatched eyes, the green and brown watching me intently. He looks totally at ease, and I'm sure El would say unforgivably sexy too. It's warm and cosy in here, and I'm tempted to light the fire.

'Nothing that radical,' I reply, deciding against a log fire in case it's too romantic as I sink onto the other end of the sofa. Fleur cocks open one eye and looks at me, before closing it and snuffling contentedly as Jake strokes her silky head. *Traitor*, I think. 'Just taking a break from dating, that's all.'

'Well, I'm sure if you put a photo of your current look online they'd all be begging to take you out.' He gestures at me, 'Baggy blue dungarees and paint-stained hair is all the rage at the moment.' His mouth curves as I glance down at myself.

'Oh, I totally forgot. I was painting the spare room. I should've changed but got distracted.'

'I think you look cute,' he mocks, 'like a little kid out at playtime.'

'Thanks.' Picking up a cushion I go to chuck it at him, but he tilts his head at Fleur, who's now fast asleep. 'You're so lucky.' I drop it. 'I'll get you next time.' Now we've decided we're definitely friends, the pressure's off and I can mess around if I want to. I can feel at ease with him, right?

'Looking forward to it.' His dimple flashes in his cheek, and I momentarily forget what I was going to say.

'Just you wait,' I mumble in the end, realising that to an outsider it might actually sound like we're flirting.

'So, why are you taking a break from dating?' Jake asks. 'Things not working out with Craig?'

'I don't want to talk about it.'

'No problem.' He raises both eyebrows and sucks in his cheeks, and, I bet, the words he wants to utter. After a moment he says, 'So, how's Henry?'

'Good. Work's still really busy, although it's becoming harder for him to handle everything. I keep trying to convince him to take on an apprentice, but he won't hear of it. He seems happy enough in his own way. This time of year is hard for him though. With Mum and everything, because families should be together, shouldn't they?'

'They should, but it's not always possible.' His face closes up.

'Jake, I wasn't getting at you. If you're not allowed Christmas off because of your job that's different. I'm talking about people who have a choice but choose to shun their families. And what's worse –' I jump up, grabbing an object from the nearby over-crammed bookshelf '– is this arrived this morning. And I just know it's from her. Another charm. I recognise the envelope and typed address.'

'Right,' Jake replies, not moving.

'How can she keep sending me gifts, torturing me like this?' I wail, thrusting the envelope out towards him, the emotions of my break-up with Craig making me raw.

'Torturing?' He frowns, shifting slightly and making Fleur groan in protest.

'She must know the only thing I've ever wanted is for her to come home – or better yet, for her never to have left. Or at least to understand why she left us the way she did. So, to keep sending me reminders of the fact that she's out there and not here, is cruel. Especially with no explanation, or news.'

'She can't change the past, Jones. No one can.'

'I was only eleven, Jake, still a kid. You can't tell me what she did was okay. You can't defend her.' My voice climbs, breaking, and blood rushes to my face.

He edges forward in his seat, scooping Fleur up and sliding her gently onto the sofa cushion next to him. 'I'm not. Of course, I'm not.' Standing up, he comes over to me, wrapping an arm around my shoulders and taking the envelope from my shaking fingers. I force myself not to squirm under his touch. That would come across as rude, when he's only trying to comfort me. 'I'm sure she has regrets,' he says calmly. 'I only mean that she can't undo it now.' He pauses. 'And I always thought you liked getting the charms, that they were special to you?' His voice is rough and I'm not sure why.

Blowing out a breath, I tug on the long silvery plait hanging down over my shoulder, speckled with emulsion, and then look down at my bracelet, tracing a finger over the charms. 'I do,' I admit, 'and they are. I guess I'm just in a bit of a funny mood. I just really miss her sometimes, that's all. I can barely remember her some days. What she looked like, what she sounded like. She used to read to me at bedtime. It's weird, but that's the thing I miss the most.' Glancing up, I realise how close his face is, and for the first time I register how absurdly long his eyelashes are.

His eyes darken, the brown one going nearly black and the green one becoming forest green rather than emerald, and I suck in a breath. They're really quite beautiful, and I'm about to blurt that out when he removes his arm from my shoulders and strides towards the back door. 'Come on, let's get some fresh air. It'll do you good.'

Without pausing, he flings the door open and walks out, leaving me trailing in his wake, flustered and wondering if he's okay. Not stopping to grab my coat, I follow him into the frost-coated garden, shivering as the winter chill hits me. The grass and trees sparkle in the sunlight and my fingers itch for a pencil or charcoal. At least redecorating the house has brought back some of my artistic inspiration. I've started work on a very special mural.

'Are you coming or what?' Jake calls, and I'm not sure if he's talking to me or Fleur as she suddenly appears beside me. He's sitting on the wooden bench at the end of the garden near the apple tree, a seat I asked Dad to install last June. That corner catches the sunlight just right in the summer evenings, and I like to have a canvas out in case the creative mood hits me.

Jogging over to him, I sit down, wishing I'd thought to wear a coat after all. The bitter wind is picking up and pierces through the thin top I'm wearing under my dungarees.

'Feeling cooler now?'

'You could say that.' My teeth chatter together. I bend over and hug Fleur for warmth, my breath hanging on the air in a fluffy cloud.

'Oh, for God's sake, Jones. You're a nightmare.' As he stands up, I assume he's going to go inside for my coat but instead he wrenches his jumper over his head and throws it at me, leaving him in a tight long-sleeved Superdry top. 'Put that on.'

Not arguing because I need warmth so desperately, I try hard not to inhale his aftershave as I pull the jumper on over my head. I fail, and Jake's scent fills my nose. Worse still is that when I'm wrapped up securely in his cable knit, I gape at the muscles I can see defined under his clinging top, before hastily glancing away. I knew he was physically fit, but ... well, El and Chloe would be having heart attacks if they were here. *Wow*. I gulp.

'Right, no more messing around. Open this,' he bosses, grabbing my hand and placing the white envelope in it.

Rolling my eyes, I tear it open, knowing he'll only go on at me until I do, and knowing there's no way I'd really hold out if he wasn't here. Of course I want to see what she's sent me. 'No letter,' I say in a dispirited voice, 'and this.' A tiny silver Christmas tree dangles from my left hand.

He gestures for me to put in on my bracelet. 'Come on.'

Hesitating, I suck my cheeks in, chewing on the inside of my mouth.

'What's the matter?'

'It sounds silly, but what if I'm like her? What if by putting it on I become more like her?'

'You've worn this for years, Jones.' He frowns at me, his brows lowering. 'You think that by wearing the charms you're going to suddenly run off one day?'

'Well, it sounds silly when you put it like that ...'

'Listen, your mum leaving is part of you, of who you are and the way you are, whether you like it or not, and you're going to have to deal with that. But it doesn't mean you *are* her, and it definitely doesn't mean you'll do what she did.'

'Fine,' I grumble, 'I know I'm being irrational.'

'You won't get any argument from me,' he jokes, taking the charm from my fingers and bending over to attach it to my bracelet.

I huff over the top of his head, but there's something about the vulnerability of seeing his bare neck pebble with goose-bumps in the cold that catches me off guard.

'There.' He sits up, his expression smug. 'It looks good. It belongs on there.'

'You can be a bit of a dick sometimes,' I blurt.

'Yep,' he nods cheerfully, 'but at least I know it. Better to be comfortable in your own skin, and accept who you are as a person, right? Besides, I don't act like a dick very often, so I'm okay with it.'

'Huh. Well I can tell you who is very definitively a dick most of the time.' I bury my face in Fleur's fur as she gets up on the seat beside me.

'Craig?'

'Yep.'

He leans towards me, the warm fog from his mouth dampening my cheek. 'So, what happened?'

I don't think about whether this is something I should share with him, I just let the words spill out of my mouth, hurt and indignation battering me. 'Short story? He dumped me. Apparently, I was too airy-fairy, with my head always in the clouds, and never paid proper attention to him or our relationship, because even when I was with him, I was thinking about something else. He said I obviously had an issue committing because of Mum. Also, I came across as *distracted and self-involved*. Am I a selfish cow?' My voice shakes.

'No! Yeah, you can be distracted at times, but if it's because you're painting that's a fair reason. You've got to do what you love and feel passionate about. What's the point in any of it, otherwise? Besides, the guy was an arse. That was clear at the concert – especially trying to take credit for the music charm we all bought.'

'He said something to upset you too, didn't he? You never told me what it was.'

He shakes his head, 'Doesn't matter now.'

'Are you sure about that?'

'Yes,' he replies, 'it's nothing important and you have a lot on your mind. You need to concentrate on putting Craig behind you, not worry about some stupid comment he made months ago.'

'Okay. If you're sure.' Drawing Fleur onto my lap because she's shivering, I rest my cheek on the top of her head. She snuggles into me, but I can tell she's still making moon eyes at Jake. 'And am I? Airy-fairy, I mean? My head in the clouds?'

'Too right,' Jake says, 'and that's exactly who you should be. Besides, who wants to live with their feet on the ground all the time, when life can be so shit down here?'

I laugh, warmed at the way he's turning Craig's insults into one of my strengths. But the trouble is, Craig's remarks hit too close to home in terms of the fears Dad had about me when I was thirteen, how he used to get so anxious if he thought I'd wandered off, the worries about my anger and penchant for running away. The trauma of what happened at my last school before we moved back. I can feel the patch of skin on my lower back tingling at the thought.

I shake it off. 'This is getting far too doom and gloom. Thanks for listening and for the reassurance, but I told you I was going to get you back earlier.' Sliding out from under Fleur, I lurch forward and scoop up some snow, twist around in one smooth motion and launch the ball at his face. It hits him smack on the nose and he shoots off the bench, eyes widening.

'You're dead!' he yells, thrusting two hands into a nearby drift and throwing twin balls of ice at me. I duck and run back inside, with his shouts of 'You're cheating' ringing in my ears.

Snickering as I bound into the kitchen, I tug off his jumper, not realising how close he is behind me until he thrusts a handful of snow down the back of my dungarees. 'Argh!' I yelp, dancing around as he laughs. Fleur bounces up and down beside us. 'It's freezing!'

'Serves you right –' he pats my back to rub it in further '– for taking aim at a defenceless man when he was least expecting it.'

'Huh,' I mutter as I undo the buttons on my dungarees so they fall around my waist, 'you're the least defenceless guy I know.' Plucking the thin pink cotton top away from the skin of my back, I steal a glance down over my shoulder to see if the skin is red. It feels sore.

'You're fine, stop making such a fuss,' he jokes, before falling silent. 'What's that?'

Before I can do anything, his fingers run over the shiny patch of skin on my lower back. Jumping away from the tingle and ignoring the heat in the pit of my stomach, I refasten my dungarees over my shoulders and straighten them over my hips. 'Nothing, just a little burn, that's all. I was a clumsy teenager.'

'How did it happen?'

'Just one of those things; it's not important.' Liar. But, it's not something I like to talk about. 'Come on, our mulled wine will have cooled down by now. Let's drink.'

***

Twenty minutes later, after we've had our festive drinks and caught up about our Christmas plans, we're in the hallway. Jake's putting his boots back on and Fleur is whining as she watches, like she's already sad he's gone.

'So, I ship out tomorrow –' Jake straightens up '– and I won't be home for a few months again. I know you'll be pining after me, but don't worry, I'll be back at some point.'

I roll my eyes. 'Yeah, whatever. I'm not Fleur.' But despite my words, inside I'm disappointed he's leaving so soon. We only get to spend fractured splinters of time together and despite how annoying he can be because he has a habit of calling me on my shit, he also has a way of making me feel better about things. 'Keep sending postcards though, won't you? I like the pictures.'

'Sure.' He smiles, eyes full of warmth.

'So how does Simone feel about you not being around for Christmas?' I ask casually.

Frowning, he grips the front-door handle. 'Why would she care?'

'Um, duh – girlfriends tend to care about that kind of stuff?'

He looks at me like I've grown horns on my head. 'You really think I want to spend time with someone who behaves like that? I took her home after the concert, made sure she was safe, called her the next day to check she was okay, and then we agreed not to see each other again. Trust me, it wasn't a great loss for either of us.'

'Oh.' He ended it with her. It makes me wonder whether I should have been strong enough to do the same with Craig. I hated the way he had a go at me for sitting on Jake's shoulders at the concert, ranting about how I'd made him look bad on national TV, because what kind of girl sat on a guy's shoulders when she was going out with someone else? But I shrugged off the overreaction and how possessive he was. I ignored the unease about how different we were as people. I don't know why. It wasn't like I was in love with him or anything. I don't think I've ever been in love, and they say that when you know, you know, right? Well, I've never *known* so I can't have been. So why did I stay with Craig, especially given that, in all honesty, when we broke up it wasn't a huge shock?

'Are you in there?' Jake raises an eyebrow, jolting me back to the present.

'Yes, sorry. I was just thinking.'

'I know.' He smiles. 'Happy Christmas, Jones, for when it gets here. Text me if you want to talk; you've still got my number.' His comment reminds me of my brutal text. I blush. 'Signal can be crap out at sea, but I'll get any messages when we dock.'

'Okay, thanks. Happy Christmas,' I whisper, fighting a sudden yearning to give him a hug or a kiss on the cheek. Instead I say, 'Take care.'

'You too. Bye, Jones.' His eyes gleam.

He lets himself out as I hold Fleur back from chasing after him, closing the door as his footsteps crunch in the snow down the footpath.

'Come on, Fleur, dinner time,' I call in a high sing-song voice, wandering into the kitchen. She follows me through but instead of panting next to her bowl with her usual excitement, she sits and gazes at me with sad brown eyes. I know exactly what she's thinking. 'Oh, don't be so wet, you silly doggy, he'll come and see you next time.'

Reaching into the cupboard, I freeze as I notice Jake's navy jumper hanging over the back of the chair where he forgot it. But rather than return it, for some unnameable reason, I simply prepare Fleur's food. Then, jogging up the stairs to the spare room, I pick up a paintbrush from the selection sitting in a jar of turps. The scent makes me momentarily feel sick, but I push the feeling away.

Switching on the overhead light, I stand back for a moment staring at the mural I'm working on, at the oily blues, greens, and purples, and the acrylic I've added in Renaissance Gold.

Then, dipping my brush in Winsor and Newton's Iridescent White, I add a patch of lighter skin to the mermaid's lower back, over the Flesh Tint I'd painted her body with earlier. Dipping the brush in the pearlescent colour again, with a steady hand I carefully add a tiny little line to the boy's face, just above his top lip. He is drowning in the sea beside a craggy archway but will be okay because a dazzling mermaid is rescuing him.

Leila

July 2013

The Holiday Charm

Glancing down at the peach wrap-dress and wedges, I sigh. I can't stand wearing heels and I don't do dresses. My favourite outfit lately is leggings and an oversized T-shirt, but I can only get away with it when working on one of my paintings. This was the best I could come up with at short notice when rifling through Eloise's wardrobe this morning, the spare key to her flat in my bag as always.

God, I hate these kinds of events. As I gaze around the white tent at all the strange faces, panic makes my stomach spin and leaves me gulping. I can't believe I let Edwin bully me into coming, but as the owner of Dorset Coastal Art Gallery and my boss, he insisted I attend for PR purposes. The gallery needs more exposure, and we need to bring in a different type of client, high-end ones with loads of money to spend, rather than OAPs on their annual summer seaside holidays. As Edwin flew out to an auction in the South of France this morning, and I'm his only employee (receptionist, girl Friday, general dogsbody, and soother of crushed artiste egos), there wasn't anyone else he could call on.

Last night he ambushed me while we were locking up, thrusting a VIP ticket into my suddenly damp hand. One he'd, in his own words, 'purloined from an event sponsor,' telling me it could be worse, and at least there was a plus one so I could bring someone with me. The only problem is, El is in Majorca this weekend for a teaching colleague's hen do, and Ethan is away for work and becoming all too distant when he is here. Dad is finishing off a massive plumbing job, Chloe's away for a dirty weekend with Owen, and Shell is working today, which makes sense given she's a professional florist specialising in wedding flowers, and it's high season.

When I'd resigned myself to attending this pretentious, noisy, awful event, and every other avenue for a plus one had been exhausted, I decided to knock on Jake's door, having caught a glimpse of him when I got home from work yesterday. I'm sure he has his reasons for not coming to see me straight away. When he answered, I felt a bit awkward, especially as I've been wearing his jumper occasionally, breathing in the scent of him whenever one of his brief postcards arrives. It's probably a bit weird, but it comforts me.

I was hesitant about asking him to come with me today. Yes, we're friends now, but he still makes me jumpy and uneasy. I don't like it, or how I feel when I think about him. How it felt when he touched the scar on my back at Christmas. The way that, even when he's teasing me, he still makes me feel better about myself than most guys I've dated.

Still, if it's a choice between coming here alone or having

him at my side and shoving those uneasy feelings aside, I know which I prefer. To my relief, he agreed readily, grinning and saying he'd meet me down here as he had other plans this morning. I bit my tongue to stop myself asking whether it was a hot date. It's none of my business; he's just a friend.

Sighing, I survey the room. Everyone looks wealthy and polished – the women in expensive sundresses and the men wearing shirts with chinos. I hope Jake doesn't show up in something too casual.

'What *are* you wearing?' A voice laughs behind me.

Spinning around, I tut at him, my cheeks filling with heat. Think of the devil, and he'll turn up. 'Thanks a lot. And I could ask you the same question.' But although not as dressed up as most men, he looks good in faded blue jeans and a navy Ralph Lauren polo top stretching across his broad chest. A pair of sunglasses hang from the vee created by the open buttons of his collar and if I didn't know him as the guy from down the road, I'd say he belongs here. The top suits his wide shoulders and brings out his eyes. For a split second my fingers itch to paint him. I stamp down on the feeling as a few women around us give him admiring looks.

He grins. 'Relax! I only mean that I can't remember ever seeing you in a dress.'

'Well, thanks for the observation, but when the situation demands it, I've been known to put a dress on.' *Lie.* Even for the Sixth Form leavers' ball, I refused to wear a dress. The tight black lacy short-sleeved top which ended just above my belly button and matching floor-length skirt are still hanging at the back of my wardrobe. Dad said I looked like I was going to a funeral, but El said I looked amazing, especially as it made my long silver-blonde hair, tipped with pink at the time, stand out so much. I think Mum always wore dresses. A different one every day. I push the thought away as Jake stares at me.

'It's not that you don't look good,' he murmurs. 'The shape suits you, it's just you're so fair ... especially with your light hair and grey eyes, and the peach makes you look washed out. You need stronger colours.'

'Since when did you become an expert on women's fashion, and start wearing designer stuff?' I say, prickly but not sure why. 'You've come up in the world, haven't you?'

When Jake's eyes flash, and the people around us turn at my raised voice, I know I've gone too far. I realise I sounded mean. 'Sorry –' I lower my volume '– I didn't mean that how it came out. I'm nervous.'

'I know.' Shrugging my grumpiness off, he turns and lifts a glass of champagne from the tray of a passing brunette kitted out in a short black skirt and white blouse. She smiles and flutters her eyelashes. He smiles politely in return before turning and handing me the drink. I notice how she walks away with a swing of her hips, but he's only looking at me.

'It's stuffy in here,' Jake says, gesturing to the bubbly. 'This will help you cool off. And to answer your question, my mate's girlfriend is a colour stylist, and whenever I see them, she talks about it. As for the designer stuff ... when you spend most of your life at sea, there isn't much opportunity to spend money, so I'm doing okay. I can afford the nice stuff. Thanks for noticing,' he finishes drily. 'By the way, speaking of clothes, did I leave my navy jumper at yours when I dropped in at Christmas?'

'Don't think so.' The back of my neck burns as I sip the champagne, avoiding his eyes.

'Okay, must have lost it somewhere then,' he muses. 'So,' he says, turning and gesturing to the knots of people chatting away and chinking glasses, 'shall we do this? I take it you're supposed to be circulating and telling people about the gallery? Let's get it done so we can relax. It's a beautiful day.'

I tilt my chin up. 'I'm not here to relax, I'm here to work.'

'Lighten up,' he says with a laugh, 'you can do both. Besides –' he leans in, and I catch a whiff of his aftershave '– it's sunny and they're serving alcohol. In an hour or two no one will be able to talk. They'll all be too pissed. Then the polo will start, and they won't give a shit about talking shop.'

'Jake,' I giggle, 'stop it!' But two girls next to us nod their heads in agreement.

He raises his eyebrows at them. 'Ladies.' Drawing me closer with an arm around my waist, he turns me to face them. 'This is my friend Leila; she runs the best gallery in Bournemouth,' he ad libs. 'Do either of you like art?'

He gives them a wide smile, a dimple flashing in one cheek. Both the girls stare at him, and I swear I hear one sigh. Something sparks in my stomach. Looks like he can be quite the charmer when he needs to be. I shrug the thought off. This is *Jake*. I bat away the shimmery feeling I had at last year's concert, when he put me on his shoulders. I push the burn of his fingers on my bare knees from my mind, and the way it feels with his arm around me now, holding me steady.

I fish business cards from my bag and hand them over with shaking hands. One of the girls, a petite blonde in a strapless pink chiffon dress, pulls a face while staring at my charm bracelet. 'Oh, look at that bracelet, how *sweet*. Where on earth did you get it from?' The tone of her voice leaves me in no doubt that because it's not designer, it's not good enough. Which makes me feel like *I'm* not good enough.

'It's a family heirloom,' Jake says smoothly. 'It'll be worth a fortune one day, won't it, Leila?'

I nod jerkily. He's trying to help but his comment hurts almost more than hers does and his rare use of my first name throws me; it's a foreign sound from his mouth. The bracelet's already worth a fortune, more than all the diamonds and riches in the world. It's a part of me, who I am, tracking my journey through life. My only connection with my absent mother, apart from our shared DNA.

Leaning closer, he whispers in my ear, 'Nice new holiday charm, by the way. I love the little palm trees against the sunset.'

The charm arrived a few weeks ago, two days after I got back from a girlie holiday with El, Chloe, and Shell to Corfu. It was a week of sunshine, laughter, shared memories, and wine, and I was sad to come home. The fact I hadn't really missed Ethan told me a lot.

Jake's lips brush my neck as he turns his head away, and my cheeks tingle with heat. 'Thanks,' I murmur in a daze, my breath catching in my throat. When did he get so *hot?*

***

I hate it when Jake's right. A couple of hours later, I've done my rounds of the room and most people have drifted outside to watch the polo. The few groups that remain in little clumps in the corners have softly slurred voices and the mood is mellow. I've had two or three glasses of champagne and I'm feeling fuzzy-headed and a bit sick. But I've given out lots of business cards and received plenty back in return, with three appointments for private viewings booked in next week. I realise that while I don't like networking, I *can* talk about art. My back and feet are aching, and my throat's sore from all the talking, but once I got going, it wasn't too bad. Edwin will be pleased with my success.

Grabbing a sparkling water from a blonde waitress who looks even more exhausted than I feel, I wander from the tent. Shielding my eyes from the sun with one hand, I gaze at the crowd, searching for Jake, wishing I'd brought sunglasses. I feel guilty he's had to spend so much time alone, but after getting me talking to the first three or four groups of people, he'd started looking a bit redundant so left me to it with a murmured 'See you later.'

Something clenches in my stomach as I spot him in the stands by the stage with a woman. Looks like he's been just fine. While I'm hesitating between going over or calling it a day and making my way home, Jake spots me and waves. Grimacing, I push my way through the crowds. There are too many people, and I feel suffocated, especially as ninety per cent of them are taller than me. Finally making my way to the row Jake and the girl are sitting in, I murmur a few 'Excuse me's before coming to a stop in front of them. Someone a few rows back mutters something and I realise I'm blocking the view.

'Move up?' Jake says to his companion, and she grudgingly slides along so he can make space for me next to him. I brush aside the dirty look she gives me. I'm obviously ruining their little party. 'So, how did it go?' he asks as I shove my handbag under the bench and roll my shoulders.

'Good, thanks.' He's close, and I fix my attention on the players, watching as they grip the saddled horses with muscular thighs. The play is energetic and aggressive, and without meaning to, I find myself drawn in.

'Only good?' Jake says, turning toward me. That earns me another huffy expression from the blonde beside him, and I wince. He's made quite an impression on her if she's feeling so possessive.

'Great, actually,' I reply in a surly tone. 'Satisfied?'

'Yeah, if you are,' he fires back, raising both eyebrows.

'Sorry. What I mean is, thanks for coming.' I'm not going to tell him the girl with him is pissing me off.

Rolling his eyes, he waves my thanks away. ''S okay.' He nods his head at the sandy pitch. 'Do you like polo?'

'I've never watched a match before, but it's better than I thought it'd be. I'm not a massive fan of the way the horses are being ridden though.' I point at a stocky player who's urging his pony on with heavy hands.

Jake squints at him. 'Yeah, maybe he's a bit full on, but the horses look quite healthy to me. Their coats are glossy, they're moving fluidly. I think they're being treated well.'

I raise my eyebrows, 'How do you know? You're not in the horse's shoes.'

'Nah, but I'm good at riding,' he jokes, elbowing my side, clearly not talking about horses.

I roll my eyes, something catching in my throat. 'If you say so. After all, you've probably had enough practice.' I'm imagining all those pretty girls in different ports. Does he send them postcards too? I hate the thought of it.

'Speaking of which, are you seeing anyone at the moment?' he asks lightly.

Twisting my head to look at him, I nod. 'Yeah, Ethan. I've been with him a few months.'

'Don't look too enthusiastic,' he mocks.

Flushing, I shrug one shoulder. 'I don't think it's going to work out,' I admit in a strained voice, thinking of Ethan's resentment when I see my friends or need to work late and cancel plans. I recall his subtle jibes about my painting, which he calls my *little hobby*. There are echoes of Craig in his behaviour. No wonder I haven't felt much like painting recently.

'I see.' Reaching out to put a hand on mine, he's interrupted by his companion clearing her throat and wrapping glossy manicured nails around his upper arm to get his attention. 'Jay-Jay, there's only two minutes of this chukka left. Can you and your friend talk afterwards?'

Jay-Jay?

He gives her a dazzling smile, and stands up. 'No need. We're off. It was nice to meet you.'

'You're leaving?' Her expression is astonished. 'Are you going to call me?'

'I'll look you up when I'm back on shore leave.' He smiles politely. 'Take care of yourself.' Leaving her gaping after him, he nudges me towards the end of the row. 'Go. Now,' he urges under his breath.

Giggling, I obey. A few minutes later we've broken free of the crowds. With a relieved sigh, I bend over and undo the straps of my wedges, hooking my fingers through the ankle loops to carry them as we fall into step along the promenade, moving away from the event. 'That poor girl, Jake.'

'It could have been worse, believe me,' he replies. 'God, if she called me Jay-Jay one more time …' He clenches his eyes shut before opening them and looking at me. 'And she wittered on and on, for the whole two hours!'

'About what?'

'Absolutely nothing, mindless stuff. I stopped listening after the first twenty minutes. It's okay to be quiet sometimes, you know? Come on,' he says, 'let's go lie on the sand and watch the sea. I know it's not Durdle Door, but—'

'Okay,' I interject quickly, not wanting to recall sad memories today.

Jumping down onto the beach, he holds his hand out to help me. Pretending not to see it and holding my dress secure with one hand, I leap down next to him. I'm not sure I can hold his hand with all the conflicting feelings swirling around inside me.

The sand scorches the bottom of my feet and I yelp. 'Ouch!'

'Hot, isn't it?' he says curtly before striding off ahead, his shoulders set.

By the time I've followed him over to the spot he's chosen,

picking my way past the noisy families and groups of friends dotted along the beach, his face is neutral, eyes hidden behind his sunglasses while facing out to sea. I've upset him, but I'm not sure how. Perhaps he felt rebuffed because I wouldn't accept his help? I didn't mean to be rude. I just need time to sort my head out.

Choosing a safe topic, and hoping to defuse the mood, I settle on the sand and put my shoes down beside me. 'Summer's a funny time of year, isn't it?'

'What do you mean?'

'Well—' I gaze at the turquoise waves rolling onto shore, taking in the crowds and music, the children laughing as they play in the sand with buckets and spades. 'Everyone in the world seems to swarm to the coast, traffic backing up and snaking everywhere in boiling lines. People start gardening or cycling to get themselves out in the sun, and there are dozens of weddings to attend or festivals to drink at. It's pretty non-stop.'

'What's wrong with that? Sounds good to me.'

Deciding to throw out an olive branch, I answer honestly. 'The whole thing is my idea of hell. Then again, other than the few good people I have around me, the ones I love most in the world, my idea of hell *is* other people. I'm sure a famous author or poet said so once. Whoever he was, he talked a lot of sense.'

'Do you know how anti-social you sound?' Jake's voice has mellowed, his tone amused.

Shrugging, I watch a seagull swooping down towards the water in search of a snack. 'I've got bigger problems than that.'

'Meaning what?'

'Nothing, it doesn't matter.'

'Okay.' He finally looks at me, pushing his sunglasses up into his thick black hair. 'But I've got to admit that when I'm out at sea and think about you, I don't imagine you at a party, wading through crowds or fighting it out for a pack of super-market BBQ sausages.'

The visual makes me laugh. 'No?' I fan my face, baking in the afternoon sun. He thinks about me when he's away. Heat prickles along my skin, and the echo of the waves beating on the sand feels like a second heartbeat thudding in my chest. *Thud-thud. Thud-thud. Thud-thud.*

'No. I think of you in your dad's back garden, quiet, with a brush in your hand and a canvas in front of you. I imagine your bracelet moving on your wrist and the charms glinting in the sunlight.' He flicks one with his finger – the round disc with the sea, setting sun, seagulls, starfish, and a boat engraved on it with a tiny blue stone – the one I received during the second half of Year 10. It's the most apt one, given our setting. 'And,' Jake adds, 'I think of you unmoving, with that expression on your face, the one you get when you're concentrating.'

'What expression?'

'Scowling and chewing your lip.'

'I do not scowl!'

'You do, I swear.' He holds both hands up to fend me off as I try to whack him.

'Whatever.' Shaking my head, I subside, digging one hand into the sand and letting the warm golden silky grains sift through my fingers. 'You're so weird sometimes. How do you know what I look like painting anyway?'

'You paint in the garden sometimes, and when I'm back on leave I can see you from my bedroom window.'

'Not the roof?' I raise my eyebrow.

'Not any more. Now, stop trying to change the subject. Whenever I bring up your painting, you—'

'Yes, enough about me, what about you?' I interrupt. 'How's work? Can you talk about it?'

'You're such a pain in the arse sometimes, Jones.' But he goes with it anyway. 'I can, as it happens. I have news.' He pauses, looking uncertain.

Doubt is a strange expression on his face, because he's usually the most confident person in the room. Or as I used to tell him, the cockiest. 'So?' I prod.

'I'm leaving the Marines.'

'What?' He couldn't have stunned me more if he tried. 'But you love it.'

'It's time for a change. It's time to come home. I'll be with Mum for a while, until I can get my own place.'

As I study his face, I wonder if there's something he's not telling me. And the thought of him being down the road all the time is both gladdening and unsettling at the same time. 'Won't you miss it? You once told me your crew, or troop, or whatever you call them, are like family.'

'They are. And nothing will ever change that, but I have another family too. Mum especially.' Jake smiles at me gently, and a look passes between us. I know we're both thinking about how I helped her, and his dad leaving. He's never returned. 'All the travelling I've been able to do has been brilliant –' for some reason he touches a hand to his left shoulder '– but as much as I love the sea, and the sense of value and contribution I get from the job, it's time to settle in one place. I know it's going to be hard living on civvy street, but don't worry, I have a plan.' He pats me on the back with a large hand to reassure me, and the force of it almost sends me sprawling into the sand. He's strong. Really strong. But then, I found that out last August when he carried me on his broad shoulders. Why can't I stop thinking about it?

Shifting away from the danger zone, I stare at him curiously. 'What's your plan then?'

'First, I'm going to do a personal-training qualification—'

'What?' I choke. There's the second shock of the day, after him leaving the Navy. 'You mean you're going to be one of those tanned, arrogant, muscle-bound guys who stride around the gym barking orders at everyone? In those little shorts and tight T-shirts, admiring yourself in the mirror and sleeping with all your female clients?'

'Wow –' he raises an eyebrow '– talk about stereotyping. I'm surprised that you of all people would be so judgemental. And what kind of gyms have you been visiting, or more relevantly, which books have you been reading, to give you that impression of PTs? Some of my mates were PTs before joining the Marines, and I'm sure some of them will be afterwards too.'

Flushing under his gaze, I grab another handful of sand and let it slip through my fingers again. I force myself to look him in the eye. The smirk on his mouth says it all. 'Okay,' I admit, 'so I haven't ever been to a gym. That's a fair point. And yes, my perceptions might be from books or magazines I've read, or an occasional TV show. But I also have friends who go to the gym and tell me about what goes on in those places. Maybe those comments were a bit unfair. Still, you're the last person I imagined working as a PT; being cooped up in a gym all day just isn't you, is it?'

'Careful, you almost sound like someone who knows me,' he answers solemnly, eyes twinkling, 'but you're right, it's not me. Which is why, if you'd let me finish, I was about to tell you I'm going to become an occupational therapist. I'll do a PT qualification to get a general grounding in fitness, and then I'll do a postgraduate course in OT.'

'Erm –' I raise both eyebrows '– not to be condescending, but don't you need a degree to do a postgraduate course?'

'Yes, Sherlock, you do. So, it's a good thing I have one.'

'Really?' I must look as astonished as I feel. 'But how? When?' Asking the questions, I realise how little I know about him, and feel guilty. Am I still so wrapped up in my own internal little world that I don't stop to ask what's going on for the people around me? It's not a comfortable feeling.

'The Armed Forces have undergrad schemes they'll fund you through. I did a business degree through Southampton Uni. I also have a level-5 Diploma in Leadership and Management.'

'That's amazing. But you hated school!'

'They weren't the best years,' he admits, 'but I just had a lot going on, and as you know, reasons for not wanting to be there.' He pauses, and we both know he's alluding to his dad. 'And actually, I like learning. You know I like to read.'

'Yes.' I stare at him, but when he picks up a stone and throws it towards the sea, I realise I've made him uncomfortable. 'Sorry.' Wanting to end the awkward moment, I stand. 'I'm boiling. Come on, let's dip our toes in.' Not waiting to see if he follows, I stride towards the water's edge, breathing a sigh of relief as the foamy sea swishes over my feet, immediately cooling me down. A slight breeze brushes my cheek, and I tilt my face towards the sun. A second later, the hairs on my arms prickle as he joins me.

'That's better.' He steps into the sea beside me.

'I know you can't tell me about any missions or exercises, but can you tell me a bit more about it?' I ask, closing my eyes to bask in the glorious summer weather. 'How you joined the Marines? Why you do it? You've never said.'

There's a pause, and then he starts speaking, his voice deep. 'When I left town and went up north, I was getting my A levels and thinking about what I wanted to do with my life. I knew I wanted to travel, and help other people, that I needed something intellectually challenging which would wear me out physically too. I needed a family as well, given ...' He trails off. 'Anyway, I stumbled across the Royal Navy recruitment website and was thinking about all the stories Ray told me and it seemed like it'd be a good fit.'

We're both silent as we think about Grandad. I still really miss him. Jake must feel like he has a hole in his heart, losing the only positive role model in his life. It makes me ashamed again about how I was with him at the wake.

'I was fit with no medical conditions and met all the entry criteria,' Jake carries on, oblivious to my guilty musings. 'I managed to get the grades I needed, got through all the tests, and panel interviews. I liked the ethos and values; it's all about excellence, integrity, self-discipline, and humility. They look for people who have courage and determination. Basically, guys who can be cheerful even in the shittiest of shit situations.'

Opening my eyes, I glance at him. 'That must be ...' I struggle to find the right words, but there aren't any to do it justice. 'Tough.'

'Sometimes. But it's really a mindset thing. You've got to be positive in the face of adversity and make strategic decisions under pressure. There was a tag-line I liked on the site about being the first to understand, adapt, and respond, and overcome. I thought that was cool.'

'It wasn't the *I was born in Birmingham, but I was made ...* tagline then?' I tease, before smiling at how much he's underplaying what he does for a living.

'It's a hard job, but the sense of satisfaction, knowing you've helped, is worth it,' he replies. 'And that's as much as I'm going to say. Because now we're talking about you, about the topic you've avoided all afternoon. What's happening with your art?'

Fixing my eyes on the white-capped blue-green sea, staring out to the horizon where the sunlight glints off the waves, I sigh. I know he won't let it go. 'Nothing.'

'What does that mean? How long's it been?'

'A while.' I squirm to think how many months it's been since I picked up a paintbrush. It was the last time I saw him, at Christmas. The mural.

'What the hell? Jones, you're so talented. You have this amazing gift. Why wouldn't you use it? For as long as I've known you, it's been your passion. It's what makes you who you are.'

'I work full-time, okay?' I say defensively. 'It's long hours at the gallery, and I'm exhausted. There's zero chance of me having the energy I need to be creative after a day at work. I need to pay the bills, and believe me, my pittance of a salary doesn't go far. Plus, I want to see my friends, go out with Ethan, spend time with Dad. And he's ...' I choose my words carefully. 'He's starting to slow down, just a little. He's in his mid-fifties and is finding the manual work harder to deal with. He's been a plumber for a long time, and his body's beginning to show it. So, I look after the house, and cook. It doesn't leave a lot of time for anything else. The last thing I need is you judging me for it. I'm doing the best I can, and you're wrong. Everything about me, what I've been through, makes me who I am. I'm not just defined by my paintings.'

'Okay, I'm sorry.' He holds his hands up in surrender. 'Look, I just don't want you to waste the gift you have. I understand you need to balance the day job with your creative side, but I honestly think sometimes you need to be a bit more selfish. The washing up can wait; your dad can cook a couple of times a week; your friends and *Ethan –*' the word has a loaded emphasis '– will understand if you ditch them occasionally. I know you get to work in the art world with your job, but it's not enough. When I think about some of your work, and how inspired it made me feel—'

'Well, maybe not everyone will feel that way,' I cut in. 'Other people might not like my drawings or paintings. I could spend countless hours painting, just to have someone tell me it's rubbish. No, thanks.' The thought scares me rigid. If I shared my art with people, exposed myself like that and they didn't like it, I'm not sure how I'd cope, if I'd ever be able to hold a paintbrush again.

'But even if it never sells, that doesn't matter. You should do it anyway. You love it, Leila, you know you do. You can't deny yourself that. You shouldn't,' he says in a fierce voice.

The way he says my first name, when he normally uses my surname, wrong-foots me. I realise how strongly he feels. My irritation and defensiveness melt away as I realise he's not saying any of this for him. It's for me. I soften my tone. 'I understand, but it's not for you to push me. It's my decision.'

He runs a hand through his black hair, ruffling it, showing his frustration. 'Fine, but I want you to think about something. One important thing.' His hand drops to his side as he turns to squint at me in the sunshine. 'Every person is a universe of possibilities.'

I blink. My emotions are all over the place, especially with things not going well between me and Ethan – the death of another relationship. I don't like crying in public, so I joke to lighten the mood, 'Every person is a universe of possibilities. What cheesy sci-fi show did you get that from?'

He waves the comment off. 'Laugh all you want, but what it means is that it's your life, your choice, and all of your choices lead onto different possibilities and paths. There's no such thing as finite. There are no limits. You can do anything you set your mind to. If you want something badly enough, you'll find a way.' His gaze is intent. 'And wouldn't you hate to be on your deathbed one day and be looking back thinking *I wish I'd painted more, and shared my art with someone?*'

This is too much. It's too close to my fears, and so far from my dreams. Art is my greatest passion, but also my greatest pain. I can't do this. Shaking my head, I turn away. 'Jake,' I say over my shoulder, 'it's summer, we're at the beach, and the weather is lovely. I appreciate the thought but let's drop it.' Why does he always try and tell me what to do? Get involved in my life? I haven't asked for his advice. He's not my boyfriend. Bending over, I scoop up my shoes and stand. As I do, my vision spins, and I stagger.

'Careful.' His hand grabs my elbow, holding me until the spots clear from in front of my eyes.

'Thanks,' I murmur, slipping my arm from his hold and edging away. 'I'm just a bit hot. I need water.'

He flushes, cheekbones colouring. 'Let's go get some then,' he answers in a stiff voice, before making his way back up the beach, skirting around towels, picnics and people with easy strides. He checks over his shoulder to make sure I'm following and leaps up the stone slope onto the promenade. Unlike before, he doesn't hold out his hand to offer me help. I don't know whether to be sorry or glad.

Leila

June 2014

The French Flag Charm

'**Y**ou've got to be kidding me.' I stare at the alert on my mobile before glancing at the half-packed case on my bed, and the garment bag hanging from the wardrobe door. The back of my neck prickles with sweat. I'm supposed to be setting off for the airport in the next hour. 'No.'

Rushing downstairs, I flick the TV onto the news channel, calling for Dad at the same time. He comes in from the garden, face flushed and looking alarmed. 'What's wrong?'

Pointing at the TV screen as if it's personally responsible for mucking up my plans, I spin around to face him. 'There's thick fog basically covering half of Europe. They've grounded all flights. What the hell am I going to do? I'm supposed to arrive tonight for tomorrow's wedding prep. Chloe will never forgive me if I don't turn up. I'm one of her bridesmaids!'

'Leila, the main thing is not to panic. Let's see if there's another way.'

We spend half an hour online working out routes and

methods of transport. We come to the conclusion that the quickest and most convenient way to travel – without me lugging a case, wedding present, and the dress around on my own from station to station – is driving. Except I'm not a confident driver. Anyone who's seen my car can attest to that. The prang with Jake in the sixth-form car park was only the beginning. There are probably more scrapes and dents on it than there is pristine paint showing. I can just about cope with town driving, or the occasional zip up the M27 to West Quay for a shopping session, but the thought of driving abroad on foreign soil on the wrong side of the road makes me shudder.

'What am I going to do?' I groan. 'This can't be happening. I can't afford another flight to a different airport, if there even are any still operating. I've spent far too much on this wedding already.' The rooms in the gorgeous chateau hotel on the shores of Lake Annecy in south east France don't come cheap, and Chloe was adamant the wedding party all had to stay there together. As it is, I've been saving for the last eight months to pay my way comfortably. I only have a bit left over for spending money. Tears spring to my eyes. The journey is going to be awful. God, what about all the fuel it's going to cost?

'I have an idea,' Dad says, standing up and leaving the room.

'Where are you going?' But he doesn't answer, and instead I hear the front door slam in his wake. He's going out *now*? During my crisis?

I'm tempted to follow him but traipse back up to my

bedroom instead. I've no choice but to drive, so I may as well start making calls to my insurance company about cover in France and roadside assistance. I've no idea about any of this stuff, but sorting it out will take my mind off my shaking hands and the stress coating my stomach. At least I have my passport ready. I'd better get on with booking the Eurotunnel too, and planning my route south from Calais. By the time I organise everything I'm unlikely to set off until tomorrow morning, meaning I'm going to have to drive all day to get there and miss out on whatever activities Chloe has planned. Hopefully she'll forgive me because it's out of my control, and at least I'll be there for the actual wedding on Friday. I should really call to tell her what's happened, but I'm not looking forward to it. 'It can wait.' Saying it aloud, I know I'm being a chicken. I throw some more clothes into my case and clamber up onto the bed.

'Jones?' Jake's deep voice makes me jump. He sticks his dark head around the open door.

'Jake?' I squeak, suddenly short of breath. 'What are you doing here?'

'Your dad came around and told me about your dilemma,' he says, stepping into my bedroom. 'Aren't you pleased to see me?'

'Of course,' I gulp. 'Hi.'

'Hi.' He smiles slightly.

I'm kneeling on top of my case trying to zip it. Walking across the room around the heaps of stuff I decided not to bring with me, he steadies me with one hand on my waist as I sway, his touch burning through my thin top. Dropping his hand, he steps closer. 'Here.' Taking the zip tab from my fingers, he leans over, eyebrows knitted together as he works on zipping the case up, my weight pinning it down.

As he bends over, I stare at his short dark hair and incredibly tanned skin. Dressed in jeans and a black T-shirt, heat is radiating off him. I always forget how tall he is when I haven't seen him for a while. His shoulders are broader than I remember, and his arms are taut with muscle.

It's been almost a year since he came to the Sandbanks beach polo with me. We hardly spoke on the journey home, and I knew I'd upset him. There's also a weird feeling in my stomach at the thought he's back for good now. Will we get to spend more time together? Will he be dating, and looking for someone to settle down with?

'Thanks.' Clambering off the case once it's zipped, I'm aware it's not the most dignified I've ever looked. 'So, uh, what did Dad say?' I'm afraid to look at him directly with the turmoil running through my head.

'He told me what happened with your flights. He thought I might be able to help, seeing as I'm going too. After all, I'm Owen's best man.'

'What are you going to do, fly me there yourself?' I joke, folding my arms across my chest as I raise my eyes to his.

'Close.' He folds his arms to mimic me. 'I'm going to drive you. I'd already booked a car and have a Eurotunnel ticket for this afternoon. I'm driving down to the Black Forest tonight and stopping over, and then driving from Pforzheim to Lake Annecy in the morning. We should get there for lunchtime tomorrow if we have a good journey.'

'We?' My voice squeaks again. Spending twenty-four hours alone with Jake? Spending tonight in a hotel with him?

'Yep, we. It makes sense for you to jump in as my passenger.'

'Why weren't you flying?' *Like a normal person*, echoes silently around the room.

'I like exploring the world, which you really should know by now, and I thought it was a good opportunity to take in some great views on the way down. And now I'll be saving your arse.'

'You're not saving my arse.'

'You'll get there at least half a day ahead of when you would have done, and you're not going to have to drive. I'd say that qualifies.'

'Isn't it great, Leila?' Dad appears, Fleur padding along behind him. He beams, happy the issue's been solved.

Glancing from him to Jake, who's immediately crossed the room to pick Fleur up, I nod. This is my best option. I'll look ungrateful and silly if I say no. 'Yeah,' I echo weakly, 'great.'

'Let's get going then. You can log on to the online site to book the hotel room while I'm loading the car. It's the Ringhotel Monch's Waldhotel. It'll take us a few hours to get to Folkestone.' Jake passes Fleur to Dad then lifts my case, grabbing the garment bag on the way to the door. 'Got your handbag? Passport? Travel insurance? Wedding gift?'

'Now?' I reply, flustered. I need some time to get my head around the morning's events. To process that Jake and I are going to spend more than a couple of hours alone together. Travelling to a wedding. The best man and the bridesmaid. Like in one of those rom-coms Shell loves so much.

251

'Yeah,' Jake says cheerfully, 'the crossing is at one o' clock. We need to get going.'

'Okay.'

'Are you ready? You've packed a sketchpad and some paints, right?'

'No. I wasn't planning to—'

'I know it'll be a busy few days, but I've heard the views over the lake are amazing. You never know, inspiration might strike. Come on.' He puts my case back on the bed, unzips it, and stares at me expectantly. 'Get your painting stuff.'

Dad stands still, his gaze moving between us. He looks amused.

'Yes, sir,' I mutter, rolling my eyes. But I walk down the hallway and into the spare room to get my supplies, careful to close the door behind me so Jake can't see the mermaid mural.

***

Letting out a two-tone whistle, I stare at the sleek black BMW. I'm not usually excited by cars and I'm not in the habit of whistling either, but Jake looks so pleased I couldn't help myself.

'Is it yours?' Moving to the passenger side, I peer in at the luxurious tan leather seats and interior.

'Nah, it's just hired for a few days. But I'm thinking of buying one so thought it'd be nice to try out. It's a seven series with a six-cylinder engine and the four-wheel drive makes it good for driving in any snow we hit. The panoramic cameras make it easy to park too.' He winks at me, nodding his head at my scraped and battered Fiat.

'Ha ha.' Opening the door and sliding in, I sigh at the comfort of the front passenger seat and the amount of legroom. Not that I need much.

Jake climbs in next to me, stretching his long legs out and starting the engine. 'You like it?'

'It's nice. It feels really spacious.'

'Good.' He sorts out the sat nav, plugging in the postcode for the Eurotunnel and checking the route for traffic. 'The only thing is right-hand drive would've been better for driving in Europe, so I should have hired it in France, but I didn't want to mess around hiring one car over here and then picking up another on the other side.'

'You really do have a head for detail, Jake. I wouldn't have even thought about it.'

'That's because you need someone to organise you,' he says, an impish expression on his face.

'Like a PA?'

'Like a boyfriend with good attention to detail,' he replies, his dimple flashing as he watches for my reaction. 'Is Ethan still on the scene, by the way?'

'I'm single at the moment and plan to stay that way for a while, so I'll have to plump for the PA.'

'Let me know what the day rates are,' he jokes. 'I have the money set aside for a car, but at some point, I may need to earn some more.'

'Ha. That reminds me, how much do you want for fuel money?' Holding my breath, I hope he doesn't come out with anything in the high triples.

'Nothing.' Jake frowns. 'You've paid for your hotel tonight, but I was making the trip anyway and your tiny frame and luggage are hardly going to add much weight to burn extra fuel.'

'Jake, I can't let you—'

'Yes, you can,' he interrupts. 'We're friends, remember? And friends do each other favours just because they can. Anyway,' he finishes, 'you'll be doing me a favour by keeping me company and sharing the views.'

'All right.' I don't want to spend the whole journey arguing about it, so I'll find a way to slip him some money afterwards.

'By the way –' he leans in close, extending his arm across my body, his hand reaching for my hip as I hold my breath and wonder what he's doing '– the chair has lots of different settings including all-over body-massage. The buttons are down here on the side.'

'You're kidding,' I breathe, going almost cross-eyed looking into his face because he's so close. Those beautiful eyes are only a few centimetres away and I wish I had something as striking about me. A quirk which makes me unique. When I see myself in the mirror, I just see ... bland. Colourless.

Still, for a moment, I wonder if he's going to try and kiss me. But he straightens, clears his throat, and puts the automatic gearbox in drive.

'Let's go.'

'Okay,' I whisper.

As we set off on our journey, I shift in my seat to gaze out of the window. That can't be disappointment flipping my stomach over, can it?

***

Staring in the mirror, I splash my face with cold water then dab it dry with hand towels, the overhead lights bouncing off the white-tiled walls. The drive to Folkestone was uneventful and we made it in two hours fifty. I know because I kept an eye on the sat nav, counting down the time until we got here so I'd be able to stretch my legs and have a few minutes away from Jake.

The journey's been a bit awkward. For me at least. I wasn't sure what to talk to him about and kept brooding over how my heart almost stopped when he was leaning over me earlier, thinking he might kiss me.

Just after we left, Jake fell into silence, rubbing his scar at regular intervals like it was hurting him. I actually fell asleep for a while in the middle, lulled by the smooth ride and massage seat. When I woke up, he handed me a bottle of water, smiling when I apologised for dropping off.

'It doesn't bother me,' he said, 'these aren't the views I wanted to share with you anyway.'

After I'd stretched my arms and yawned, I rooted through my bag for my phone. Calling Chloe while sitting next to Jake wasn't a good idea as I had no way of knowing what she might say within his earshot, so I messaged instead.

Chlo, hope everything's going according to plan at your end :) My plane was grounded by fog so I won't be flying in tonight or need picking up. I'm so sorry. But not to worry, Jake's giving me a lift and we'll be arriving 2moro lunchtime. Sorry I'll be a bit late! Ahhhh – you're getting married in 2 days! SO EXCITED :) :) :) xxxxx

Her reaction wasn't quite what I expected, but being with Owen over the past few years has definitely mellowed her.

Sorry you'll miss the boat trip tomorrow morning, but at least you'll be around for the spa! Massages & facials all around! If you're with Jake, I'm not worried. He's a good guy, and I'm so pleased he's Owen's best man :) 48 hours to go! xxxxxxxxx

I've never really thought about how much time she must spend with Jake when he's home, because of Owen. It suddenly strikes me as strange that we don't do more together as a group. Why is that? I almost texted her to ask, but decided to talk to her face to face. Besides, I have other more worrying stuff on my mind.

'Ready?' Jake's leaning against the wall outside the Ladies' at Folkestone terminal, holding the sandwiches and crisps we picked out.

'Yes.' I hesitate.

'What's up?' He hands me my food.

'Have you ever been in the Eurotunnel before?'

'No. You?'

I shake my head slowly. 'Never. Do you know how long it takes?'

'About half an hour, I think. What's the matter?'

'I'm worried,' I confess, falling into step with him as we make our way across the terminal.

'About what?'

'Well, what if it springs a leak?'

'What do you mean?' He looks puzzled as we step outside through the doors.

'The tunnel. It's in the sea,' I say, earnestly, 'so what if it springs a leak and then with the pressure and everything it could flood and crush us—'

Jake throws his head back and guffaws so loudly I swear half the people in the car park turn to look at him. 'Jones, you are hysterical!'

'What?' I hiss, feeling my cheeks flush bright red. I curse my stupid milky-pale skin.

'I— No, I can't …' he stops and splutters, bending over and holding his stomach with glee. When he straightens, it looks suspiciously like he's wiping tears away from the corner of his eye. 'The tunnel is under the sea bed, about 40 metres, I think. It's not on the floor of the sea, it's buried underneath it. So, the chances of it springing a leak …'

'Oh.' Scrunching my eyes up, mortified, I blab, 'I always wondered how they built it without all the water getting in.' Even as I open my eyes and say it, I realise how silly I sound and start sniggering.

'Jones, you make me laugh.' Taking the key fob from his pocket, he unlocks the car, shaking his head. With a mischievous grin he starts humming 'Under the Sea' from Disney's *The Little Mermaid*.

Elbowing him, I join in before saying, 'Well, at least I'm good for entertainment value.'

'You certainly are.' Wrapping his arm around my neck, he

brings me towards him and plants a kiss on my forehead before I can do anything, 'And I love that you can laugh at yourself. Don't ever stop.'

Dropping his arm, he gets in the car, leaving me staring after him at the affectionate gesture. I can't work out whether it was brotherly or something else, and am too afraid to ask.

***

In the end, the Eurotunnel's quick and easy although a little hot, and we decide to stay in the car in the train carriage to eat our food rather than get out. There's not exactly a lot of room to walk around, given how they pack in the vehicles bumper to bumper. A few times Jake shakes his head and chortles, and I know he's remembering my gaffe. I good-naturedly ignore him, choosing to read instead.

'I hope that's not a premonition about our trip,' Jake gestures at the paperback's title: *The Accident* by C. L. Taylor.

'Hardly, it's a psychological thriller about a teenage girl who steps out in front of a bus. I think we're safe.' My tone is wry.

'Is it good?'

'Yes. I love her voice.'

'The author's?'

'Yes. It's what makes a book so unique, isn't it? It's why you could give a story with the same plot, descriptions, and character to two writers, but they'd write two totally different books. It's the way they tell it.'

'Like a signature, or a fingerprint.'

Surprised at his acuity, I glance at him, 'Exactly.'

'It's the same with artists, isn't it? Everyone has their own distinctive style: the paints they use, the way they mix the colours and how they use them, the way they sketch shapes and perceive things. I could ask you and another artist to paint the beach or a house—'

'Or a house on a beach,' I add playfully.

He smiles. 'And the two paintings would be different. Yours would be better, of course.'

'Obviously.' Pausing, I gather my courage. 'You think of me as an artist?'

'Why, don't you?'

'I guess I always think artists make their living selling their art. I don't do that. So, I think of myself as a painter.'

'That's bullshit,' Jake says, 'painters are people who paint walls or fences for a living. You create art – pieces that tell stories. I've told you before, I'm not sure I would have got through some of my teens if I hadn't had those doors to escape through or your wonderland to hide beneath.'

It touches me, even though I still cringe a bit about him seeing pieces I created for myself when I was so young.

'I mean it, Jones,' he says as he shifts around to face me, laying a hand on my arm, his skin warming mine, 'you're an artist. You have the imagination, passion, and discipline to put brush to canvas and create something special.'

'Not so sure about the discipline bit, but I am painting more, partly because of what you said last summer. About having regrets if I don't share my art. So, thank you.' Dropping my gaze, I stare down at his tanned hand on my pale one, the strength of his long fingers overlaying mine. His skin makes mine tingle, and I bite my lip.

'You are?' Lifting his hand away, he grips the steering wheel instead. 'What have you done?'

'I'm working on a series of oil paintings based on mythical creatures. I've completed three so far. I'm thinking there'll be another two.'

'Which creatures?'

'I have you to thank actually. The first is a unicorn.'

He grins, looking delighted. 'What I called you at the concert. What else?'

'A dragon,' I admit as it dawns on me how much Jake's inspired me. I didn't realise.

'I said you were the Mother of Dragons for helping Mum.' His grin widens, that familiar dimple creasing his cheek. 'So, you must have done a mermaid then, the most mythical creature of all.'

'Nope,' I blush. The mural is far too personal to show anyone, and it didn't feel right painting a different mermaid, or my mermaid in a different setting. I tick the other three off my fingers, 'Phoenix, Pegasus, and Valkyrie.'

'Who does the Valkyrie look like?'

'Eloise. The black hair, big blue eyes and statuesque figure – it had to be her really. She agreed to sit for me.'

'What was that like?' Jake asks as the tannoy in the carriage announces we're five minutes from Calais.

'Painful, for both of us. She found it hard to keep still, even to be immortalised in art.'

'Wel,l if you ever need a male muse, let me know. I was trained to sit still for hours.'

'Thanks.' Immediately my mind flashes to a visual of Jake sitting on a stool with his top off. To bat it away, I say, 'I didn't think of that, you needing to sit still for hours. There must have been times the job was really tough.'

He waves my comment off, unwilling to talk about it. 'What are your plans for the series? Are you going to ask Edwin to sell them, or explore other options?'

'I don't know. I'll see what happens.'

My vague reply obviously doesn't satisfy him, because he narrows his eyes at me. 'What are you scared of?'

'That's a bit blunt. But any number of things,' I say as the fears flow from my mouth: 'that people won't like them, that they won't be good enough, or won't sell.'

He looks thoughtful. 'Or that they will sell, and all the attention will be on you? You're an introvert, Jones, and I know you'd find it difficult, but talking about your art goes hand in hand with painting it. Anyway, you talk to people about art all day long at the gallery.'

He's too perceptive at times.

'That's different. I'm talking to them about other people's work, the spotlight isn't on me. I don't like anything that's too showy, or where there are too many people. Like Sandbanks last year.' I can't believe it'll get any better if I do eventually sell paintings and make a name for myself. I'll still feel out of place, silly and scratchily self-conscious, never knowing quite what to say and stumbling over my words. Praying for it to be over so I can go back to hiding behind my canvases.

'Speaking of pictures –' I deliberately change the subject '– thanks for all the postcards. I guess now you're home for good, you won't be sending them.'

'That's the plan.'

As he answers, it strikes me that I'll miss them. There are another four postcards in my drawer from the last year, secured in their bundle with the purple ribbon. Pictures of sandy beaches and teeming ports. He'd listened to the complaint I levelled at him at the concert, and instead of a generic sentence saying he hopes I'm well or describing the weather or saying to tell Dad hello from him, he instead includes inspirational quotes that are personal to me.

I am not afraid of storms, for I am learning how to sail my ship, by Louisa May Alcott. Or my favourite, which was about setting your course by the stars, and not by the light of passing ships. That one made me feel reassured, like Jake was saying it's okay to be different and you should live your life according to something bigger and not worry about what everyone around you is doing.

Those postcards gave me comfort, and I'm sad at the thought of them ending.

'Isn't it time to go?' I ask, shrugging off the sadness. The train's pulled up on French soil while we've been talking, and the vehicles in front of us are pulling away.

Jake starts the engine and rolls the car forward. 'If you ever want any moral support at art events, or anything,' he offers, returning to our previous subject, 'don't forget I'm home now. I'll be around.'

Something in my body pings at the thought, and all the

questions I've been asking myself crowd in my head clamouring to be heard, but I simply say, 'I'll bear it in mind, thanks.'

***

'This is lovely,' I breathe, a very tiring seven hours later, staring out of the car window at the lush forest surrounding both sides of the curving grey road.

Jake just smiles, rolling his shoulders and stretching his neck from side to side to work the kinks out.

'You've been driving for ages. You must be exhausted.'

'I'm used to long hours.'

By mutual consent we drove straight through St-Quentin and Reims, past Metz, and arched over the top of Strasbourg so we could reach our hotel in time for a late dinner. It's been a long day, and while I've only sat here staring through the windows, listening to music or occasionally playing a game with Jake to stave off boredom, I'm desperate to eat and fall into bed. There's something about sitting in a car for so long that makes you lethargic.

'Thank you.' The words come out of my mouth on impulse. 'You've been brilliant today. It can't have been an easy drive, but you haven't moaned or grumbled once. Even when I thrashed you at Animal, Vegetable, or Mineral,' I joke.

'Well, there's loads of other stuff I'm better at than you,' he quips.

'True,' I concede. 'Except painting.'

'Except painting,' he agrees.

As we fall silent, he slows down and turns into a wide driveway. Winding along it, we arrive in a small car park on an incline, cars lined either side, with a chalet-style hotel sitting at the top with a turning circle out front. Jake slots the car neatly between an Audi and another BMW, and I climb out, massaging my lower back. Gazing up the hill, I take in the multi-tiered building, all rectangular boxes and sharp corners but with terraces of colourful flowers to soften the look. The overall effect is quaint and pretty, and it fits perfectly into the surrounding landscape.

I love it even more inside, once Jake's grabbed our cases and we're checking in at reception. It's all warm tones and chandeliers, antler horns and dark wooden furniture. A hunting lodge with a modern twist.

'What do you think?' Jake nods at the lobby and the seating area I can see leading off it.

'I love it.' I smile. 'Shall we eat?'

'Sure,' he says easily, 'do you want to go and get changed first?'

'It's nearly nine. I'd rather just grab a drink at the bar and have dinner, if that's okay?'

He staggers back, clutching his chest in a pretend heart attack. 'You mean you don't want to shower, change, do your make-up, and style your hair? Put some heels on and make an entrance?'

'Like a normal woman would, you mean?' There's an edge to my voice. 'You should know by now I'm not that type of girl.'

'Well, I definitely know you're not normal.' Jake comes over

264

and slings an arm around my shoulder. 'But what's normal anyway, and who is? As far as I'm concerned, your lack of vanity makes you the perfect travelling companion. Not like some of my ex-girlfriends.' He mock shudders.

As we stroll through the carpeted rooms into a small but perfectly formed bar with mint tones and antlers hanging on the wall, I try and ignore the weight and warmth of his arm. He's just being friendly.

While we wait for our table I climb onto a barstool, which takes me three galling attempts. I turn to him once there's a chilled half pint in my hand. 'Do you think I don't make an effort with my appearance?'

'What?' He looks surprised, then shakes his head. 'No, I just mean you don't go overboard like some women. I prefer natural beauty any day and you really don't need make-up to look good.'

'Oh. Thank you,' I whisper, swallowing back the instinct to push away his words, never having been comfortable with compliments. 'I guess I feel I look washed out sometimes because of my colouring, like you said once.'

'Your colouring is gorgeous,' he says immediately. 'Loads of women would kill to have your hair, and the only way they can come close is from a bottle. And yes, you're fair but with your dark grey eyes it makes you look like a fairy. So ethereal. Like the girl in the wonderland, right?' We share a smile at the thought of the creation under my old bed.

His words warm me, making me feel special. No other guy has ever described me like that, or made me feel this way about myself.

'All I meant that time was that pastels –' he points at my light-yellow top '– don't do you any favours.'

'Go on then, Gok Wan,' I say, amused, 'what colours should I be wearing?'

'Well, on the basis that Dan's girlfriend would probably say you're a "winter", I'd go with bold or strong colours – deep purple, turquoise, navy, black, hot pink.'

Nodding, I hold back a grin. He'll approve of my bridesmaid dress then.

Gesturing at my baggy jeans, he carries on, 'I also notice you wear a lot of T-shirts and don't really wear clingy stuff. You do like your figure, don't you, Jones?'

'Jake!' Hissing it at him, I look around to see if anyone heard, but there's only a lone businessman sitting on the other side of the room, frowning at his phone. 'You can't ask things like that.'

'Why?' His black eyebrows draw together.

'Because,' I splutter, 'it's rude.'

Shaking his head, he puts his drink down and gazes at me. 'I just want to make sure you're not underselling yourself, that's all. I know you're not a big fan of dresses, but you seem to hide yourself.'

'I hardly think denim cut-offs and a vest top is draping myself in fabric from head to toe.'

'True, and you look really sexy in those, but other times ...'

He thinks I'm sexy?

'I'm explaining myself badly.' He pushes a hand through his thick hair, leaving it stuck up in tufts. Idly, I wonder if that's what it looks like when he rolls out of bed in the morning. 'All I mean is, you've got a lovely body and loads of girls would kill to have it.'

Battling a blush at the comment, I blurt out, 'You think I should show off my non-existent bum and tiny chest?'

'Not every bloke is in love with the Kardashians, Jones.'

'Whatever. It's easy for you; you've got bags of confidence. You're fit and you know it.'

Tilting his head, he leans towards me. 'You think I'm fit?' he crows, his eyes gleaming. 'Jones, is that a chink in your armour?'

'I mean physically fit,' I race on. 'Don't go getting cocky again.'

'I wouldn't dare.' He slides from his stool as the barman indicates our table is ready.

We wander through and settle at a table. It's romantic, replete with white tablecloth, silver cutlery, wine glasses, and a burning candle, and I tell myself not to get carried away into a world which doesn't exist for us. We're friends.

***

Jake sets aside the wine glass and puts his elbows on the table. 'Do you really still think I'm cocky?' His face is troubled, eyes inquisitive.

As much as I'd love to keep him guessing, it'd be mean. 'No.' I play with my fork, aware we're the only people in the restaurant as it's so late. 'I don't. I only say that to wind you up. I mean, you're confident, but you haven't been cocky for a long time. It's just that you're so tall and well-built, and women stare at you. You definitely know it.'

'Not always,' he mutters. 'And you'd be surprised. People aren't always as confident as they seem.'

'You?' I say, surprised. 'You're the most self-assured person I know. And you're always telling me what to do!'

'I know who I am; I have that core of resilience, but I'm not confident about my looks. Women stare at me because I'm different. I've been told more than once I'm a nice bit of rough.' He laughs, but there's pain behind the sound rather than joy. 'As for the well-built thing, it's part of the job, and –' he hesitates, '– when I was growing up, I promised myself I'd be big and strong one day.'

'Your dad,' I murmur, not needing to say anything else. 'Oh, Jake.' I've never seen this vulnerable side to him before, not really, but rather than making him seem weak, I admire the strength it takes to confess his biggest fears. Things feel more equal between us at his admission, because *I've* always been the one telling *him* about the things I'm scared of.

Leaning forward, I study the curve of his eyebrows, the dark stubble, his unusual eyes, and the scar. How can he not think he's attractive? No matter what it costs me, I can't let him keep carrying that around with him. 'Jake, you're a good-looking guy. And if women make those 'bit of rough' comments, it's only because your scar gives you a rakish air, and because you were in the Marines and it's a profession seen as big and tough. You have nothing to worry about, believe me.'

He goes quiet at my words, but after a moment murmurs, 'Thanks.' Straightening in his seat, he picks up the menu and studies it, before clearing his throat. 'As for telling you what to do, I just want to make sure you're happy. I want to protect you from all the bad stuff life can throw at you.'

'Oh.' I've always felt, or assumed, that his being overbearing was part of the cockiness, of thinking he knows best because he's older. But when he talks about protecting me ... something clicks. 'Like you've always tried to protect your mum?'

Raising his eyebrows from the menu, he winces. 'Tried and failed.'

'Oh,' I repeat, slowly, drawing the word out. So, it's not bossiness, or control, or thinking he knows better than me. All these years, he's been trying to look after me. I've always felt so suffocated by it, so hemmed in. But the whole time he was just trying to make sure I was happy ... and protect me from harm. The realisation loosens something inside me, uncoiling a knot of tension I hadn't realised was there. 'Thank you,' I say impulsively, reaching across the table to hold his hand. 'You're a good friend.'

Looking at me strangely, he sighs. 'Sure.'

'As for your mum,' I race on, 'you did everything you could, Jake! You were barely more than a child, and then as an adult you tried to get her out. She just wasn't ready yet. You can't beat yourself up about it.'

'You managed to save her.'

'She saved herself. I just opened the door and put the choice in her hands.'

'And I'll never stop being grateful for that.'

I shrug his comment off, wondering if gratitude is what's really kept him by my side these last few years.

***

'What a view,' I comment to Jake the next morning, standing at the wooden balcony and gazing out across the lush forest which goes on for miles in every direction. After a solid night's sleep and a speedy breakfast so we can get on the road early, we're about to check out.

'We'll have to come back another time, for longer,' he suggests, leaning on the railing and taking a deep breath. 'It's peaceful here. I like it.'

'Yes.' It's not clear whether I'm agreeing about coming back or that it's peaceful, but I'll leave him to figure out the ambiguity. Ever since our conversation in the bar last night I feel off balance, and a tiny part of me wants him to feel the same. 'Do you need peace?' I ask, curious. 'I mean, are there things you saw overseas you need headspace to deal with?'

Gripping the railing, he keeps his gaze on the forest. 'It was tough, and I lost people and saw some horrific things, but I was one of the lucky ones. I found ways to cope, and I didn't come back with PTSD.' He pauses, admitting, 'Sometimes it makes me feel guilty, like I got off lightly.' Pushing back from the railing, he brushes past me. 'Time to get on the road.'

I grab his arm. 'I didn't mean to pry or upset you. I'm sorry.'

His eyes darken. 'I don't like to talk about it, Jones. I prefer to focus on the future. Don't you?' Placing his hand over mine, he squeezes it and then moves away. 'I'll meet you in reception.'

***

A few hours later, after we've traversed the western edge of the Black Forest Nature Park, swooping along winding passes and roads Jake took great delight in putting his foot down on – making me alternatively grimace and laugh – we cross the border into Switzerland. Jake goes off the planned route with my agreement, turning towards the centre of the country so we can drive through the Swiss Alps.

'It's not the quickest route, but it'll have the best views. We'll probably arrive at two, rather than noon. Do you think Chloe will mind?'

Feeling reckless, I nod. 'Probably, but we'll just say we set off late and hit traffic. I'm willing to take the heat if you are.' We grin at each other like naughty schoolchildren as Jake flicks the indicator, steering us off course.

We stop at a gravel parking spot at the top of a snow-capped mountain. 'It's absolutely stunning.' I gape at the panoramic view.

'It really is,' he agrees in a quiet voice, standing next to me, our arms brushing.

I shiver in my denim cut-offs and white T-shirt, a pendant hanging round my neck and the charm bracelet on my wrist jostling with the movement. I can't bring myself to spend time rifling through my case for a cardigan when I can take all this in instead. I don't want to miss a moment. 'I could stay here for ever. It's so ... breathtaking,' I whisper, 'so vast and epic. Photos can't do it justice.'

We've driven up grassy knolls on zig-zagging roads and swept along craggy passes, climbing ever higher, peering down at the hints of civilisation getting smaller and smaller. We've seen goats and cows lazily chewing grass on the sides of hills and watched birds of prey circling on the air currents above us.

But this. *This.* Staring at the mountains and valleys surrounding us, I shake my head in wonder. Not all the mountains are snow-capped; some are green and have rows of trees running along their ridges and dips, with boulders sitting in piles at cave mouths. The one straight across the valley from us has a sparkling waterfall running down from its peak, wending a bubbling, splashing route down the mountain and into the alpine village at its base. Along with the view, there is a profound sense of peace and a deep calm. A resounding quiet. In this moment, I know that none of the petty worries back home really matter.

'I'm not a spiritual person,' I murmur, 'but this high up and being part of something so awe-inspiring, I can believe in God.'

'Like it's been touched by the hand of God,' Jake says.

'Yes.' I can't help it. I burst into tears. Messy, noisy sobs.

'Aww, Jones, what's the matter?' Alarmed, he grabs me in a hug, holding me against his hard chest as he strokes my hair.

'I'm sorry, it's just so amazing ... I don't know, it's made me emotional, I guess.' Leaning back, I wipe my face with one hand, 'And to think I almost didn't see it. I would've just caught a glimpse of the mountain range from the air if my flight hadn't been cancelled.'

'Are you crying because you're sad, or happy?'

'Both, I guess. Happy that I came here, sad we don't have more time.' Stepping back, my arms drop to my sides. 'And scared I'll never come back here again.'

'You just need to make a promise to yourself you will, and then make it happen.'

'Right, because life is that easy,' I say with a snort.

'It can be.' He looks serious. 'If you want something enough you can make anything happen.'

My eyes are tearing up again and I open my mouth, but he gets there first.

'Now –' Jake pats me on the back '– sort yourself out, you soppy mess, and let's take a selfie of us standing in front of the Alps. You'll want a memory to take home with you.'

But I know I don't need a photo. This memory will stay etched in my head – and my heart – for ever. The fact I'm with Jake makes it feel even more special. Which confuses me, because for some reason it makes perfect sense.

***

Spinning the BMW's wheels along the shingled driveway, Jake turns into the car park and I read the sign. *Le Palace De Menthon*. We made good time so hopefully I'm not in too much trouble with Chloe. I texted to let her know we were a little delayed.

Jake climbs out of the car and pushes his Oakley sunglasses further up the bridge of his nose. 'Go on. You'll get points for turning up earlier than anticipated.' Clicking open the boot, he unzips my case and stands back. 'If you grab the stuff you need for this afternoon, I'll take your case to reception. Have fun.'

'Thanks.' Rooting through my luggage, I find a bag of goodies I packed, plus my bikini and wash-bag, assuming the spa will supply towels and robes. I step back, holding them against my chest. 'Don't you want to come down to the spa and say hi to Chloe?' For some reason, I'm reluctant to leave him.

'Nope, I'll say hi to the bride-to-be at dinner,' Jake replies. 'I'd better find Owen and see if I have any best-man duties to catch up with.'

'I guess I'll see you later then.' I go to leave and then stop. 'Thanks, Jake. It was a lovely trip. I've enjoyed spending time with you. Thanks for the mountains too.' I'm not just saying it out of politeness – I really mean it.

'Sure, Jones. See you this evening.'

'Yes.' The thought of that makes me happy.

***

'You made it!' Chloe races along the side of the pool and flings her arms around me, hugging me tight. 'I'm so glad you're here.' Her eyes are sparkling, skin tanned and glowing, and her dark brown hair is hanging in a ponytail down her back.

'Sorry I'm late,' I say, easing back. 'You look amazing. All twinkly. I don't need to ask if you're having second thoughts about marrying Owen tomorrow.'

Grinning, she bounces on her heels, reminding me more of Eloise than the sometimes dour Chloe I shared my teens with. 'Nope, none at all,' she sings. 'No cold feet for me, no siree!' Slapping her hand over her mouth, she giggles, 'I may also be a bit twinkly because El brought four bottles of champagne.'

'Oh, God. She's not showing me up in bridesmaid duties, is she?'

'Nope, and anyway, I'm just happy you're here. And she may have said something about divvying up the bill between you, her, and Shell.'

Pulling a face, I grimace, thinking of my diminished funds. 'Gee, thanks, El.'

'I'm just teasing,' Chloe says quickly. 'Are you okay?'

'Yes, sorry. Bit of a fraught twenty-four hours,' I share, flashing a look over her shoulder. I can see the rest of the girls from the bridal party in the round hot-tub, hair up in buns and champagne flutes in their hands. They smile and wave, beckoning us over. 'But that doesn't matter now. I'm here, you're getting married tomorrow, and I couldn't be more excited. Let's have some fun!' Opening up the bag hanging off my arm, I scoop out little gift-wrapped clear bags of her favourite sweets – lemon Refresher bars – tied with hot pink ribbons, and hand them to her. Then I fish around and bring out a plastic tiara with fake pink jewels in it. She bends over so I can carefully push it into her wet hair and thanks me.

When I draw the next item out, her eyes widen. 'Oh God, no.'

'Oh God, yes,' I hand her dangly pink penis earrings.

'Oh, all right then.' Laughing, she threads them into her earlobes.

Next are some drinking straws with penises at the top. 'So we can sip our champagne and get drunk quicker,' I add.

'Of course! You're such a lovely friend.'

I pull away so I can see her face. 'Even though I got here about fifteen hours late?'

'Even though.' She nods. 'Now, I managed to juggle things around so you can have a facial in about ten minutes, and a back massage later. Go and say hi to the girls, grab a champagne, and then relax. Down the hallway to the left for the treatment rooms.'

***

By dinner time, I'm feeling very relaxed. My face is glowing after my facial, my muscles loose after my massage, and I'm light-headed after champagne in the hot tub, but in a good way.

Everyone's dressed up for dinner and I break tradition by putting on a floral dress with spaghetti straps and a fitted bodice. I bought it a few weeks ago and really wasn't sure about it, but now I'm glad I threw it in my case, especially after Jake's comment last night. Not that I have anything to prove to him. It surprises me, though, how girly and pretty I feel in the dress, with my hair tied in a high ponytail and my charm bracelet swinging from my wrist.

Owen wolf-whistles and Jake raises both eyebrows when I enter the restaurant and make my way towards Shell, Eloise, and Jonny. Then Owen stands up, raising his glass in a toast. 'Little Leila Jones, putting on a dress for us,' he cheers. 'Now I *really* know I'm getting married in the morning.' There's a round of applause from the whole table, as I sit down blushing. *I'll get you back*, I mouth at Owen. He just winks at me, and elbows Jake.

My gaze is drawn to Jake more and more over dinner, and I keep hoping I'll catch his eye, but he seems to avoid looking in my direction. Maybe I'm being paranoid.

***

Chloe and Owen's wedding day dawns sunny, clear, and beautiful. After El, Chloe, her sister Amanda, Shell, and I breakfast together in the bridal suite, we set about doing each other's hair and make-up. Popping open some fizz, we pause what we're doing when there's a knock on the door. We throw each other panicked looks because we're all in tiny underwear under thin silky robes, not planning to get dressed until just before the ceremony. Chloe's worried about something being spilt on our bridesmaid dresses, which are all the same gorgeous colour but each with a slightly different neckline.

I'm closest to the entrance of the suite, which has a small hallway area, so I volunteer to answer, checking to make sure no one inside the suite is visible as I crack open the door and peer through it. I see one green eye and one brown. 'Morning,' Jake.'

'Jones,' he nods, his gaze slipping momentarily down to my chest before meeting my eyes again.

I flush and pull the robe tighter, aware my strapless balconette bra is lacy and see-through. Anyone could walk down the corridor while we're talking.

'Nice hair.' His mouth twitches.

'Thanks.' Putting my hands to the large rollers pinning my long tresses up, I say, 'Chloe wants us all to have extra body.'

'Does she now?' He chuckles, looking at my cleavage again.

'Ahem, if you two can stop flirting, I am still here?' A voice sounds from behind Jake's wide shoulders. I recognise it straight away.

'Judy?' I squeal.

'That's me.' A bejewelled hand moves Jake to one side. 'Excuse me, handsome, but I'll be needed in there. Off you pop, now.'

Jake blushes as she pats him on the bum to shoo him away, and I stifle a laugh behind my hand as he leaves, shaking his head. I've never seen him look so bemused before.

'What a nice look, Leila.' Judy steps into the room and closes the door behind her, patting my cheek and smiling fondly at me.

This woman pretty much raised me, when I wasn't with Dad. 'Thank you,' I say, striking a pose, one hand on my hip, 'I thought so.'

Spinning around, I lead her into the bedroom. 'El, your mum is here,' I announce. 'And she looks amazing.'

Everyone turns around, champagne flutes in hand.

'Mum,' Eloise says, beaming, 'you made it. I love the outfit too.' She indicates the pearly lilac dress Judy is wearing. 'What are you doing up here?'

'I couldn't let Chloe get ready without a mother of the bride.' Judy looks at Chloe with soft eyes. 'If you'll let me be that for you? You girls practically grew up at my kitchen table, so I sort of feel like your other mama. I know it must be hard without your mum here today.' She holds open her arms, and Chloe flies into them with a sniffle. Amanda gulps down tears in the background. They lost their mum to cancer when Chloe was ten and Amanda was eight. It's one of the things that's always bound us together – the absence of a mum. Judy filled that gap to some extent. She always had a warm welcome for us and a ready supply of tissues, advice and food.

Watching them, I wonder if she'll do the same for me on my wedding day. Then I wonder if, with my record, I'll ever get married. Putting my fingers to my eyelids, I press back tears. Today isn't about me. 'Oh, no. This is too sweet. Stop it, or we'll all cry.'

Chloe raises her head, laughing and stepping from Judy's embrace.

'Yeah, that's a lovely idea, Mum, but let's not get the waterworks started,' El teases.

'Thank goodness we hadn't started on the mascara yet,' Shell says.

Judy shows Chloe over to a padded velvet chair. 'Right, what's next then?'

***

The rest of the morning goes smoothly. The professional photographer arrives as planned, flitting around taking photos of us in various stages of preparation. The receptionist calls to confirm the band have arrived and are setting up down on the lawn to play the entrance music. They're using the large circular wooden arbour right on the water's edge for the ceremony. The Wedding Breakfast will be in one of the three reception rooms, but Chloe wants to get married by the lake. It's the spot where Owen proposed to her last year, going the traditional route by getting down on one knee, having asked her dad's permission first. It's so romantic we could all burst.

Now, walking down the grassy aisle created by the two columns of chairs set out in front of the arbour, murmuring *step-together, step-together* under my breath, I feel something rise up inside me at the sight of Jake standing next to Owen at the front. They both look incredible in well-cut black tuxes, hot pink ties, and buttonhole roses pinned to their lapels. But it's Jake's eyes I search for, and as our gazes tangle and I see the warm appreciation on his face, I stumble.

'Watch it!' Eloise hisses behind me, not unkindly.

Steadying myself, I look around at the guests instead, smiling at them like the bride asked me to, ignoring the nerves at being centre of attention. *Step-together, step-together*. I'm the first bridesmaid in the line, much to my chagrin, but Chloe wanted us in height order to look neat. El, Shell, and Amanda are next in single file, followed by Chloe on her dad's arm. He looks like he could explode with pride, though we all know it's a bittersweet day for their family.

Overhead, the sky is a bright blue – Winsor and Newton's

Manganese Blue Hue – the lake is a shimmering Cobalt Turquoise, and the trees lining the shore are Winsor Emerald. Jake was right. I'm inspired and desperate to paint the scene. My fingers curl tighter around the flowers I'm clutching in front of me.

With relief, I reach the front without any further mishaps, moving to my designated place over to the side and waiting for the other bridesmaids to join me.

Sighing, I watch as Owen catches sight of Chloe for the first time. If his face is anything to go by, he's as awestruck as we all were earlier when Chloe was finally ready. Her white satin wedding dress has a strapless sweetheart neckline and a fitted bodice, with a full princess skirt, puffed out by two hoops underneath. She looks stunning. Like a princess, especially with her dark brown hair trailing down over her left shoulder, a spray of flowers and jewels securing it away from her face above her right ear, classic red lipstick coating her mouth.

The ceremony is brief but moving, and I tear up countless times at seeing my friend so happy. Eloise takes hold of my hand and squeezes, and I look out over the crowd to stop from breaking down completely, my bottom lip wobbling.

And then Jake is stepping forward to hand Owen the wedding rings, but instead of looking at his best friend, his focus is on me. Staring at the strapless hot pink dress – Permanent Magenta – clinging to my body, which crosses over on the bodice and hugs my waist and hips before falling in a waterfall to the ground at my heels. Running his eyes over my long silvery blonde tresses which are falling in gentle waves down my back almost to my waist, a circlet of tiny roses and jewels perched on my head, giving me the fairy-tale princess style Chloe was aiming for.

Wow. He shapes his mouth around the word, and I nod at him. *You too.*

Surely friends can compliment each other.

Owen coughs to get Jake's attention, and Jake turns to him. 'Sorry, mate,' we all hear him mutter, as he hands over the rings.

Owen clasps him on the shoulder, glancing over at us bridesmaids. 'No worries,' he says and laughs.

Chloe takes it all in, and then looks from me to Jake, eyebrows raised. She shakes her head, but then gives me a little smile before turning to face Owen so they can say their vows. Shuffling my feet, I feel like I've been caught out in front of everyone.

***

The wedding breakfast feels endless. It's the wedding of one of my best friends and I don't want to seem ungrateful, but I can't wait to go outside on the lawn, take in the view, and get some fresh air. All of the bridesmaids are sitting at the round table nearest the head table with Jonny and Amanda's husband, Darren. Their son Toby is being looked after by Judy to give them both a break. Shell and I are the only single ones at the whole wedding, it feels like.

Chloe and Owen are sitting in the middle of the head table, with her dad, his brother, and his parents on either side, and

Jake sitting next to the groom. Jake does a spectacular job with his speech, talking about when he first met Owen, how their friendship has grown over the years, what a good guy Owen is, and the way Chloe and his best friend complement each other. It's funny and moving, joyful and poignant. Parts of it remind me of the letter he wrote to Grandad, or the postcards he sent me. 'All we have is time,' he finishes, looking meaningfully at the bride and groom while raising his glass, 'and I am thankful you've found each other and can make every minute count on this incredible journey together. Please stand as we offer a toast to the bride and groom,' he says, his voice carrying to the back of the room, 'wishing them all the happiness in the universe.'

Everyone stands, holding their prosecco aloft, repeating after Jake in a choral symphony of voices. There are very few dry eyes as people resume their seats.

'Oh my God, I can't cope,' Eloise dabs her big blue eyes with a tissue she pinched from her mum earlier. 'That was just bloody brilliant. Who knew Jake was such a poet?'

Biting my tongue to stop myself saying, *I did*, I get to my feet. 'Anyone up for a wander in the grounds? It's hot in here and I could do with some air.'

Shell stands too. 'I'm done, and I heard Chloe say something to the waiters about music and drinks on the lawn, so I think we're about to move anyway. I'll go check.'

As she goes over to the head table, I catch Jake watching me, his jacket on the back of his chair now his speech is over. There are three empty flutes and a whiskey glass containing an inch of amber liquid in front of him. He waves at me, a sloppy grin on his face, and I can tell he's on his way to being drunk.

Shell returns. 'I was right. Chloe says we can go outside now.'

'Does she need help with anything?' Amanda asks.

'Oh, yeah –' Shell turns to her '– she asked if you could go hold her hoops so she can finally visit the bathroom.'

'I get all the best jobs,' Amanda rolls her eyes. 'I thought I'd bottomed out with smelly nappies and potty training a two-year-old, but apparently the rung below that is helping a grown woman wee.'

We all laugh as she lets out a mock long-suffering sigh and heads off to her sisterly duties. We gather our drinks and belongings, skirting around tables, chairs, and chattering people to reach the exit. As El and I leave the room ahead of Shell, who's wandering along speaking with Darren, she leans her head towards me and says in a low voice, 'You could do worse than Jake, you know.'

I blink. 'I-I don't know what you mean.'

'We've been friends for over twenty years if you count our time at primary school. I know you. I've seen the way you look at him.'

'You're wrong, El. It's not like that between us.'

Letting out a *pah* sound, she eases me over to a corner, away from the human traffic. 'Is that because you think that, or because you think he does?' she says in a low voice. 'You *like* him, like him. If you don't do something about it, then someone else will. He's lovely. He's gorgeous. He's always been there for you. Why wouldn't you want him?'

Mouth open, I click it shut. 'I don't. I don't like him like that.' But my voice wobbles and I sound weak. Jake *is* lovely, and has always been there for me, even when he irritated me, or I thought he was being bossy and overbearing.

I think of our shared history. He kept me company in the park that lonely week before I left Bournemouth. He covered for me at school and got expelled. I saved his life, and we floated in the inky sea together beneath the stars. He's funny, kind, caring. He supports my art. He makes me feel good about myself. He came in search of me when I lost the baby. He gave me a rainbow charm to give me hope for the future. His touch makes my skin tingle and I get breathless when I'm near him. I wear his jumper and keep his postcards and letter in a bundle in my bedside drawer. His charms – the book, the rainbow, and the musical note – hang off Mum's bracelet next to her charms, which are so precious to me.

But he kept leaving, like Mum. But not exactly, I realise, because he kept coming back. And now he's back for good. The thought terrifies me, because it means I have to face how I feel.

'Oh my God,' I stare at her. 'I do,' I whisper, holding a hand to my chest and leaning against the wall, 'I *do* like him.' Shaking my head, instinct kicks in. 'But even if I do, I'd just be making a complete idiot of myself when he tells me yet again he's my friend.'

'Well, I've always got the impression he'd like there to be something more. And didn't he kiss you once?'

'Yes,' I say softly, 'but it was years ago when he was comforting me, and he's never tried again.' I pushed him away.

His timing was awful. And I didn't *see* him back then, not the way I see him now.

'Well, you won't know unless you try, will you? Come on.' She links her arm with mine, raising her eyebrow at my expression. 'Let's get another drink.'

***

A warm hand lands on my bare shoulder, sure and steady, but nonetheless it sends a tingle along my skin, raising the hairs on my arms. I spin around to find Jake smiling down at me. The breath catches in my throat. 'Hey,' I croak, 'you okay?'

'More than.' His mouth crooks a little lopsidedly.

I can tell he's on the wrong side of tipsy. His sleeves are rolled up and the hot pink tie is dangling undone around his neck. He looks deliciously decadent.

'But you,' he continues, 'are wearing ridiculous shoes. Those heels are too high and I've been watching you hobble around in them all day. To be honest, I'm surprised you're not crippled.'

'I'm fine.' My tone is a little stiff. I've observed him floating around the wedding talking to women all day and have hated the jealous twinges I've felt. 'I can take the pain.' I add, 'To be honest, I'm too scared of what Chloe might do if I take them off.'

He throws back his head, laughing, and I notice how tanned and muscular his throat is, and how broad his shoulders.

'Yeah, right.' He grins. 'Come on, time to take them off.'

'What? No!' Looking around at the other wedding guests,

who are swaying to the music, I see none of them are shoeless. 'I can deal with a pair of heels, for God's sake.'

'Hah! Not if your expression is anything to go by,' he jokes, before bending over and grabbing my ankle. 'Deal with it, it's happening.'

As I squeak in protest, hanging onto him for balance to stop myself falling over, he slides first one shoe off, then the other. 'Jake, my feet!'

Throwing the strappy heels aside under a nearby table, he grabs me around the waist. 'Relax, we're just dancing barefoot in the grass. Well, you are anyway. But just in case you're worried about your poor little feet, here. Is this better?' Dragging me close, he stands me on his shoes so our bodies are pressed together. When he shifts, I shift. There's nowhere for me to go when he's holding me so tightly. I have to admit, my poor crushed toes feel better already.

But, bracing myself, I try to push away. Whatever El said earlier, whatever I've been thinking, I'm not ready for this.

'Where are you going? Just relax.' Pressing a tender kiss to my forehead, he loosens his grip a little and sways to the music. The band have just broken into an acoustic rendition of John Mayer's version of 'Free Fallin'', the singer's voice smooth and melodic. I can't help it, my hands uncurl on Jake's shoulders, and I lean into him. Letting him lead, holding me tight.

'My dad used to do this when I was little,' I whisper, 'before Mum left. At weddings, parties, and stuff.' Pausing, I gulp. 'We never really danced after that. Once she was gone, I guess he didn't feel like dancing.'

Jake says nothing, just pulls me closer, and I lay my head against his heart. The picturesque lake beside us is tranquil despite the noise of the wedding, and the mountains circling it stand shoulder to shoulder as if protecting us from the outside world. Above us, the sky stretches upwards and outwards for ever, a deep velvet navy with pinpricks of light from a glittery scattering of stars. It's beautiful, idyllic, and reminds me of the wonderland under my bed from all those years ago, the one I stuck day-glow stars on to keep me company and let me live in another place, just for a bit. The creation did the same for Jake. It also reminds me of the starry sky that night above Durdle Door when I saved the life of the boy who's turned into the man holding me. Could a shared history as friends, I wonder blearily, fuzzy with alcohol, turn into a joint future as something more?

As the tension leaves my body, ebbing away like a low tide, I sigh, and start to notice that as well as a sense of peace, I also feel aware and on edge. Energised. Just as I'm starting to think too much about it, along with the way Jake's hands feel resting on my hips, the song reaches its peak and he spins me around, finishing by dipping me backward, low over his arm. My back's arched in a curve with my pale hair streaming down towards the grass, and if he let me go now, I'd be in trouble – or at least, lying in an undignified heap. Staring down at me, his eyes soft, he strokes my cheek with his forefinger, drawing an invisible line down it. The touch makes my skin feel scorched. We're so close. I feel safe and, at the same time, like I'm in danger.

'Leila,' he whispers.

I can see from his gaze that Eloise is right; he wants something more. We're having a moment. I can't deny it, but I'm breathless and confused. As he rights us again, I step backwards off his feet deliberately, placing a hand on his chest to create some space between us. His shirt is crisp under my fingers and he smells amazing. But this is Jake. *Jake*. I shake it off, too afraid to make the leap. If I mess this up, it will be another person who leaves me. I can't risk losing his friendship. I won't.

'No, Jake. It's just the drink and the atmosphere. It's a wedding. You're the best man, and you're supposed to pull a bridesmaid.'

'It's not that.' He shakes his head. 'It's more, and you know it.'

'No. I—' Overhead, a purple firework blooms in the sky with a bang and a sizzle, cutting off my words. I gaze upwards. *Boom, boom, boom*. In quick succession, the fireworks launch and explode, lighting up the celebrations. When there's a brief pause between them, I glance at Jake to find him watching my face rather than the dazzling display.

'I'm sorry,' I say. 'I just need things to be ... as they are. I'm not ... I mean, I can't ...' I bite my lip. 'Shit! I can't deal with change right now.'

Hands moving to grasp my elbows, he steps closer. 'Leila,' he whispers urgently, his warm breath fanning my face as fireworks start whizzing overhead again, 'the only constant in life is change. You can't control it. Nothing is ever certain. *Nothing*. And it's only what we do when we're faced with that fact that makes us who we are.'

His beautiful impassioned words get to me. But I'm resentful, scared. Even despite the amazing experience we had in the mountains this morning, when the peace touched me at my core. Fire spits out to cover my vulnerability. 'Maybe I don't share your optimistic view of the world, or believe in happy ever afters. You know me, how floaty and unreliable I am.' I break my arms free, knowing the alcohol is clouding my judgement and unleashing a torrent of emotion. 'Perhaps I'm meant to be alone,' I cry.

He stares at me, struck by my aggressive defence. 'I don't know what to say to you any more, Jones.' Stepping backwards, he shakes his head, looking defeated and leaving me cold. 'I need another drink.'

'Yes, that's it,' I lash out at how easily he's been pushed away. 'Hit the bottle like your dad. That'll help.'

He flinches. 'Not cool, Jones. Not cool at all.' His censure is almost more than I can bear, and I feel horrible. 'Unlike him, I can handle my drink,' Jake remarks. 'Can you?'

Shame burns through me as he strides away. I stand, barefoot in the crisp green grass, arms wrapped around myself, watching as he goes.

***

It's past midnight when I stumble up the concrete stairs to the main entrance of the hotel. After my blow-out with Jake, I found my friends, determined to shake off his words and have fun. We danced and drank some more, Jonny laughingly swinging me around to a *Dirty Dancing* song, and all the bridesmaids linked in a circle around Chloe, then pumping our fists to a Beyoncé tune after the swing-band had finished and the DJ came on. The bride forgot to throw her bouquet until the end of the night, and then tossed it from the arbour in an alcoholic haze. We all jumped to catch it but she miscalculated and it sailed over our heads, into the lake.

'Noooo!' Chloe cried, almost bursting into tears at the loss of such lovely flowers.

Owen came running over, comforting her with hugs and kisses, telling her it didn't matter. When he saw her distraught drunken face, he rolled up his trousers and waded into the water to retrieve it, much to everyone's entertainment. I caught sight of Jake watching, a smile on his face, ready to get in and help if required. He didn't turn my way once.

'My hero.' Chloe threw her arms around her new husband as he triumphantly brought the flowers back to her.

'My princess.' He kissed her nose as she put them down on the concrete floor, promptly forgetting about them when the DJ started playing Avicii.

Blowing out a breath as I arrive on the terrace, I pause to take in the moon over the lake one last time. It's been a brilliant day and I'm so lucky Jake was able to bring me here, no matter what's happened between us tonight.

'Is your carriage about to turn back into a pumpkin?' he asks, stepping out of the shadows.

'Oh!' I jump. 'Jake. I thought you went up to bed a while ago.'

'I wasn't ready for the night to be over yet.'

Approaching him, I touch his arm. His skin is warm, sleeves

still rolled up in the heat, and his jacket thrown over the balustrade. 'I'm sorry about earlier.' I force myself to look into his eyes. 'I shouldn't have said that about your dad. Are you okay?'

'I'm tired of talking.' Wrapping an around my waist, he brings me in close, gaze on my mouth. I can feel the heat of his hard body burning through my thin dress. 'Come on, Leila Jones, make my day.'

'Only your day?' I can barely get the words out.

'My week, my month, my year,' he says gravely.

Lust pulses through me, and my lips move nearer to his.

'You'll have to kiss me this time.' His breath is warm on my mouth and does funny things to my stomach. 'I'm not making that mistake again. Go on, do it. I dare you.' There's a gleam in his eyes.

I plant both hands on his chest, all my insecurities and fears rising up between us. 'It's just a game? Because I rejected you that time?' Breaking free, I back away from him. 'You're obviously only trying it on because you've had too much to drink. I'm the girl you came with and you're single. Or is it the bridesmaid thing after all? Quick, Shell might still be down there.' I point to the lawn, where fairy lights are still twinkling, and music is pounding.

His mouth drops open, and I don't think he's faking the astonishment on his face. 'How can you say that?' His tone is one of disbelief. 'For over twelve years, I've been— Oh, forget it. I'm *done*.' Storming from the terrace, he slams through the glass doors and is gone in an instant.

I stand staring after him, a leaden feeling in my chest,

knowing I've pushed him too far. I also know I was right: the risk of losing his friendship is too great. Because if this is how awful I feel watching him walk away from me when we've not even kissed properly, imagine how devastated I'd be watching him walk away if we were a couple.

***

At breakfast the following morning everyone is rowdy, high on talk of the wedding before Owen and Chloe depart for their honeymoon in Nice. In contrast I'm subdued, staring down at the food, which feels like hamster-cage bedding in my mouth.

I was hoping Jake would ask me to drive back to England with him so we could talk and make sense of what happened last night – God, we were both so drunk – but when I asked after him at reception a few minutes ago, the petite French woman said he checked out early this morning. Racing to the car park, I was deflated to see the BMW gone.

'Are you okay?' Chloe stops by our table, wearing tight jeans and a vest top with *The New Mrs Plaitford* emblazoned in diamanté. 'You look a bit pale. Well, paler than usual.'

Forcing a smile, I nod. 'Yeah, all good. Shell and I are heading off to the airport after lunch.' The fog's cleared, so the return flights we originally booked are taking off this afternoon. 'Yesterday was such an amazing day. I can't wait to see the professional photographs. I was having such a good time I didn't take any.' For me, that's when you really know an event has been good, when you're so caught up with it, in living it, you forget to take your phone out and post all over social media. I know Jake would say the same. It bothers me I know that about him, how these thoughts slip into my mind so readily.

'Me too. We'll see you guys when we get back. I'm hoping we'll have the photographer's photos by then. Are you coming out front to see us off?'

'Absolutely.' Shell and I stand, while Eloise stays sitting down, cradling her head in her hands, badly hung over. Jonny's rubbing her back and she keeps snapping at him to get off her. 'Come on, El.'

Groaning, she gets to her feet, swaying. 'Why did I drink so much?'

'Because you were at our wedding,' Chloe says with glee, squeezing Owen's hand.

Owen just smiles, his gaze resting on my face. I wonder if he knows what happened between me and Jake, and I wince. Does he blame me for driving his best man away? Or maybe that's egotistical of me. Jake said he was planning to drive the whole way back in one go, so perhaps it was always his plan to leave early. Still, he'd mentioned leaving tomorrow, not today.

'Come on, ladies,' Chloe prompts as Amanda walks over to us. 'Time to say goodbye.'

***

The day after we get back from the wedding, I go to Jake's door and press on the bell with insistent buzzes. He doesn't answer. The hire car isn't there, and his mum doesn't seem to be either. I return later that evening and try again with no success.

Texting him, I get no reply.

It feels weird returning to real life – the wedding and everything that happened in Annecy feels like a faded dream. But I go into the spare room and start a painting of the chateau by the lake in bold acrylics, and when I close my eyes the scene is vivid behind my lids: the rolling manicured gardens with perfectly trimmed trees, the sparkling lake, the gorgeous hotel next to the shoreline.

Alongside that, I begin a sketch of the mountains where we stopped along the way, wishing I had the picture of Jake and me together at the viewing point. But it's on his phone, not mine.

The following morning, I wander up his front path and shove an envelope through the letterbox. It contains a wodge of bank notes for fuel, and a post-it.

Thanks for taking me. I had fun, even if you no longer feel the same. Jones x

I'm on proverbial tenterhooks for the next few days, expecting him to text or call me, or knock on the door for a chat. Something. *Anything.* I have a weird anxious feeling in my stomach that won't go away, like an itch begging to be scratched, and I can't stop thinking about Jake. Lying in bed at night trying to read, failing with every turn of the page, I wear his jumper, which no longer smells of him.

My mind keeps picking through memories of us together,

even when I don't want it to. I'll be musing over a completely different subject – hoping Chloe and Owen are having an amazing honeymoon, wondering what time Dad will be home for dinner, playing with Fleur – and I'll suddenly realise I've slipped back into thinking about Jake again.

About how handsome he looked in his suit, and how he made me feel when we danced barefoot on the grass together beside the lake, the way my head spun when he dipped me over beneath all the stars. The look on his face when I pushed him away, scared of losing him if things didn't work out.

Despite being away at sea all those years, he's always come back to me. Always. Is he going to this time?

I have the sickest feeling that I've made a huge mistake.

Then I catch sight of a photo on Facebook that someone posts of us at the wedding, dancing together on the jade-green grass, my small bare feet planted on his shoes, his arms holding me tight. His face is full of joy and my grey eyes are soft as I gaze up at him.

The sick feeling surges through me again, stronger this time. I run to the window and push aside the curtain, craning my head to stare down the street at his house. But his car still isn't there. I go to bed with a sense of gnawing frustration and unease.

The next evening, when I get in from a hot, sticky day at the gallery, I pick up a heap of letters Dad's stacked on the bookcase. One of them is the envelope full of money, and with it there's a handwritten note.

Thanks, but no thanks. And this is for you. J

Inside is a charm for my bracelet, a heart in the design of the French tricolour flag to honour our trip together. I'm touched. Then fear trickles into my veins as I notice the lack of kisses on the note, and the curtness of his words. Shivers run along my skin as I recall his words that night at the wedding, *I'm done*. Is the charm a parting gift?

The thought makes me gasp. It terrifies me so much logic flies out the window and emotion takes over. Without pausing to rationalise, I race out of the house and down the garden path, then along the short bit of pavement separating our homes.

I bang on his front door, and when he opens it, surprise fills his face. Before he can say anything, I jump up into his arms and wrap my legs around his waist. Grabbing his face between my hands, I give him the hot passionate kiss he's been waiting for.

As scared as I am of losing his friendship, and as fearful as I am of things not working out, I have to take the chance. I can't let him slip away without trying. Without knowing.

I kiss him deeply, revelling in his touch, and realise that *nothing* has ever felt so right.

Jake

June 2014

The Painter's Palette Charm

When Leila shows up at his door and leaps into his arms, Jake is shocked. But he soon loses himself in her touch. In the feel of her soft lips against his mouth, demanding his total attention as her tongue seeks his. In the weight of her slight body as she curls herself around him, like she can't get close enough. The scent of strawberries fills his nose as the waterfall of her hair swings around their faces. His stomach dips when her thighs tighten around his hips, her fingers curling into his thick dark hair to bring him nearer, consuming him. Her pert breasts are mashed against his chest and he can barely breathe. Not because she's crushing his lungs, but because he's been waiting so long for this, too long. It's overwhelming. Years of waiting, and the moment is finally here. This is it. He's kissing her, *kissing Leila.*

Adrenaline surges through him as their kiss deepens. Stepping backwards, he kicks the front door shut behind her, sinking down onto the bottom step of the stairs, shifting her legs so she's straddling him. His eyes slide closed. For a while he loses himself in her again, in the heat of her body and the way she moans when he bites her bottom lip. Wrapping his arms tighter around her, his hands sweep down her back to curl over her narrow hips. When she moans again, he tears his mouth away, breathing heavily.

She stares down at him, moving her hands to cup his jaw, stroking his stubble. Her mouth is a deep, dark red, cheeks flushed, eyelids heavy. She traces the scar above his lip with a tender finger. 'This is so sexy.'

There's another funny dip in his stomach at her words. His whole life feeling self-conscious about his scar, of trying to ignore people staring at it, and she likes it. A tiny bit of the weight he's always carried on his shoulders slips away.

She frowns when he doesn't say anything. 'Why are you stopping?' she whispers. 'Isn't this what you want? I thought—'

'Don't!' He tightens his grip as she tries to move away. 'Of course it is,' he rushes on. 'You must know by now ...' He gulps as she shifts on his lap and brushes against him. 'I want this. I want you. But what do you want? Why are you here, Jones, and doing this? Are you just feeling bad about how we left things?' He keeps his arms around her to show how much he wants her here, with him.

Her grey eyes meet his. They're clear and honest. 'I do feel bad about how we left things,' she says slowly, 'and I'm sorry about the night of the wedding. I'm also sorry that you left without saying anything the next morning.' When he goes to reply she places a finger against his lips to quieten him. 'I'm sorry if I upset you,' she says in a soft voice. 'Your friendship means a lot to me.'

'Oh.' He jerks his head away from her touch and braces himself to untangle their bodies. He can't do this. It's too difficult.

She sees his intention and leans forward to pin him down with her weight, clamping one arm around the railing of the stairs so he can't move her. 'Wait! I don't want to lose your friendship, that's true. But I've realised something important over the last few days.'

'Which is?'

Her breath's warm on his cheek, her expression both tender and scared at the same time. 'I miss you when you're gone. You make me feel like no one else does. You've always been there for me, even when I was being a pain in the arse. I want more. I want this.' She kisses him gently. 'It scares the shit out of me,' she admits, 'but I want *you*, Jake. I've made the choice to come to you. *I've* kissed *you*, just like you asked me to.'

'Finally.'

'Yes. Sorry I took so long.' Even on such a serious subject, she looks impish, eyes dancing. She looks happy, at ease, but at the same time, surprised to feel that way.

'There's nothing to be scared of,' he says in a fierce voice, 'it's just me. It's just *us*. I know it's a risk, but you need to trust me, and yourself.'

She nods, hesitating. 'I think I can do that. At least, I can try.'

At her words, his body surges and he makes a muffled sound against her collarbone, planting a kiss on the soft skin there.

She groans, but looks down at him intently. 'I'm trusting you not to hurt me. Not to leave me, Jake.'

301

'Never.' Seeing her so vulnerable makes him ache for the hole her mum has left in her life, and in her heart. With time, he hopes he can show her that not everyone walks away. Bending his head, he kisses her neck once more.

She groans again, then suddenly giggles. 'God, please tell me your mum's not here!'

He shouts out a laugh and raises his eyes to meet hers. 'No, she's away for the day with a friend. She has those now –' he nods '– partially thanks to you.'

'I'm glad.' Then her expression changes. 'So, are you going to make my day, Jake Harding –' she echoes his own words from the wedding back at him as she runs her hands along his broad shoulders, grinning '– and take me to bed?'

He returns the grin. 'Try and stop me.'

***

It's nothing like he imagined, nothing like he planned. Instead of slow and tender, of taking the time to explore each other's bodies once they're alone in his room, of working out how to please each other, of him showing her how much she means to him, it's the opposite. It's impatient and instinctive, like they've been together for years and know exactly what to do. Their clothes get stripped away and thrown to the floor. She pins him against the door, surprisingly rough, her hands on his broad, hairy chest, eyes widening as she sees him naked for the first time. She kisses and touches him like she can't wait for the next moment. Like she's been waiting as long as he has and can't wait any longer. He runs his hands through

302

her gorgeous hair and then wraps it around one fist, pinning her head back so he can kiss her throat then devour her mouth. She moans and grinds herself against him, so he releases her hair, picks her up and throws her on the bed, almost stumbling over his own feet. He's strong, but she makes him feel weak.

When he joins her on the mattress, she pulls his body down between her thighs, thrusting her bare breasts towards him. He drops his head to pull her sensitive skin into his mouth. She wraps her arms around his head and her hips pulse against his.

'*Jake*,' she says in a strained voice.

'You're absolutely beautiful.' He lifts his head to stare into her dark grey eyes. 'You do know that?' He curves a hand over her cheekbone and then along her neck and down her body, ending by curling it around her hip to draw her closer. His index finger traces the small burn on her lower back, wondering again what happened to put it there.

She wriggles slightly to dislodge his hand. 'I do feel beautiful now.' Her eyes gleam. 'And you are too.'

He shakes his head at her words, but smiles. It's the only pause, the only slow beat before they're tangling themselves around each other again, rolling on the bed and kissing, touching, groaning. They can't get close enough. They're desperate for each other, and as he drives himself into her and her nails bite into his shoulders, she moans. It's a sound of passion, of pleasure, and he loses himself in her again.

***

Afterwards, she's quiet and he's drowsy. He's hardly slept over the past few nights and tiredness slams into him. The release of adrenaline and happiness has drained his tension away. Still, he needs to stay awake to be with her. She's not helping, fluttering her fingers gently over his chest in little patterns as he lies on his side facing her, watching her despite his heavy eyelids. The sheet is around their hips and he loves being naked with her. It feels so right.

'What happened to my doors?' she says after a while, gesturing to the magnolia walls.

'My father painted over them one day, when he realised how much I liked them.'

'Oh. Sorry,' she answers in a small voice. 'And where did you go after the wedding? You didn't come straight home.'

'Wasn't safe to drive that day,' he mumbles, 'so I found somewhere to pull over and slept a few hours. Then I decided to spend some time driving back slowly through Europe.'

'I knew it.' She pauses, then, her voice rising, 'You went back through the mountains?'

'Not without you.' He opens one eye to squint at her.

Her pale silky hair is spread in a tangle over her shoulders and slithers down over her body almost to her waist. Her chest is flushed a deep rosy pink and her bottom lip appears bruised. She looks gloriously happy.

'Stop staring at me like that,' she murmurs, while gazing at his ridged stomach. 'It's my turn to look at you.'

'I can't help it,' he whispers, 'you're so lovely.'

Leaning forward, she kisses him before drawing back. 'Is it weird, that this doesn't feel weird?'

He huffs out a laugh, drowsiness still trying to drag him down. 'Not for me. I always knew we'd be good together. It just took you a while to work it out.'

She snorts. 'You're not kidding. To think of all those losers I dated.' She rolls her eyes, tone playful. 'And all this time, I could have been in bed with you.'

He can see what she's doing, trying to make light of the situation, unsure what happens next, uncertain as to what this means. He goes to tell her, to make it clear what he wants – more of this, a future together – but she grabs his shoulder and rolls him over so he's lying on his front.

'I caught sight of something earlier—' Her voice catches as she sees the black ink covering his left shoulder blade and muscular upper back, 'Oh, Jake. Wow. I didn't know you had a tattoo.' Her fingers stroke over his skin, tracing the map of the world laid out in a flat image like the open pages of an old-fashioned geography book, so you can see every country and continent. 'The calligraphy is amazing. You have stars. I have them in my tattoo as well, on my hand. But mine are outlines instead of filled in. What do yours mean? Wait, are they—'

'Everywhere I've ever visited,' he murmurs, burying his face in the pillow.

'Yes, I recognise some from the postcards. You've been to so many places.' Her index finger touches each star in turn, wonder in her voice.

'I told myself I wanted to see the world, and travelling with the Navy was great, but really I was looking for a home,' he says drowsily. 'It took me a long time to realise it was the one I left behind.'

'And you're definitely here to stay now?' Her voice quivers as her finger presses on a particular point which he knows is the slightly larger star marking out Bournemouth. 'You're doing the PT qualification?'

'Yes ...' His voice drifts off. 'Yes, definitely.'

'Good.' She places a kiss on his shoulder. He smiles, hardly able to believe it's Leila doing it. How did he get so lucky?

Moving to lie down next to him, she snuggles into the warmth of his body. After a few minutes of silent contentment, she whispers, 'Thank you, by the way.'

'For what?' His eyes are closed. He's fighting sleep, half in the land of the living and half in the land of dreams.

'My French flag charm.'

He senses rather than sees her lift her arm to look at the bracelet. There's motion and sound as she plays with the charms. 'S'okay,' he mumbles, unable to fight any more. He always could sleep anywhere and anytime when he was in the Navy. It was a useful skill when he needed rest, but now it's about to undo him. As he slides away, he hears himself whisper, 'But of all the ones I've bought you, it's not my favourite. The sea charm is, with the blue gem in it.'

'What?'

'What?' His eyes fly open and he sits up, yanked from the beginnings of unconsciousness.

They stare at each other and he winces. Her normally pale skin is snow white, her grey eyes so dark they're almost black.

'What do you mean, *of all the ones you've bought me*? And about the sea charm? That's from Mum.' Her voice is icy, and a chill runs down Jake's spine. She pulls the sheet across her body to cover her nakedness.

What had he said, something about his favourite charm? He struggles to make sense of it. He's so tired and blurry.

'Jake?' Standing up, she whips the sheet off him and wraps it around her, leaving him lying there cold. 'Of all the charms you've bought me? You've only bought me the book one when you returned *Pandora* and the rainbow one after I lost the baby. You helped pick out the music charm for my birthday at the Coldplay concert, but you didn't buy that for me alone. But you mentioned the sea one, with the blue gem.' Holding up her wrist, she yanks the bracelet around to stare at the charm in question. It's the first time he's ever seen her be rough with it. 'This one arrived like the others,' she says in a shaking voice, 'in an envelope with a typed address, or an L on the front.'

Jake doesn't know what to do, what to say. He rubs his hands over his face and shakes his head to clear his foggy brain. Shit. Not now, not like this.

'Tell me,' she demands, her voice trembling, 'right now. Don't you dare lie to me.'

'I won't,' he says, 'I wouldn't. I always meant to tell you, but I was finding the right way, the right time. I did try a few times, when we were younger.'

'Tell me what?' She shivers, teeth chattering even though it's summer and the room is warm. From the expression on her face she knows what's coming.

He clears his throat and looks her straight in the eye. She deserves that. 'I bought all of your charms and sent them to

307

you, Leila. Apart from the heart one that came with the bracelet from your mum.'

'None of them were from her?' She is immobile. 'She never sent any of those?'

'No. I'm sorry.' He pushes himself off the bed to go to her, but she stops him with a warning glower.

'All this time, I thought she was thinking of me, that she'd somehow found a way to know what was going on in my life, and the charms were her way of showing me that. Like little messages.' She says it through dry lips, her voice rising. 'I thought she loved me. That she hadn't forgotten me after all.' Then she unfreezes, lifting her arm again and staring at the bracelet like it's a foreign object, rather than a part of her. 'Noooo ...' she wails, before crumpling to the floor. Breaking into loud sobs, she wraps her arms around herself.

Jake stares, horrified. Leaping off the bed, he tries to scoop her up into his arms, but she erupts in fury. 'Get off! Don't fucking touch me!' she screams. 'You tricked me! All this time I thought it was her, that she and I were connected.' She scrambles up, rushing over to her clothes and yanking them on, knickers shoved into her pocket, her top pulled on without a bra. 'But we weren't. It was never her.' Tears roll down her face. 'It was just you. How could you betray me like that, when you must have known how much it meant to me? What was it, some twisted way of trying to get close to me?'

'What?' Glancing around, he grabs his boxers and fumbles them on. 'No! How can you say that? Don't try and twist something beautiful and well-intended into something ugly.'

But she looks devastated and he can tell she's not really

listening. 'I've always cared for you, and when I started sending them, I just wanted to make you smile,' he explains. 'I could tell how much you liked your bracelet, so I wanted to make you happy by filling it. I wanted to thank you too. For giving me hope and helping me.' She backs away towards the door and he follows her, knowing he's losing her. 'Then as we got older, it meant more, but when you talked about your mum sending the charms and I twigged what was going on, I didn't want to upset you. I knew it might break your heart. It was too late to say anything. So, I thought it was kinder to—'

'To let me believe she was thinking of me all those years, even if she couldn't be bothered to come back?' she sobs. 'You never should have given me false hope!' Reaching behind her, she twists the door knob, yanks open the door and flees the room.

Dumbfounded but giving chase, Jake thunders down the stairs behind her, intent on making her listen to everything he has to say. She has to understand what he did and why.

She's thrusting her feet into her shoes and reaching for the front door latch.

'Leila.' He tries to remain calm, calling on years of training to slow his breathing and heart rate. It's difficult where she's concerned – his emotions always get the better of him. 'Wait. You've got to believe me. I just wanted to do a good thing. Besides, isn't it better to have some hope, rather than none at all?'

'No, Jake, it isn't.' Her face screws up, tears coursing down her blotchy cheeks. 'Not when you haven't got a fighting chance of your dream ever coming true.' She flings open the door.

'Besides, this wasn't just about helping me, was it? You've admitted it was something you did for *you*, to thank me. And don't try and deny there wasn't an ulterior motive, that you didn't ever imagine a scenario where you told me you'd bought all the charms and I flung myself at you, exclaiming how romantic it was you'd been sending me the charms all this time.'

Jake winced, and opened his mouth ready to deny it, but couldn't. He was only human. He'd thought about it, and during all those years at sea away from her he'd been comforted by the thought of her wearing the bracelet, of them being connected. Still ... 'It wasn't like that, I swear.'

'I don't want to hear it.' She barges through the doorway and onto the sunny path. As she turns to face him, the sunlight catches her silvery blonde hair and sets it on fire. As she slips through his fingers, she's more beautiful than ever.

'Wait.' He follows her out, uncaring that the neighbourhood can see him in his underwear. 'I'm sorry, Leila. I never meant to hurt you.'

'It's Jones to you. Actually, it's nothing,' she spits. 'It's too late.' She pauses on an indrawn breath, her eyes furious. 'Goodbye, Harding.'

With that, she turns and runs away. Jake watches her go, knowing she's too full of rage and shock to reason with. Terrified that after the magical hour in bed together, he may never get the chance to hold her again.

***

The days drag. He misses her, but while he knows he might've got it wrong, that he should have told her about the charms sooner and not let it go on so long, he also knows it's too soon to go to her. He also thinks she's in the wrong as well, and he's sick of their relationship being so one-sided. He loves her but she needs to grow up. It's true he upset her and if he could have a do-over and tell her when they were teenagers, he would. Yet she acted like he's committed murder, or ripped her heart out. But perhaps in her eyes he has. Still, maybe she needs to come to him this time. Jake fears he might be waiting for ever.

He throws himself into his PT qualification, spending hours poring over the workbooks and studying the course material, putting together his portfolio and training for the assessment days.

A week passes and Leila doesn't make contact. In the second week, while he's out on a run one morning with his earbuds in, she passes in her car on the way to work. She must know it's him because her face is turned resolutely away. He sighs, beginning to lose hope. Maybe his pride is getting in the way. Maybe he should go and apologise again.

But that night he hears something in the front garden. When he rushes to the door, his mum is standing there with a confused look on her face, staring down at a bundle of dark material on their doorstep. Bending over, she picks it up and shakes it out. His navy jumper, one he hasn't seen since Christmas a year and a half ago, unfurls.

'Yours?' she asks dryly, raising an eyebrow.

Since she's been alone without the shadow of his father

standing over them, gone is the meek woman she used to be. In her place is someone who meets your eyes when she talks to you. Standing in front of him is someone who has redis-covered life. Whatever happens between him and Leila, he'll always be grateful for the gift she gave his mum. One he could never manage. Freedom. Jake sometimes wonders where his father is and what he's doing, but he doesn't think he'll come back and that's enough for him.

'Yeah, it's mine.' Taking the jumper from her, the scent of strawberries floats up, and he smiles. He should probably be worried Leila's returned it, as if she's cutting ties. But instead he focuses on the fact she kept it for eighteen months, even though she denied having it last summer. He also muses over the fact she could have taken all his charms off the bracelet and returned them too, but hasn't. At least, not yet. He frowns. 'What do I do, Mum?' He's told her about them sleeping together, about his stupidity and the argument. How badly Leila reacted.

Closing the door, she motions with her chin toward the kitchen. He trails after her as she walks down the hallway. When she gets there, she opens the fridge and takes out two long-necked bottles of beer. After twisting both caps off, she hands one to him. 'Well, first you have a drink.'

'And then what?'

'Then you remind yourself you have a good heart, and that she'll calm down eventually. Yes, you let it slip in an unfortu-nate way, and far too late, but you meant well. God, what that girl has put you through.' Shaking her head, she looks trou-bled. 'You've always been so patient with her. When I think of everything you've done for her—'

'She's done things for me too,' he jumps in. 'Including helping you ... And she was the one who painted all those amazing doors in my room, before Dad ... before *he* painted over them. The point is—'

'The point is that you love her.' His mum smiles.

'Yeah.' He runs his hand through his hair. 'She's it. She's the one.'

'Then you'll have to be patient. Although perhaps it wouldn't hurt to say sorry again.'

He hesitates. 'I feel like I need to make a grand gesture.'

'No. Don't do anything big. The best thing you can do now is be honest. Just talk to her. That's all. Give her a bit longer though. She's upset about her mum but I'm sure she'll come around.'

***

Another busy week passes, and Jake decides it's time. There's been nothing since the jumper, and he's yearning to see her, even if it's just her shouting at him again. As he knocks on her front door, he's uncharacteristically nervous. It swings open, and her dad's standing there.

'Hi, Henry. Is Jones— I mean, Leila here?' He feels like the kid he used to be, asking if his friend can come out to play.

The man looks at Jake sympathetically. 'She is ... but I'm not sure what reception you'll get. She's calmed down, but I'm not sure she's ready to talk yet.'

Leila's told her dad what happened. He grimaces. 'I never meant to hurt her.'

Henry surprises him by laying a hand on his shoulder. 'I

know.' Sighing heavily, he says, 'I always knew it wasn't Amelia sending the charms. Ray told me, but I didn't have the heart to tell Leila either. I didn't want her to be any angrier or more disappointed than she already was, especially after what happened when she was thirteen. She always seemed so happy when the charms arrived. I didn't want to spoil that. So, this is my fault too.'

The two men exchange a look, and Jake shakes his head. 'What *did* happen when she was thirteen? Is it anything to do with that scar on her back?'

Henry looks shocked. 'She's never told you?' His brows draw together. 'Too ashamed, I guess. The guilt's still there, I can tell, and I often wonder if the reason she seems to feel she doesn't deserve happiness is because of that.'

'Doesn't deserve happiness?'

Henry sighs again, 'Look, Jake. She needs to tell you herself. For the record, she's lucky to have you, and I've told her that. I know you sent those charms because you care. She's my daughter and I love her, but she needs to learn to see things from other people's points of view.'

Jake feels a lump fill his throat, and nods in gratitude at the older man.

Fleur trots up, and seeing who's visiting, wags her tail and starts panting. Her pink tongue lolls out of her mouth as she doggy grins at him. As Henry steps back into the hallway to invite him in, Fleur immediately jumps into Jake's arms and licks his chin. 'Thanks,' he says, 'I think.' He imagines if Leila was down here to see this, she'd be shaking her head at the dog and muttering *traitor* under her breath. The thought makes him smile. Setting Fleur down and taking his trainers off, he asks where Leila is.

'Spare room. Painting.' Henry answers, reaching for the lead hanging on a wall hook. 'Come on, Fleur. Walkies.' Winking at Jake, he pushes his feet into walking boots and grabs some keys off the sideboard.

'Thank you.' As the front door closes behind Henry and Fleur, Jake takes the stairs two at a time and strides towards the box room next to Leila's bedroom. When he pushes open the door, the breath leaves him. He stands in the doorway, stunned.

Leila spins around, her gaze unfocused before it sharpens on him. 'Jake!' She's flustered, eyes widening. 'What are you doing here?'

Moving fast, she puts her body between him and the painted wall behind her, arms outstretched to hide it. He steps to the side, and she matches him, trying to block his view. But he's taller and sees it spread out in the way she must visualise it in her head.

'It's us,' he says in awe. 'The party. The night you ...' His voice trails off. It's all there. The vast night sky dotted with stars, the rocky outcrop of Durdle Door archway stretching into the sea, the multi-hued shingle on their favourite beach. The sea, the shining moon hanging above its surface. The curve and sweep of the chalk cliffs. The only thing missing is the other teenagers who were there that night. It's just the two of them in the sprawling image covering almost a whole wall.

She's painted him struggling in the dense blue-grey sea,

one arm above his head reaching for the sky. His scar is tiny but noticeable, and she's captured his black hair and mismatched eyes perfectly. One green, one brown, and the right way around. She's holding him with an arm around his shoulders, and is a glowing mermaid with an iridescent scale-covered tail and seashells covering her breasts. She's swimming on her side and he can see Leila's painted her own scar on her back, in the same shade as his. She's added glitter to her long pale hair and there's a small smile on her red lips.

'You weren't meant to see this. It's not for you.' She flaps her hands, but he just captures one and holds it tightly, turning to her.

'The hell it isn't. It's amazing. Thank you.'

She blushes. 'I don't know what you're thanking me for. I've just said, I didn't paint it for you.'

'Thank you anyway.' He looks down at their joined fingers and strokes the stars and swirls tattoo on the back of her hand. 'And I'm sorry. For not telling you about the charms sooner.' Gazing into her eyes, he sees a softening there, and lifts her hand to his mouth. Kissing it, he adds, 'I got it wrong.'

'Yes, you did.' Sliding her hands away, she lowers her head, her voice quiet. 'Can you go, please?'

His stomach pitches and he feels sick. Lowering his voice, he asks, 'You really want me to leave? After this? I know you're angry but—'

'Angry isn't the right word any more,' she says, backing away, 'now it's disappointed, or sad. I feel like you've stolen something precious from me. Something I can never get back.' Her voice hitches.

'It's not me who took your mum away from you, Jones. She did that all on her own. I haven't stolen anything from you.' Now it's his heart that hurts. He can feel it thudding and tearing apart in his chest. 'I've given you *everything*.' Spinning around, he leaves the room. She calls his name as he thunders down the stairs, but he doesn't stop.

***

As he strides along the pavement, he hears footsteps racing up behind him. He doesn't wait, just keeps going. 'Jake!' Leila's hand wraps around his arm, pulling him to a stop. She's out of breath as he turns to her. Her cheeks are flushed, her expression panicked.

'What?' he asks.

'I'm sorry. I was just so flustered about you seeing the painting. I hadn't planned to show it to you. I also wasn't ready to see you yet.'

'Yet? So, you were thinking about seeing me?'

'I just needed a bit more time.'

'What's going on out here?' His mum throws open the door and stares at them both. 'Hello.' Maggie raises both eyebrows at Leila. 'I see you haven't taken it off.' Pointing at Leila's wrist.

'Mum ...'

'It's okay.' Leila tilts her chin up. 'Maybe she's entitled to give me a bit of a hard time. She is your mum after all, and she loves you.'

Jake's mum sighs, her face softening. 'You should speak inside. Come on.'

Leila glances at Jake, and he nods. They go into the house and through to the living room. After a moment, they hear rustling, a few footsteps and then a voice calls out, 'I'm going out. Talk. *Properly.*' The door slams shut behind Maggie as she leaves.

Jake's mouth curves.

'What are you smiling at?' Leila raises one eyebrow as she settles uneasily on the black sofa opposite where he's standing.

'Just thinking about how good both our parents are at making themselves scarce so we can be together.' He snorts. 'It would be easier if we moved out. Maybe we should do that and leave them in peace.'

'Hang on, we've only slept together once, and I'm still pissed off with you, and you want us to live together? You're racing ahead a bit.'

Jake stares at her. 'What?'

Leila blushes a deep red, 'Nothing.'

'No, wait.' He throws himself onto the sofa beside her. 'You thought I was suggesting we get our own place together?'

'No ...' She avoids his eye, staring over his right shoulder as if fascinated by something on the far wall.

He laughs. 'Jones, if I ever asked you to move in with me, it would be a better offer than that, and believe me, there would be no confusion.' She squirms but stays silent, her skin deepening from red to puce. 'But I take it as a good sign you thought that and haven't run screaming.' When she continues to avoid his gaze, he gently grabs her chin and forces her to look at him. Reluctantly, her grey eyes flit up to his. 'And you're pissed off with me now, rather than being the furious girl who ran out of here without any underwear on?'

'Jake!' She punches his shoulder but a smile tugs at her lips and her blush starts to fade. 'I'm not ready to joke about it yet.'

'Okay, sorry.' He drops his hand from her chin and slips his arm around her shoulders. 'But can we talk about it, please?'

'I've probably said enough,' she murmurs, but doesn't move away, 'judging by what everyone else has told me. But that comment I threw at you at the house was unfair,' she admits. 'You're right. I can't take my anger with her out on you. It's just the charms have always been such a huge part of who I am, and my relationship with Mum. Finding out they mostly came from you made me feel I was losing her all over again.' She gulps, tears misting her eyes. 'I reacted badly. I said some horrible things. I'm sorry. I know your heart was in the right place.' Placing her hand on his arm, she gazes at him, 'I ... I am glad that if they're not from Mum, they're from you. They mean a lot. My bracelet means a lot to me.'

'Thank you. I really was only trying to make you happy. But my timing was really bad. I didn't mean for it to happen that way, I was just half asleep and it slipped out. I hadn't slept properly for days because of how it was left between us at the wedding—'

'You were that upset about it?' Her eyebrows draw together and she drops her hand from his arm, shifting back to see his face better.

'Of course. I hated how we left it. You're my best friend.'

'I am?'

'You didn't know that?'

'You have lots of friends from the Marines, and you have Owen.'

'Owen is my best friend, in a blokey way. But I talk to you about stuff I've never shared with other people. You've seen the best and worst parts of me.' He shifts nearer, picking up her hand, the one with the stars and swirls on it. He rubs his thumb over the tattoo. 'When we're together I feel closer to you than I ever have to anyone else. And when we're apart I worry about you. I care about you, which is why when I was at sea, I sent texts and the postcards. I wanted you to know I was thinking about you. I told you in Germany, I just want you to be happy, Jones. It's why I sent you the charms.'

She leans in to him, watching him intently. 'So where does that leave us?'

'What do you mean?'

'You just want to be best friends? None of the, you know ...' She wiggles her eyebrows.

'Kissing?' he teases.

'Well, yes ...'

'I want to be with you, properly. Best friends should always be the basis for that.'

'It should?' Shaking her head. 'I feel like I'm being really dense.'

'You didn't feel that way about any of the guys you dated?' A nerve pulses in his cheek. 'That they were the person you wanted to spend the most time with? That you laughed with them no matter how shitty life was? That they got you like no one else did?'

'No. Never. It always felt so ... hard. Like I had to make such an effort. None of them really got it about my painting. You're the only one who's ever pushed me to pursue my passion.'

'Then let me show you how a proper relationship is supposed to be.' Dropping his head, he places a soft sweet kiss on her lips, and her head tilts back to return it. She reaches up to wrap her arms around his shoulders and their kiss quickens. She makes a sound deep in the back of her throat.

He pushes her back gently. 'Not so fast. I'm glad you've calmed down and have decided to forgive me, but I have a few questions.'

She huffs playfully but moves back to rest against the red scatter cushions. 'Such as?'

'Why weren't you going to show me that painting? *Our* painting?'

'It was painted just for me. I needed to let it out.'

'That's the only reason?'

'Yes.' She meets his gaze, but he feels like she's hiding something.

He decides not to push it. 'Okay.'

Her fingers squeeze his thigh and she kisses the corner of his mouth. 'I told El about us.'

'And what did she say?'

'Well, lots actually, especially after something she said to me at the wedding.' Leila rolls her eyes, lifting her hand from his thigh to tick items off on her fingers. 'She said, "Thank God." That it's always been there in the way you look at me, but I was blind to it. She thinks deep down I was aware of how you felt but wasn't ready for you. She told me that because of Mum leaving, and failed relationships, I've always been untrusting. Not just with men. She said I kept her at arm's length for a long time too and have a way of retreating into my own world, whether it's with a book, a sketchpad, or a canvas. I put barriers between myself and everyone else.'

'And what do you think of all that?'

'I was miffed with her for a while, but it was food for thought and I had to do some long hard thinking about myself. Then I realised she was right.' Blowing out a breath, she purses her lips. 'It's not been comfortable, I'll admit that.'

'What hasn't?'

'Having to acknowledge I'm a total idiot.'

He laughs, 'Well not a total one. Maybe just a little one.'

She flicks his arm then adds, 'I do need to work on my trust issues, and as Dad would say, try to spend more of my time in the real world.'

'Did your dad say anything else?' He hugs her, full of happiness.

'He told me I was stubborn, too stuck in my own way of looking at things, that I needed to accept – however hard it might be – that Mum might never come back. That I had to stop running away, and had I learnt nothing since I was thir-teen?' She glosses over the last bit, speaking fast. 'Above all, that I should be grateful you've always been there for me.'

'Aww, that's nice. Thanks, Henry.'

'He said one other thing, when I told him something had happened between us.'

'What was that?'

'"Well, it's about time."' Bringing his mouth down to meet hers, she murmurs against it, 'And now, I completely agree.'

His questions about her thirteenth year are swept away by her soft lips beneath his, and the warmth of her hands on his body.

***

Hours later, when they're lying in his bed curled around each other, Jake broaches a tricky subject. He knows he might be pushing his luck, but can't stop himself.

Propping himself up on one elbow, he strokes her face. 'So, I know this is going to be a sore spot for a while, but I kind of did something.'

Sitting up, she stares down at him. 'Jake, no. What now? What did you do?' Her expression's worried, as if the happiness of the last few hours might be snatched away. 'No more secrets, okay? Just honesty.'

'I bought you another charm,' he says sheepishly. 'I saw it and knew it was meant for you. Especially after our conversation on the way to Annecy about your mythical creature paintings. I was hoping to give it to you myself this time. No envelope, no mystery. Just something from me to you. Is that okay?'

Taking a deep breath, she lets it out slowly. 'That's a relief.' Nodding, she purses her lips. 'Okay. I'm going to be sad it's not from her, but I need to move on.'

'If you're ready.'

Pushing her hair behind one ear, she gulps. 'Not completely, but I'm trying. So yes, please, I'd like my charm.' She holds her left hand out politely like a child waiting for a present, the charms jingling on the bracelet around her wrist.

He reaches across to his nightstand and pulls out a small black box tied with a baby pink ribbon. Turning to her, he places it on her palm.

Untying the ribbon, she opens the gift. 'Oh, Jake,' she breathes, her grey eyes wide. Holding up the tiny charm, she smiles. It's a painter's palette with tiny coloured gems to denote the different shades of paint, with a little paintbrush sitting on top of it.

'You like it?'

'Yes. It's perfect.' Leaning forward, she kisses him hard before resting her forehead against his. 'Thank you.' There's an inflection on the last word, telling him she appreciates it coming from him directly, no pretence. Drawing back, she extends her arm. 'Put it on, please.'

Obeying happily, he finds an empty link and attaches the new charm to the bracelet. 'Promise me you're going to sell those paintings. You need to get serious about your art. It will make you happy. Or if not, at least you'll have tried.'

Her face is solemn. 'You'll be there to encourage and support me? To pick up the pieces if I fail?'

'Always. Just tell me what I need to do to help.'

'Then yes, I will. *Thank you.*' Linking her arms around his neck, she beams. 'This feels like a new beginning.'

'They're the best kind,' Jake says, grinning as he tumbles her onto the pillows.

Her expression turning serious, she stares up at him. Looks at her palette charm. Runs the fingers of her right hand across all the charms. 'You really get me,' she whispers, her tone full of wonder. More bravely, she asks, 'Do ... do you love me, Jake Harding?'

He stares at her in astonishment. 'Absolutely, Jones.' Stroking her hair away from her pink cheeks, he goes on, 'But, you know, not for that long. Only since you were about eleven. I remember thinking you looked like an angel on the day we met. And then I saw the magical doors and your wonderland under the bed and ... that was it, I was a goner, even though I was too young to really know what that kind of love was.'

Her grey eyes are wide. 'I love you too,' she replies shyly.

Jake's chest fills with a warm glow as he squeezes her tight. Now he's heard those words, he doesn't need to hear anything else.

'That's why I didn't want to show you the mermaid picture,' she confesses, clutching his shoulders.

'What do you mean?'

'I thought you'd know, that you'd be able to tell from looking at it.'

'Tell what?'

Her grey petal irises are dark, but clear. 'That I'm completely in love with you. I think it started that night I rescued you from the sea. I just didn't know it at the time.'

Leila

February 2015

The Valentine's Charm

'**I**t's our first Valentine's Day together next week,' I murmur to Jake, lifting my head from his broad chest in the early morning sunlight, 'and our seven-month anniversary. Shall we do something special?'

'More special than you finally making our relationship Facebook official?' he teases, sliding from under me and out of bed. Padding over to the drawer I've set aside for him in my dresser, he pulls out some boxers and a black T-shirt and picks his jeans up off the floor where they were dropped last night.

'Jake, I'm serious.'

'Yeah, course we can. Let's go for dinner or a drive. But whatever we do, every day is special with you.'

Sticking two fingers in my mouth, I make gagging noises. 'You're so soppy.'

'Would you have me any other way?' Turning, he raises one eyebrow.

I drop my hand. 'No.' Blinking, I drink in his toned, naked

body, and smile broadly. I'll never get tired of looking at him and some days I kick myself for wasting so many years. After so long thinking he was just a friend and that I didn't fancy him, it feels all too natural to spend as many nights as possible in bed with him. It's all we seem to do now: get naked, have sex, spend hours in bed, go to work, eat, and then start all over again. Although, we talk too, long into the night, and laugh together a lot. When I sold all five of my mythical creature paintings, he bought me a bottle of vintage champagne and told me how proud he was of me. Then he arranged a celebration dinner with my friends and family, and all of us spent the night chatting and toasting each other. At one point, Eloise leaned over to me, whispering in my ear, 'Aww, you guys are adorable. I love the way you look at each other.'

I've never known anything like it. I just love being with him. It's so easy, even when we disagree about something. The last seven months have been a revelation, and despite thinking I knew him when we got together, he still surprises me.

Over the past few months I've learnt he always sleeps on the left side of the bed, but likes to sprawl his leg over me to be close; his favourite colour is sky blue; he prefers the DC universe to the Marvel one; he loves both rom-coms and action films; his favourite time is at sunrise when the promise of a new day is just beginning; he sings in the shower, though he denies it; he reads widely, in no preferred genre; snorts with laughter at Joe Lycett, and hugs me every night we're together. He buys me flowers or makes me a tea when I'm feeling down, and he understands when I say I don't want to talk about what happened when I was thirteen, every time he prods me about it.

What took me so long to realise how amazing he is? He deserves every single bit of happiness I can bring to his life. Because of that, I'm hoping he'll like the Valentine's gift I'm creating for him. I smile to myself.

'Earth to Leila.' He waves a hand in front of my face and plants a kiss on the end of my nose. 'I don't know what you're smiling about, but I've got to grab a shower. If I don't get on the road soon, I won't make it to my first lecture. Thank God it's a 10am start.'

He drives to Plymouth every week for his occupational therapy postgrad degree course, lodging with a family near campus for three days before coming back to me again. It's not too bad given it's only for a year and we're already more than halfway through it. It worried me at first, with my abandonment issues, but when he first started staying away, he'd call me every night to put my mind at rest. After a while I told him he could just message instead, that I was okay. I guess I'm finally learning to work through my issues instead of avoiding them.

'Can't you wait ten more minutes? Come back to bed.' Fluttering my eyelashes, I drop the quilt around my waist and fluff my long hair down over my boobs. I'm body-confident in a way I never have been before.

His eyes heat up, but he steps back. 'Stop that! I can't be late. You need to get up soon too. You can't be late either.'

'Okay, Jake.' I haven't told him I've got the day off to paint. I'm still working at the gallery, but Edwin has stepped back a bit and semi-retired, often leaving me in charge. I'm thoroughly enjoying it, and while I haven't made enough money from my paintings yet to be able to go part-time in the day job – which is the aim eventually – I'm not in a rush to do that right now. I've managed to convince my boss to update the decor and install air-con, and already business has picked up.

Jake grabs his bag from the corner. 'I'll get dressed in the bathroom and then make tracks. Say bye to your dad for me. Tell him he's a saint.'

'I will.' I tilt my head back for a kiss, and say 'bye' to him as he shoots out the door.

We're normally here at my house when Jake's in town. We stay at his occasionally, but Maggie's started dating so we like to give her space. Sadly, there's no sign of Dad doing the same. It goes unspoken between Jake and me that we can't go on like this for ever. Plus, at almost twenty-five, I should really think about moving out. But what will Dad do without me and Fleur to keep him company? I'm loath to leave him alone.

Besides, the thought of Jake and me sharing a house, with Fleur bouncing around our ankles, still scares and thrills me at the same time.

***

'Happy Valenversary,' I sing, meshing together valentines and anniversary as I throw my arms around Jake.

'You too.' He returns my hug and eases back. 'Thanks for such a great day.'

'My pleasure.' We spent the day at Winchester Science Centre, playing like kids with the experiments and interactive games, before sitting in the darkened planetarium and watching a show which flew us through the universe in 3D. Holding hands, we gasped and wondered at the sights above us. When we came out it took us a while to reorient ourselves and come back to earth.

'Are you sure you didn't want to go out to a fancy restaurant?' my boyfriend asks, looking worried. Jake's my boyfriend! It still doesn't seem real.

'No, here is perfect.' Maggie's away overnight with a group of single friends who decided to get away from all the romantic fuss. While she's getting herself out there, she hasn't found anyone special yet. 'Plus, I have these gorgeous flowers to stare at over dinner.' I gesture to the bunch of lush red roses Jake bought me. He said he knew they were traditional, and maybe a bit cheesy, but they're as vibrant as I am. He's so sweet.

He's set the table properly, with a tablecloth, napkins and candles, glass flutes and a silver wine bucket full of ice with a bottle of prosecco resting in it. He's also placed candles in jars all around the room. 'This is lovely,' I say, 'thank you. Now, is dinner nearly ready?' I tease, 'or am I going to have to call for Chinese take-away?'

'Cheeky!' He disappears into the kitchen.

Later, after we've eaten a delicious meal of chicken parmigiana and dauphinoise potatoes with green vegetables, and delighted in a berry trifle, he slides a box over the tablecloth toward me.

'Happy Valenversary. I know it's a bit predictable –' he rubs the scar above his lip with his finger, making me want to kiss him '– but it's what I do. And it's us.'

'It is.' Picking up the box, I open it on a gasp. 'Oh, it's beautiful. Thank you.' Inside nestles a tiny heart-shaped charm with filigree detailing and a heart-shaped diamond in the middle. 'I love it.'

'Good.' Without being asked, he takes the charm out of the box and fixes it to a link on my bracelet. 'I know you have other hearts, the one from your mum and the one with the anchor and cross, but I just wanted to get you one that represented our love.'

'You really are soppy.' I shake my wrist and the bracelet tinkles satisfyingly. 'Wow, there are so many on here now.'

'Still plenty of links to fill though,' he quips. 'I'd better get this qualification finished so I can get my first OT job and keep buying these for you.'

'No rush,' I reply. 'Besides, I've been thinking: maybe, one day, I should buy one? To mark an achievement or something. Perhaps when I earn enough from my art to scale back the day job. I'm a modern girl, so I'm quite capable of buying myself jewellery.'

'Of course, you are,' he says, eyes twinkling, 'but there's one type of jewellery you're banned from buying yourself.'

'What's that?'

He doesn't answer, but simply picks up my left hand and rubs a fingertip over my ring finger.

I gulp. It's way too soon ...

'Don't worry, I'm not proposing.' He's responding to the

expression on my face. 'I'm just letting you know what lies in our future.'

'Well, let's take it one step at a time.' I jump up, smiling too brightly. 'Now, it's time for your present. Stay there.'

A minute later, I return to the kitchen carrying a large canvas under one arm. Balancing it on the chair, I straighten the cloth covering it. 'Are you ready?'

'I can't wait.' He watches solemnly as I pull the cloth away to reveal the painting.

He's silent for such a long time I get nervous. 'This is your favourite maritime port, right? Alexandria, in Egypt?' I bite my lip. 'Did I get it wrong?' It's taken me hours and hours of painstaking work over the last two weeks, my neck and back aching for days, my left hand curled into a claw from holding the paintbrush so long. 'That time last Christmas when you were naming all the stars on your tattoo for me, I thought you said—'

'No. This is it. I'm just ... stunned.' Getting to his feet, he comes over to the painting for a closer look. He peers at the white arched buildings, spires and multitude of windows. 'It's so detailed. You've captured its history so brilliantly. It's one of the oldest ports in the world.' He lifts his eyes to mine. 'You usually paint in oils, but this is watercolour.'

'I thought I'd try something different.'

'It's almost like I could be there. It's amazing, Jones, thank you. I'm hanging it in my room facing my bed so I can see it before I go to sleep and when I wake up in the morning.'

'Aww –' I blush '– it was nothing.'

He hugs me. 'It's everything. It must have taken ages. You

Ella Allbright

managed to keep it a secret from me too. Thank you. I love you.'

'I l-love you,' I stutter, still finding it hard to say the words as easily as he does. With his comment about proposing squeezing tension into my neck, it's even harder.

***

We slip into March and his comment about proposing still niggles at me. While imagining a future with Jake makes me happy, there's anxiety in the pit of my stomach. What if I'm not cut out for that kind of life? For a home, white picket fences, marriage, and a family? What if I'm like my mum? What if with the pressure I break, and run?

Where before I was relaxed and happy in Jake's company, now I feel like I'm living on borrowed time, quivering with anticipation. But not the good sort.

My creativity dries up, and no matter how hard I try, no matter how many times I go into the spare room and stand in front of a blank canvas, I can't put brush to paper. Nothing will come. I am confused and frustrated.

'What's got into you?' Jake asks one evening while we're drying dishes after dinner.

'Nothing.'

'Why are you so irritable?'

'Excuse me?' I step back, putting my hands on my hips.

He tilts his head to one side. 'Something's bothering you. What is it, Jones? You might as well tell me. Resistance is futile.'

'You're really going to quote *Star Trek* at me?'

'It's worth a try, isn't it?' His dimple flashes in his cheek.

I make a growling sound and flick the tea towel at him. 'You're so annoying.'

'That's my gift,' he jokes, 'now stop avoiding the subject. What's up?'

I sigh. 'I can't paint.'

'Why not?' He comes over to me, squeezing my hands.

'I don't know.'

'What's holding you back?'

'I don't know!' Tugging away, I pace around the kitchen, pulling a face at the disgusting dark cabinets. Why on earth haven't we ripped it all out and started again? It's so old-fashioned.

'Then you need a bit of time and space to figure it out,' he says sympathetically. 'How about a day trip to Lulworth Cove and Durdle Door tomorrow?'

I stop pacing and stare at him. It's Saturday tomorrow. Just the thought of walking down to the shingle beach at Lulworth with an ice-cream in my hand, and then panting up the steeply stepped hill along the cliff path to Durdle Door is enough to make me feel lighter.

Walking over to him, I slide my arms around his waist and rest my head against his beating heart. 'That sounds like a great idea, thank you.'

***

We have a magical day in each other's company. The coastline as stunning and rejuvenating as always. By the time we get back to mine, windswept and giggling, I feel better than I have in weeks.

But almost a week later, I still haven't painted anything, and the frustration starts to build again. Then, one Saturday morning as Jake and I are eating scrambled egg on toast with Dad, an envelope plops through the letterbox, landing on the mat. Fleur rushes to the hallway, panting, and trots back in holding the envelope proudly in her mouth. Whistling to her, I exchange it for a corner of toast and pat her on the head. 'Good girl.'

Flipping the envelope over, I peer at the scrawl on the front. It's addressed to me, but I don't recognise the writing. Ripping the flap open, I tug out a folded piece of paper and unfold it. '*What?*' I whisper in disbelief.

'What is it?' Jake frowns, putting his knife and fork down.

'Here. I don't want it.' Thrusting the letter at him, I jump to my feet, catching my thighs on the edge of the table. 'Shit!'

'*My darling girl,*' Jake reads aloud, eyebrows pulling together. His mouth straightens into a line and the scar above his lip turns white. He and Dad exchange a look.

Rage makes me dizzy, and a wave of heat scalds my face. I start shaking. 'I'm not her darling anything,' I spit. 'It's too late.' Snatching the letter from Jake, I tear it up into small pieces and throw them like confetti onto the table.

Marching into the hallway, I push my feet into my trainers and fling open the door. 'I'm going for a walk.'

Jake and Dad follow me out in their socks. Dad looks ill at ease. 'Wait, Leila. Don't leave like this.'

Jake's face is full of understanding. 'Do you want one of us to come with you?'

I can tell they're both worried I might not come back. 'Oh, for fuck's sake,' I snap, 'I'm going for a walk to clear my head. I'm not a kid any more. And I'm not running away from home.'

Dad winces. 'Leila!'

Jake studies me with concern. 'Okay. If you need picking up or anything, just call.'

I soften. 'I will.' Thrusting my hands into the pockets of my jeans to check I have my phone, I nod. 'Don't look so worried. I'll be back.' Setting off down the garden path, I sense their eyes on me. But I don't turn around.

***

Three days later, I'm still unsettled and swinging between fury and regret. I can't believe she had the cheek to write to me after all this time and call me her darling girl. She doesn't have the right. I also can't believe I tore the letter up without reading the rest of it and wish I hadn't been so hasty. The first time in almost fourteen years she contacts me – something I've always been desperate for – and I mess it up.

When I slope into the spare room, planning to brood over a blank canvas and the mural of me and Jake, I stop dead. The letter's propped up on my easel, stuck back together, tape holding fast the tiny pieces in lines and ragged edges.

Swallowing down a huge lump in my throat, I approach it.

Intuitively I know it's Jake who's repaired it for me. Picking up the letter with a shaking hand, I begin to read.

My Darling Girl,

You probably think this letter is years too late, but for me it is almost too soon. It's taken me a long time to feel whole enough to write to you, to make contact and try to explain. Still, I find I can't. Not quite.

You will never know how sorry I am for leaving you and your father, how I regret how much I have missed over the years, but at the same time, it was the right thing to do, for all of us. I couldn't stay.

So this is just me reaching out to you. Saying hello. I've decided there are some things that should be said face to face. So, I'm coming back, my darling. Not just yet, but soon. I'll let you know when.

Love, Mum x

As I finish reading, tears are trickling down my face and itching my neck. I wipe them away with my sleeve. I'm sad but incensed. How dare she write to me to say, well, basically nothing at all, and that she's coming back, but without offering any timescale? It shouldn't be hanging over us all, causing upset and tension. As if we've got nothing better to do than sit around waiting for her. My mother hasn't changed; she's as selfish as always. 'Arghhhh!' I swipe at the letter and send it, with the easel, crashing to the floor. I kick the skirting board for good measure and then whimper as pain shoots through my toes. 'Fuuuckkk!'

Picking the easel up in a rush, I slot a canvas onto it, before grabbing my paintbrush and palette. The letter crumples satisfyingly under my feet as I begin to paint a vision of a stormy sea and a dark heart beneath it. Shame, rage, sadness, all those raw emotions pour out of me onto the canvas.

When I stop hours later, I notice Jake sitting quietly on the floor in the corner of the room, reading a book. 'I didn't notice you come in,' I whisper.

'I know.' Placing the book down, he opens his arms. 'Come here.'

Putting the palette aside, I check my clothing for paint before going over and crawling into his lap. He holds me close, his chin propped on my head. 'Feel better?'

'Yes. I do. And now even more so,' I snuggle into his chest.

'It's brilliant, Leila.'

Jake using my first name touches me, and I tip back my head to land a kiss on his mouth before gazing over at my creation. It's colourful but dark, a chaos of explosive feeling laid out on canvas in teal, red, and black oils. The tension flows out of me, and my mouth curves, exhaustion buzzing along my nerve endings.

Two weeks later, it's hanging in a London gallery after much badgering from my boyfriend and a day trip to the capital. Three days after that there's a sold sticker in the corner of it and I've taken an exciting phone call. Then it gets a critical review from an up-and-coming art journalist.

The passion, love, and rage practically drip off the canvas.
Leila Jones is a bold and promising new talent.

'Well,' I remark bitterly to Jake and Dad at dinner that night, 'we may not know exactly when she's coming back, but at least Mum's good for something.'

Jake

June 2016

The House Charm & The Champagne Bottle Charm

Jake can't believe over a year has passed since he and Leila celebrated their first Valentine's Day together. In that time, they've also celebrated their first anniversary as a couple, Jake's twenty-seventh birthday, and Henry's fiftieth last month. They've attended weddings, baby showers, and christenings together, holding hands and then later watching each other across a packed room, and sometimes Jake still feels like he's seeing Leila for the first time.

He loves the concentration on her face as she talks to someone, giving them her whole attention, which he knows isn't always easy for her because her mind often drifts off into other worlds. Even more, he enjoys the way she looks for him when he hasn't been at her side for a while, like she misses him.

He thinks it's funny how people use these events and milestones to mark the time, when every moment should be lived in and feel exciting. What he can't believe is that, while he'd put aside any thought of proposing given how skittish she'd been after his comment on their Valenversary, he's managed to get her to move in with him. They've actually bought their own house together. And of all the ways in which he thought it might happen, with him just starting out in his new career and Leila's fledgling art company getting off the ground last year, there was no way he could have predicted the path that would lead them here.

He thinks back to when Leila's mum turned up with no warning the previous summer. Of all days, she'd chosen Leila's twenty-fifth birthday and the seventh anniversary of her own father's death, although of course she hadn't known the latter at the time. She wasn't what he'd been expecting: a short, dark-haired woman in a sensible beige suit and lace-up shoes. The way Leila had always described her, Jake had anticipated a vivacious but flighty woman in a bold dress, a woman who was loud and talkative with a hint of wired tension beneath the surface.

What had followed were tears of recrimination and anger on all sides.

It'd been a long, emotional, and exhausting afternoon as Amelia described a history of severe depression. She'd known she hadn't been coping as a wife and mother, known she was doing both her husband and daughter a disservice. She hadn't been able to look after them, and it had been killing her to try. It'd been going on for years. She'd had to get away. The thought that Leila had been about to start secondary school, about to enter the teenage years with boys and exams and peer pressure, had been too much for her. She hadn't felt able to ask her own father, who'd always been so stoic, for help. So she'd fled.

'So, it was my fault?' Leila had demanded.

'Of course not! It was mine. I couldn't cope.'

It'd killed Jake to see his girlfriend and her dad in bits, held hostage by the return of the stranger they'd lost, but he'd sat quietly letting it happen as it needed to, rubbing Leila's back or holding her hand in silent comfort.

'So, what's changed?' Leila asked, stony-faced but, Jake knew, hopeful.

'I eventually got better, and fell in love with someone who understands and helps me manage my illness.'

'I could have done that, if you'd talked to me,' Henry choked.

'I know. I'm sorry. I owe you an apology, one bigger than I can ever put into words. I shouldn't have left the both of you wondering all this time ... I'm sorry. So sorry. But I want to make a fresh start. I've moved back to the UK with Tom, and I'd like to get to know you again, Leila. If you'll let me. I hope we can be civil, Henry, and I hope that you'll –' her eyes clouded with tears and uncertainty '– let me go?'

Henry paused. 'I should have let you go a long time ago, Amie,' he said gruffly, 'but because I never knew where you were or what'd happened to you, I never could. Now I know you're okay, and have someone, I think I can. I'll give you a divorce.' Placing an arm around his daughter's shoulders and squeezing, he had peered down into her face. 'Leila, love, perhaps we can have a fresh start. All of us?'

Leila had stared back at him and then studied her mother's tear-stained cheeks, before turning to gaze at Jake. 'I think I'd like that.'

During the following months, Amelia had fought hard to earn Leila's trust, turning up every Saturday morning without fail for a visit, calling her twice weekly for a catch-up, offering to help her at the gallery before she'd quit to paint full-time. She'd also shown up alone on Christmas Day, knowing Leila wasn't ready to meet her new partner yet, happy to be patient.

Jake knew Leila found it difficult, and at times a bit stifling, but with every week that passed she'd thawed, letting her mum in a little at a time. She'd softened too, becoming less defensive with people, more able to see other people's perspectives.

Still, when Amelia had told her daughter in February she had a lump sum of money for her – thousands she'd saved up and scraped together with Tom's help – and that she wanted to help Leila and Jake buy their own place, Leila baulked.

'It will take us years to save up,' Jake pointed out reasonably over dinner one night. 'Why not let her help? She probably thinks she owes you after all these years.'

Leila crossed her arms. 'My love can't be bought. And she owes me time, not money.'

'We both know that, so you just need to tell her. Besides, she's doing her best to make up for the lost time.' Pausing, he'd smiled at her gently. 'Look, it's your decision, but why not let her make up for some of the past, by helping us step into the future?'

A few weeks later, Leila had half-heartedly agreed to accept her mum's gift. Initially not excited at the thought of house-hunting, she'd soon thrown herself into it, thrilled when they'd found a two-bedroom house they both loved, with a long narrow garden for Fleur and an airy brick-built conservatory with lots of windows which she could use as her studio. All just three roads away from her Dad's.

***

On the first night in their new home, Jake sits Leila on a red beanbag on the lounge floor, settling Fleur in her bed.

'You've made me really happy,' he says, kneeling and holding a box out to her. 'This is for you.'

'You've made me happy too.' She blows him a kiss, before frowning. 'But I haven't got you anything.'

'Doesn't matter. Open it.'

Grinning, she flips the lid open and then rocks back on the beanbag. 'Oh, they're so cute! I'm glad we've carried on with this.'

She'd asked Amelia once over a Sunday family dinner why she left the bracelet for her with one charm on it, and then never sent any more.

'Oh.' Amelia had looked blank. 'I just wanted to get you something a little more grown up, and I thought you and your dad could fill it together. It was something you could share, with me gone.'

Later that evening, Leila had remarked to Jake that it showed just how differently she and Amelia thought about things. All that time and significance Leila had given to the bracelet and how it was binding her and her mother together, when all along Amelia had never given it a second thought.

'You really like them?' Jakes asks Leila now, bending over to unfasten the tiny house and the small champagne bottle charm from their velvet bed.

'Yes! But why are you giving me two?'

'Because,' he explains as he fixes them onto the bracelet, 'we have double reason to celebrate. Firstly, we're now home-owners, and secondly, I get to wake up with you every day.'

Pulling a face, she jokes, 'Is that a blessing or a curse?'

'I guess only time will tell.' He smiles. 'You might hate living with me.'

He kisses her, moving forward and playfully unbalancing her so they fall onto the carpet together, wrapping their arms around each other. In their new home. *Their home.*

***

Kodaline are singing about 'High Hopes' as Jake moves through the house topping up drinks and greeting people. After debate, and worrying they'd spoil their lovely new house, they decided to have a housewarming party. It's worth it, Jake thinks, to have his and Leila's friends and family here to celebrate this happy event in their lives, though they've defi-nitely misjudged how popular they are from the numbers that've turned up and the gifts lined up on the counters and tables. He feels so grateful, and lucky.

Owen's manning the BBQ with Jonny at his side, a circle of old schoolfriends reminiscing with them as Jake reloads the outside fridge with beer. As he walks into the lounge, Eloise, face glowing and cradling her small bump, is standing with Shell and Chloe, laughing in the corner. Chloe's arm is thrown around Leila's shoulders.

'Hey, gorgeous Jake! Aren't you proud of your new house-mate, doing so well with her art business?' El yells across the room.

Waving, he laughs. 'Of course I am! The commissions are rolling in.' Leila's paintings are really taking off and her work is in hot demand. Jake keeps telling her she's only a few steps away from world domination.

As the crowd gets rowdier, Jake feels his phone begin to vibrate. Digging into his pocket to take it out, he frowns at the screen. It's a number he doesn't recognise. 'Hello?'

'—ou there?' A no-nonsense voice says. 'Hello, I'm trying t—'

Someone beside Jake laughs, and he sticks his finger in his left ear to try and hear better. It's no good, it's too noisy in here. 'Hang on, please.' Stepping into the hallway, he moves toward the front door, unlocking the latch and easing into the front garden. He sits down on the low grey wall, bracing his feet on the pavement. 'That's better. I can hear you now. Sorry, I'm at a party. Who's this?'

'I'm trying to reach a Jacob Marcus Harding,' a female voice says, her tone steady and quiet. 'Is this him?'

There's a sinking feeling in his stomach. This sounds official. 'Yes. I haven't been called Jacob in years, but that's me.'

'Can you please just confirm a few details, so I know I'm talking to the right person?'

'I guess so. But first, who is this please?'

She pauses. 'I'm with the Manchester Coroner's Office. I'm

calling in connection to a Terry Lee Harding. Do you know him?'

Coroner's office? Surely that can only mean one thing? 'Yes, he's my –' the word sticks in his throat '– father.'

After running through some checks, she identifies herself as calling from the Natural Deaths team.

'Just tell me,' he urges, bracing his feet more firmly on the ground in front of him. A small but strong hand lands on his shoulder and he knows without looking it's Leila, the scent of her shampoo wafting across his face as she leans close to listen in.

'Of course. I'm sorry to break this to you, but your father suffered a massive heart attack in the street this afternoon. Despite the paramedics' best efforts, he couldn't be revived. He died in the ambulance on the way to hospital.'

'You're sure it's him?'

'Yes.' She pauses, 'You're listed as his next of kin. I am sorry this has happened. There are a few practicalities which need taking care of ...'

Jake's not sure what type of man it makes him, but all he feels is relief. Terry is dead, and can never hurt any of them again.

***

Nine days later, Jake and Leila sit in an unfamiliar church together, hands entwined, his mum on one side. He knew she'd thought twice about coming, but they both needed to say their goodbyes, for their own benefit.

Jake's still waiting for a shadow of grief to touch him, for a tug of regret, but it hasn't come yet. He's not sure it ever will.

He's worn a suit out of habit, but his mum's in a bright orange wrap-dress, a silent and defiant two-fingered salute to the man who kept her in the dark for so long. She refuses to mourn. Leila has put on a more conservative navy dress, her long silvery hair pinned up in a bun.

After the short service, as Jake leaves the church with his mum walking on ahead and his girlfriend by his side, Leila turns to face him. 'Are you okay?' She touches his cheek, palm resting against his stubble.

'I am.' He kisses her hand. 'I never saw eye to eye with him, and now I'll never get the chance to understand why he was like that, but I can live with that.' He moves her on from the church, then cranes his head back to watch as a plume of smoke rises from the chimney. *Goodbye, you bastard*, he thinks.

'Are you really okay?' Leila repeats, her grey eyes soft.

'Yes,' he says firmly. Tucking her arm through his, he walks them towards the car. 'Besides, why dwell on the bad, when you can celebrate the good? I'm happy to leave this part of my life behind and move forward with you. Now, let's go home.'

Jake

30 August 2017

It's taken Jake hours to work out the locations he wants to use for Leila's birthday treasure hunt, and write up the clues. He just hopes she can figure them out and doesn't end up going around in circles. Every place is somewhere important to either one or both of them – a location she loves, or a significant part of their history. Little gems strung along the Dorset coast, like the charms on her bracelet. If all goes according to plan, they'll meet in their favourite place so he can give her this year's birthday gift. The best one yet, he hopes.

He's driven all over the county today, sticking the clues up in clear plastic wallets to protect them from any rain that may come. He can't wait to see her face, thinking back over the last year of happiness together. He's been working as an OT in a small practice to get some general experience before moving on to working with children, and she works from home, happily taking commissions and spending weeks on each piece of art, paint in her hair and under her short finger-nails. She doesn't like doing the publicity and interviews her agent urges her to, but overall Jake's never seen her so fulfilled.

Now there's just the matter of their next step together and he hopes he hasn't got it badly wrong.

When he gets home that evening, she's in a funny mood: excited about her birthday but quiet, brooding.

'What's up?' he asks over dinner.

'Where were you today?' She slides into the chair across from him, studying his face.

'At work. Why?'

'I called the office earlier because you weren't answering your mobile. Gina said you had the afternoon off.'

For pity's sake, couldn't Gina have said he had back-to-back client appointments? He wants the treasure hunt to be a surprise. 'Oh, right. Well, I might have finished early to go and collect your birthday present.' He hopes she won't keep digging. He's not good at lying to her. Not after the charms. 'But that's all it was.'

'Promise?' She looks into his eyes, as if searching for something.

'Promise,' he says solemnly. 'You can't get rid of me that easily.'

'Okay.' She pauses, 'I saw that picture you liked on Facebook earlier, of El's baby, and the comment you wrote.'

'Right.' *She's gorgeous. Can't wait to have some bambinos of our own.* He'd posted it in a rush at work, not thinking about Leila seeing it. Or perhaps wanting Leila to see it?

'Is that why you still haven't unpacked your gym equipment in the spare bedroom? Because you're saving it for a nursery?' Her face is pale, sweat beading her upper lip.

'I just haven't got around to setting it all up yet,' he replies evasively, taking a deep swallow of his water. 'But yeah, I guess in a couple of years' time, I'd like to think we'll be trying. It isn't a pressure to do it now,' he says quickly. 'We're still young.'

'I'm not sure, Jake.'

'Not sure about what? Trying in a couple of years, or trying full stop?'

She flinches at his tone, her expression uneasy as she scans his face. 'You must remember what I went through with the miscarriage. I'm not sure if I could go through that again.'

'I understand, but you wouldn't be alone this time. You'd have me. And just because it happened before, it doesn't mean it would again. Don't you remember about the rainbow baby?' He points to the tiny multi-coloured charm on her bracelet.

'It's not just that,' she interjects, flushing. 'What kind of mum do you think I'd be? I didn't have a role model around to teach me.'

'What about my own parents and the poor role models they were? Mum's been great over the years since he left, but I'm hardly a poster child for a happy home, am I? Not everyone gets what you had with your father and Ray. And now you have your mum back, and you're becoming close. I know how much she hurt you, but you don't get to keep hugging that hurt to you, using it to stop us from moving forward.'

She inhales sharply. 'Jake ...'

'I'm just being honest about what I want and what I'd like us to have together.' Standing up, he scrapes his chair back and transfers his still full plate from the table to the counter top with a clatter. At the noise, Fleur comes bounding in, intrigued to see what all the fuss is about. She lays her head on Leila's knee and watches Jake.

Stepping back, he swipes his hand through the air, hurt at Leila's view of things. 'I need to know that one day you're going to stand on firm ground with me so we can build a life together. Which means babies, a family.'

'How can I build a life with you, when I almost destroyed someone else's?' she cries.

'What are you talking about?' he asks, bewildered.

And in a rush, she finally tells him all about what happened when she was thirteen. Everything she's been holding back. About the frustrated and rage-filled girl she was, so angry at her mum for leaving, so full of hormones and a burning sense of injustice. Staying after school one day to paint, she'd been alone and lost her temper when she couldn't get the angle on a vase right and flung a jar of turpentine across the room. It'd smashed into pieces and sent turps trickling along the lino floor. Grabbing some blue hand-towels from the dispenser in the corner, she'd stumbled back across the room, catching her hip on the teacher's desk, knocking her teacher's handbag over. Hesitating, Leila had picked up a pack of matches that'd fallen from the bag and carried them over to the spilt liquid almost in a daze.

'I wasn't thinking properly.' She looks haunted as she relives the past. 'It was an impulsive act, a stupid moment. I was just so furious all the time, and wanted to see it burn ...'

'So, you set it alight?'

She nods, gulping. 'The turps caught so quickly, and raced

354

across the classroom, consuming wooden desks, stacks of paper and art supplies. Before I knew it, the room was full of dense smoke and heat, and was coming to get me. I started choking, turned to run away but stumbled over something and fell. Mrs Green got back just in time and pulled me out.' She shudders, 'My back was on fire and she had to put it out with her hands, rolling me on the corridor floor.' Sobbing, she drops her head into her hands. 'She came off worse than me and had to have skin grafts. She almost lost her job for leaving me alone in the classroom, and for having the matches in her bag. She was a smoker. But it was my fault, all mine.' Raising her face as he steps forward to comfort her, she puts a hand up to stop him. 'I don't deserve your comfort. The day after they let me out of hospital I ran away from home.' He's shocked, unable to speak. 'Dad was frantic. I was gone for two days, hiding out at a shelter in the park. The police brought me home and put the fear of God into me. Shortly afterwards, we moved back to Bournemouth. It's why Dad was always worried about me running –' she sniffs '– and why he's always been worried about me drifting off. He thinks the fire was set by accident, that I wasn't paying attention. But the truth is much worse, and almost cost someone dearly.'

Moving to her as she finishes her tale, he puts his arms around her shoulders and holds tight, resisting when she tries to push him away. Compassion flows through him as he finally understands her. Why she doesn't like losing her temper. Why she reacts when people accuse her of being like her mum. 'You were a mixed-up, angry kid. Teenagers are known for acting on impulse; it's part of the way they're built. Okay, someone was hurt, but did your teacher actually get fired? Did she lose the use of her hands?'

'No.' She lifts her face. 'The last I heard, she kept her job and recovered. I sent her a sorry card, but never heard back. Then we moved. I-I looked her up on Facebook once. She's still at the same school. It didn't stop me feeling so awful and guilty though.'

'You've carried it around for years, haven't you? Is that why sometimes you don't paint for long periods? Because the smell of turps brings it back?'

'I—' Her eyebrows pull together. 'I've never put it together like that, but yes, I guess, in a weird way, sometimes it does.'

'Well, it's time to forgive yourself, Jones.' A small smile tugs the side of her mouth at the use of her old nickname. He calls her Leila nowadays. 'You deserve to be happy and need to live your life. Put it behind you. Come on.' Lifting her from the seat, he gives her a quick kiss.

'Where are we going?'

'We're going to bed, where I'm going to hold you and kiss all your troubles away and run my lips over that scar on your back. It's as a much a part of you as anything else, a piece of your history that's made you who you are.' Easing her toward the door, he adds, 'Besides, I can't have you being upset the night before your birthday. So, I guess I'll just need to cheer you up with my strapping body and smooth moves.'

Picking her up as she reluctantly laughs, he heads for the door. She places a finger on the scar above his lip as he carries her up the stairs. 'Thank you. I can't get over it just like that, but it's a start, and I feel better talking about it.' She pauses. 'I love you millions.'

'Me too.'

That night, they make love delicately, savouring each other and the life they share. Finally, there's no reason to hold back and she gives everything to him, and he to her. They fall asleep holding each other, and Jake can't remember ever feeling happier.

***

The next morning, Jake wakes Leila up early. 'Happy Birthday,' he whispers into her neck, before straightening up.

'Huh?' She opens bleary eyelids, taking in his suit and tie. 'You're going already?'

'I'm afraid so. You know how important this interview is. I wouldn't leave you otherwise, today of all days.' He gestures to the tray on the bedside unit. It contains a teapot, mug, sugar, and crispy bacon sandwich slick with tomato ketchup, just the way she likes it. 'But I made you a birthday breakfast.' There's a single red rose too, and a card propped up against it.

'Aww, thank you. No fair that I didn't get to wake up with you in bed though.' She yawns, dragging herself into a seated position and pushing the mass of hair away from her face.

'I know,' he says sympathetically, plucking the card up and handing it to her. 'But follow this today, and I'll see you later this afternoon.'

'Follow it?' she looks puzzled.

'It'll make sense when you open it. I've got to go, or I'll be late. Speaking of, are you okay? About Ray and the anniversary?'

'Yes.' She nods. 'I'm okay.'

'Good. I love you millions.' He kisses her pale, slim shoulder and then her forehead, before backing out of the bedroom with a wave.

The sound of her voice follows him down the stairs. 'Love you millions,' she echoes. He grins as he leaves home, excited about the day ahead.

Leila

31 August 2017

I can't believe Jake has organised a treasure hunt for my birthday. It's so sweet. He really is one in a million.

I know that now more than ever, because he was so supportive last night when I finally told him about that terrible day when I was thirteen. I've carried it around with me for years, the guilt gnawing away, and had built it into such a big thing in my head, but Jake's words helped me see I've been too hung up on it. I need to let it go. It was stupid, and irresponsible, but I learnt from it. I learnt to control my temper, and I learnt that actions have consequences, and that running away from your problems doesn't solve them. If anything, it makes them worse.

I'm so glad I stopped running from my feelings for Jake; stopped running from my fears about losing him as a friend. The last three years have been incredible. We've built a home together, a life, and when I look at him, I feel happy and at peace. He's still my friend but so much more, especially after everything we've been through together. He makes me a better person.

He's the love of my life.

It really is true that life is never quite what you think it's going to be. It can take you by surprise and lead you to the most unexpected places.

Today has been brilliant so far. I've spent hours driving around following Jake's handwritten clues across the county, reminding me of how beautiful Dorset really is, from windswept beaches to fields and forests.

I could sense the clues were coming to an end when this last one led me to my second favourite place in the world. Arriving at Lulworth Cove after an arduous hour's drive from West Bay in the summer traffic, I decided to walk down to the beach at the bottom of the path before hunting for the next clue.

Now, standing here savoring the breathtaking view, my mouth curves at how Jake calls this my 'calm place'. The horseshoe-shaped cove has arching cliffs on one side and high green hills settled over chalk cliffs on the other. People walk their dogs along the shore or stand eating ice creams from one of several kiosks. It's hard to believe *World War Z* was shot here, masquerading as Nova Scotia.

Some of these Dorset beaches remind me of the northern French coast, and thinking of France takes me back to Chloe and Owen's wedding at Lake Annecy. How beautiful but how fraught it all was, and how it was part of the catalyst for bringing Jake and me together at last. Smiling, I play with my French flag charm, forever grateful Jake was so patient and waited for me.

Raising my arm, I study my silver bracelet. It's mine and Jake's now, ours. The thought of how many more precious memories we have to make together, and the charms he'll buy me to represent those, brings joyful tears to my eyes and a lump to my throat.

I frown as I realise the clasp is caught on the inside of my sleeve. As I'm trying to untangle it from the fine knit of my cardigan, my phone starts ringing. Digging the mobile out of my front pocket, I accept the call before sticking the phone between my shoulder and ear as I fiddle with my bracelet.

An unknown voice in my ear asks for Miss Jones, peppering me with questions as I undo the bracelet in order to set it free. My brain, distracted trying to split itself between two tasks, finally settles on the person on the other end of the line as my bracelet undoes. I grip the phone with my suddenly free hand.

'What did you just say?' I whisper numbly.

When she answers, I spin around and sprint towards the car, churning up stones as I go.

Jake

31 August 2017

Jake's hands grip the steering wheel, zipping the silver Hyundai along the M3, weaving in and out of traffic. The interview at Southampton General Hospital for an OT position has gone well, and after a quick lunch he's set off back down south to find Leila. What he hasn't counted on is the volume of traffic, with the end of the summer holidays.

He has a cool-box in the boot he'll fill with food she loves, and a bottle of champagne he'll get ice for. It'll make her happy. Hopefully she'll be even happier with what happens after the picnic. Although there's still a part of him worrying it'll make her feel like running, especially after the disagreement about babies last night. He can understand why she's worried about starting a family, or why she's not ready yet, especially with the fears about her fitness to be a mother after the legacy her own has left her with. Either way, they'll figure it out together. They always do. He hasn't loved her for so many years to throw it all away now.

Foot pressing down on the accelerator, he indicates as a gap appears in the lane next to him, unaware of the overloaded articulated lorry pulling out three cars behind him.

He just wants to get back to the woman he loves. To the girl with the charm bracelet on her wrist and the stars in her eyes. The girl who's always brought such magic and wonder into his life.

Leila

31 August 2017

Screeching to a halt in Southampton General Hospital car park, I leap from my Fiat, unable to think about parking or tickets or anything else but getting to Jake. I don't even know how I got here; I can't remember the drive. He has to be okay.

Racing into reception, I launch my question at the woman there. 'Where's Intensive Care?'

I'm panting, shaking, sweaty, hair stuck to my forehead. Smiling kindly, she gives me directions in a calm clear voice. 'Are you ok—?' she starts to ask as I back away, but I'm already gone, pounding the hallways and stairs with heavy legs which I urge to run faster.

Arriving at a set of heavy doors, I shove them hard, expecting to be able to burst through them. But they're locked and I ricochet off, nearly falling over. I peer through the tiny glass windows, pounding on the doors, holding my breath as a nurse walks towards me from inside the ward, holding a finger to her lips.

As she opens the door, I'm already spilling in. 'I'm here for

Jake Harding.' It erupts in a rush, the words running together. 'Where is he?'

But before her lips can frame an answer, I catch sight of Maggie over the nurse's shoulder. Her eyes are red and swollen, the lines of her face etched into grooves, making her look twenty years older than the last time I saw her a few days ago.

I run towards her, clutching her arm as I reach her side. 'Where is he? What happened?'

She doesn't have to answer though. I see the truth in her eyes. But still she says the words that'll haunt me through thousands of days and nights. 'He's gone, Leila. Jake's dead.'

'No,' I howl, crumpling into a fractured ball at her feet. '*No*.' My heart tears apart; life doesn't make sense any more. Sobbing, I fall into darkness as she mumbles incoherently about a car crash, about how it was quick and he died at the scene despite all the people who tried to save him. Someone is sobbing and shouting, someone is being told to calm down by the medical staff, and firm hands grip my body and lift me from the floor. But it can't be me making those horrendous sounds; it can't be me they are half carrying to a nearby bed.

Because I am dead. I can't be in the world if Jake isn't.

Leila

September 2017

The next few days pass in a haze. I flutter between numbness and abject pain, denial, and grief.

Maggie identified Jake's body alone at the hospital. Isn't it odd, the way you have to do that? The way you're expected to look at someone through so much pain and say, *yes, this is them. They were mine*. To claim them. As if those words can ever come close to conveying everything they meant to you, who they were to you.

I tried to go with Maggie but couldn't cope and had to be sedated. When I came round a while later, Dad and Maggie were at my side.

'It's him,' she said, simply.

I started crying again but scrambled from the mattress, tugging the IV line from my arm and finding the floor with my feet. 'Where is he?' I demanded. I had to get to him, I didn't want him to be alone. Over the years, he'd left me to travel for work, but he'd always been with me, somehow.

When I found Jake after a scramble through corridors and down stairs, he lay in the centre of a quiet, pale green room on a bed of some kind, a blanket tucked up beneath his chin.

It was him but it wasn't him. He looked like he was sleeping, at peace, but his face was different. Slack. I shuffled toward him and placed a hand on his forehead. His skin was cool where it had always been so warm, and I knew then it was really true. He was gone. Everything we'd been to each other, all the memories we shared were no longer contained in the person in front of me. He was somewhere else now, far away, perhaps in the stars which had once shone so brightly above us the night I rescued him.

I sat with him for hours, holding his chilled hand. I spoke about the story of our life together, about all the aspirations and dreams I'd had for us and our future, all the things I knew he'd have achieved had he not been ripped away from us. I wept, I laughed, I smiled. And then I thanked him for everything he'd given me and for supporting my dreams. I whispered that I was grateful for his love; he'd helped me become a better person.

When there was a gentle knock on the door, I knew my time was up. *Our* time was up.

Sniffling, I placed a kiss on his cheek. Then I picked up his right hand to run his fingers over the charms on my bracelet one last time. I sucked in a breath when I realised it was missing, but the enormity of his death overshadowed the loss.

Tucking his hand tenderly away beneath the blanket, I stepped back. 'Goodbye, Jake,' I whispered. 'I'll see you amongst the stars one day.'

***

I survived in a fog during that time. I missed Jake's presence with a physical ache, the gap he left behind too vast to make sense of.

'I don't want to do this. *Please* don't make me,' I told Dad fiercely when he walked me into the chapel the day of Jake's funeral. 'I can't say goodbye.' I was dressed in a riot of colour – the way Jake would have wanted – despite the fact I felt like wearing black from head to toe.

Dad tightened his hand on my arm as if I'd run away, like I used to. 'I don't want to either, but we have to, love, for him.'

I let him lead me up the aisle to the front pew, where I joined Maggie. We gripped hands tightly, and my friends eased into the row behind us. It was enough to know they were there, like at Grandad's funeral. Jake had looked so handsome in his full uniform that day. I almost uncoiled at that thought, but clenched my teeth. Mum appeared by my side, gazing at me questioningly, Tom standing a foot away. I nodded to the row behind, to indicate she could join Shell, Chloe, Eloise, Jonny, and Owen. Mum hadn't earnt a place in the front row. *Yet*, I could almost hear Jake saying silently in my head, being my conscience. *She hasn't earnt her place yet, but she will do someday.* I hoped it was true.

There are parts missing then, and I'm not sure where I went in my own head, but suddenly Maggie had spoken about Jake, and so had Dad on behalf of Ray and himself, and I'd no idea what they'd said. My name was being called, and my legs, as if they belonged to a stranger, carried me to the altar. As I gazed at all the people who'd come for him, there was still a part of me thinking it wasn't real. That at any moment,

Jake would fling open the chapel doors and grin and say, 'Gotcha, Jones.'

But he didn't, although I waited for a long minute, during which people shifted in their seats uncomfortably. I saw Eloise rising from the bench to check on me and that finally made me lift my chin and begin to speak. I could do this. It was only a tiny part of what I owed him.

'I loved Jake completely,' I said simply. 'It took me a lot longer to get there than him, but what we shared was a great love. *Is* a great love. He was my best friend, my soulmate, my advocate, my partner in crime, my best support, and my greatest passion. I will miss him for ever. Words can't do Jake –' my voice broke and tears clouded my vision '– justice. So, I won't even try. This is my eulogy to him, and my goodbye.' I moved to the side of the altar and dragged an easel across to the centre of the space. Dad had kindly brought it up for me the day before.

Pulling away the cloth, I stared at the piece I'd spent so many nights on since Jake had died. I'd felt compelled to paint him, to hold on to one last part of him before bidding him farewell. Painting without my bracelet around my wrist made it even more bittersweet, and panic had snaked down my back every day at the thought I might never get it back. I'd placed ads everywhere three days after Jake died, craving my charm bracelet in the way I was craving him. I needed it back – our shared history and a precious physical reminder of our story.

The room was silent as they took in my creation, and I smiled once, briefly. Jake was walking along Durdle Door beach with his back to us, the craggy archway in front of him and to the right. His head was turned in profile so you could see his scar and the slight curve of his lips. He looked happy. Wearing jeans and a T-shirt, the top edge of his back tattoo was visible and I'd painted a red heart on his sleeve. He'd never been someone who was afraid to share his thoughts or how he was feeling.

The night sky sprawled inkily above the stony beach, a multitude of stars represented by pinpoints of shining light. A quarter moon hung illuminating the calm sea and, in the distance, you could see a tiny mermaid floating among the swells out in the deeper water. Her face and silvery hair were illuminated by the lunar glow. Slightly ahead of Jake, where the archway seemed to meet the land, there was a painted doorway. I'd given him one last door to walk through. It was partially open, and white, with a yellow shimmer coming from within. Hundreds of tiny stars sparkled around the edges of it. I'd used the brightest, deepest colours I owned to reflect the vibrancy of the person he'd been to so many people.

He was turning away from us, yes – *leaving* us – but he would be okay.

It was those of us left behind, I thought, who would not.

Leila

December 2017

The Rings Charm

Months have passed since that sad day, and while the acute agony is no longer with me, every day feels like a torturous passing of time, hours on a clock I have to run down before I can see him again. My friends and family have tried their best to keep me company, to give me motivation to get out of bed in the morning, to help me see life goes on even if I don't want it to. Dad pops around for dinner most nights, and to catch me up with his day. Maggie and I walk a lot with Fleur, anywhere we can, over fields and through woods, along windswept beaches and muddy rivers. Being outside helps, and talking about him helps, but it hurts too. I miss Jake so much.

I haven't painted since the funeral, and I know he would hate that, but it doesn't feel right. Like I'd be moving on and leaving him behind if I created a new piece. Besides, the world doesn't hold much colour or joy for me any more, and there are no scenes in my head begging to be painted. Mum called all my clients for me, surprising me with her practicality, explaining the situation and that I was taking a break. No new commissions would be accepted and any that were outstanding would have to wait. They could have their deposit back if they wanted. No one asked. Mum has also moved in with me. She cooks and cleans, helping to shape a routine, forcing me to read and watch funny movies and go out with my friends or chat to them when they call round. Still, I'm living a half-life, and while I'm aware everyone around me is frustrated and worried, I don't know who I am, or how to move forward. The fact I'm still missing my charm bracelet makes everything so much worse. I need it back. Despite this, I can't bring myself to revisit Lulworth Cove and resume my birthday treasure hunt. I'm terrified of the emotions it might bring back, and how I'd survive them.

As I sit on the modern grey sofa Jake and I picked together, staring into space, there's a knock on the front door. I glance at the time on my phone and wait for Mum to answer. It'll be Dad.

Smiling wryly, I hear their voices floating along the hallway and some doors opening and slamming, mixed in with the sound of Fleur's excited panting. She's in heaven having all these visitors, although she doesn't drift far from my side. She lies on me pretty much every time I sit down, like she can't get close enough. It's lovely but is getting a bit weird now. Perhaps it's because I have some extra padding to cuddle up to nowadays, from all of Mum's stodgy comfort food.

'Hi, love.' Dad strides into the room.

'Hi, Dad.' I play with the cuff of my cardigan, the one I was wearing the day Jake died.

'Right. Up you get then.'

'Huh?' Lifting my head, I notice his frown, the line carved between his eyebrows.

'This can't go on. We can't bear to see you like this.' He and Mum exchange a look. 'I hope this will make it better. I'm not sure it could get any worse.'

'What are you talking about?' I ask vaguely, unable to summon the energy to even be curious.

'Up you get,' he repeats as Mum leaves the room, returning a moment later with my coat and boots. Holding my coat out, she gestures for me to push my arms into the sleeves, before nodding at my Uggs. Dutifully I obey, wondering what they're up to.

She walks into the hallway as Dad grasps my arm gently, nudging me into the kitchen and through the back door into the garden. A moment later, Mum follows in her fur-trimmed coat. The air is chilly. Fresh. There's a bonfire crackling away, and we sit in front of it together on the bench I brought with me from Dad's when I moved. Mum and Dad sit either side of me like parental bookends.

'What's going on?'

'Here.' Dad looks at me searchingly, before extending his hand. There's a wrapped present on his palm.

My hand flies to my mouth. 'I— Jake?'

Nodding, he sighs, 'It was with his belongings. Your birthday present. Maggie's been hanging on to it until, well—'

Mum interjects, 'We've been waiting for you to be strong enough ... Maybe you are, maybe you aren't, but we've decided we shouldn't wait any longer.'

'We?' They've been talking about me. They're really concerned. I have to show them I can do this. *Be brave, Jones*, I hear Jake whisper in my head. Taking a deep breath, I lift the present from Dad's hand and shiver, despite the warmth of the nearby flames. It's like receiving a gift from a ghost. But I can't think of Jake that way; he was never quiet or faded. He was alive, energetic, compassionate.

Tearing into the paper in a rush exposes a velvet box. Pausing, I take another deep breath and flip the lid open. It's a silver charm – two tiny rings entwined. 'Oh, God,' I whisper, tears filling my eyes, 'Oh, *Jake*.' It's bittersweet and lovely, but I have no bracelet to hang it from. Breaking down, I bend over and sob with pain, at the unfairness of the world, at my loss. Dad rubs my back as I keen, and Mum strokes my hair from my face. They say nothing, simply letting me grieve. I'm never going to see him again, and now there is only one charm left, because I know he would have hidden one for me at the final location.

My tears last for a while, and when they're spent, I straighten up.

'Thank you.' I murmur, staring at the charm again. Then, clicking the lid shut, I go to slide it into my pocket.

Dad stops me. 'Look underneath.'

'Underneath?' I frown, puzzled.

'Under the sponge,' he points to the box.

Re-opening it, I move the charm aside carefully and pull up the velvet bed, exposing a glint of metal. My eyes widen and I gasp. Plucking it between trembling fingers, I hold it up to the light of the fire.

It's a platinum engagement ring, a solid circle with diamond-encrusted leaves curled into it with a larger round diamond on top. It's pretty and quirky, and totally me.

'He said he'd see me later that day. He was going to join me at the end of the treasure hunt. He had it with him. He was going to propose,' I breathe. The pain is fresh and rushes back on me. Everything we could have had, everything that might have been. I'll never see him kneeling in front of me, face hopeful and arm outstretched. I'll never get to say, '*Yes!*' Never get to excitedly announce our engagement to our family and friends. Never get to walk down the aisle towards him or promise to stick by him in sickness and in health, for better for worse, till death us do part. He has already been parted from me. 'He wanted to marry me.'

'Of course he did, love. He was devoted to you.'

'He asked your dad for permission,' Mum says. 'I thought that was a lovely touch.'

'It is. It was,' I sigh. A lone tear traces its way down my cheek. It's different to the tears which came before. 'He would have been worried about proposing,' I go on, 'because of my commitment issues.' Glancing at Mum, I can see in her eyes she knows that's her legacy. 'He would've been wondering if it was going to scare me away. I made him wonder. I made him doubt me.' I shut my eyes. 'I made him feel ... less.'

'No!' Mum says fiercely, 'He knew how much you loved him, and you'd already committed to him. You'd bought a house together, set up home.'

I nod, opening my eyes. 'It's not fair. This isn't the life I imagined for us. This wasn't how it was supposed to be. We were going to grow old together. We didn't get enough time.'

'Love, I know,' Dad replies. 'But you also had fifteen years together, from when you first met. That's longer than some marriages last.'

'Your time together may be over, Leila. But *you* still have time. To live. To love. You know Jake would have wanted you to use it well, and wisely.'

It sounds so much like something Jake would say that my mouth falls open at Mum's words. 'How ...'

Mum smiles, 'I read some of the letters between Jake and your granddad. I wanted to feel closer to Dad and found the box in the spare room the other day. I hope you don't mind?'

'No,' I reassure her, 'they were as much Grandad's as Jake's. You have an equal right to them.'

Her confession distracts me from my sadness. Falling silent, I tuck the ring away inside the box, resettling the charm on top of it. Pushing it deep into my coat pocket, I hold my hands out towards the bonfire, feeling the heat on my fingers and palms.

'Now, there's something else we need to talk to you about, something important.' Mum starts to describe what she's noticed, her suspicions. At first, I shake my head in disbelief, then I start to shake as things fall into place. I think maybe she's right, and I don't know whether to be terrified or excited, or both.

Leila

December 2017

... *When you contacted me last night, Caitlin, to tell me you'd found my bracelet and to ask for a detailed description, it felt like fate. Especially after the events of yesterday, when Mum and Dad gave me Jake's gift, along with hope for the future too. A way that Jake and I still get to have a future together, even if it's not the way we planned. A path that was confirmed this morning, news which gave me the strength I needed to return to Lulworth Cove and find the last clue.*

That same strength also allowed me to write this email to you, detailing every charm through not just my eyes, but how I know Jake would have told you his side of the story too. He told me enough times over the years what life had been like for him, all the things he'd done for me, to make me happy. What he was thinking in the time we were apart, and what every charm meant to him. I'm only sorry you won't get to meet him. Everyone liked Jake.

Earlier, after I parked up at Lulworth, I walked down to the beach and stood on the same spot I'd been on when the nurse called me on my birthday about Jake. I gazed out to sea, recalling how happy I'd been in the moments before my phone rang, how much I was looking forward to seeing him. I have lost so much since that phone call, but I have gained something too. An appreciation of how short life is, and how we can't waste what time we have. And writing this email to you, while sad – and through tears at times, but laughter too – has revived Jake, has brought him back to life for a short while, reminding me of everything we went through together and what he taught me. Bringing our love sharply into focus, along with the charm bracelet.

It's helped me see as well that I'm stronger than I was a few months ago. Strong enough to do what comes next.

Earlier today, recalling the last clue from Jake (about a sweet tooth with Brad Pitt), I trudged up the beach and along the path running next to the small stream, until I came to a small, old-fashioned sweet shop. Stepping inside, I asked the grey-haired woman behind the counter for a hundred grams of my favourite sweets, pear drops. She went to reply automatically, then stopped and eyed me searchingly. 'You're not Leila, are you?'

'Yes.'

Reaching down behind the counter, rather than going over to the rows of wall-shelves stacked with jars, she brought a container of pear drops out. 'I was expecting you months ago. I kept it just in case, because he was lovely and seemed so excited about what he was up to.'

'It took me a long time to get here.' I smiled, not offering

any further explanation. 'Thank you for keeping it. May I?' Holding my hands out.

She nodded, passing me the container. Flipping it over, I found a note taped to the base of it. Typical Jake. Laughing softly, I peeled it away, carefully unsticking and then unfolding it.

OUR FAVOURITE PLACE.

J X

'Of course,' I muttered, 'yes.' Lifting my head, I smiled at her, ignoring the naked curiosity on her face. 'Thanks so much, again,' I said, backing away. 'It means more than you know.'

'Wait!' As I turned to leave, she came out from behind the counter, eyes kind. 'He bought these for you.' She pushed the box of sweets into my hands.

'Really?' I laughed, 'I hardly need fattening up. But thank you.'

She floundered with her mouth open, unsure what to say. I took pity on her and shook my head. 'Never mind. Take care.'

'Have a good day,' she replied, giving me an odd look.

Returning to my car, I drove to the car park above Durdle Door, and have been sitting in my Fiat in the gravelled area above the steep path that curves down to the beach. I've been here for hours, writing this email to you, and when I'm done – once I press 'send' – I'll remain here for hours more. With hope in my heart.

And so that's it, Caitlin. Every charm on my bracelet,

every sweet memory, every precious important minute. Jake's story, my story. Our story. It's taken me months to feel brave enough or strong enough to finish the treasure hunt. Now, there is just one tiny bit left to go. One more charm left to discover. If you believe me, Caitlin, if you believe what I've told you, every memory I've brought back to life – for myself, for you, for Jake – then please meet me at Durdle Door with my bracelet. Below is my number. You can call me, text me, email me, whatever you want. It's in your hands, it's up to you.

I truly hope you believe the bracelet is mine now … and maybe you can help me find the last charm.

Leila x

Leila

December 2017

The Charm Bracelet & The Treasure Chest Charm

Durdle Door has always been the anchor point that drew Jake and me together, holding us steady. The one place we had in common, where we shared hopes, fears, dreams.

As I sit here after my meandering walk down from the car, the pain which struck my heart when I first stepped down onto the shingle beach and saw the famous rock archway recedes. The tears in my eyes dry away. It's hard being here without him, but at the same time I feel closer to him than I do anywhere else. It may be tinged with sadness, but this place is still beautiful.

The air is crisp, the winter sky a clear blue so bright it almost hurts my eyes. The Door still stands solid and immovable, and I know it will be many years before it gives up and crumbles away to be claimed by the sea.

Smiling, I picture the tiny multi-coloured rainbow charm I'll see again soon. Caitlin's got to believe me. All those memories, my whole life stretching behind me, with enough space on the bracelet to mark the events that will form my future, will be with me once more. Until a day ago I wasn't sure I'd have a future, but now I know differently.

My phone pings in my hand. It's an instant message from an unfamiliar number, the paragraph of white writing filling a rectangular blue bubble.

Dear Leila, got out of lectures and spent the whole afternoon reading your emails. The charm bracelet is on the desk in front of me. Thank you for taking me on your journey. Your story – and Jake's – made me laugh and cry, has touched me and held me, and at times tore me in two. Yes! I believe it's your bracelet. Something tells me you're still at Durdle Door. If you are, wait for me. Will be there in 40 mins. Yours, Caitlin x

Some time later, a girl of about twenty steps down onto the beach, walking slowly towards me. As she approaches, I see she has wavy red hair hanging down her back, brilliant blue eyes and freckles dusted across her nose. Her expression is open, her eyes pink-rimmed.

'Leila?' she asks hesitantly.

I nod, just once, and begin to smile. 'Caitlin.'

As she comes closer, stopping a few feet away, I see over her shoulder a tall man with similar red hair. He looks at me with suspicion.

'My older brother, Cian. He wouldn't let me come alone, just in case ...' She looks sheepish.

'I understand.' When I push myself off the ground to stand up, my coat falls open.

Caitlin's gaze is drawn to my stomach, to the barely-there bump pushing against the fuchsia knit of my jumper. Her eyes widen. 'Oh. You're having his baby,' she breathes.

'I am.' Grinning, I touch the neat mound with my hand. 'I didn't know for sure until this morning. I hadn't realised ... I put the weight gain and the nausea down to grief. I missed some pills in the weeks before he died.'

'So, he didn't know then.' Caitlin bites her lip.

'No,' I answer softly, 'but I believe that somehow he will. If there's any atom or speck of him out there, he'll know.' I pause. 'Thank you for coming, Caitlin. Can I please have my bracelet now?'

'Sorry.' She flushes. '*Yes*, you can.' Pulling a piece of paper from her pocket, she unfolds it with great care. As she does, I catch sight of my prized possession, the silver links and all the tiny charms, and reach out eagerly. Before I can swoop it up, she closes her hand slightly, staring at me. There are tears in her lovely blue eyes. 'I'm so sorry you lost him.'

A hand lands on her shoulder, making her jump, and she looks up at her brother. 'I'm fine,' she responds to his unanswered question. Wiping her eyes roughly with her free hand, she shrugs him off to step closer to me. 'Here,' she holds my bracelet out, 'let me put it back on your wrist. Back where it belongs, just like you said in your email.'

'Thank you,' I answer, relieved. Holding my left arm out gladly, I push my coat sleeve up. She loops the bracelet together and fastens the clasp, testing to make sure it's secure. With gratitude, I feel the weight of it around my wrist, and run my fingers over all the silver charms, breathing freely for the first time in months.

'You know,' she says, lifting her chin, her eyes gazing into mine, intense, vulnerable, 'reading your email, I feel like I've aged fifteen years in a day. But in a good way. One day, I hope I have what you and Jake did. It was special.'

'What we still have,' I say firmly. 'It'll never leave me. That kind of love doesn't. Not really.' Thinking of the last clue from Jake, I murmur, 'Our favourite place.'

'Is that what the final clue said?' Caitlin demands, taking a step back and gazing across the beach.

'Yes. Do you want to help me find the last charm? It isn't really the last one, because this one would have been.' I take the box with the engagement ring concealed in it and I hand it to her, knowing I can trust her. 'But it will be the last one I find from him.'

Nodding, she flips open the lid and takes out the charm with two rings entwined and attaches it swiftly to my bracelet. She hesitates with the box in her hand. 'Is the engagement ring ...?'

'No,' I shake my head. 'That's at home safely tucked away, fastened on the ribbon that ties all his postcards together. I wasn't taking any chances after losing this.' I indicate my bracelet.

Mouth curving, she hands me the box back and I tuck it away. 'So, the other charm, where would he have hidden it?'

'It would have to be somewhere tucked away, where other people couldn't easily find it.' We look around at the beach, at the Door and the steps leading away from it. Even Cian is scanning the scenery, his brows drawn together. 'Somewhere out of sight ...' Trailing away, I study the base of the cliffs, noticing the little nooks and crannies. Caitlin follows my gaze.

'The caves!' we say together.

All three of us set off for them, plodding our way over the shifting stones, hunching our shoulders against the chill. The temperature has dropped, and darkness is starting to creep along the edges of my vision. We search fruitlessly for a few minutes, climbing the shelves of chalk and sticking our heads into sheltered alcoves and narrow recesses, until with a shouted 'Here!' Cian makes the discovery.

Both rushing over to him, my heart swoops as I see the envelope, a familiar *L* written on the front of it, stuck to a mini champagne bottle.

Sliding the envelope from Cian's grasp, I look up to see them watching me expectantly and pause.

'Don't worry,' Caitlin says, smiling, 'you don't have to open it in front of us. This is just for you and Jake. We'll leave you to it. Will you be okay here on your own?'

'I'm not on my own.' Briefly, I lay a hand on my stomach. 'But yes, I'll be fine. I'll go home soon, and it's not dark yet. I have time to reach the car.'

'You're sure?' Cian pipes up, and there's compassion in his eyes.

'Definitely.' Nodding, I gesture them away. 'Thank you so much for bringing my bracelet back to me, and for helping me. It means so much.' I turn to face the sea, the envelope clutched between my fingers, impatient now to open it.

'Okay,' Caitlin says, reluctant to leave.

Cian nudges her with his elbow. 'Come on, she wants to be alone.'

Looking at her, I smile widely, gratefully. 'Thank you, again, Caitlin.'

With that, and a wave of our hands, we part. They tramp along the shingle towards the steps, arms linked. I watch them for a moment, before making my way towards the shore. Standing a few feet from the sea, I inhale the briny air deeply, the cold stinging my nostrils.

Just as I'm about to open Jake's envelope, there's the sound of running feet and Caitlin reappears at my side.

'It's not the last charm,' she blurts, tears in her eyes.

'Pardon?'

'It's not the last charm. Well, it is from Jake but ... the point about the bracelet is that it's a way of capturing memories, right? That's why it's always been so precious. But your life doesn't stop just because his has. If there's one thing I've learnt about Jake in all this, it's that he wanted the best for you, always. He wanted you to be happy and that means he would want you to keep living and making memories. Your story carries on. So, you have to buy yourself the next charm. For him.' She squeezes my arm, her face earnest.

I step back, gulping. 'I ... I don't know, Caitlin.'

'I do,' she replies, her voice intense. 'So much of what you wrote included things Jake told you from his perspective during the last fifteen years of your journey together. You gave him so much, and he helped you become someone better. So now you must be brave, for him.' Her hand brushes against my belly for a fleeting instant. 'You have to be brave for this baby. And that doesn't mean half measures; it means going all in. Keep making memories and keep adding charms so that one day you can share them all with the child you made together. You must paint again, too.'

My face crumples, but I hold back tears. She's wise beyond her years. Pausing, I realise she is also right. Jake would have wanted all of that, and when I mentioned buying charms once, all he said was that I couldn't buy myself a ring. Gulping, I whisper, 'Thank you, I'll try. Take care.'

We hug, tight and quick, and then she leaves, properly this time.

At last, I sit down on the stones and open the envelope. Inside is a treasure chest charm with minuscule multi-coloured gems in its open lid. I think of Jake's rainbow charm letter, and the part about having to treasure life. And even though it shouldn't be possible, with the sky darkening and barely a touch of rain in the air, I see a rainbow in the distance and know he's out there somewhere. I hold the rainbow charm between my fingers, thinking of his words, which are engraved on my heart.

Always look for the rainbow, Jones. You have to treasure life – no one else is going to do it for you.

Jake is still with me. I can feel him here beside me in the whisper of the breeze on my cheek, in the light of the setting sun on my face. I have his baby, his legacy, our memories, our love. We'll share a future together, even if it's not the one we planned. When I look into his child's eyes, I will see him there. No matter what else I go on to do in my life, that will remain.

Leila & Mia

March 2020

The Baby Charm, The Cocktail Glass Charm, & The Red Heart Charm

It's an early morning in mid-March and the weather is wintry despite the fact it's almost spring. The sun hasn't long been up over Durdle Door, casting a dim light over the bleak grey sky.

A gust of wind sweeps my hair across my face. Grabbing hold of its pale length with one hand, I twist it into a bun and tuck it in my hood, the way Jake used to.

I hoist Mia higher up on my hip, her solid weight making my arm ache. I abandoned the pushchair at the top of the steps with Dad and carried her down. Pointing at the rocky archway, I tell her, 'Your daddy jumped off the top of that once. It was a silly thing for him to do, wasn't it?' Mia babbles in response, just a toddler, not yet two years old. 'I'm glad he did though.' I tighten my hold on her. 'It gave me the chance to save his life. And if I hadn't done that, I might not have got to know him so well, or had you.'

It's bittersweet, but at least I can laugh now instead of just

cry. The last few years as a single parent have been tough.
There are times I miss Jake unbearably, times when my heart
aches. But I'm still young, though older now than Jake was
when he died. This year I'll be thirty, an age he'll never get
to reach. I can be glad we had what we did, though, and I
can be happy Caitlin was right and that I owed it to him to
keep making memories. I meet her for coffee once a month,
and she's one of my biggest champions. I'm sure Jake brought
us into each other's lives for a reason. I'm painting again too,
and earning a good living from it. Jake was right: sharing my
art with the world makes me happy.

I shake my left wrist and the sunlight glints off my bracelet
and its many charms. It holds three new ones: a tiny baby I
bought for myself the week after Mia was born; a silver cocktail glass with a cherry in it from Eloise, who took me for my
first night out when Mia was six months old and got me
drunk on Cosmos despite my better judgement; a red heart
from Mum, who said it was to show she always loved me and
held me in her heart when she was away, no matter where
she was.

Mia chatters away nonsensically, reaching out her chubby
fingers to play with the bracelet as her father used to. I take
it as a sign. 'We have lots more memories to make together,
Mia,' I say with confidence, 'lots of charms to add to the
bracelet.' I smile up at the sky, visualising Jake with his broad
shoulders, his scar, and mismatched eyes – one green, the
other brown – remembering how special he always made me
feel, how good he was. 'One day, I'll buy you a bracelet of
your own and you'll follow your own journey,' I tell our

daughter. 'Then later, when I go to join your daddy up in the stars, our bracelet will be yours. And you'll hold both of us with you, for ever.'

Hugging her close, breathing in the strawberry scent of her thick black hair, I gaze down into her extraordinary green eyes as she lifts her head to look at me, and we both smile. Then, I turn back towards the steps, ready to go home.

Ready to keep living life as best as I can, with mine and Jake's charm bracelet upon my wrist.

THE END

Acknowledgements

Firstly, thank you dear reader for buying this book and reading it. I truly hope you enjoyed it and that you took something special away from it.

When my lovely Editor, Charlotte, called and asked me to come to London in early 2017, I had no idea that the concept she was about pitch to me would be so hard to write or would affect me so profoundly.

It has been a pleasure and privilege (and sometimes, a pain!) to create this world and these characters, and to do justice to that initial concept about a lost charm bracelet and an epic love story. Living with Jake and Leila in my head for two and a half years and following them on their journey has been joyful and touching, but often sad.

Grief is always difficult to write about, especially as it struck me like lightning when my grandma (always known as Meme to our family) passed away suddenly in March 2016. It took me a long time to pick myself up, and writing *The Last Charm* put me back in touch with all those thoughts and emotions, so it wasn't always easy.

However, it also taught me a lot, which I hope I can pass

on to others struggling with grief. I've learnt that life goes on regardless of death, even when at times you don't want it to, but that there's always something worth living for. And after a while, it doesn't all feel quite so difficult.

I didn't write for six months after Meme died, but one of the things that helped was knowing she'd want me to carry on writing, and how proud she'd be if I carried on getting books published and making connections with other people. So this book is also in memory of Connie Moorcroft, the toughest woman I had the pleasure of knowing and being related to. We still miss you.

I am truly grateful as always to everyone – including my fabulous agent Hattie Grünewald at The Blair Partnership, family, friends, work colleagues, the writing community who I shared many a Facebook post/Tweet/conversation with – who helped and encouraged me in the writing of this book. I have to mention the lovely bloggers and reviewers who helped publicise *The Last Charm*, including the incredible Rachel Gilbey of *Rachel's Random Resources*; your hard work is always appreciated. Thank you, of course, to the lovely One More Chapter team, who fly the publishing flag so brilliantly.

I'd also like to thank David Bunting, my secondary school English Teacher at St. Peter's in Bournemouth. He was a wonderful teacher and encouraged me to write, telling me I had talent. Well, I kept writing! Seriously, Mr Strickland, the English teacher in this book, is *nothing* like Mr Bunting. Thankfully.

A giant thank you to my close friend Juliette, who with her

beautiful daughter's agreement let me borrow the name Ella. You're both stars.

And a special mention to my friend Jake Wyatt, for letting me use his name – thank you.

Lastly, I hope I've done you proud, Charlotte. We got there in the end! Thank you for everything.

Author Q&A

1. How did you come up with the idea for this story?

As mentioned in the Acknowledgements section, the charm bracelet concept for this story actually came from my lovely editor, Charlotte Ledger at One More Chapter, the digital-first fiction imprint for HarperCollins. We met at The News Building in London, and she asked me to write an epic love story set around the concept of a charm bracelet and all the charms on it. Charm bracelets are so personal, and so popular, that she thought it would be amazing to build a love story around one, and I completely agreed.

That was the opening brief. We then spent about an hour and a half together throwing ideas around. Who would the two main characters be? How old were they? Where did they live? What might happen to keep them apart? How could their story develop? By the time I left, we had a loose story arc agreed. I was on my way to the airport to spend a long weekend in France with Mark (at Lake Annecy, which later made it into the book as the setting for a very special event) and couldn't stop the ideas from flowing, so kept emailing Charlotte with suggestions and names over the next few days! A few weeks later, I'd sent her a twenty-chapter outline, and we'd agreed on the structure. Over the next couple of years we emailed regularly, spoke on the phone and met to discuss *The Last Charm*. It was great working with Charlotte in such a collaborative way, and I know she has always been as passionate about this book as I am.

2. Why Dorset, after writing a romance series set in London?

I love London, especially its diversity, and so really enjoyed the research I did for the Love London series (as Nikki Moore). However, when Charlotte and I discussed a new standalone book in the Commercial Women's Fiction genre, one of my first questions was whether I could set it in Dorset. I'd been told by an agent previously (not the one I signed up with) that only cosy crime was set in Dorset, but I was determined to bust that myth, and also wanted the chance to showcase my home county. We have such an amazing quality of life here, and there truly are some hidden gems strung along the south coast. From forests to fields, rivers to the sea, there are some views that take my breath away and that I wanted to share with readers. If you get the chance, please do come to Dorset – www.visit-dorset.com!

3. How long did it take you to write from start to finish?

From the initial concept to handing in my absolutely final polished and edited Word version, was three years. However, I actually handed in a proper first draft (which had the bulk of the story in it but with about 30,000 extra words!) in about two and a half years.

I wasn't writing five days a week every week during that time though, as I had a day job, and there were periods where I stopped writing for a few months at a time due to several bereavements. I actually wrote about 50,000 words of the book over two consecutive Julys. Every year I go off to a writing retreat in Devon for 4–5 days and closet myself away, writing between 6–8,000 words a day. If you paid close attention, you may have noticed Leila stop off in a little village called Sheepwash ... If you're interested in the retreat, Debs and the team are fabulous – you can find out more here: www.retreatsforyou.co.uk.

4. Tell us more about the structure of the book.

We knew straight away that we wanted to have multiple viewpoints in the book, as we needed to see the story through both Jake and Leila's eyes, hence the alternating chapters. I also knew pretty early on that is was going to span most of their teens and early twenties, so around a 15–20 year period. The loss, and finding, of the charm bracelet was the hook to get the story started and I knew immediately there had to be an advert and then a letter or email from Leila to whoever had found the bracelet for her. I wanted to use that device to tell the story of each and every charm. Jake has fewer chapters in 2017 because his story is coming to an end.

When we first started out, the structure was going to have the chapters muddled up in terms of year i.e. not in chronological time order, however some early feedback we got was that it was a little confusing, so I rearranged all the chapters to span from the earliest memory up to present day and it definitely made for a stronger story.

5. Who is your favourite character in *The Last Charm*, and why?

Leila will of course always have a special place in my heart – and she does have a few of my worst traits, namely the inability to park a car without putting a ding in it, and a tendency to be distracted when dreaming up creative ideas – but Jake is my favourite. I don't really think of my characters as ones I've deliberately created, they're more like friends who talk to me, so for me Jake is a living, breathing person. That might sound slightly odd to non-writers!

I love his resilience after his difficult upbringing, his thoughtfulness, his positive outlook and generally pragmatic disposition. I like too that he's not afraid to say what he thinks or how he feels – something I genuinely admire in people, because it takes courage to truly own who you are. I also admire the way he supports Leila with her art; something my fiancé has always done for me with my writing.

6. What's your writing routine like? Do you write full-time?

I've mostly had a full-time job in Human Resources since being published, apart from a brief 6-month stint when I reduced to four and a half days a week (but to be honest I ended up doing housework instead of writing!) so I went back to full-time. I write on weekends and some evenings, trying to squeeze in 3–4 hours here and there. When I'm up against deadline I'll write for between 7–10 hours on a weekend, and past midnight in the week. It can be really painful to tear myself away sometimes to go back to normal life! I also have to squeeze in social media and marketing activities.

If I know what's going to happen in a chapter, then I can write quickly, averaging 1000 words an hour. A lot of my writing actually takes place in my head before I physically sit down at the laptop. While I'm driving the car, doing housework and walking the dog, I'm thinking, *What if x happened?* Or, *What if x did this?* I also spend a lot of down time dreaming up dialogue between characters.

7. Where do you write?

Mark and I have a box room which we've converted into an office, so I tend to write in there, unless I'm at the lounge table to keep an eye on our beagle puppy, Luna – who stars as Fleur in the book. However, I can write or edit pretty much anywhere nowadays, including in cars, on trains, on holiday, and in the canteen during my lunch break from the day job. I make the most of any time I have to cram some writing in.

8. What do you do in your spare time?

Ha! Around the day job, housework, writing, seeing friends and family, life admin etc. I don't have much spare time. However,

I read as much as possible; it really helps me relax and I love being transported into other people's worlds. I try and leave as many reviews on Amazon as possible and connect with authors on Twitter, because I know how much it means to me when readers do this. I also love watching films – I'm a sucker for rom-coms and action films, but am very partial to the DC and Marvel universes.

9. What's next?

I'm currently writing another commercial women's fiction novel, partially set in Dorset but with an amazing road trip around Italy playing a major part. So now I have two new main characters to fall in love with; Will and Izzy.

10. Where can we find you?

I love to hear from readers, so please come and find me via Twitter at @NikkiMoore_Auth, or on Facebook at Facebook. com/EllaAllbrightWrites. I also have a YouTube channel where I vlog about getting published and my writing journey – just look up Nikki Moore – Author By The Sea.

The Last Charm Playlist

For me, when I look back over the years and have to evoke a sense of time and place, it's always music, TV and films that were popular at the time which give me the feeling of that decade/year. In light of that, these are the songs I listened to (in no particular order) when I was writing *The Last Charm*, largely covering 2001 to 2017.

Avril Lavigne – *When You're Gone*
John Mayer – *Free Fallin'*
Tinie Tempah – *Written In The Stars*
The Script – *For The First Time*
Scouting For Girls – *Love How It Hurts*
Coldplay – *Fix You*
Oasis – *Stand By Me*
Snow Patrol – *You Could Be Happy*
Stereophonics – *Indian Summer*
Kodaline – *High Hopes*
Birds – *Wings*
Adam Levine – *Lost Stars*
Kodaline – *The One*

Ella Allbright

Gabriella – *The Scientist (Coldplay cover)* on YouTube
Tom Chaplin – *Quicksand*
Maroon 5 – *This Love*
Ed Sheeran – *Perfect*

Book Club Questions

1. What do you think are the core themes of *The Last Charm*?

2. What do you think the author is trying to tell us about (a) grief and (b) fulfilling your dreams?

3. Jake gives Leila a lot over the years, not just charms but advice and support too. What do you think Leila offers him in return?

4. Do you think that Jake was right to give Leila some of the charms and let her believe they were from her mum? Why? / Why not?

5. How much of an impact did Amelia leaving on the eve of Leila's eleventh birthday have on her daughter, and in what ways did this affect Leila?

6. Did you always think that Leila and Jake were going to get together? If not, why not?

7. Was the ending what you expected? How could it have ended differently?